KINDRED IN DEATH

KINDRED IN DEATH

J. D. ROBB

**Doubleday Large Print
Home Library Edition**

G. P. Putnam's Sons

New York

This Large Print Edition, prepared especially for Double-day Large Print Home Library, contains the complete, unabridged text of the original Publisher's Edition.

PUTNAM

G. P. PUTNAM'S SONS
Publishers Since 1838
Published by the Penguin Group
Penguin Group (USA) Inc., 375 Hudson Street,
New York, New York 10014, USA • Penguin Group
(Canada), 90 Eglinton Avenue East, Suite 700,
Toronto, Ontario M4P 2Y3, Canada (a division of
Pearson Penguin Canada Inc.) • Penguin Books Ltd,
80 Strand, London WC2R 0RL, England • Penguin
Ireland, 25 St Stephen's Green, Dublin 2, Ireland
(a division of Penguin Books Ltd) • Penguin Group
(Australia), 250 Camberwell Road, Camberwell,
Victoria 3124, Australia (a division of Pearson
Australia Group Pty Ltd) • Penguin Books India Pvt
Ltd, 11 Community Centre, Panchsheel Park, New
Delhi–110 017, India • Penguin Group (NZ),
67 Apollo Drive, Rosedale, North Shore 0632, New
Zealand (a division of Pearson New Zealand Ltd) •
Penguin Books (South Africa) (Pty) Ltd, 24 Sturdee
Avenue, Rosebank, Johannesburg 2196,
South Africa

Penguin Books Ltd, Registered Offices: 80 Strand,
London WC2R 0RL, England

ISBN 978-1-61523-670-1

This is a work of fiction. Names, characters, places, and
incidents either are the product of the author's imagina-
tion or are used fictitiously, and any resemblance to
actual persons, living or dead, businesses, companies,
events, or locales is entirely coincidental.

While the author has made every effort to provide accurate telephone numbers and Internet addresses at the
time of publication, neither the publisher nor the author
assumes any responsibility for errors, or for changes
that occur after publication. Further, the publisher does
not have any control over and does not assume any responsibility for author or third-party websites or their
content.

Welcome, kindred glooms!
Congenial horrors, hail!
—JAMES THOMSON

A lie which is half a truth is
ever the blackest of lies.
—TENNYSON

KINDRED IN DEATH

She'd died and gone to heaven. Or better, because who knew if there was really good sex and lazy holiday mornings in heaven. She was alive and kicking.

Well, alive anyway. A little sleepy, a whole lot satisfied, and happy the end of the Urban Wars nearly forty years before had resulted in the international Peace Day holiday.

Maybe the Sunday in June had been selected arbitrarily, and certainly symbolically—and maybe remnants of that ugly period still littered the global landscape even in 2060—but she supposed people were entitled to their parades, cookouts, windy speeches, and long, drunk weekends.

Personally, she was happy to have two days off in a row for any reason. Especially when a Sunday kicked off like this one.

Eve Dallas, murder cop and ass-kicker, sprawled naked across her husband, who'd just given her a nice glimpse of heaven. She figured she'd given him a good look at it, too, as he lay under her, one hand lazily stroking her butt and his heart pounding like a turbo hammer.

She felt the thump on the bed that was their pudgy cat, Galahad, joining them now that the show was over.

She thought: Our happy little family on a do-nothing Sunday morning. And wasn't that an amazing thing? She had a happy little family—a home, an absurdly gorgeous and fascinating man who loved her, and—it couldn't be overstated—really good sex.

Not to mention the day off.

She purred, nearly as enthusiastically as the cat, and nuzzled into the curve of Roarke's neck.

"Good," she said.

"At the very least." His arms came around her, such good arms, in an easy embrace. "And what would you like to do next?"

She smiled, loving the moment, the lilt of Ireland in his voice, the brush of the cat's fur against her arm as he butted it with his head in a bid for attention.

Or most likely breakfast.

"Pretty much nothing."

"Nothing can be arranged."

She felt Roarke shift, and heard the cat's purring increase as the hands that had recently pleasured her gave him a scratch.

She propped herself up to look at his face. His eyes opened.

God, they just *killed* her, that bold, brilliant blue, those thick, dark lashes, the smile in them that was hers. Just hers.

Leaning down, she took his magic mouth with hers in a deep, dreamy kiss.

"Well now, that's far from nothing."

"I love you." She kissed his cheeks, a little rough from the night's growth of beard. "Maybe because you're so pretty."

He was, she thought as the cat interrupted by wiggling his bulk under her arm and bellying between them. The carved lips, the sorcerer's eyes, and sharp, defined bones all framed in the black silk of his hair. When you added the firm, lanky body, it made a damn perfect package.

He managed to get around the cat to draw her down for another kiss, then hissed.

"Why the hell doesn't he go down and pester Summerset for breakfast?" Roarke nudged away the cat, who kneaded paws and claws, painfully, over his chest.

"I'll get it. I want coffee anyway."

Eve rolled out of bed, walked—long, lean, naked—to the bedroom AutoChef.

"You cost me another shag," Roarke muttered.

Galahad's bicolored eyes glittered, perhaps in amusement, before he scrambled off the bed.

Eve programmed the kibble, and since it was a holiday, a side of tuna. When the cat pounced on it like the starving, she programmed two mugs of coffee, strong and black.

"I thought about going down for a workout, but sort of took care of that already."

She took the first life-giving sip as she crossed back to the platform and the lake-sized bed. "I'm going to grab a shower."

"I'll do the same, then I can grab you." He smiled as she handed him his coffee. "A second workout, we'll say. Very healthy. Maybe a full Irish to follow."

"You're a full Irish."

"I was thinking breakfast, but you can have both."

Didn't she look happy, he thought, and rested—and altogether delicious. That shaggy cap of deer-hide hair mussed about her face, those big dark eyes full of fun. The little dent in her chin he adored deepened just a bit when she smiled.

There was something about the moment, he thought, moments like this when they were so much in tune, that struck him as miraculous.

The cop and the criminal—former—he qualified, as bloody normal as Peace Day potato salad.

He studied her over the rim of his cup, through the whiff of fragrant steam. "I'm thinking you should wear that outfit more often. It's a favorite of mine."

She angled her head, drank more

coffee. "I'm thinking I want a really long shower."

"Isn't that handy? I think I want the same."

She took a last sip. "Then we'd better get started."

Later, too lazy to dress, she tossed on a robe while Roarke programmed more coffee and full Irish breakfasts for two. It was all so . . . homey, she thought. The morning sun streamed in the windows of the bedroom bigger than the apartment she'd lived in two years before. Two years married next month, she thought. He'd walked into her life, and everything had changed. He'd found her; she'd found him—and all those dark places inside both of them had gotten a little smaller, a little brighter.

"What do you want to do next?" she asked him.

He glanced over as he loaded plates and coffee onto a tray to carry it to the sitting area. "I thought the agenda was nothing."

"It can be nothing, or it can be something. I picked yesterday, and that was lots of nothing. There's probably something in the marriage rules about you getting to pick today."

"Ah yes, the rules." He set the tray down. "Always a cop."

Galahad padded over to eye the plates as if he hadn't eaten in days. Roarke pointed a warning finger at him, so the cat turned his head in disgust and began to wash.

"My pick then, is it?" He cut into his eggs, considering. "Well, let's think. It's a lovely day in June."

"Shit."

His brow lifted. "You've a problem with June, or lovely days?"

"No. Shit. June. Charles and Louise." Scowling, she chewed bacon. "Wedding. Here."

"Yes, next Saturday evening, and as far as I know that's all under control."

"Peabody said because I'm standing up for Louise—the matron of honor or whatever—I'm supposed to contact Louise every day this week to make sure she doesn't need me to do something." Eve's scowl darkened as she thought of Peabody, her partner. "That can't be right, can it? Every day? I mean, Jesus.

Plus, what the hell could she need me to do?"

"Errands?"

She stopped eating, narrowed her eyes at him. "Errands? What do you mean by errands?"

"Well now, I'm at a disadvantage having never been a bride, but best guess? Confirm details with the florist or caterer, for instance. Go shopping with her for wedding shoes or honeymoon clothes or—"

"Why would you do that?" Her voice was as thoroughly aggrieved as her face. "Why would you say these things to me, after I rocked your world twice in one morning? It's just mean."

"And likely true under other circumstances. But knowing Louise, she has it all well in hand. And knowing you, if Louise wanted someone to shop for shoes, she'd have asked someone else to stand up for her at her wedding."

"I gave the shower." At his barely smothered laugh, she drilled a finger into his arm. "It was here, and I was here, so that's like giving it. And I'm getting a dress and all that."

He smiled, amused by her puzzlement—

and mild fear—when it came to social rites. "What does it look like, this dress?"

She stabbed into her eggs. "I don't have to know what it looks like, exactly. It's some sort of yellow—she picked out the color, and she and Leonardo put their heads together on it. The doctor and the designer. Mavis says it's mag squared."

She considered her friend Mavis Freestone's particular style. "Which is kind of scary now that I think about it. Why am I thinking about it?"

"I have no idea. I can say that while Mavis's taste in fashion is uniquely . . . unique, as your closest friend she understands perfectly what you like. And Leonardo knows exactly what suits you. You looked exquisite on our wedding day."

"I had a black eye under the paint."

"Exquisite, and absolutely you. As for etiquette by Peabody, I'd say contacting Louise wouldn't hurt, just letting her know you're willing to help out should she need it."

"What if she does need it? She should've asked Peabody to do this instead of having her second in command, or in line. Whatever the thing is."

"I think it's called bridal attendant."

"Whatever." With an impatient hand, Eve waved the term away. "They're tight, and Peabody really gets into this . . . female thing."

The insanity of it, as far as Eve was concerned. The fuss, the frills, the frenzy.

"Maybe it's weird because Peabody used to date Charles, sort of, before she hooked up with McNab. And after, too." Her brow furrowed as she worked through the tangles of the dynamics. "But they never banged each other, personally or professionally."

"Who Charles and McNab?"

"Stop it." It got a quick laugh out of her before she thought about errands and shopping. "Peabody and Charles never got naked when Charles was a pro. Which is also weird that he was a licensed companion when he and Louise hooked up, and the whole time they're dating—*and* getting naked—it doesn't bother her that he's getting naked with other people, professionally. Then he quits without telling her and trains to be a therapist and buys a house and does the proposing deal."

Understanding, Roarke let her run it through, fast words and jerky logic as she shoveled in eggs, potatoes, bacon. "All right, what's all this about really?"

She stabbed eggs again, then put the fork down and picked up her coffee. "I don't want to screw it up for her. She's so happy, they're so happy—and this is a really big deal for her. I get that. I really do get that, and I did such a crap job on ours. The wedding thing."

"I'll be the judge of that."

"I did. I dumped everything on you."

"I believe you had a couple of murders on your hands."

"Yeah, I did. And of course you don't have anything to do but sit on your giant piles of money."

He shook his head and spread a bit of jam on a triangle of toast. "We all do what we do, darling Eve. And I happen to think we do what we do very well."

"I wigged out on you, pissed you off, the night before the wedding."

"Added a bit of excitement."

"Then got drugged and kicked around at my own drunk girl party at a strip club before I made the collar, which was fun in retrospect. But the point is, I really didn't do the stuff, so I don't know how to do the stuff now."

He gave her knee a friendly pat. For a woman of her sometimes terrifying courage, she feared the oddest things. "If there's something she needs you'll figure out how to do it. I'll tell you, when you walked toward me that day, our day, in the sunlight, you were like a flame. Bright and beautiful, and took the breath right out of me. There was only you."

"And about five hundred of your close friends."

"Only you." He took her hand, kissed it. "And it'll be the same for them, I wager."

"I just want her to have what she wants. It makes me nervous."

"And that's friendship. You'll wear some sort of yellow dress and be there for her. That will be enough."

"I hope so, because I'm not tagging her every day. That's firm." She looked at her plate. "How does anyone eat a full Irish?"

"Slowly and with great determination. I take it you're not determined enough."

"Not nearly."

"Well then, if that takes care of breakfast, I've had my thought."

"On what?"

"On what to do next. We should go to the beach, get ourselves some sand and surf."

"I can get behind that. Jersey Shore, Hamptons?"

"I was thinking more tropical."

"You can't want to go all the way to the island for one day, or part of one day." Roarke's private island was a favored spot, but it was practically on the other side of the world. Even in his jet it would take at least three hours one way.

"A bit far for an impulse, but there are closer. There's a spot on the Caymans that might suit, and a small villa that's available for the day."

"And you know this because?"

"I've looked into acquiring it," he said easily. "So we could fly down, get there in under an hour, check it out, enjoy the sun and surf and drink some foolish cocktails. End the day with a walk along the beach in the moonlight."

She found herself smiling. "How small a villa?"

"Small enough to serve as a nice impulse holiday spot for us, and roomy enough to allow us to travel down with a few friends if we've a mind to."

"You'd already had this thought."

"I had, yes, and put it in the if-and-when department. If you'd like it, we can make this the when."

"I can be dressed and toss whatever I'd need for the day in a bag in under ten minutes."

She leaped up, bolted toward her dresser.

"Bag's packed," he told her. "For both of us. In case."

She glanced back at him. "You never miss a trick."

"It's rare to have a Sunday off with my wife. I like making the most of it."

She tossed the robe to pull on a simple white tank, then grabbed out a pair of khaki shorts. "We've had a good start on making the most. This should cap it off."

Even as she stepped into the shorts, the communicator on her dresser signaled. "Crap. Damn it. *Shit!*" Her stomach dropped as she read the display. Her glance at

Roarke was full of regret and apology. "It's Whitney."

He watched the cop take over, face, posture, as she picked up the communicator to respond to her commander. And he thought, *Ah well.*

"Yes, sir."

"Lieutenant, I'm sorry to interrupt your holiday." Whitney's wide face filled the tiny screen, and on it rode a stress that had the muscles tightening at the back of her neck.

"It's no problem, Commander."

"I realize you're off the roll, but there's a situation. I need you to report to Five-forty-one Central Park South. I'm on scene now."

"You're on scene, sir?" Bad, she thought, big and bad for the commander to be on scene.

"Affirmative. The victim is Deena Mac-Masters, age sixteen. Her body was discovered earlier this morning by her parents when they returned home from a weekend away. Dallas, the victim's father is Captain Jonah MacMasters."

It took her a moment. "Illegals. I know of Lieutenant MacMasters. He's been promoted?"

"Two weeks ago. MacMasters has specifically requested you as primary. I would like to grant that request."

"I'll contact Detective Peabody immediately."

"I'll take care of that. I'd like you here *asap.*"

"Then I'm on my way."

"Thank you."

She disengaged the communicator, turned to Roarke. "I'm sorry."

"Don't." He crossed to her, tapped his fingertip on the shallow dent in her chin. "A man's lost his child, and that's a great deal more important than a bit of beach. You know him?"

"Not really. He contacted me after I took Casto down." She thought of the wrong cop who'd gone after her at her wedding eve party. "MacMasters wasn't his LT, but he wanted to give me a nod for closing that case, and taking down a bad cop. I appreciated it. He's got a rep," she continued as she changed the holiday shorts for work trousers. "A good, solid rep. I hadn't heard about his promotion, but I'm not surprised by it."

She tidied her choppy cap of hair by raking her fingers through it. "He's got about twenty years on the job. Maybe twenty-five. I hear he draws a hard line and sticks to it, makes sure those serving under him do the same. He closes cases."

"Sounds like someone else I know."

She pulled a shirt out of the closet. "Maybe."

"Whitney didn't tell you how the girl was killed."

"He wants and needs me to come in without any preconceptions. He didn't say it was homicide. That's for me and the ME to determine."

She picked up her weapon harness, strapped it on. Pocketed her communicator, her 'link, hooked on her restraints. She didn't bother to frown when Roarke offered her the summer-weight jacket he'd selected out of her closet to go over her sidearm. "Whitney's being there means one of two things," she told him. "It's hinky, or they're personal friends. Maybe both."

"For him to be on scene . . ."

"Yeah." She sat to pull on the boots she preferred for work. "A cop's kid. I don't know when I'll get back."

"Not an issue."

She stopped, looked at him, thought about bags packed just in case, and walks in the tropical moonlight. "You could fly down, check this villa out."

"I've work enough I can see to here to keep me busy." He laid his hands on her shoulders when she rose, laid his lips on hers. "Get in touch when you have a better handle on the situation."

"I will. See you then."

"Take care, Lieutenant."

She jogged downstairs, barely breaking stride when Summerset, Roarke's man of just about everything and the pebble in her shoe, materialized in the foyer.

"I was under the assumption you were off duty until tomorrow."

"There's a dead body, which unfortunately isn't yours." Then she paused at the door. "Talk him into doing something that's not work. Just because I have to . . ." She shrugged, and walked out to meet death.

Few cops could afford to live in a single-family residence on the verdant edges of Central Park. Then again, few cops— well, none other than herself—lived in a freaking castle-manor estate in Manhattan. Curious about how MacMasters managed his digs, she did a quick run on him as she navigated the light holiday morning traffic.

MacMasters, Captain Jonah, her dash comp told her, born March 22, 2009, Providence, Rhode Island. Parents Walter and Marybeth nee Hastings. Educated Stonebridge Academy, further education Yale, graduated 2030. Married Franklin, Carol 2040, one offspring, female, Deena, born November 23, 2043. Joined NYPSD September 15, 2037. Commendations and honors include—

"Skip that. Finances. Where's the money come from?"

Working . . . Current worth approximately eight million, six hundred thousand. Inherited a portion of grandfather's estate. MacMasters, Jonah, died natural causes June 6, 2032, founder Mac Kitchen and Bath, based in Providence. Company's current worth—

"Good enough. Asked and answered."

Family money, she thought. Yale educated. Ends up an Illegals cop in New York.

Interesting. One spouse and a twenty-year marriage, commendations and honors on the job. Promoted to captain. It all said what she already knew of him.

Solid.

Now this solid cop she barely knew had specifically requested her as primary in the investigation of his only child's death. Why was that? she wondered.

She'd ask.

When she reached the address she pulled in behind a black-and-white. As she engaged her On Duty light, she took a survey of the house. Nice digs, she thought, and got out to retrieve her field kit. And, though she was in danger of overusing the word, it struck her as solid.

Pre–Urban Wars construction, nicely rehabbed so it maintained its character, showed a few scars. It looked dignified, she thought, the rosy brick, the creamy trim, the long windows—currently shielded with privacy screens, every one.

Pots of colorful flowers stood guard on either side of the short flight of stone steps, a pretty touch she supposed. But she was more interested, as she stepped over and crossed the sidewalk, in the security.

Full cameras, view screen, thumb pad, and she'd bet voice-activated locks with a coded bypass. A cop, and particularly one with good scratch, would be sure to fully protect his home and everything— everyone in it.

And still his teenage daughter was dead inside.

You could never cover all the bases.

She took her badge out of her pocket to flash the uniform at the door, then hooked it to her waistband.

"They're waiting for you inside, Lieutenant."

"Are you first on scene?"

"No, sir. First on scene's inside, along with the commander and the captain and his wife. My partner and I were called in by the commander. My partner's on the rear."

"Okay. My partner will be arriving shortly. Peabody, Detective."

"I've been apprised, Lieutenant. I'll pass her through."

Not a rookie, Eve thought as she waited for him to pass her in. The uniform was both seasoned and tough. Had Whitney called him in, or the captain?

She glanced to the left, to the right, and imagined people in the neighboring houses who were awake and at home keeping watch, but too polite—or too intimidated—to come out and play obvious lookie-loos.

She stepped in to a cool, wide foyer with a central staircase. Flowers on the table, she noted, very fresh. Only a day, maybe two old. A little bowl that held some sort of colored mints. Everything in soft, warm colors. No clutter, but a pair of glossy purple sandals—one under, one beside a high-backed chair.

Whitney stepped out of a doorway to the left. He filled it, she thought, with the bulk of his body. His dark face was lined with concern, and she caught the glint of sorrow in his eyes.

And still his voice was neutral when he spoke. Years of being a cop held him straight.

"Lieutenant, we're in here. If you'd take a moment before going up to the scene."

"Yes, sir."

"Before you do, I'll thank you for agreeing to take this case." When she hesitated, he nearly smiled. "If I didn't put it to you as your choice, I should have."

"There's no question, Commander. The captain wants me, he's got me."

With a nod, he stepped back to lead her into the room.

There was a little jolt, she could admit it, when she saw Mrs. Whitney. The commander's wife tended to intimidate her with her starched manner, cool delivery, and blue blood. But at the moment, she appeared to be fully focused on comforting the woman beside her on a small sofa in a pretty parlor.

Carol MacMasters, Eve concluded, a small, dark-haired beauty to contrast Anna Whitney's blonde elegance. In her drenched black eyes, Eve read both devastation and confusion. Her slight shoulders shivered as if she sat naked in ice.

MacMasters rose as she came in. She judged him at about six-four, and lean to the point of gangly. His casual dress of jeans and T-shirt coincided with returning from a brief holiday. His hair, dark like his wife's, had a tight curl and remained full and thick around a lean face with deep cheek grooves that may have been dimples in his youth. His eyes, a pale, almost misty green, met hers levelly. In them she saw grief and shock, and anger.

He moved to her, held out a hand. "Thank you. Lieutenant . . ." He seemed to run out of words.

"Captain, I'm very sorry, very sorry for your loss."

"She's the one?" Carol struggled up even as tears spilled down her cheeks. "You're Lieutenant Dallas?"

"Yes, ma'am. Mrs. MacMasters—"

"Jonah said it had to be you. You're the best there is. You'll find out who . . . how . . . But she'll still be gone. My baby will still be gone. She's upstairs. She's up there, and I can't be with her." Her voice pitched from raw grief toward hysteria. "They won't let me go be with her. She's dead. Our Deena's dead."

"Here now, Carol, you have to let the lieutenant do what she can." Mrs. Whitney stood up to drape an arm around Carol.

"Can't I just sit with her? Can't I just—"

"Soon." Mrs. Whitney crooned it. "Soon. I'll stay with you now. The lieutenant is going to take good care of Deena. She'll take good care."

"I'm going to take you up," Whitney said. "Anna."

Mrs. Whitney nodded.

Starched and intimidating, Eve thought, but she would handle a grieving mother and a devastated father.

"You need to stay down here, Jonah. I'll be down shortly. Lieutenant."

"You're friends with the victim's parents off the job?" Eve asked.

"Yes. Anna and Carol serve on some committees together, and often spend time with each other. We socialize. I brought my wife as a friend of the victim's mother."

"Yes, sir. I believe she'll be a great help in that area."

"This is hard, Dallas." His voice leaden, he started up the steps. "We've known Deena since she was a little girl. I can tell you she was the light of their hearts. A bright, lovely girl."

"The house has excellent security from my eyeball of it. Do you know if it was activated when the MacMasters returned this morning?"

"The locks were. Jonah found the cameras had been deactivated, and the discs for the last two days removed. He touched nothing," Whitney added, turning left at the top of the stairs. "Allowed Carol to touch nothing—but the girl. And he prevented his wife from moving the body or disturbing the scene. I'm sure we can all understand there were a few moments of shock."

"Yes, sir." It was awkward, she thought, and uncomfortable to be thrust in the position of interviewing her commander. "Do you know what time they returned home this morning?"

"At eight-thirty-two, precisely. I took the liberty of checking the lock log, and it confirmed Jonah's statement to me. I'll give you a copy of the statement from my home 'link log. He contacted me immediately, requesting you, and requesting my presence if possible. I didn't seal the scene—her bedroom. But it is secure."

He gestured, stood back. "I think it best if I go down, let you proceed. When your partner arrives, I'll send her directly up."

"Yes, sir."

He nodded again, then sighed as he looked at the open bedroom door. "Dallas . . . It's very hard."

She waited until he'd turned away, started down the stairs. Alone, she stepped to the doorway and looked at the young, dead Deena MacMasters.

2

"Record on. Dallas, lieutenant eve, at scene, MacMasters, Deena, victim."

She scanned the room first as she took Seal-It from her field kit to coat her hands and boots. A large space, bright and airy with triple windows—privacy screen activated—along the park-view wall. A padded bench, mounded with colorful pillows, curved under the glass. Posters of popular musicians, actors, personalities covered walls done in a dreamy violet. A little clutch tightened Eve's stomach as she studied one of her friend, Mavis Freestone, blue hair swirling, arms lifted in triumph, titled *Motherhood Rocks!*

On it, she saw Mavis's big, bold handwriting.

YO, DEENA,
YOU ROCK, TOO!
MAVIS FREESTONE

Had Deena pushed the poster at Mavis at some concert or event, and Mavis—laughing, bubbling—signed it with Deena's purple pen? Noise, lights, color, Eve imagined, and life. And a thrilling memory for a sixteen-year-old girl who couldn't have known she would have so little time to treasure it.

A portion of the room was designed for studying and schoolwork with a glossy white desk, shelves, a high-end comp and com center, disc files—all ordered and tidy. A second area, suited for lounging, probably hanging out with girlfriends, also sat tidy and apparently undisturbed with plump cushions, soft throws, a scatter of stuffed animals likely collected throughout childhood.

A hairbrush and hand mirror, a few

colored bottles, a bowl of seashells, and a trio of framed photos stood on a dresser in the same glossy white as the desk.

Thick, boldly colored rugs flashed over a gleaming wood floor. The one nearest the bed, she noted, skewed out of alignment. He'd knocked it or skidded against it, or she had.

A pair of panties—simple, white, unadorned, lay near the rug.

"He stripped off her underwear," Eve said aloud, "tossed them aside."

The nightstands beside the bed held fancy, frilly lamps with tasseled shades. Again, one of the shades sat crooked on its base. A bump by an arm or elbow. Everything else around the bed itself showed a delight in order and precision, a love of pretty, girlish things.

A young sixteen, to Eve's mind, but maybe she was projecting. At sixteen she'd been counting the days until legal adulthood and escape from the foster system. There had been no pink, no frills, no fuzzy teddy bears beloved since childhood in her world.

And still, she felt this was the room of a girl still firmly in childhood, just barely approaching the woman she might have been. One who had died living a woman's worst fear.

In the center of the pretty, cheerful room, the bed held vicious violence. The tangle of pink and white sheets ruined with rusted bloodstains wound around the body's legs like rope. He'd used them to bind her feet to the footboard, to keep her legs open for him.

She'd fought—the bruises and raw marks on her ankles, her thighs where her purple skirt was rucked showed she'd fought, showed he'd raped her violently. At the side of the bed, Eve leaned in, angled down to peer at the police restraints binding the victim's hands behind her back.

"Cop cuffs. Vic is a cop's daughter. Evidence of struggle in bruising and lacerations on wrists. She didn't go easy. No signs of mutilation. Some bruising on the face indicates physical blows, bruising on neck indicates manual strangulation."

She eased open the victim's mouth, used her penlight and magnifier. "Some threads and fabric in her teeth, on her tongue, blood on her lips, teeth. She bit her lip, deeply. Some blood and possibly saliva on pillowcase. Looks like he used it to smother her. Clothes are askew but not removed, some tearing at the shoulders of the shirt, buttons missing. He pulled at them," she continued as she worked her way down the body. "Pulled them out of his way, but he wasn't interested over-much in the rapist's foreplay."

With care and deliberation, even as her mouth went dry and the back of her head pounded, she examined the damage caused by violent rape.

"Torture—choke, smother, rape, choke, smother, rape. Vaginally and anally. Repeatedly by the amount of bruising and tearing." She felt her breath hitch as her lungs tried to shut down, and forced air out. In. Out again. "Blood from vaginal area indicates victim might have been a virgin. ME to confirm."

She had to straighten up, had to take a few more calming breaths. She couldn't afford to switch off the record and settle herself, couldn't afford to let the record show how much her hands wanted to shake, how much her stomach wanted to roil.

She knew what it was to be helpless like this, abused like this, terrified like this.

"At this time it appears the security was engaged. Cameras were subsequently turned off, and all discs removed from premises. There is no visible sign of break-in—Crime Scene Unit to confirm. She opened the door; she let him in. Cop's kid. She knew him, trusted him. Face-to-face rape and murder. He knew her, wanted to see her face. Personal, very personal."

Calmer, she got out her gauges to determine time of death. "TOD three-twenty-six. Primary determines rape-homicide to be confirmed by ME. Dr. Morris is requested if available."

"Dallas."

It showed Eve how deep into the moment—and into the past—she'd gone—too deep to hear her partner's approach. She schooled her face to neutral lines and turned to where Peabody stood in the doorway.

"The kid died hard," Eve said. "Fought hard, died hard. No tissue under her nails that I can find, but plenty of trace from the sheets. It looks like he held the pillow over her face, she bit it and her own lip. As it's most likely multiple rapes, he may have gotten off on the struggle. Choked her, too. We should be able to get his handspan from the bruising."

"I kind of knew her."

Instinctively Eve stepped over, blocking Peabody's view of the body, forcing her partner to look at her instead. "How?"

Sorrow, simple and sincere, shone in Peabody's dark brown eyes. "When I was a rookie, we did this kind of public service thing in schools." Peabody cleared her throat, pressed her lips together. "She was my liaison, like a student guide. A really sweet, smart kid. I guess she was about eleven or twelve. I was new to New York, too, and she gave me some tips on where to shop and stuff. And, ah, last year she did a report on Free-Agers for school." Peabody paused, busied herself sealing up. "She got in touch, and I helped her out with some background and personal anecdotes."

"Is this going to be a problem for you?"

"No." On a breath, Peabody pushed

her dark hair back from her face, threading her fingers once through the sassy flip she wore. "No. She was a nice kid, and I liked her. A lot. I want to find out who did this to her. I want in on taking the son of a bitch down."

"Start by checking the security, the electronics through the house. Look for any signs of break-in." Big house, Eve thought. It would take a while, long enough to put Peabody into cop mode. "We need all 'links checked, all logs copied. I need the sweepers, but I want it designated Code Yellow. This isn't a media blackout, we can't go there with a cop involved, but I don't want the juice poured out either. I want Morris unless he's not able."

"He's back?"

"Scheduled to be back from leave tomorrow. If he's in town and willing, I want him."

Peabody nodded, pulled out her communicator. "Given it's a cop's kid, I think we want Feeney."

"You think right, and go ahead and tag your bony-assed cohab. Feeney's going to need McNab on this anyway, so let's get our EDD team up and running now."

"He's on standby. When Whitney contacted me, I asked him to wait for my signal. If you're ready to roll her, I'll give you a hand."

Eve heard the message under the words. *I need to do this. Need to prove I can.*

Eve stepped back, turned to the body. "He didn't remove her clothing. Tore it some, pulled it out of the way. Another indication it wasn't sexual, and that it wasn't about humiliation so much as punishment, violence, or causing pain. He didn't care about stripping her, about exposing her. On three," she said and counted out so they rolled the body facedown together.

"God." Peabody breathed in, breathed out. "That blood's not just from rape. I think . . . she was a virgin. And those are cop restraints. Using them, keeping her hands bound behind her back? He's making a point, don't you think with the first, and causing her more pain with the second. Look at the way they dug into her wrists, pushed into them from the weight of her body. He could have cuffed her to the headboard. Bad enough."

"It's about pain," Eve said shortly. "Pain gives the inflictor more control over the victim. Do you know anything about her friends? Boyfriends, men?"

"No, not really. When I was helping her with the report, I asked about boyfriends, the way you do."

As she spoke Peabody began to scan and study the room. Coming back, Eve judged, sliding back into cop mode.

"She got flushy and said she didn't date much since she was concentrating on her schoolwork. Ah, she was really into music and theater, but she wanted to study philosophy and alternate cultures. Talked about joining the Peace Corps or Education For All after college."

Shy, Eve thought, using Peabody's impressions to help her form a picture of the dead. Idealistic, serious about education.

"And I remember," Peabody continued, "when we met at this cyber joint for the research, McNab hooked up with me at the end. She was really shy with him—flushy again. I guess she was shy around guys yet. Some girls are."

"Okay. Go get started on the rest. I'll finish here."

Shy around boys, Eve thought. Parents away for the weekend. Idealistic often went along with naive, especially in the young.

Maybe take the leap, let boy/man in. She studied the ruined clothes again.

Pretty skirt, nice top. Could be the victim dressed up a little just for herself, but wasn't it likely she'd gone to the trouble for a date? Earrings, bracelet—that must have added yet more pain rubbing against the restraints. Painted toenails and finger-nails. Facial enhancements, Eve noted after slipping on microgoggles and peering closely into the face. Smudged from tears, the struggle, the pressure of the pillow.

Did young girls paint up their faces for an evening at home?

Had she gone out, brought someone home with her—date or pickup gone wrong?

"Let him in or came home with him. No sign of any cozying up down in the parlor, but maybe elsewhere. You wouldn't have been able to tidy up. Came in, kicked off your purple sandals, at some point in the day or evening. Maybe he tidied up down-stairs. Did you bring him up here, Deena?

Up to your bedroom. Doesn't quite fit the sexually inexperienced teenager, but there's always a first time. No signs of struggle here either, outside the bed—and even that's consistent with struggle after bondage. Did he tidy up here, too? Why would he? No, he brought you up. No," she said slowly. "No, you didn't kick off your shoes. You're too inherently tidy. They fell off, came off when he forced you—or carried you—upstairs. Flag tox screen and expedite."

She took another breath. It was easier now, she thought, easier after dealing with Peabody, after finding the right corner inside herself to bury the past, again.

She turned away from the body, and began to search the room.

Good clothes, she noted, good fabrics and the usual baffling—to Eve—collection of shoes. An even larger collection of books on disc—fiction and nonfiction. An enormous collection of music discs, and a quick flip through the menu of a purple Tunes revealed countless music downloads.

No secret diary hidden away from parental eyes and no personal PC. Or 'link.

She replayed the last communication on the desk 'link and listened through a chatty conversation between the victim and a girl she called Jo about shopping plans, music, Jo's annoying younger brother. Not a word about boys. Didn't teenage girls obsess about boys?

And no discussion about plans for Saturday night.

The bathroom continued the violet and white theme and the order and tidiness. She found the enhancements—many, many tubes of lip dye partially used. No condoms or birth control of any kind hidden away. No sign the victim had been contemplating engaging in sex.

And still, Eve thought, she'd let her killer in or brought him home.

She started out, paused once more by the side of the bed. "Victim to be bagged and tagged and transported to the morgue." After she left the room she assigned one of the uniforms to stand outside it until the sweepers and dead wagon arrived.

She took her time assessing the other rooms on the second floor. The master had soft, soothing colors, a large bed with cushioned headboard. Two overnight cases lay beside a deep, scooped chair as if they'd been dropped or knocked over.

MacMasters likely brought them up, she thought, while the wife walked toward the daughter's room to check in. Scream, shout, MacMasters drops the bags and runs to his daughter's room.

None of the other rooms—two home offices, a casual media room, two more baths, and what she took for a guest room—appeared to have been disturbed.

Downstairs, she set a marker by the sandals, then sought out Peabody.

"The way I read it," Peabody said, "the security and locks were disengaged from inside. There's no sign of tampering. EDD may find otherwise, but it looks like they were re-engaged again from the inside, then the cameras shut down right at the source. The last disc there is from Saturday. I ran it back on my PPC. It shows the victim coming home, alone, at just after eighteen hundred. She had a pair of shopping bags, both from Girlfriends. It's a high-end boutique, focused on teens and the college crowd. It's on Fifth at Fifty-eighth."

"We'll check it out, see what she bought,

and if she shopped alone. She had arrangements to hook up with a friend for Saturday shopping. I haven't found her personal 'link or PC, and no coms on her desk unit other than one with a girl-friend, two from her parents over the last forty-eight. I found eight handbags all empty."

"She was carrying a white straw French strap with silver buckles on the disc."

"I didn't see anything like that in her room. Check communal closets and stor-age. These are tidy people. Maybe they have a spot for that kind of thing. Was she wearing purple sandals?"

"The ones in the foyer? No, blue skids."

"Okay."

"Dallas, the other thing. The control room? It's passcoded. No signs of tamper-ing there I can see either. Either she did the shutting down, or she gave him the code. Or he's really damn good with bypassing."

"She'd have told him anything if he said he'd stop. But we'll have the experts check for tampering."

"There was one glass on the kitchen counter. I bagged it. Everything else is put away, so it struck me as off. Plus, I ran the log for the AutoChef. She ordered two single pizzas at eighteen-thirty last night. One veggie, one meat. She had company, Dallas."

"Yeah, she had company. I'm going to talk to MacMasters and his wife. The sweepers should be coming in any minute. Ride herd on that, will you?"

Eve went back to the parlor. Anna Whitney sat beside Carol, an elegant guard dog. MacMasters sat at her other side, kept her hand clutched in his. Whitney stood, staring out the front window.

Mrs. Whitney looked over first and Eve saw, briefly, the guard dog unguarded. Abject grief burned in her eyes, and with it a plea Eve read clearly.

Help us.

MacMasters straightened when Eve came in, going ramrod straight.

"I'm sorry to intrude. I know this is a very difficult time."

"Do you have children?" Carol asked dully.

"No, ma'am."

"Then you can't know, can you?"

"Carol." MacMasters murmured it.

"You're right," Eve said as she sat

across from the trio on the couch. "I can't. But I know this, Mrs. MacMasters. I'll do everything in my power to find the person responsible for what happened to your daughter. I'll see to it that everything that can be done is done. I'll take care of her, I promise you."

"We left her alone, don't you see? We left her."

"You called her twice. You made sure she was as safe as it's possible to make her," Eve said even as Anna drew breath to speak. "It's my job to observe and analyze, and from my observations at this point, you're good and loving parents. You're not responsible for this. I'm going to find the one who is. You can help me now by answering some questions."

"We came back early. We were going to surprise her and all go out to a big holiday brunch, then to a matinee. She loved to go to the theater. We were going to surprise her."

"When were you due home?"

"We'd originally planned to get home late this afternoon," MacMasters answered. "We left Friday afternoon, took a shuttle to Interlude, an inn in the Smoky Mountains in

Tennessee. Carol and I were taking a quiet weekend to celebrate my promotion." He cleared his throat. "I made the reservations ten days ago. We'd been there as a family before, but . . ."

"Deena wanted us to have the trip by ourselves," Carol managed. "We usually go together, but this time . . . We should have insisted she stay with the Jenningses. But, she's almost seventeen, and so responsible. She'll be going to college next year, so we thought, we just thought—"

"Are the Jenningses family friends?"

"Yes. Arthur and Melissa. Their daughter, Jo, is Deena's best friend." As she answered, Carol's lips trembled. "Deena wanted to stay on her own, and we thought, we both thought we should respect that, trust her, allow her that independence. If—"

"Can you tell me the names of her other friends?"

Carol drew in a shuddering breath. "Jo, and Hilly Rowe, Libby Grogh from school. They're the closest. And Jamie, Jamie Lingstrom."

Eve went on alert. "The late DS Frank Wojinksi's grandson?"

"Yes." MacMasters nodded. "I was friendly with Frank, and Jamie and Deena have been friends for years."

"Boyfriends?"

"Deena wasn't interested in boys, not in that way, as yet."

As MacMasters spoke, Eve caught the look in his wife's eye. "Ma'am?"

"She was shy around boys, but interested. I think there was one in particular she liked."

"Who?"

"She never said, not directly. But in the last couple of months she took more interest in how she looked, and . . . I'm not sure I can explain it, but I knew there was a boy who'd caught her eye and interest. Enough so that I had another talk with her about sex."

MacMasters frowned at his wife, a look of bafflement more than annoyance. "You never said."

She glanced at her husband, and her trembling lips tried to curve. "Some things are private, Jonah, and just between girls. She hadn't been with a boy yet. I'd have known. And she'd have told me. We discussed birth control and safety. She knew

I was ready to take her to the clinic should she want to choose a birth control method."

"Do you know if she kept a diary?"

"More a journal or a notebook. She'd record thoughts, or observations, complaints, I imagine, sometimes bits of poetry or song lyrics." As her eyes continued to stream, Carol dug for another tissue. "She loves music. She keeps it in her purse, always."

"And she has a PPC, a 'link?"

"Yes. They'd be in her purse, too."

"She has a white straw bag, with silver buckles."

"Her new summer bag. We bought it last month. It's her new favorite."

"Where does she keep it when she's not using it?"

"In her room, on the hook on the inside of the closet door."

The empty hook, Eve thought. Her killer had taken it, and everything in it.

"I have to ask. Did Deena use illegals?"

"She did not. I don't say that with absolute certainty simply because she was my daughter and due to my position." MacMasters kept his gaze steady on

Eve's. "I know all the signs, Lieutenant. And I'm well aware of how susceptible a girl of Deena's age can be to peer pressure or the urge to experiment. She was strongly opposed to illegals, not just because they're against the law but because she had a deep respect for her body, her health."

"She's very aware of nutrition," Carol added. "In fact, I often felt guilty for drinking coffee or indulging in junk food. She works out six days a week—yoga, jogging, resistance training."

"What gym did she use?"

"She doesn't like gyms. We have a little area on the lower level. And if she wants to jog outside, she uses the park. The secured trails. She carries a panic button, and knows self-defense. Jonah saw to that. She's been using the park more recently, with the good weather. Illegals would never be a choice for her. She respects herself and her father too much."

Present tense, Eve thought, all present tense. Deena was still alive for her. Would it be another nightmare when reality fully set it?

She hesitated, trying to find the right

tone to direct toward the father without hastening the nightmare for the mother. That flicker translated itself to the other cops in the room.

"Carol." MacMasters tightened his grip briefly on his wife's hand. "Could you and Anna make some coffee? I think we could all use some."

"I'd appreciate that," Whitney said.

"Of course we can." Obviously understanding the ploy, Anna rose, held a hand out for Carol. "I'd love some coffee."

"Yes, all right. I should have offered . . ."

"We'll take care of it." Anna firmly led Carol from the room.

"You want to know if there've been any threats against me or my family," Mac-Masters began. "Anything from the job that might have led to this. There's always a chemi-head who mouths off, a dealer who tries to toss his weight around, save face. I have a file of what I consider the more serious threats. We took down a major operation two months ago. The moneyman, Juan Garcia, made bail." His face shifted into a look of disgust. "Shark lawyer, a pile of money. He's wearing a bracelet, but it wouldn't stop him."

"We'll check him out."

"Yeah. Yeah. But . . . this isn't his style." MacMasters rubbed his hands over his face. "He'd go for me, or the other cops on the bust. He'd slit my throat, or have it slit in a blink if he thought he could get away with it, but I don't see him doing this, or ordering it. Plus, if he went for my family, he'd want me to know who did it."

"We'll check it out anyway, and look into the rest of your file. I'll need a copy."

"You'll have it. I know we can never be sure—" He broke off a moment, seemed to struggle. "Never sure if or when something might come back on our family through the job, but I know I haven't been tailed. This is a good neighborhood, and we've kept everything in Carol's name, on public records. Word gets out, I know, but the house is secured, and we've drummed safety and awareness into Deena since she was a toddler."

"Something closer to home?" Eve suggested. "An argument or dispute with a neighbor?"

"No. Nothing." MacMasters spread his hands. "Everyone gets along. Deena, especially Deena, was well liked. She—

she ran errands for Mrs. Cohen down the block when she was laid up with a broken ankle. She fed the Rileys' cat when they went on vacation. She . . ."

"You haven't noticed anyone unfamiliar hanging around the area?"

"No. No. In any case, she'd never open the door for a stranger, especially when alone in the house. I looked—while I was waiting for the uniforms. I couldn't find any sign of break-in. There's nothing missing or disturbed. It wasn't a burglary gone wrong. It was direct and deliberate against my girl. And it was someone she knew."

"At this point in the investigation I agree with you, Captain. We'll still cover all the ground. I'm going to talk to her friends. If there was a boy who caught her eye," Eve continued, using Carol's phrase, "she may have been more forthcoming with them."

"It wasn't a . . . a date gone wrong. It wasn't an impulse."

"No, sir, I don't believe it was."

"Then tell me what you believe."

Eve glanced at Whitney, got a nod. "At this very early stage I believe she may have made a date, planning to entertain a friend—someone she may have met outside her circle. Someone who may have targeted her. I believe he may have incapacitated her. There's a glass, the only thing out of place in the kitchen, which we'll have tested."

"Drugged her." Emotions scraped the words raw.

"Possibly. Captain, I can't as yet draw conclusions, and I'm not entirely comfortable outlining speculation. I will promise to keep you in the loop. I will promise my partner and I, and the team I've already started to assemble, will work diligently to find the answers."

"I asked for you, Lieutenant, because I have no doubt of that." He pressed his fingers to his eyes. "For the record, and to repeat the statement I gave the commander: My wife and I returned early from a two-day holiday. The locks were secured. The cameras, I discovered later, were off. I didn't notice this immediately. We went directly upstairs. I took our bags to our bedroom while Carol went to Deena's room to see if she was awake. She screamed. My wife screamed, and I ran directly to her. I found her trying to lift Deena from the bed. I could see . . ."

"There's no need, Captain. I can refer to the statement you gave the commander."

"No, we all know it needs to be repeated. I could see Deena was gone. I saw the evidence of sexual and physical abuse—the blood, the bruising, the restraints. I pulled my wife away from our girl because . . . I knew I had to. She fought me, but I was able to get her out of the room and into our bedroom where I used both force and intimidation to keep her in there while I contacted the commander. I realize this isn't procedure. I should have called for uniforms, but . . ."

"I would have done the same."

"Thank you." His chest shuddered as he fought for control. "I related the situation to the commander. I asked for his help. The uniforms he dispatched arrived. No, that's not accurate. I went back into Deena's room first. I had to see . . . I had to be sure. I convinced Carol to come downstairs, and at that time I checked the security and looked for signs of break-in. Then the uniforms arrived. The commander and Mrs. Whitney arrived shortly thereafter. At that time, the commander and I went back to . . . to the scene. I then requested you as primary."

"Thank you, Captain. I've dispatched two uniforms to do the door-to-door. With the commander's permission I'll copy you on all reports."

"Permission granted. The ME's team is here," Whitney added when he saw the wagon pull up outside. "It would be best if we kept Carol in the kitchen."

"I'll go back with her." MacMasters got to his feet. "If you're done with me for now, Lieutenant."

"Yes. The sweepers will be all over the house soon. Is there somewhere you and your wife can go for the time being?"

"You'll come home with us," Whitney said.

MacMasters nodded. Eve thought the cop was beginning to fade. His hands trembled, and even as she watched, the lines at the corners of his eyes seemed to cut deeper.

"I'll be in contact, Captain. Once again, I'm very sorry for your loss."

When he walked out, a man in a daze now, Whitney turned to Eve. "Conclusions?"

"Speculations is more accurate. She let him in, planned to do so. Impossible to say at this time if she brought him home with her from some outside meet or if he came here on his own. She ordered him food from the AutoChef. Most likely they ate. If he drugged her, left the glass on the counter, it was deliberate."

"He wanted us to know that much," Whitney concluded.

"Yes, sir. It was personal, planned, and deliberate. The rapes were very violent, the facial bruising feels like an afterthought, like show. I believe he choked her, smothered her, maybe taking her in and out of consciousness to prolong the event, and her pain and fear. He wanted the pain and the fear. TOD is after three this morning. Everything I've learned this far indicates the victim wouldn't have let anyone in, even a boy she had a crush on, in the middle of the night."

"No. No, I don't believe she would have done that. Unless. . . if she believed someone needed help. Someone she knew."

"It's a possibility. More likely he was here for some time, a considerable amount of time. Unless the sweepers find evidence to the contrary, I believe all the violence took place in her bedroom, and after he had her restrained. He didn't take any chances. He came here to accomplish a specific thing, and he did so."

"Check like crimes," Whitney began, then stopped himself. "I'm telling you how to do your job. Instead, I should let you do it."

"I'm going to start with her friends. We may get lucky there, get a name, a description. I'm having the glass Peabody bagged sent straight to the lab. I've requested Morris as ME. Feeney, McNab, and whoever Feeney assigns out of EDD will handle the electronics. We'll also do a sweep of the park where she jogged. If she met her killer there, someone might have seen them together. We will check out Garcia, though I tend to agree with the captain on that."

"Keep me informed," Whitney told her, then glanced over as his wife came in.

"I wanted to give them a few moments in private. And to give this to you, Lieutenant." Anna offered Eve a memo cube. "The names and contacts of the friends Carol told you about."

"Thank you."

"I know you need to get started on what comes next, but I'd like to say something. Carol and Jonah are dear friends, and Deena was . . . lovely in every way. I don't always like your style, Lieutenant. Jack," she said with an impatient glance when he started to interrupt. "Please. I often find you abrasive and difficult to understand. But Carol and Jonah are dear friends, and Deena lovely in every way. If Jonah hadn't requested you to lead this investigation, I'd have used every influence I had with your commander to get you so assigned. Get the bastard. You get the bastard."

She broke down, walked straight into her husband's arms, and wept.

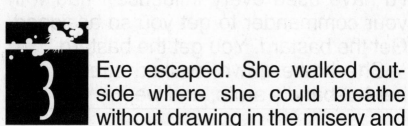 Eve escaped. She walked out-
side where she could breathe
without drawing in the misery and
grief. And where she could reestablish the
locks on her own memories and emotions.

She spotted the two uniforms she sent
out on the knock-on-doors crossing back
toward the victim's home.

"Officers. Report."

"Sir, we covered the block, and were
able to speak to all but four residents.
Others confirmed the family two doors
east is out of town, and has been for three
days. Two others are reportedly attending

a Peace Day rally this morning, and the whereabouts of the remaining resident is unknown at this time."

"I want the name of the question mark. We track him down and interview. The same with the rally attendants. Everyone on this block in residence for the last twenty-four hours is to give a statement."

"Yes, sir. Those we spoke with noticed nothing out of the ordinary yesterday or last night. No one saw anyone but the victim enter or leave the scene." The female officer taking the lead flipped out her memo book. "A Hester Privet both saw and spoke to the victim yesterday morning at approximately ten-fifteen. The victim was, at that time, watering the plants at the entrance to the house. They spoke briefly. The victim mentioned she had a few errands to run that day as her parents were due back the following afternoon. Privet states she then jokingly asked if the victim had a big party planned for the evening. The victim seemed slightly flustered, but laughed and stated she thought she'd just have a quiet evening instead. Privet then continued east on foot."

Over the uniform's shoulder Eve

watched a big orange dog lead its young couple into the park, spotted a jogger in bright red shorts heading out.

"The witness passed by the house later in the day, she believes about three in the afternoon when she took her children to the park, and again at approximately five when she took them home. She is certain the security was engaged at those times as she deliberately walked by to check as she was aware the parents were out of town. She did not, however, see the victim at either time."

"Good. Let me know as soon as you've located and gotten statements from the others."

After dismissing the uniforms, she stood where she was and watched the morgue attendants bring Deena out in the anonymous black body bag. Then she moved to intercept a woman, blond hair flying, who rushed toward the house.

"Ma'am. This is a crime scene, you can't enter at this time."

"It's Deena, isn't it? They wouldn't say what happened, the police. Just that there'd been an incident. I couldn't believe. . . Is it Deena? What happened?"

"I'm unable to give you any information at this time. Are you a friend of the family?"

"Yes. A neighbor. Hester Privet. I spoke with two officers earlier this morning, but—"

"Yes. I'm Lieutenant Dallas. You spoke with Deena yesterday."

"Yes, right here, right out front. Is she—God—is she in that bag?"

No point in evading. It would all hit soon enough. "Deena MacMasters was killed last night."

The woman stumbled back a step, then wrapped both arms around her torso. "But how? How?" Tears gathered in eyes gone wide with shock. "Was there a break-in? She's so vigilant with the alarms and locks. She babysits my twins, my boys—and she lectures *me* about making sure the house is secure. Oh God, my God. My boys adore her. What will I tell them? Can I do something, anything? Jonah and Carol. They're away. I have the contact information. I can—"

"They returned this morning. They're inside."

Hester closed her eyes a moment, took several breaths. "I—I almost went over and knocked. To check? To make sure she didn't want to come over and hang, have dinner. But I talked myself out of it. I wish I'd . . . Is there anything I can do? Anything?"

"Did Deena ever have anyone over when she watched your children? A friend?"

"Sometimes Jo came with her. Jo Jennings, her best friend."

"Any boys?"

"No. God." She used the backs of her hands to wipe her wet cheeks. "Against the rules, and Deena didn't really date."

"Did she always follow the rules?"

"Yes, from what I could tell. I often wished she'd break one." Hester swiped at another tear. "She seemed, to me, so young and innocent for her age, and on the other hand so mature. Responsible. I trusted her absolutely with my sons. I should have checked on her more while her parents were gone, kept a closer eye. I should've insisted she come over for dinner. But it was only a couple of days, and I didn't think. Just didn't think."

"Did she ever talk to you about a boy?"

"No one specific. We did talk about

boys now and then, in general. She has—had—such a good relationship with her mother, but sometimes a girl can't say things to her mom. And we were closer in age. Plus, I pried," Hester admitted with a twisted smile. "I think she had a crush on someone because I'd noticed she was taking more care with her wardrobe, her hair. And . . . well, there was just a look in her eye. You know?"

"Yeah."

"I commented on it, and she just said she was trying some new things. But there was this look in her eye. This I've-got-a-secret look. Did some boy hurt her? Did some . . ." Realization and horror struck her face. "Oh God."

"I can't give you details at this time. I'm going to give you my card. If you think of anything you saw, anything she may have said to you, I want you to contact me. I don't care how inconsequential it may seem, I want to hear it." Eve passed over a card. "One thing. Did you happen to notice when you saw her yesterday morning if she had her nails done? Painted fingers and toes?"

"She didn't. I would've noticed as she rarely did. And she was barefoot. Watering the plants there, in her bare feet, so I'd have noticed."

"Okay, thank you."

"I have to tell my husband, and our boys. They're only four. I don't know how to tell them."

Peabody came out as Hester walked away. "EDD's on the way, and the sweepers are on it. Mrs. Whitney's packing a few things up for Mrs. MacMasters. They'll stay at the Whitneys' for a day or two, depending."

"We'll leave them to it then. We need to interview the friends. It's too late in the day to scope the park, the jogging trails. Her habit was to run there between eight and nine on weekends, the same weekdays when she didn't have school. We'll hit that tomorrow. We'll take Jamie first."

"Jamie? Our Jamie?"

"Lingstrom. He was a friend."

"It's a damn small world when it sucks."

Couldn't argue.

She knew Jamie was home for the summer, and staying with his mother. She kept tabs—loosely. He was the grandson of a dead cop—a damn good cop, and a boy who'd lost his sister to murder when he'd been sixteen.

He was no stranger to death.

And at sixteen, he'd intrigued her husband by using a homemade jammer to bypass Roarke's home security enough to gain access to the estate.

She knew Jamie had a job in one of Roarke's R&D departments for the summer—just as she knew Roarke harbored a bit of frustration that the boy's goals were toward the Electronic Detective Division and cops rather than the private sector.

"Since they were friends, and knowing Jamie, he's going to want in."

Eve picked her way through the holiday traffic. Gathering crowds, souvenir and snack stands prepared for the afternoon parade.

"That'll be up to Feeney." There was a connection there, too, as Feeney and Jamie's grandfather had been tight back in the day. "More to the point, he is in. He's on the short list of the vic's friends, and the only male on it."

"You think they were involved, romantically?"

"The parents don't think so—but according to one of the neighbors, and the mother—there was somebody. Somebody fairly recent that the vic was keeping to herself."

Peabody pondered a moment. "If she had a thing for Jamie—and he had one back—I don't think she'd have kept it to herself. He's just the type the parents would approve of. He's smart, responsible, has the cop connection. He's on scholarship to Columbia, and had plenty of other offers from top-level colleges. He took Columbia so he could stay close to home, not leave his mother too much alone."

At Eve's sidelong stare, Peabody shrugged. "He chats up with McNab, which is also how I know Jamie's been dating the field the last few months. No one girl, nothing serious. I don't think he's even mentioned Deena. I'd've remembered, since I knew her. Plus most college guys don't go for high school girls, or not for long."

"What do high school girls go for?"

"Boys. A college boy would be a big status coup. But . . . Deena wasn't the type. She was kind of sweet and serious and shy."

"Vulnerable. A guy pays attention, knew how to play it. She got her nails done."

"Huh?"

"Sometime Saturday, she did her nails or had them done. She dressed up—skirt, nice shirt, jewelry, put on makeup. If you're hanging at home for the evening, alone, what're you wearing?"

"My pajamas or sweats, probably my rattiest."

"She didn't just let him in. She was expecting him." Eve pulled over to the curb of the modest town house.

She'd done all this before, walked this same path to tell Brenda Lingstrom her daughter was dead.

This time Jamie answered the door.

When had he gotten taller? She had to shift her gaze up to meet his, an odd sensation. He'd let his hair grow a little longer so it tumbled around his face in blond disarray. His jeans were full of holes, his T-shirt baggy with the faded faces of what she recognized as a popular trash rock group sneering out.

His face had fined down since she'd last seen him, and had gone handsome on her. Another mild shock. She wasn't looking at a boy anymore, she realized, but a man.

His sleepy eyes brightened in friendly pleasure, then immediately went blank. He said, "Oh shit."

"Nice to see you, too."

"Who's dead? You're not at the door because you were passing by. Who's— my mother."

Panic leaped, even as his hand shot out and gripped her arm hard enough to bruise.

"No. She's not here?"

"She and Grandma left Friday to hook up with some friends for a girl week, take advantage of the holiday. They're okay?"

"As far as I know. We need to come in, Jamie."

"Who is it? Tell me who it is."

No point trying to soften the blow. "Deena MacMasters."

"What? No. No. Deena? Oh God. Oh, god*damn*!"

He turned away, strode into the living area that had changed little since she'd brought death into it almost two years before. He paced it, veering around tables, chairs, circling like a cat in a cage. "Give me a minute, okay? Give me a minute."

Eve gestured Peabody to a chair herself, and remained standing while Jamie took his minute.

He stopped, turned, with an air of weary resignation at odds with his youth. "When?"

"Early this morning."

"How?"

"We're going to talk about that. When's the last time you saw her?"

"Ah." He rubbed the space between his eyebrows. The gesture seemed to steady him a little. "A couple weeks ago. Wait." He lowered to the arm of a chair, then stared hard into space for a few minutes.

And Eve watched him pull control and composure back. If he decided to pursue law enforcement, he had the spine to make a cop, she thought.

"Tuesday, two weeks ago this coming Tuesday. A bunch of us went to see this new group—Crusher—play at Club Zero. I asked her to come along because we hadn't seen much of each other in a while, and she's into music. All kinds, even the old stuff. It's an underage club, so she could get in, no prob. They sucked extra large, so she and I split off after the first set and went for pizza, caught up some. I took her home, got her home before midnight. She's got a curfew."

"What did you talk about?"

"All kinds of shit. School, music, vids, e-bits. She's not much into the e-scene, but she liked to hear me talk about it. We've known each other forever. Grandpa knew her dad, and she was looking hard at Columbia for next year. We talked about that since I've done two semesters."

"Did she talk about her boyfriend?"

"What boyfriend?" His eyes went on alert. "She wasn't tuned into anybody I knew about. She wasn't hooked up. She got all spazmotic when it came to guys, hardly ever did the one-on-one."

"One-on-one?"

"Dating, you know? She didn't think she was pretty, but she was. And she said she couldn't think of what to say or how to say it. Mom said how she was just self-conscious and shy, and she'd grow out of it. Now she won't." Bitterness coated the words. "What happened to her, Dallas?"

"Her parents were away for the week-end." Eve kept her tone brisk and neutral. "Sometime yesterday, she let someone into the house. It appears she expected him, and given what we know of her at this point, we conclude she knew him and trusted him."

He'd get the details soon enough, Eve knew. Better to hear them now, and from her. "He restrained her. He raped her. He killed her."

His gaze didn't waver from hers. Fury snapped into it as he got to his feet, then his eyes went cold. Yeah, he'd be a good cop, she decided.

"She was harmless. I want to say she was the kind of person who'd go out of her way not to hurt anyone. But she was strong and fast, and smart. She knew self-defense. She took me down a few times when we practiced. He wouldn't have been able to restrain her without a fight. You've got to have some trace."

"It may be he slipped her a drug to in-capacitate her so he was able to restrain her and prevent her from causing him any harm. She fought, Jamie, and hard, but it was too late."

"If she let someone in, she knew him. You're right there. We haven't been as tight since I started college, so I don't know everyone she might have . . ."

"What?"

"When we peeled off from the group, were hanging out over pizza, she asked me what college guys looked at in a girl. I made some crack like the same thing every guy looks for. But she wanted to know, like, if it was looks or common ground, and if we all really expected sex. We could talk like that because we didn't have that kind of thing."

He eased back down on the arm of the chair. "I think I said it wasn't expected, it was hoped for. Pretty much always. But I didn't score with every girl I went out with. I said how she could worry about college guys when she was a college girl. She smiled. I didn't think anything of it, the way she smiled and bounced off topic. She wasn't just talking about guys. There was a guy. Son of a bitch."

"Who would she have told about him?"

"Jo, if anybody. Jo Jennings. BGP-FAE."

"Sorry?"

"Ah, best girl pals forever and ever. They've been hooked since grade school. But Deena could keep things tight when she wanted or needed. Plus, she'd rather listen than talk. She didn't like to stand out, got wizzy if people paid too much attention to her."

"All right. We're going to be talking to Jo Jennings."

"What about the security?" Jamie demanded. "She wouldn't have turned off the cams, not even for someone she knew. House rule, h and f—hard and fast. Cams on and activated twenty-four/seven."

"It appears the killer deactivated them, and removed the record discs."

"Then he'd have to access the control room, and it's passcoded. He had to know how. He had to know . . ." Already pale, his face seemed to whiten to bone. "He planned it, right along. He scoped her. Did he jam them first?"

"We haven't gotten that far."

"Even if he figured how to delete the hard drive, took the disc—and he'd have to have some skills on the e-side for the delete, he'd be on there. He'd still be on there in shadows and echoes. You have the captain on this? You have Feeney?"

"He should be there now, with a team."

"I want in. Dallas, you have to let me in."

"I don't have to do anything," she said coolly. "Captain Feeney will have autonomy on e-details."

He got to his feet again, every line in his body tensed. "You won't block me."

"Is that a question or a statement?"

He remembered himself—and her. "A request."

"As I said, e-detail is under Feeney's province. The work's harder when it's someone you care about. You already know that."

His throat worked as he nodded. "When Alice was murdered, Deena was a rock for me. I didn't want to talk to anyone, but she just kept being there until I had to. I'm going to be there for her now. I can handle it. In three years when I'm finished college, I'm joining the force. College first, that's the deal I made, but then I'm going for the badge. I can handle it."

"Deal with who?"

"With Roarke, since he's picking up the freight the scholarship doesn't cover. And you didn't know that." The faintest smile came back to his eyes. "I guess he knows how to keep things tight, too."

"Apparently. If Feeney gives you the nod, I've got no problem with it. I'm sorry you lost your friend, Jamie."

"Do her parents know?"

"They found her this morning."

He sighed. "I'd like to go over. Not just for the work, but I may be able to help them."

"They're with the Whitneys."

He nodded. "I'm going to go over anyway, speak to the captain. Ask him to let me in."

"Clean up first. Even e-geeks should have some standards."

"McNab will be there." Peabody spoke for the first time, then rose. She crossed to Jamie, hugged him. "You could toss some stuff in a bag, and hang out at our place if you don't want to be alone here."

"Maybe. Thanks." He sighed again. "Yeah, maybe."

And when he laid his head on Peabody's

shoulder Eve saw there was still a boy in there. "I went to a party last night. Maybe if I'd asked her to go. Maybe—"

"You couldn't have changed anything." Peabody drew him back. "We go from here."

He nodded. "From here."

He's going to be thinking of his sister, too," Peabody commented when they were back in the vehicle. "He won't be able to help it. Most people get through their lives without violent death touching it. He's eighteen, and dealt with it three times."

"Working with EDD might help him deal. If you had a secret guy, would you keep him secret?"

"I had such crap luck with guys for such a long stretch a serious date would have been cause for taking out an airtram ad. But Jamie's right—at least it jibes with my sense—she could keep things tight."

Eve pulled up at the next address— a well-maintained multi-family building. "She was only sixteen, and going by our current theory very likely infatuated with an older boy. Jaime said she asked about college guys. She had to tell someone something. I vote for the BGPFAE."

The Jennings's apartment took up the corner on the third and fourth floor. The woman who answered the door appeared to be harassed. The root might have been, Eve concluded, the shouted argument in full swing. Furious voices—a girl, a boy—blasted down the stairs.

"Yes. What is it?"

"Mrs. Jennings?"

"Yes."

"Lieutenant Dallas, NYPSD, and Detective Peabody."

"God, are the neighbors complaining?" She held out her hands, wrists together. "Will you arrest me if I just go up and bash their heads together? Please, please do. I could use the quiet."

"May we come in?"

The woman gave the badges the briefest of glances. "Yes, yes. I don't even know what they're fighting about now. They've been at each other most of the morning about one thing or the other. Peace Day, my ass," she said with weary bitterness. "Their father's golfing. Bastard," she added with the smallest hint of a smile.

"Maybe you could just arrest them, then I could have five minutes of *peace!*"

She shouted the last word, aiming for the stairs. It didn't make a dent in the noise.

"Mrs. Jennings we're not here about a complaint." Why didn't she tell them to shut the hell up? Eve wondered. "We're Homicide."

"I haven't killed anyone. Yet. Was there an incident in the building?"

"No, ma'am. We're here about Deena MacMasters?"

"Deena? Why would you . . . *Deena*?"

Eve watched it sink in, but pushed through. "She was killed early this morning. We understand she and your daughter, Jo, were friends."

"Deena?" she repeated, backing up. "But how?" She reached up as if to push at her hair. It was already pulled back in a tail, and her fingers stayed at her temple. "Are you sure?"

"Yes."

"We understand this is a shock, Mrs. Jennings," Peabody said. "If we could have a few minutes with Jo, it might help us."

"Jo. Jo doesn't know anything. Jo's been home all morning, fighting with her brother. She doesn't know anything."

"She's not in any trouble," Peabody assured her. "We're talking with all of Deena's friends. It's routine. You knew Deena for some time?"

"Yes. Yes. They've been best friends since they were eight. She's—they—oh God. My God. What happened?"

"If we could speak with Jo," Eve interrupted. "You're free to remain in the room."

"All right. Yes. All right." She walked to the base of the stairs, gripped the banister until her knuckles went white. "Jo! Jo! I need you down here. Right now. Do I tell her? Should I—"

"We'll tell her." Eve heard the clump that translated into resentful feet, then a girl with an explosion of brown curls and violently angry brown eyes appeared. She wore knee-length black shorts and, in a fashion that baffled Eve, had layered a trio of tanks so the blue peeked out from the red, and black peeked out from the blue.

"Why is it always me?" Jo demanded. "He started it. He won't . . ." She trailed off, flushing deeply when she spotted Eve and Peabody. "I didn't know anyone was here."

"Jo, baby—"

"I'm Lieutenant Dallas. This is my partner, Detective Peabody."

"Police? Are you going to haul that *freak* off?"

"You're the freak." A boy, curly brown hair shagging in the current style, eyes just as violent as his sister's, snarled as he stormed down the steps.

"Stop! Both of you! Now!"

At last, Eve thought. Obviously stunned by the tone and the order, both kids stopped and stared at their mother as they might a two-headed alien.

Eve stepped up, pointed to a chair. "Sit."

"Am I in trouble? I haven't done anything. I swear."

"Freak," the boy muttered under his breath, then visibly shrunk under Eve's frigid stare.

Eve turned back to Jo. "I'm sorry to inform you that Deena MacMasters was killed this morning."

"Huh?" It was knee-jerk disbelief.

"What?" And the tears welled and spilled instantly. "Mom? Mom? What is she saying?"

Though Eve preferred to leave weepers to Peabody, she sat across from Jo, kept their faces level as the mother squeezed into the chair to put her arms around her daughter.

"Someone killed her. Someone she knew. A boy she's been seeing secretly. What's his name?"

"She is not *dead*. We went shopping on Saturday with Hilly. Why are you saying that?"

The brother moved to her other side, all anger forgotten.

"She let someone into the house while her parents were away. Who was she dating?"

"Nobody."

"Lying doesn't help her now."

"Lieutenant, please. Can't you see how upset she is? We all are."

"Her parents are upset, too. They came home and found their daughter dead. Who was she seeing, Jo? What's his name?"

"I don't *know*. Mom. Mom. Make her go

away." She turned her face, pressing it to her mother's breast. "Make it go away."

"It can't go away." Eve said it coldly, before Mrs. Jennings could speak. "It happened. Were you her friend?"

"Yes. Yes."

"I'll get her some water," Peabody murmured, and turned away to find the kitchen.

"Tell me everything you know. It's the only way to help her now. If you're her friend, you want to help her."

"But I don't know. I really don't. I never met him, or even saw him. She just called him David. She said his name was David, and he was wonderful. They met in the park a few weeks ago. She ran there a couple times a week. More sometimes."

"Okay. How did they meet?"

"She liked to run, and this one day he was on the same path, and he tripped. He went down pretty hard, so she stopped to see if he was okay. He was all embarrassed, and he'd banged his knee a little, turned his ankle, you know? And he told her he was fine, not to stop, but when he tried to get up, his water bottle was broken and spilled all over, and he was *more* embarrassed because it got her shoes wet. They went over to sit on the grass, started talking a little, so she could make him feel better. And he was really cute."

"What did he look like?"

"I don't really know. She just said he was really cute. Adorable squared, and he was from Georgia and had an accent that just made her go wizzy. He was clumsy and really sweet and courteous. Old-fashioned. She really liked that about him."

Peabody brought in a glass of water. Jo stared at it. "Thank you. I don't understand. I don't understand."

"Why did she keep him a secret?" Peabody asked gently.

"It was romantic. She didn't even tell *me* until, like, last month, and only because she said she'd *burst* if she couldn't talk about him. And . . . well, she knew her parents would ask questions, and he told her he'd gotten in some trouble back home in Georgia when he'd been in high school. With illegals. Her father wouldn't have liked it, even though he told her straight out, and he'd done his rehab and community service and everything. She wanted some more time before she said anything about him."

"But you never met him either," Eve pointed out.

"He was shy, and he said—I think—how he liked it just being the two of them for a while. They didn't *do* anything. Honest, Mom, they didn't . . . you know."

"It's all right, sweetie. It's all right, Jo."

"They just met in the park sometimes, or went for walks or rides on his board, and they went to see a couple vids and talked on the 'link a lot. It was weeks before he even kissed her. And he was nineteen. She was afraid her parents wouldn't like that he was older."

"Did they have a date last night?"

Jo nodded, miserably. "She was going to have him over, just to eat and hang out a while because he was going to take her to a show. She liked going to the theater, and he got tickets to *Coast to Coast*. It's why we went shopping, especially. She wanted a new outfit. She bought this really mag purple skirt—it's her favorite color, and new shoes to go with it. She was really excited."

Eve thought of the shoes near the table

by the stairs, the purple skirt rucked up on the bruised thighs.

"She went out yesterday afternoon for a mani and pedi." Eyes streaming, she burrowed into her mother. "She tagged me to see if I could meet her, but we had to have dinner at Gram's and Poppa's. She wanted it to be special. She was so happy. He wouldn't have hurt her. He was nice. There has to be a mistake."

"Who else did she tell about him?"

"Nobody. She wasn't supposed to tell me, they'd made a promise to each other to keep it just the two of them, at least for a while. But she couldn't, she was so happy she just wanted to talk to me, to tell me. I had to swear absolutely not to tell, not even Hilly or Libby. And I didn't. I didn't tell. He was so mag, she had to tell somebody. And we're best friends. There has to be a mistake," Jo insisted. "Please? There has to be a mistake."

There'd been one, Eve thought as they walked back to the car. And young Deena had made it. David from Georgia—and what bullshit that was—had played her right from the first meeting in the park. Shy, clumsy, sweet—with just that one shadow in his past. Irresistible to a girl like Deena.

He'd created the boy of her dreams.

But why?

 **4** "Was she a target before he saw her running in the park habitually, then set up the play," Peabody wondered, "or before even that? I mean, specifically Deena MacMasters rather than just a teenage girl, maybe one with certain physical characteristics?"

"It's a good question."

"It seems like, if it was luck of the draw, he'd have backed off when he found out her father was a cop. Easier prey out there."

"Which may have been part of her appeal to him," Eve said. "She'd make a challenge. He knew enough about her at the setup meeting. He'd already done or at least started research on her. He knew her father was a cop when he staged the meet—cute. Knew her tastes. Shy boy, awkward boy, gentle boy."

"Specifically her then." Peabody frowned. "So why was it a good question?"

"Because we can't rule out the other option. I'm going to drop you off at the next pal's, leave that one to you. I think Jo was being straight when she said nobody else knew about this guy—but we'll cross the Ts. When you finish interviewing the friends, head down to Central. I'll book a conference room. I want EDD to come in with a prelim report asap.

"They went for walks," Eve murmured, thinking of what Jo had said. "You can bet he didn't walk with her in her own neighborhood. Nowhere they'd be likely to run into someone who knew her. To vids, where it's dark. Keep it all a secret. It's more romantic, and I'm ashamed of my minor transgression. I'm shy. A few weeks, Jo said. A long time to play out the string. Patient bastard."

"Young, if he's really nineteen."

"Maybe he is, or maybe he knows how to look nineteen." She swung to the curb. "We'll run like crimes. I'll start on that after I go by the morgue."

"Tell Morris . . . well, just tell him welcome back." Peabody climbed out.

Hell of a welcome, Eve thought, but bulled her way back into traffic. The barricades, the swarms of pedestrians trooping toward Fifth for the parade, the seas of entrepreneurs with carts and wheeled cases loaded with souvenirs jammed the streets and sidewalks.

Within blocks her bulling slowed to inching. She narrowed her eyes at the throng of tourists and locals forming impenetrable walls—and thought if she saw one more person sporting a peace sign or waving a flower flag, she might just pull her weapon and give them one good zap.

I've got your peace right here, she thought.

She glanced at the time, blew out a breath, then used her dash 'link to contact Roarke.

"Lieutenant. I take it this isn't to let me know you're on your way home."

"No. I'm fighting through freaking Peace

Day mayhem. If these people want peace, why the hell don't they stay home?"

"Because they want to share goodwill with their fellow man?"

"Bullshit. Because they want to get drunk and cop feels in the crowd."

"There is that. Where are you heading?"

"The morgue. It's a bad one."

"I'm sorry. Can you tell me?"

"Sixteen-year-old daughter of a decorated cop, one who recently earned his captain's bars. Rape-murder, in her home. Her parents found the body this morning when they returned from a weekend holiday."

"I'm very sorry." Those intense blue eyes searched her face looking, she knew, for cracks.

"I'm fine."

"All right. Is there anything I can do?"

You just did it, she thought, by asking. "I'm trying to fit the pieces together. One of them is Jamie."

"Jamie? How?"

"They were friends."

"Surely you don't think—"

"No, I don't think. I'll check out his alibi simply because I don't want to leave any blanks, but he's not a suspect. She had a secret boyfriend—one it's looking like targeted her, laid all the groundwork. I'm on my way to the morgue to see if some of the pieces in my head fit the evidence. After that, I'm hitting the lab."

She saw a minute break in traffic, gunned it, flipped her vertical, soared over—she *loved* this new ride—and swung west.

"I asked Whitney to order Morris in today. Then I'm convening a briefing at Central. We need to run like crimes, go through the electronics, start a sweep on her areas of interest, so—"

"I believe I'll come down and watch you work."

"Look—"

"I can stay out of the way if that's what you want. But you won't keep Jamie out. I may be some help there. You've said her parents—one a police captain—returned home to find her dead. But you don't mention security discs or the system. One assumes a veteran cop would take all necessary means, including strong security, to protect his family. There's some e-work here."

"That's Feeney's aegis."

"I'll be contacting him then."

Knew you would. "Wouldn't you like a nice quiet Sunday at home?"

"I would, if I had my wife here. But she's having a different sort of day."

"Suit yourself. Question. Why didn't you tell me you were supplementing Jamie's scholarship?"

"Busted." He looked mildly disconcerted. "It's not a crime."

"Well now I'm not altogether sure, as you'd see it as a bribe, wouldn't you, to lure him into one of my companies?"

"Isn't it?"

"Damn right, and a fine one, too. But the boy's determined to be a cop. If he's still of that mind when he's finished at university, your gain is my loss. He's bloody brilliant."

"As good as you?"

Those wild blue eyes sparkled. "No, but a good deal more honest. I'll see you at Central."

"Don't take Fifth. Jesus! I wish you could see this. There's some asshole dressed like a peace sign. He's a big yellow circle, with naked limbs. People are so damn weird. I'll see you later."

She'd known he'd come, just as she'd come to know how useful it was to have a thief—former—help analyze the bypassing of locks and codes.

Deena might have given her killer the passcode for the control room, if she'd had it. But if he'd shut down the cameras, wiped the hard drive, accessed the discs, he'd needed more than the code. He'd needed excellent e-skills.

And there her thief—former—was unsurpassed.

"Bloody brilliant," she muttered, using Roarke's own term.

A skeletal holiday shift manned the morgue, and those who remained behind to deal with the dead wore colorful shorts under lab coats. Music danced jauntily out of offices and cutting rooms.

She doubted the residents cared overmuch one way or the other.

She paused long enough to scowl at Vending. She wanted a tube of Pepsi, and didn't want any bullshit from the damn machine.

"You!" She jabbed a finger at a passing tech, and the gesture had his face going as white as his bony legs. "Two tubes of Pepsi." She pushed credits at him.

"Sure, okay." Dutifully, he plugged them in, made her request. Even as the tubes plopped into the slot, and the machine began the soft drink's current jingle, Eve snatched them out.

"Thanks." She strode away.

The first sip was shockingly cold, and exactly what she was after. She continued down the white tunnel, chased by the echo of her own boots and the sticky hints of death that clung to the air under the blasts of citrus and disinfectant wafting out of the vents.

She paused outside the double doors of the autopsy suite not to brace herself to face that death, but the man who studied it.

She drew a breath, pushed through the doors.

There he was, looking the same.

He wore a clear protective coat over a suit of moonless night black. He'd paired it with a shirt of rich gold, and a needle-thin tie where both colors wove together. She frowned at the silver peace sign pinned to his lapel, but had to admit on Morris it worked.

His ink-black hair drew back from his exotic face in a single, gleaming braid.

He stood over the dead girl he'd already opened with his precise, almost artistic Y cut.

When his dark eyes lifted to Eve's, she felt her belly tighten.

He looked the same, but was he?

"I guess this is a crappy welcome back." She crossed over, offered the second tube. "Sorry I had to pull you in early, and on a holiday."

"Thank you." He took the drink, but didn't crack the tube.

Her tightened belly began to jump. "Morris—"

"I have some things to say to you."

"Okay. All right."

"Thank you for finding justice for Amaryllis."

"Don't—"

He held up his free hand. "I need to say these things before we go back to our work, our lives. You need to let me say them."

Feeling helpless, she stuck her hands in her pockets and said nothing.

"We deal with death, you and I, and with that death leaves grieving. We believe—or hope—that finding the answers, finding justice will help the dead, and those the dead leaves grieving. It does. Somehow it does. I no longer believe it, or hope it, but know it. I loved her, and the loss . . ."

He paused, opened the tube, drank. "Immense. But you were there for me. As a cop, and as a friend. You held my hand during those first horrible steps of grief, helped me steady myself. And by finding the answers, you gave me, and her, some peace. It's a day to remember peace, I suppose. The job you and I do is often ugly and thankless. I need to thank you."

"Okay."

"More, Eve." He rarely used her first name, and using it now, he closed his hand over her arm to keep her still. "Though it discomforts you." And smiled, just a little—just enough to loosen the tightest knots in her belly. "Thank you for suggesting I speak to Father Lopez."

"You went to see him?"

"I did. I had thought to go away, stay away until . . . Until. But there was nowhere I wanted to be, and frankly, I felt closer to her here. So I stayed, and I went to see your priest."

She had to fight not to squirm. "He's not mine."

"He gave me comfort," Morris continued over her flustered response. "He's a man of unassailable faith, with a flexible mind and limitless compassion. He helped me with those next difficult steps, and helped me accept I'll have more to take."

"He's . . . good, but not a pain in the ass about it. Much."

Now the smile reached those dark eyes and eased more of her tension. "An excellent summary. And thank you for trusting me when I wasn't sure I trusted myself."

"I don't know what you mean."

"Before your request came in this morning, I was going over the reasons— excuses—not to come back yet. Another week, maybe two. I wasn't sure I was ready to be here, to face this place, to handle the work. But you asked for me. You trusted me, so what choice do I have but to trust myself?"

"She needs you." On that single point Eve had Lopez's unassailable faith. "Deena MacMasters needs you. You have a good team here, good people. But she needs *you.* She needs us."

"Yes. So . . ." He stunned her by brushing his lips, very lightly on hers. "It's good to see you."

"Um. Likewise."

He gave her arm a quick squeeze, then released it. "And where is the estimable Peabody?"

"Field work. We've got a lot of ground to cover."

"Then we'll begin. I know MacMasters, of course. He's solid. This will have put a hole in him."

"He's maintaining."

"What else is there? Her name is Deena." He glanced at Eve, got her nod. "Sixteen-year-old female in exceptional health prior to her death. She took care of herself, and was cared for. The scan showed no prior injuries of any note, and confirms excellent nutrition. Her last meal, consumed at approximately six-thirty p.m., was pizza with a topping of peppers, mushrooms, black olives, and about six ounces of cherry fizzy. As you flagged tox, I've determined the barbiturate she ingested with the meal was mixed with the drink."

"He drugged her."

"I can't say, only that she ingested the barb, and there are no signs of regular use of same in her scan. All to the contrary. Given her weight, and the assumption she wasn't accustomed to taking drugs, the dose would have been enough to render her unconscious, for perhaps as much as an hour."

"Plenty of time for him to get her upstairs, restrained, then shut down the cameras and take the discs. If he did so in that order. Plenty of time. She'd have been groggy, disoriented when she came to."

"Yes. She ingested another dose—smaller—at about midnight."

"A second dose?"

"Yes. Her hands were cuffed behind her back at the wrists—there's deep bruising, lacerations indicating she struggled against them, quite violently. The marks on her ankles indicate a different restraint. Probably cloth."

"Bedsheets."

"That's consistent. She fought those, too. And if you look." He paused to pick up a second pair of microgoggles, gave them to Eve. "Here." They bent over the ankles together. "The bounds were extremely tight, digging into the skin. Here, here, here."

"Tied, retied, tied again." She saw it in her head as well. "Tied, raped, untied, turned, *tied,* sodomized. Untied, turned, raped again?"

"It would be my conclusion. Multiple rapes, multiple sodomy, all extremely violent. As you can see . . ."

He moved up the body. A line of sweat, icy cold, slid down Eve's spine. But she moved with him, slammed more locks on her memories, and studied the damage.

"The tears, the trauma. Her hymen was intact before the rape. So young," he murmured. "And so mercilessly used. I found no semen. He sealed up, and was cautious enough to do so with each rape.

We've no trace of him in or on her. I'd speculate he removed his own genital hair, possibly all his body hair before the act. Otherwise, even sealed, with multiple, violent rapes, we should have found a stray hair. There's some bruising on her legs, her torso from his hands. Deeper bruising on her shoulders where it appears he held her down more forcibly. On her throat—"

"He choked her. Watched her face while he did. Watched until she passed out. Between the rapes, between them because he wouldn't want to risk going too far, taking her out too soon, spoiling the fun."

She could see it, in the room with the soft violet walls and the glossy white furniture. See the terror, the horror. Feel the pain.

"He chokes her while she struggles, fights for air, goes out. Then he unties her legs, shoves her over, secures her again. And waits for her to come to so she can feel him sodomize her. No good if she's out. He wants to hurt her. Needs to hurt her. Maybe he gets off that way. On her pain, her struggles, her pleas."

"You've gone pale." Morris touched her arm. "Step back, sit."

She shook her head, brushed him off. She *would* get through it. Staring into her own past as much as Deena's, Eve swiped the cold tube over her brow.

"Then what he does, when he's finished, however many times he feels inclined, when she's lying there, quivering or when she's gone somewhere else, somewhere she can't feel the pain, he pushes her face into the pillow, holds her down, smothering her until she passes out again. Then he can turn her over, tie her again. He worked her for about eight hours, a full day's work. So he could let her lie there a while until he could get it up again.

"Maybe he promised to let her go if she gave him the passcode for the control room. But I think he may have already taken care of that. Either way, lots of time. She'd ask him why, why he was doing this. He'd tell her, tell her exactly. Because he was going to kill her, and he'd enjoy telling her why."

"Why?" Morris spoke softly, watching her face.

"Don't know. Not yet. But he'd make sure she knew it wasn't because he *wanted* her. Not because he liked her. If he made all this time, took all this effort to hurt her physically, again and again, wouldn't he want to hurt her emotionally, mentally? Break her down, carve her away, every inch. In addition to the rape, and all that does to your body, your mind, your fucking soul, he'd want to make sure she knew she meant nothing. That he'd played her. Taking her out, holding her hand, being a shy guy. Making her feel like a fool? Nice bonus."

She kept her breathing even, she could do that, even if she couldn't stop the pulse from hammering in her head.

"Mask's off. No need for it now. He'd want her to see who he was. He'd want her to know what's inside her when he rapes her, what's tearing and ripping her. Young healthy girl, strong girl, so he can drag it out for hours, until the last time he put his hands around her throat, the last time she looks in his eyes as he starts to squeeze. Until he ends it."

She did step back now. She didn't tremble, though she wanted to. Still, she took a long, slow drink of the now-lukewarm Pepsi. "He leaves the cuffs. Cop cuffs. Standard issue. He unties her legs, but leaves her hands cuffed. Because that's a message to her father. That's an extra punch to the gut. It wasn't her, not about her. She was just an instrument. A weapon. He could've killed her dozens of times before this, in dozens of ways. He wanted it to be in that house, inside the house where the cop believed his little girl would always be safe."

She studied the face. "The second dose, that was for MacMasters, too. He wanted to make sure we found the drug in her system. As far as he knew, at the time of the murder, her parents weren't due back until the afternoon, mid- to late afternoon. We wouldn't have gotten to a tox yet on that time frame. We wouldn't have gotten to one until evening, even flagged and expedited. Just another boost to make sure we found it. That's why he left the glass."

"Glass?"

"It'll be her glass he left on the counter in the kitchen, and there'll be traces of the barb there for the lab to find. It's like . . .

thumbing his nose. An insult to kick it all down. Look what I can do in the sanctity of your own home, to your precious daughter, using the very thing you work against every day of your life. It wasn't about her, about Deena. That's worse, isn't it?"

She looked at Morris again, composed again. "It's worse for MacMasters knowing it wasn't about her. She was just the conduit."

"Yes. It would be worse." *And what were you?* he wondered. *What were you to the one who used you this way?*

But he didn't ask. He knew her too well, understood her too well, to ask.

Later, she stood outside, breathing in New York, drawing in the sticky heat of a day that decided to soar to summer. She'd gotten through it, she told herself, gotten through what should be the worst of it. She got back in her car and drove to the lab.

She expected to butt heads with Chief Lab Tech Dick Berinksi. In fact, she looked forward to the tension relieving ass-kicking she hoped to give the man not so affectionately known as Dickhead.

"He's a fuck, but he's the best," she'd say about him.

She found the lab empty but for a handful of lab rats tucked in their glass cubes or dozing over paperwork. And the egg-shaped head plastered with thin black hair of the chief bent toward a comp screen while his clever, if creepy, fingers played over both screen and keyboard.

"Status." She said it like a dare.

He shot her a resentful glare. "I had tickets to the ball game. Boxed seats."

Bribes, no doubt. "Captain MacMasters had a daughter. Now ask me if I give a flying shit about your box seat."

"She wouldn't be less dead if I was chowing on a dog, sucking down a brew, and watching the Yankees on freaking Peace Day."

"Gee, you're right. It's too bad she got raped, sodomized, raped again, terrorized, and choked to death on freaking Peace Day just to inconvenience you."

"Jesus, chill." The murderous gleam in her eye must have gotten through his own ire as he waved those spider fingers in the air. "I'm here, aren't I? And I already ran the glass. You got cherry fizzy and barbs. The mickey comes up as Slider, liquid form, with a small kick of powdered Zoner."

"Zoner?"

"Yeah, just a touch. Didn't need it, not with the Slider, but the combo gives the user freaky dreams. Usually, you wake up with a mother of a migraine. I don't see an upside to sucking down this particular cocktail, but it takes all kinds."

"So, she'd have suffered even when she was out. And come back in pain."

"He'd wanted to just knock her out, the Slider'd do it. You have to figure he wanted the edge. I got DNA and prints, and both match the vic's. I was just sending it over. You could've saved yourself the trip."

"What about the sheets, her clothes?"

"I'm not a freaking machine. I've got them logged in, and I'm going to run them. Sweepers lit them up on scene—just like I figure you did—no semen. He suited up most like. But we'll give them a full scan. If his suit sprang a leak the size of a pinhole, or he drooled, we'll find it. Before you ask, the cuffs are standard issue. I took a gander and they look new. Or at least they hadn't seen any use to speak of before this. Blood and tissue match the vic's. No prints. Fibers caught in them, probably from the sheets. Harpo can take those in the morning."

She couldn't argue. He'd done the job. "Send the report on the glass—and another as soon as you finish with the sheets, her clothes."

She left it at that and headed to Central with the low hum of a headache at the base of her skull.

Even on Peace Day, cruising toward evening, Central buzzed. Protect and serve meant 24/7, and peace be damned. Bad guys, in their various forms, on their various levels, didn't take time off. She imagined there were precincts across the island filled with not-so-bad guys who'd had too much holiday brew, indulged in some holiday pushy-shovey, or had their wallets lifted in the parade crush.

She took the glides rather than the faster elevators to give herself just a little more time to level out.

She wished she had something to pummel. Wished she could take twenty to swing into one of the on-site gyms and tune up a sparring droid. But eight hours after the tag from Whitney, she strode into the bullpen in Homicide, and straight through to her office.

Coffee, she thought—the real deal— would have to substitute for the release of punches and sore knuckles.

He sat in her visitor's chair, one she knew was miserably uncomfortable because she didn't want anyone to settle into her space too long.

But he sat, working on his PPC, his sleeves rolled up, his hair tied back as it was when he prepared to dive into some thorny task or was already in the thicket.

She shut the door.

"I thought you'd be with Feeney."

"I was." Roarke sat where he was to study her face. "They haven't been back from the scene long. They're setting up in the conference room you booked."

She nodded, walked straight to her AutoChef to order coffee. "I just want a minute to organize my thoughts for the briefing. You can tell them I'm on my way."

She'd wanted to brood out her skinny

window while downing the coffee, but brooding required being alone. Instead, she turned to walk to her desk.

He'd risen and stepped behind her. He made less noise than their cat. And he took the mug of coffee out of her hand to set it aside.

"Hey. I want the kick."

"You can have it in a minute." All he did with those strong, seeking blue eyes on hers was touch his fingertips to her cheeks.

"Okay." Letting go, just letting go, she stepped into his arms. She could close her eyes and be enfolded, be held, be loved and understood.

"There now." He turned his head to press his lips to her hair. "There."

"I'm okay."

"Not quite. I won't ask if you'll pass this on. You wouldn't even if a colleague hadn't asked you for help." At the shake of her head, he kissed her hair again, then eased her back so their eyes met. "You need to prove you can get through it."

"I am getting through it."

"You are. But I think you forget you need to get through nothing alone."

"She was older than I was. Twice my age. Still . . ."

He stroked her back when she shuddered, just one hard tremor. "Still. Young, defenseless, innocent."

"I'd already stopped being innocent. I was . . . When I was at the morgue, I looked at her, and I thought, that could've been me on the slab. If I hadn't put him on one first, it could've been me. He'd have killed me sooner or later, or worse, turned me into a thing. Putting him there first had to be done, and that's that. She didn't have a chance, not even the chance I did. A good home, parents who loved her, and who'll be broken, some pieces of them always broken now. But she didn't have the chance I did. I could never pass her on."

"No, you never could."

She held and was held another minute, then stepped back. "I was wishing I had time to go beat the living crap out of a sparring droid."

"Ah." He had to smile. "A never-fail for you."

"Yeah. This was better."

He picked up her coffee, handed it to

her. "Taking a blocker for the headache would be better yet."

"It's not so bad, not so bad now. I'll work it off."

"The pizza I ordered should help."

"You ordered pizza?" The part of her that yearned warred against the part of her that wanted to maintain discipline. "I've told you not to keep buying food for my cops. You'll spoil and corrupt them."

"There's only one cop I'm interested in spoiling and corrupting, and pizza happens to be a weakness of hers."

She drank her coffee doing her best to scowl at him over the rim. "Did you get pepperoni?"

5 Feeney chomped down on a loaded slice. He stood at the conference table, focused on the pie while Jamie and McNab attacked a second one. Her former partner, now captain of the Electronic Detectives Division managed to balance what was left of the slice and what appeared to be a tube of cream soda while studying crime scene photos Peabody had yet to tack to the murder board.

He'd had his hair chopped recently, Eve noted, but it did little to combat the spring of ginger and wires of gray that spooled through it. His face, weathered and worn, drooped like a sleepy hound's. She figured he'd bought the shit-brown jacket he'd paired with wrinkled trousers before his best boy, McNab, had been weaned from his mother's tit.

In contrast, the young EDD ace and Peabody's cohab sizzled in atomic red cargos and a tee the color of radioactive egg yolks scrambled with lightning bolts. His long blond hair was tucked back from his thin, pretty face in a slinky braid.

Since it was there, Eve scooped up a slice.

"You okay having Jamie work on this?" she asked Feeney.

"He's going to push on it anyway. It's better if he does it where I can keep my eye on him." He took a swig of cream soda. "He's going to be rocky right off, but he'll steady up. I knew Deena, too. Good kid." He kept his eyes on the crime scene photos. "Sick fuck. This one's going to spread through the department. You'll have more cops lining up for detail on this than you can use."

"How well do you know MacMasters?"

"We worked a few together, knocked back some brews together. Good cop."

It was, she knew, Feeney's highest praise.

"You look at this, Dallas, and you think—as a cop, as a father—you can do everything right, do the job, keep it clean, and you still can't protect your own kid from something like this. You think you can, even though you know what's out there, you have to think you can. Then something like this brings it right home, right in the front door. And you know you can't."

He shook his head, but it didn't budge the anger on his face. "We want to believe we can protect our own." Then he paused, took another long drink. "I was going to head out with the wife to New Jersey this afternoon, a cookout at our boy's. New Jersey for Christ's sake," he added with the deliberate disdain of a native New Yorker.

"Well, look at it this way, traffic would've been a total bitch."

"That's fucking A. Anyway, the wife's bringing me back a plate." He looked down at Deena again. "This little girl had a lot more than a holiday barbecue taken from her."

"He went for her, Feeney, knew how to

get to her. There has to be a reason. We work from there."

"Payback." Feeney nodded. "Could be. He's been a cop a long time, LT of Illegals near ten years, I guess. Captain now. He closes cases and doesn't take any bullshit. Good cop," he repeated. "Good cops make enemies, but—"

"Yeah, I've been working on the 'buts.' Let's get started here, and we'll go through them. Screen on," she ordered.

The command signaled the others, and the briefing began.

"The victim is Deena MacMasters, female, age sixteen. ME has confirmed homicide by manual strangulation. The victim was raped and sodomized multiple times over a period between six and eight hours. Traces of barbiturate—street name Slider—mixed with a small amount of powdered Zoner found during tox screen indicate she was drugged."

"That's Wig."

Eve paused, lifted her eyebrows at Jamie.

"Sorry, Lieutenant. I wanted to inform you the freaks call that cocktail Wig because it, well, wigs you out. If you take enough to conk, you go into weird-ass nightmares. They're supposed to be really real, and you have one bitch of a headache after."

Feeney jabbed a finger at Jamie. "How do you know so much about it? If you're playing around with that shit at college, I'm going—"

"Hey, don't look at me. I'm clean. I get one bust I can lose my scholarship. Plus, Jesus, if I want a nightmare I'll eat a burrito and watch a horror vid at midnight."

"Damn right."

"Jamie confirms what I learned from Dickhead at the lab. As there are no defensive wounds, no sign of struggle prior, we believe she was drugged with this combination, then taken to her bedroom where she was restrained. Cuffs on her hands, sheets used as ropes on her ankles."

"He wanted it to start for her even when she was unconscious," Peabody murmured.

"And while she was unconscious, he may have taken the time to run the plates and his glass through the sanitizer, may have accessed the control room. He would then have time to return to the bedroom before she'd come around.

"Except for her underwear, her clothes were not removed but pulled away during the assaults. There are some tears on her shirt, but they don't indicate much force. This shows a lack of rage, of frenzy, and a deliberation."

Eve cut her gaze toward Jamie as he started to speak. It was enough to have him subsiding. "Minor bruising on the face, the torso indicates she was struck, but not with serious force. Bruising on the biceps, shoulders, indicates she was held down. The bruising and lacerations on her wrists, her ankles mean she fought, and fought hard.

"Her killer took his time, incapacitating her by choking or smothering until she passed out, at which time we believe he removed the ankle restraints, turned her over, and retied. He most likely waited for her to regain consciousness before raping her again. It appears he repeated this pattern more than once."

She glanced toward Jamie again. His face was very white, his eyes very dark, but he said nothing.

"This tells us a lot," she said, and waited.

"Um. He didn't waste time and energy smacking her around," Peabody began. "He wasn't interested in hurting her that way. He didn't bother to strip her because he didn't care. It wasn't about that kind of humiliation."

Eve nodded. "It's more insulting to leave her dressed. It makes the act more base than it already is. Penetration. Dominance. Pain."

Her heart fluttered, a quick beat of panicked wings. And she looked at Roarke, straight into his eyes, to calm it again.

"The lab has confirmed a glass left on the kitchen counter contained the same drugs found in her system. Also confirmed, the restraints used on her wrists were police issue. Only her blood and tissue have been found on the cuffs. Thus far, Crime Scene has found no trace of the killer on scene. There is no DNA of the killer on or in the vic's body. He sealed up. Peabody, witness statements."

"The lieutenant and I spoke to two of the victim's known friends, as well as Jamie. I also spoke with two others on the list given us by the vic's parents. Of these, only Jo Jennings stated any knowledge of a man the victim had been involved with. He is reported to be nineteen years of age, and apparently told the victim he was a student at Columbia, originally from Georgia. They met several weeks ago in the park where Deena routinely jogged, and began dating secretly. All subjects interviewed stated that the victim had a PPC, a pocket 'link, but neither were found on scene or on the premises. We conclude the killer took them as there may be communications between them thereon. None of Deena's friends or family met or can identify this man, according to their statements."

"According to Jo's statement," Eve continued, "the vic told the UNSUB her father was a cop, an Illegals cop. He then told the vic he'd once been arrested for illegals use, and appears to have used that to convince her to keep their relationship from her friends and family."

"She'd have gone along." Jamie glanced at Eve, got her nod. "If he said he was embarrassed or weirded out by that, she'd have gone along so he wouldn't be uncomfortable. She didn't like to put any-one on the spot, you know?"

"Added to it," McNab said, "a secret boyfriend? Pretty juicy for a kid that age."

"By all appearances the vic not only let him in on the night of the murder, but was expecting him. Again from Jo's statement, the vic believed the killer was coming by to have something to eat, then taking her to the theater. The log on the AutoChef rec-ords two single-serving pizzas—one meat while the vic's was a vegetarian—ordered at about eighteen-thirty. She ingested her first dose of drugs, through her soft drink."

"First dose?" Feeney asked.

"She ingested a second dose around midnight. I believe the killer knew when her parents were due back, which was late this afternoon. I believe this second dose was given to ensure it showed clearly on the tox screen. He couldn't know her parents would decide to come back several hours earlier than planned. He left the glass on the counter to be sure we'd run it, and find the drugs."

"A slap at MacMasters." Feeney

frowned at the tox report on the wall screen. "It follows, but . . . if you go after a cop, you go for the cop. If you're going to go at him through his family, where's the signature? You'd want him to know, no doubt, it was payback. Plus, Christ knows this fuck couldn't have taken the kid out before today. Getting Deena to play along with the secret, that's risky. A kid that age talks. She told one friend parts of it."

"More fun this way." Eve switched the image on screen to Deena's ID photo—young, fresh, smiling. "More personal. Not only in the house, in the girl's pretty bedroom. And she opened the door. Confirmed?"

Feeney nodded. "No sign of tampering, of bypass on any door or window in the place. Our prelim time line matches yours. Locks disengaged, from the inside and with proper procedure, at eighteen-twenty-three, and immediately re-engaged, again from the inside and with proper procedure. She let him in, then locked back up. At twenty-three-eighteen, the door to the control room was opened, with passcode, and the cameras disengaged with proper procedure."

"He'd worked on her for about four hours by then." Eve thought, couldn't stop herself from thinking what it was to be raped and abused for hours. "She'd have given him the passcode. He didn't have to work it himself. He worked her instead."

"She was a cop's kid," Jamie objected. "And she was smart. I don't think she'd make it that easy for him."

Couldn't see, Eve concluded. How could you when you've never been there? "Four hours being raped and terrorized, choked, smothered. He tells her, okay, I'm going, but I need to turn off the cameras, get the discs. Maybe she says no the first time, or the first few times. So he hurts her again, again. Give me the codes, Deena, and all this stops."

"She didn't give him the code to get the discs, not the right one anyway." McNab spoke up. "It may be she didn't have them. No reason for her to have them. He hacked that, but it didn't take him long. Ten minutes maybe, so he's got some skills or some good equipment. The discs were removed according to the log at twenty-three-thirty-one. The hard drives were wiped and corrupted, but we dug out the time. And we may be able to reconstruct the data, with images. It's not going to be a walk, but we've got a shot. The system's ultra. The more ultra, the more fail-safes, the better chance at reconstructing a wipe and bypass."

"That's a priority," Eve said. "Once he had the discs, did the wipe and disengaged, he went back up and went at her for another two hours."

"He left by the front door," Feeney put in. "Opening the locks from inside, resetting them at oh-four-three."

"Giving him a space after TOD to clean up, do his own sweep, leave the glass. No hurry, no panic, just one step at a time. Bet he had a checklist," Eve muttered. "He leaves early enough not to be noticed or seen. Yet he arrived in daylight, and we've got no one who saw him. Blends well, moves well. There're a couple of subway stops within three blocks. I've ordered copies of all security. But . . ."

She didn't like the odds. "If he's smart enough to do all this, he's too smart to get caught on security at a station close to the scene. On foot most likely. If his hole is any distance from the scene, maybe he rides or cabs it within ten blocks, any direction. Takes the damn bus. He could have his own transpo."

"Walking's best," Roarke commented. "Saturday evening, the city's busy. It was good weather. Who'd notice a boy—or a young man—walking along? Dressed well, I'd expect, but not so well as to draw attention. Sunny out, so he'd be wearing shades, maybe a cap or hoodie. Maybe have an earbud in so it looks like he's listening to music, or he's using his 'link as a prop, so it looks like he's talking or texting. The opportunity comes along, he might slide in with a group of people— if he hits on some about his age. Less noticed yet if he's with others. It's best, if you've a mind to do crime in a neighborhood, and show yourself beforehand, you blend in—disappear as it were into the fabric. What I'd do, in his place, is use that 'link a couple blocks back, to call the target."

Eve narrowed her eyes. "Let her know you're nearly there. Can't wait to see you. Just up the block. We're still on, right? That sort of thing."

"Aye. Then wouldn't she be right there,

keeping watch for him while they talk a bit more? Right there to open the door even before he starts up the stairs. He's in, a matter of seconds." Roarke shrugged. "Well, that's how I'd have played it out."

"And she's got her 'link, right there," Eve added. "He's going to need to take that, and this way he wouldn't have to look for it if she didn't put it back in her bag. That would be smart, efficient. That would fit him."

She tapped her fingers on her thigh as she paced a moment. "We still hit the rest of the neighborhood. And the park. The park's the best bet. Peabody, we're on that in the morning. Feeney, your team's on the electronics. Focus on the security. I'm going to run like crimes, and I'm pulling Mira in for a profile. Currently I have officers doing the rounds on all her usual haunts, and a pair doing a check on one Juan Garcia, a chemi-dealer."

Feeney lifted his chin toward the crime scene photos. "That type doesn't operate like this."

"Agreed, but we'll eliminate him, and any others who pop up out of MacMasters's file or memory. The likelihood is slim that he went with her where she was known. After the initial contact, he'd need to steer her away. For walks—out of her perimeter, to the vids—but not her usual spots—the park? Probably moved to a different sector for meets after he'd established."

"If it was payback . . ."

She nodded at Feeney. "We'll be going over MacMasters's cases, and I'm going to talk to him again, go back with him. Jamie, would she recognize a gang type?"

"I think so, yeah. She was smart, like I said. Really street aware, just sort of . . . not self-aware? Is that right, do you get it? She knew to be careful, what types to avoid."

"What type would draw her?"

"Well . . . he'd have to be clean. I don't just mean cleaned up. He'd have to look right, sound right. Jo said he told her he went to Columbia? That might hook her since I do, and she'll be going next year. It's an opening, you know? And, ah, manners. Like, he'd be polite. If he came on too strong, he'd scare her off."

Plenty of other schools in New York, Eve thought, but he hits on the one where one of her closest friends goes, where she plans to go. Eve didn't see it as coincidence.

"He studied her, stalked her, researched her. And he took his time." No, it wasn't some illegals dealer or one of his spine-crackers. "MacMasters made the reservations for this trip ten days ago. This bastard was ready. This was his opportunity. She'd have told him her father got promoted."

"She texted me, the night after he got informed," Jamie told her. "I think she tagged everybody she knew. She was really proud. I was surprised she didn't go on the trip, like a family celebration."

"A girl, in the first weeks of a romance," Peabody said. "She doesn't want to go off with her parents for the weekend when she can stay home and see the guy. Even if she was on the fence about it, one word from him, how he'd miss her, and she stays."

"We work the lines we have. Peabody, contact somebody at Columbia on the off chance he told her the truth. I want a list of every male student—and add in any staff—

currently enrolled or employed, or who have been enrolled or employed within the last five years who are from Georgia. Age range eighteen to thirty. While that's running tag Baxter, he and his boy are back on the roll. I want them to take Garcia, then follow up on all door-to-doors, and expand same to a three-block radius of the scene."

In her office she ran like crimes, and did a full-scan search through Feeney's brain child, IRCCA, to take it global, and run the data through off-world as well.

While her computer labored, she set up a second murder board in her office. Deena's image—alive and dead—would stay with her while she worked.

"Smart girl," Eve murmured as she pinned images, reports, time lines. "Cop's daughter. Everyone says that. But under it you're still just a girl. A nice-looking boy pays attention, says the right things, looks at you just a certain way. You're not smart anymore."

She hadn't been, Eve thought. Not a cop's daughter, but a seasoned cop—a cynic, a badass herself. And Roarke had paid attention, said the right things, looked at her in that way. She couldn't claim she'd been smart. She'd bent her own rules, taken chances, fallen for a man she'd known was dangerous, one who'd been a murder suspect.

No, she hadn't been smart. She'd been dazzled. Why would anyone expect Deena to be otherwise?

"I know what you felt, or thought you felt," Eve murmured. "I know how he got to you, broke down your resistance, your defenses, your better judgment. Me, I got lucky. You didn't. But I know how he got under your guard."

So now, instead of thinking like the girl, she needed to think like the pursuer.

She turned toward the AutoChef—stopped.

Coffee, she remembered. Roarke's first gift to her had been a bag of coffee. The real deal. Irresistible to her, and worth more to her mind than a fistful of diamonds.

Charming and thoughtful—and exactly right.

Had there been a token given? she wondered. Something small and exactly right?

She stepped back to her desk, studied

Deena's photo. Music and theater, she recalled. Big interests. And reading. All those
music discs, she thought. Maybe he put together a music mix, designed just for her.
Or poems—didn't women get off on poetry, especially if it was from a man?

Wanted to join the Peace Corps or Education For All. But damned if she could
think of a token that applied there.

Her computer signaled the first search
was complete. Letting the other angle
simmer, Eve sat down to read case files
on rape-murder.

Nothing popped, though she read, analyzed, ran probabilities for more than an
hour. The search through IRCCA gave her
the same results. She had a handful of
long shots to track down, but her gut told
her it was just for form. Had to be done.

She'd eliminated half the long shots
when Peabody stepped in.

"I got a partial list from Columbia—the
currents. It's going to be tomorrow before I
can get the formers. At this time there are
sixty-three male students from the great
state of Georgia, and four instructors, one
security guard, and two other employees.
The guard's on the high side at thirty, a

groundskeeper at twenty-four, and a main-tenance tech, twenty-six."

"We'll do background runs on them, all of them."

"It just doesn't feel like he'd have given her that much truth."

"I think he gave her enough truth, so if she played cop's daughter, checked him out, it would fly. He's too careful to leave himself open."

Peabody gestured toward the AutoChef, got a nod. "You think he's a student there?" she asked as she walked over to program coffee.

"I think he may have set it up so if she checked, he'd pop up as a student. He may have already taken care of that, wiped the record. Here's what you could do, if you were being careful. You find a student, clone his ID, take his name, or change it—dealer's choice. You can bet your ass he had what would look like stu-dent ID. You get discounts, right, when you go to vids, theater, concerts. He took her out, he'd have to show it—and it would have to pass the scan."

"I didn't think of that. Which is why you get the slightly less crappy bucks than

I do." She passed Eve fresh coffee. "So maybe, one of these sixty-three is his dupe. Or . . . it could be he had a partner."

"He works alone. A partner means you have to trust. Who could he trust this much? No loose ends if you work alone. I'm going to bet one of those students had their ID stolen or lost it within the last six months. He clones it, replaces the photo with one of himself, tweaks the basic data if necessary. If Deena gets a buzz, and checks, she's going to find he's registered as a student. For now, we run them. Dot every i. Tomorrow, we check to see if any of them replaced their ID. Take the top thirty," she ordered. "I'll take the rest. Work here or at home, and report to my home office in the morning, oh-seven-hundred."

"Where are you going?"

"I want to go back to the scene, walk through it, then I'll pick up the runs at home. Copy the data from Columbia to my home unit."

"Okay. If I hit anything, I'll let you know."

Eve downed more coffee, and tagged Roarke. "Any progress?"

"This won't be quick or easy."

"I'm done here. I'm going to go back to the scene, do a walk-through, then take the rest home."

"I'll meet you in the garage."

"Not quick or easy, remember?"

"With the captain's blessing, I'm having some of the units sent to my lab at home. I've got better equipment. Five minutes."

He clicked off.

She loaded up what she needed, sent copies of all reports, notes, files to her home unit. On the way to the garage she took a tag from one of the officers on the knock-on-doors. All residents on the victim's block had been located and interviewed. And not one of them had seen anyone enter or exit the MacMasters home, save Deena herself, over the weekend.

Maybe Baxter and his faithful aide, Trueheart, would have better luck, she thought. Or she and Peabody would get a hit from the morning circuit of the park. But when a man left no trace of himself at a rape-murder, when he took hours to complete the task and left nothing behind, the likelihood of him being careless enough to be seen with his victim was low.

Still, someone somewhere had seen them. Remembering was a different matter.

They'd walked, talked, eaten, played in the city, and over a number of weeks. She only had to find one venue, one person, one crack in the whole to pry open.

She walked to her car, leaned back against the trunk as she took out her memo book to key in more notes.

Columbia. Student ID.

Georgia. Southern accent.

Truth or lie? Why truth, why lie?

Missing pocket 'link, PPC—possible e-diary?—handbag. Other contents of handbag important? Protection and trophy?

She looked up when Roarke crossed the garage. "When you worked a mark, did you ever fake an accent?"

"A cop shop's an odd place to discuss such matters from my standpoint. Since you're working, I'll drive."

He waited until they were in the vehicle before he answered the question. "Yes, now and then, tailoring such to suit the mark. But more often the Irish suited well enough. I might layer it on—switching to a thicker West County brogue, or posh it up with public school tones."

"But, especially if it was a long con, or some job that would take several weeks and a lot of communication with the mark, it would be easier and safer to stick close to natural. Posh it up or thicken it up, but stay with the basics."

"That's true enough," he agreed as he headed uptown. "One slip and the whole thing can fall apart."

"Guy tells her he's from Georgia. She likes the accent, tells her friend that part. He's smart, so the smart thing is to use what you have, what you're comfortable with. Maybe he lived in the south, at least for a while. He tells her he goes to Columbia, so maybe he did, or he knows enough about it to be able to speak intelligently when she says, hey, I have a friend who goes there. No point in getting tripped up on those kinds of details. It's hard to believe he's nineteen, and has this kind of patience and control, this kind of focus."

She glanced at Roarke. "Though some do."

He switched lanes to slide into a narrow gap in traffic. "At nineteen I had a lifetime behind me, of being a street rat, of running games, thieving, and aiming toward getting the fuck out. So by then I'd honed some skills, and learned the need for that patience and control."

"Murder's different from thievery."

"It is indeed entirely different. And more yet when it's the deliberate murder of an innocent girl. It would be all in the motivation, wouldn't it? To plan it, run it, execute it this way would take a strong motive. But for some, the motive's all in the thrill, isn't it?"

"It doesn't feel like a thrill killing. It's too exacting for that. And too cold."

He said nothing for a few moments as he nipped around a Rapid Cab and through a light seconds before it flashed red. "When I went for the men who'd tortured and killed Marlena, it was cold. Cold-blooded, cold-minded. Some might have looked at the results and thought otherwise, but there was no thrill involved in it. None of it."

Eve thought of Summerset's young daughter—a girl Roarke had thought of as a sister, and who'd been used and murdered as a warning to him. "Deena wasn't executed. If there's a similarity it's between her and Marlena. The payback. It keeps ringing for me. On the other hand, he could have taken her out other ways, at other times. Abducted her, put MacMasters through that agony before killing her."

"He liked playing the boyfriend, you're thinking. Stringing it out, making her care. He likes the game maybe. If there was a thrill, it would've been in that stage of it. Cold blood and a cold mind. You'd need both to be able to romance a girl, to use that for the express purpose of taking her life."

When he pulled up in front of the Mac-Masters home, Eve got out to stand on the sidewalk.

"It's later than it would've been when he walked here. He had to walk, nothing else makes sense. He could've come from either direction, even through the park. Until we find somebody who saw him that night, we can't know. He had the cuffs, he had the drug. Warm night, but he could've been wearing a jacket. A lot of kids wear them more for style than need. Restraints in a pocket, maybe, same with the drug. But he'd need tools, wouldn't he, for the security. Maybe he had a satchel, a bag, a backpack. Or he's just got the tools in another pocket. McNab wears pants that have a million of them."

"With a jacket you could hook the cuffs in the back, cover them, as cops often do."

"I think he strode along, a young guy with somewhere to go. Just another teenager or college type, good-looking, clean, upscale clothes. Nobody pays attention. I think he tagged her from a block or two away, got her on the 'link, the way you said. Maybe just to say, 'I'm nearly there,' maybe, yeah maybe to pretend he wasn't sure of the house. That would be smart. She'd guide him in, keep her eye out for him, open the door to greet him even as he makes the turn for the steps."

"She would want him in quick and smooth, too, wouldn't she? Wouldn't want one of the neighbors mentioning to her parents how they'd seen the boy visiting while they were away."

"Good point." Eve narrowed her eyes. "Yeah, good point. They may have even worked it out ahead, when he talked her into having him over. 'I'll tag you when I'm close, so you can watch for me.' Their little secret."

She saw it in her head as she went up the steps, broke the police seal, used her master to open the locks.

"Still, somebody might see. He's not worried about anyone mentioning it. She'll be dead, game over. But he'd have to take precautions about *what* they see. So yeah, I'm betting jacket, probably a cap, shades. Keep your head down, hands in your pockets, using an earbud or headset. Maybe they can ID the clothes, but you'd ditch those. Maybe they can give a general idea of your height and build. Your coloring. So what? Even eye wits rarely get it just right. He's just a boy going to see a girl."

She stopped to stand in the foyer, to keep it rolling through her head. "She's excited. He kisses her hello. Still the shy guy, still the sweet boy. He needs to keep that up so he can take her without a struggle, so she doesn't have a chance to fight or get away or scrape any pieces of him off. She's got music on, she likes music. They like music. Maybe show him some of the house, at least take him back to the kitchen so you can get the drinks, the food."

She walked back, with Roarke beside her. "It's fun, it's exciting to have dinner, just the two of you. He's careful not to touch anything, or if he has to touch something to make note of it and wipe it down after. But hands in the pockets again. Shy guy. You're kids so you eat in here, in the kitchen. Right over there."

She walked over to a bright blue table with padded benches that offered a view of a small courtyard backed by a high wall.

"Sit across from each other so you can talk. So you can look in his eyes as you talk. Eat, laugh, joke, flirt. Oh hey, do you want another fizzy? Sure he does, and when you go to get it, he slips the drug in your drink. It's so easy. You feel woozy for a minute, you feel off, but with the Zoner to kick it, mellow, too. You just slide out, slide under. And he carries you upstairs.

"She weighed one-thirteen and change. Deadweight, but not that much for a young, healthy man to carry up a flight of stairs." She continued as she followed the path to the kitchen stairs. "Makes more sense to take her up the back. Why waste the energy? If he'd scoped out the house, and he damn well would have, he'd know which room was hers. He'd have seen her through the window anytime she didn't use the privacy screen. Even if he wasn't sure, it's so easy to make which room is hers. The color, the posters. It's all girl."

Roarke said nothing, not yet. He knew what she was doing, walking it through as both victim and killer. "You'd want to restrain her first, take no chances. The cuffs, the sheets. Tight on the sheets; you want her to feel it. You want to leave marks. You hope she struggles. She will. You know she will. So you go down and clean up. Dishes, but for her glass, in the machine. Run it on sterilize, wipe out any trace. Check out the security door. No point working on that. She's going to give you the code. You'll make sure of it. Strip down, seal up."

She circled around, shook her head in annoyance. "No, no, out of order. You'd do that downstairs, even before you bring her up. Nothing of you up here. All your things in a neat pile, careful, very careful. After you finish with her, get her bag, check the contents, take it down to put it with your stuff. Upstairs again, go through the room, make sure, very sure there's nothing of you, nothing on her comp, on the bedroom 'link. Any-where . . ."

She paused, wandering the room, opening drawers she'd already searched. "Would he take something to make sure he got hard? Multiple rapes take a lot of energy, a lot of wood. That's a thought, that goes in the wonder pile. Maybe he doesn't need it. Maybe her thrashing around trapped in the nightmare he gave her, helpless and scared, even uncon-scious, maybe that gets him up.

"Then she starts coming around, and the fun begins."

"Don't put yourself through that." It

clawed through his heart, left it bleeding. "We know what happened then, so don't."

"It's part of it. Has to be. She's . . . bewildered. The drug makes her mind musty at first, then the headache, the stabbing pain of it."

She looked at the bed, stripped down to the mattress now. "It occurs to me he could've made it easier. Given her a dose of Whore or Rabbit. That was a choice. He didn't want her to participate, even under a date rape drug. He wanted her terrified and hurting. Does he tell her what he's going to do, or is it right down to business? I can't see him yet. Just can't figure him yet. She cries. She's only sixteen, and that part of her cries and asks why, and doesn't want to believe the sweet boy is a monster. But the cop's daughter knows. The cop's daughter sees him now. He'd want her to.

"She fights—that has to be satisfying— even during the rape she fights. She fights even while she screams and cries and begs. She's a virgin; nice bonus. She bleeds from where you've broken her, from her wrists, from her ankles. She's strong and she fights hard."

He stood by, his guts in knots, as Eve went through it, step-by-step, horror by horror. She moved around the room, circling the bed where that obscenity had taken place. Even as she described the last moments of a young girl's life, her voice stayed steady.

He didn't speak again until she'd finished and had started another search of the room.

"Even after all this time with you, I don't know how you can do it, how you can put yourself in these places, make yourself see these things the way you do."

"It's necessary."

"That's bollocks. It's more than an objective, observational sort of thing. You do what you do, how you do it for them. You do it for Deena and all the others who've had their lives stolen. It's more than standing for the dead, which is vicious enough to bear. But you walk with them through it. With all I've done in all my life, I don't know if I'd have the stomach to do what you do, every day."

She stopped for a moment, let herself stop, pressed her fingers to her eyes. "I can't not do it. I don't know if it was ever a choice, but I know it's not one now. I can't see him. It's not just because we haven't found anyone alive who has. It's who he is, why he is, why he did this and in this way. I can't see him. He's murky. Walking through it helps clear some of the murk."

She rubbed her eyes again, refocused. "How long would it take you to retrieve the discs from a system like the one here, and wipe the hard drive?"

"It has two fail-safes, and requires a code for disc retrieval. But I know the system."

"Yeah, one of yours, I checked. But he'd know it. Bank on that."

"Well then, it would take me about thirty seconds for the retrieval, and another one or two to do the wipe. But he infected it to corrupt. We've got that much from today's work. A complicated virus to corrupt the drive and wipe out the data and imagery, and that would take some time to upload, and skill or money to obtain."

"He's not as good as you—not a pat on your back, but he doesn't have your experience. If he passes for nineteen, I doubt he's hit thirty. So maybe two or three times longer for the retrieval, maybe twice on the wipe since he's using a virus."

"What are you looking for, Eve? If I had an idea I might be able to do more than stand here."

"I don't know. Something. You gave me coffee."

"Sorry?"

"A token, something to charm her. A little gift, nothing too important. You sent me coffee right after we met."

"And you interviewed me as a murder suspect."

"It worked. The coffee, I mean. Hit the right button. So what did he give her? What . . . I knew it. I fucking knew it." She held up a music disc taken from the hundred or so in a holder. "Happy Mix 4 Deena, that's the label. And look here, she added this sticker thing—a big red heart, and initials inside."

"DM, for her, DP for him."

"For the name he gave her anyway," Eve confirmed. "David, Jo said. Never as smart as they think. He should've looked for this, taken it. It's a link, and the only one so far."

She bagged it.

"I have to say the odds of tracing that disc—as it's a common sort—are astronomical."

"He made it. A link's a link." She looked around again, satisfied for now. "Okay, the scene doesn't have any more to tell me. At least not now. I need to go work it."

**6** As summerset made no appearance when they walked into the house, Eve lifted her eyebrows. "Where's Mister Scary?"

The look Roarke sent her managed to be both resigned and mildly scolding. "Summerset has the night off."

"You mean the house is Summerset-free? Damn shame we have to waste it with work."

He slid a hand down her back, over her ass. "A break wouldn't be uncalled for."

"Nope. I've got over thirty runs to do. Plus I put off reporting to Whitney hoping we'd catch a miracle." She started up the steps, then stopped dead when she spied the cat sitting on the landing, staring at her with unquestionably annoyed eyes.

"Jesus, he's almost as bad as your goon."

"He dislikes being left on his own."

"I'm not going to start hauling him to crime scenes. Deal with it, pal," she told the cat, but stopped to crouch and stroke when she reached the landing. "Some of us have to work for a living. Well, one of us has to. The other one mostly does it for fun."

"As it happens I need to go have a bit of fun. After which I'll put in some time in the lab."

"Work, on Peace Day—or pretty much Peace Night now, I guess."

"A little something I started this morning when my wife left me on my own."

They continued up together with the cat prancing between them.

"Can you make a copy of this disc?" she asked him. "I need to keep the original clean."

"No problem." He took the evidence bag. "We're eating in two hours," Roarke decreed as he walked past her office toward his own. "Meanwhile, you can feed the cat."

She didn't bother to scowl, it was energy wasted. She moved through her office, and again stopped dead when she saw the stuffed cat Roarke had given her—a toy replica of Galahad—sprawled on her sleep chair.

She looked at the toy, at the original, back to the toy. "You know, I don't even want to know what you were doing with that."

In the kitchen she fed the cat, programmed a pot of coffee.

At her desk she booted up her comp then sat to organize her notes, the reports, and start the first ten runs from the Columbia list. While the computer worked, she looked over the report she'd drafted for Whitney.

She refined it, read it again. Hoping he'd be satisfied, for now, with the written, she sent copies to both his home and office units.

She ordered the computer to display the runs, in order, on screen. Sitting back with her coffee she studied data, images.

Young, she thought, all so young. Not

one of her initial runs had so much as a whiff of criminal, no juvie bumps, no illegals busts, not even so much as an academic knuckle rap.

She ran the rest, then started over from another angle.

"Computer, run current list for parents, siblings with criminal record and/or connection to MacMasters, Captain Jonah, as investigator or case boss."

Acknowledged. Working . . .

Payback, if payback it was, came from different roots, she thought. While the run progressed, she rose to set up yet another murder board.

Data complete . . .

"On screen."

Now there were some bumps and busts, and a few whiffs. Eleven on her list had illegals hits, some more than one. And yet, she noted, none of those had any connection to MacMasters.

Considering, she ordered a run on the investigating officer or team. Maybe the connection with MacMasters was more nebulous.

Once again, she hit zero. And paced.

She'd ask MacMasters directly. Maybe

one of the investigators was an old childhood friend, or a third cousin once removed.

Waste of time, that wasn't it, but they'd cover the ground.

She recircled the murder board, coming from another angle, but saw nothing new. She shook her head as Roarke came in.

"Daughter," she said. "Payback—if we run with that—was to kill MacMasters's daughter. Is it a mirror? Is MacMasters somehow responsible—in the killer's mind—for the rape or death of his own daughter—child. Make it child as Mac-Masters only had a daughter."

"If the killer is anywhere near the age he pretended to be, he'd be a very young father. What if he's the child, and Mac-Masters is, to his mind, responsible for the rape or murder of his parent? Or, for that matter himself. He might perceive himself as a victim."

"Yeah, I'm circling those routes, too." She dragged both hands through her hair. "Basically, I'm getting nowhere. Maybe taking that break, clearing it out of my head for an hour, is a good idea."

"I copied the music disc."

Something in his tone had her looking away from the board, meeting his eyes. "What is it?"

"I ran an auto-analysis while I was working on the other e-business. It's both audio and video, which is very unusual. Performance art is often a part of a disc like this. But there was an addition made this morning at two-thirty, and another at just after three."

"He added to it. Son of a bitch. Did you play it?"

"I didn't, no, assuming you'd disapprove of that."

She held out her hand for the disc, then took it to her comp. "Play content from additions, starting at two-thirty, this date. Display video on screen one."

Roarke said nothing, but went to her, stood with her.

The music came first, something light and insanely cheerful. The sort of thing, she thought, some stores play in the background. It always made her want to beat someone up.

Then the image slid on screen—soft focus, then sharper, sharper until every bruise, every tear, every smear of blood on Deena MacMasters showed clearly.

She'd been propped up on the pillows so that she reclined, half-sitting, facing the camera. Probably her own PPC or 'link, Eve thought. Her eyes were dull, ravaged, defeated. Her voice, when she spoke, slurred with exhaustion and shock.

"Please. Please don't make me."

The image faded, then bloomed again.

"Okay. Okay. Dad, this is your fault. Everything is your fault. And, and, oh God. Oh God. Okay. I will never forgive you. And I hate you. Dad. Daddy. Please. Okay. You'll never know why. You won't know, and I won't. But—but I have to pay for what you did. Daddy, help me. Why doesn't somebody help me?"

The image faded again, and the music changed. Eve heard the cliché of the funeral dirge as the camera came back, panned up, slowly, from Deena's feet, up her legs, her torso, to her face. To the empty eyes.

It held on the face as text began to scroll.

It may take you a while to find this,

play this. Your dead daughter sure liked her music! I played it for her while I raped the shit out of her. Oh, btw, she was an idiot, but a decent piece of ass. I hope our little video causes you to stick your weapon in your mouth and blow your brains out.

She didn't deliver her lines very well, but that doesn't diminish the truth. Your fault, asshole. If it wasn't for you, your deeply stupid daughter would still be alive.

How long can you live with that?

Payback is rocking-A!

For the crescendo, the audio blasted with Deena's screams.

"Computer, replay, same segment."

"Christ Jesus, Eve."

"I need to see it again," she snapped. "I need it analyzed. Maybe he said something that we can pick up, maybe there's something that picks up his reflection." She moved closer to the screen as it began its replay.

Roarke crossed over to open the wall panel. He pulled out a bottle of wine, uncorked it.

"There's no mirror, no reflective surface. Her eyes? The way he's got her sitting, maybe he can get a reflection off her eyes."

"Alive or dead? I'm sorry," Roarke said immediately. "I'm sorry for that. Truly."

"It's okay."

"It's not. She's so young, and so afraid, so helpless."

"She's not me."

"No. Not you, nor Marlena. But . . ." He handed her a glass of wine, then took a long drink from his own. "I'll see if I can get something off it. I'd have a better chance with the original than a copy."

"I need to log that in, in Central, run it through Feeney." Time, she thought, it all took time, but . . . "No shortcuts on this."

"All right then." Roarke gestured to the screen. "You won't show this to the father."

"No." She drank because her throat was dry. "He doesn't need to see this."

Because he needed to, needed the contact, Roarke took her hand in his as they studied the screen together. "It seems revenge, your payback, holds as motive."

"It had to. I couldn't see it any other way." Again, and again, she read the final text, that ugly message from the killer.

"It's boasting," she said quietly. "He couldn't resist digging in the knife. Leaving the music disc wasn't the mistake. But adding this, that's a big one. He doesn't care about that, but it's a mistake."

"It wasn't enough even to torture that child, to force her to say those words—her last—to her father. He had to add his own."

"Exactly right. That's a crack in control, in logic, even in patience."

"The kill," Roarke suggested. "For some it's a spike, a rush."

"That's right. He was so damn pleased with himself. All those weeks, those months of preparation coming to a head here, in what he sees as his victory. So he has to do his little dance. It's a mistake, a weakness," she said with a nod. "He put too much of himself in there, couldn't resist claiming that much responsibility for her. It's the kind of thing that gives us a handle."

Personal, she thought. Deeply personal. "He needed MacMasters to know, and to suffer for the knowing. It gives us a focus. We concentrate on MacMasters, his case files, his career. Who has he taken down, what cops has he kicked over the years. Everything he did up to that was cold, controlled. This part? It's cocky, and even while it's smug, it's really pissed off. It helps."

Because he'd had enough, maybe too much, Roarke turned away from the screen. "I hope to God it does."

"We'll take a break."

"Which you're doing now for me."

"About half." She ordered the screen off, ordered a copy of the disc. "You're right, it hits really close to home. I need it out of my head for a little while."

He went back to her wondering why he hadn't seen how pale she'd gone, how dark her eyes. "We'll have a meal. Not in here. We'll step away from this. We'll have a meal outside, in the air."

"Okay. Yeah." She let out a breath that eased some of the constriction in her chest. "That'd be good. I need to inform

Whitney, and the team. I have to do that now."

"Do that, and I'll take care of the meal."

When she came down, stepped out on the terrace, he stood with his glass of wine on the border between stone and lawn. He'd switched on lights that illuminated the trees, the shrubs, the gardens so they glimmered under the moon. The table was set—he had a way—with flickering candles and dishes under silver covers.

Two worlds, she supposed. What they'd closed away inside for a while, and what was here, sparkling in the night.

"When I built this house, this place," he began, still looking out into the shimmering dark, "I wanted a home, and I wanted important. Secure, of course. But I think it wasn't until you I put secure in the same bed as safe. Safe wasn't a particular priority. I liked the edge. When you love, safe becomes paramount. And still with what we are, what we do, there's the edge. We know it. Maybe we need it."

He turned to her now, and he was both shadow and light.

"Earlier I said I didn't know how you could bear doing what you do, seeing what you see. I expect I'll wonder that a thousand times in a thousand ways through our life together. But tonight, I know. I don't have the words, no clever phrases or lofty philosophy. I simply know."

"When it's too much, bringing it home, you have to tell me."

"Darling Eve." He stepped to her, danced his fingertips over her messy cap of hair. "I wanted a home, and I wanted important. I managed the shell of it, didn't I? An impressive shell for all that. But you? What you are, what you bring into it—even this, maybe due to this, you make it important. And for me, for what I might add to it? Well, it might balance the scales a bit."

"Are you looking for balance?"

"I might be," he murmured. "So." He leaned down to brush a kiss over her brow. "Let's have our meal."

She lifted one of the silver tops and studied the plate below. A chunk of lightly grilled fish topped a colorful mix of vegetables with a spray of pretty pasta curls.

"It looks . . . healthy."

He laughed, kissed her again. "I wager it'll go down easy enough. Then you can wipe the healthy out with too much coffee and some of the cookies you've stashed in your office."

She gave him a bland look as she sat down. "Stashed indicates concealed. They're just put away in such a manner that certain people whose names rhyme with Treebody and McBlab can't grab them and scarf them down." She stabbed some fish, ate it. "It's okay."

"As an alternative to pizza."

"There is no alternative to pizza. It stands alone."

"Do you remember your first slice?"

"I remember my first New York pizza— the real deal. Out of school, of age. Shook myself out of the system and hit New York, applied to the Academy. I had a couple weeks, and I was walking the city, getting my bearings. I went into this little place downtown, West Side—Polumbi's. I ordered a slice. They had a counter that ran along the front window, and I got a seat there. I bit in, and it was like, I don't know, my own little miracle. I thought, I'm free, finally. And I'm here, where I want to be, and I'm eating this goddamn pizza and watching New York. It was the best day of my life."

She shrugged, stabbed more of the delicately grilled fish. "Damn good pizza, too."

It both broke his heart and lifted it.

For a time they spoke of inconsequential things, blessedly ordinary things. But he knew her, her mind, her moods.

"Tell me what Whitney said. It's inside your head."

"It can wait."

"No need."

She toyed with the vegetables. "He agrees there's no point in showing MacMasters the disc, or—at this time—informing him of it. We'll focus on Mac-Masters's cases, current and prior, see if we can hook any of them to his threat file. But . . ."

"You're thinking he's too smart to have threatened outright."

"He's made one mistake, he'll have made another. But I don't think we'll find him there. Baxter and Trueheart hit the one name MacMasters came up with, a dealer he'd helped bust. There's nothing there," she said with a shake of her head. "It doesn't play. When you . . ."

He angled his head when she trailed off and scooped up more fish. "Finish it off."

She looked into his eyes, already sorry she would take him—them—out of the shimmering night and into the blood and pain of the past. "Okay. The men who killed Marlena, who brutalized her and killed her to strike at you . . ."

"Did I let them know I intended to hunt them down and kill them?" he finished. "It makes you—what's the most diplomatic word under the circumstances— uncomfortable to ask, or to delve too deep into the fact that I did hunt them down, and I did kill them. Everyone who'd tortured and raped and beaten and broken her."

She picked up her wine while the raw edge of his tightly controlled anger stabbed at her. But she kept her eyes steady on his. "Comfort isn't always a part of this, what I do, what we are."

"What was done to that girl we watched on the screen upstairs was done to another, even younger girl. By more than one. Over and over, again and again. For the same reason, it seems. To strike out at someone else. With Marlena, it was me. She was family to me, and they ripped her to pieces."

"I told you to tell me when bringing it home is too much. Why the hell don't you?"

He sat back making an obvious—it was so rare for it to be obvious—effort to settle himself. "We're too entwined for that, Eve. And I wouldn't change it. But there are times, Christ Jesus, it's like swallowing broken glass."

It struck her suddenly, and made her want to spring up and punch him. "Goddamn it, I'm not comparing what you did to what this bastard's done. You didn't kill an innocent to punish the guilty. You didn't act out of blind revenge, but—whether or not I agree—out of a sense of justice. I asked, you idiot, because you were young when it happened, and youth is often rash, impatient. But you countered that *with* patience, with focus until you'd . . . done what you'd set out to do. Which wasn't, for Christ's sake, raping and murdering a kid to get your rocks off."

He said nothing for a moment, then gave an easy shrug. "Well, that's certainly telling me." Even as she scowled at him, candlelight flickering between them, he smiled. "The fact, the singular fact, that you can know what you do of me and accept is my great fortune."

"Bollocks," she muttered, and made him laugh over her co-opting one of his oaths.

"I adore you, every day. And I realize I needed more than the meal and the break. I needed to get that out of my system. So, to your question, Lieutenant."

"What the hell was the question?" she asked.

"Did I threaten or boast or transmit to the men who'd killed Marlena that I intended to make them pay for it? No. Nor did I leave any trace so any of those involved would know the why of it."

"That's what I thought." Calmer, she nodded. "But then, it wasn't like this. It wasn't revenge. That's part of the difference, and part of the need here. The reason for the video, the message."

"Aye. I'd agree. That kind of revenge? It's thirsty."

"Thirsty," she murmured, and ran the message back through her head. "Yeah. That's a good word for it."

"Generally you'd leave enough so the target of that revenge knew which quiver the arrow came from. Otherwise, there's no point in that victory dance."

"Yeah, but we have to check it out. We'll need to comb through the university, that's an angle. And we'll analyze the disc. Feeney needs to take that."

"Am I being demoted?" Roarke asked lightly.

She arched her brows. "We're too entwined for that," she said. "But it's a cop's kid. We need to be careful. I want the head of EDD in charge of that piece of evidence. We've got an unlimited budget, unlimited manpower—and there will be those, in the media, even in the department, who question that."

A faint line of annoyance rode between her eyes. "How come this case gets so much time and effort? Why didn't Civilian Joe get the same treatment? The answers are simple. You come after a cop or a cop's family, we come after you. And it's more complex. You come after a cop or a cop's family, it puts us all in the crosshairs and makes it goddamn hard to do the job for Civilian Joe. We live with that, but this intensifies. MacMasters had partners through the years, and as a boss, men under his command. How many of them might be vulnerable? And more, when we catch this bastard, every piece of evidence, every point of procedure has to be above reproach. We can't have anything questionable in court, nothing some defense attorney can hang us on."

She ate a bite. "That said, if you had the time and the inclination to work with the copy, nobody's stopping you. As expert consultant, civilian, assigned to EDD, you report to Feeney."

"Which isn't nearly as fun as reporting to you. But message received."

"One of the most valuable things you do is let me bounce stuff off you. Listen, give opinions. Just talking it through opens up angles for me. That's why I asked the question."

"Understood. Now you have another, so bounce."

"Okay, I have to play all the lines—pull, tug. One of them that keeps circling for me is the Columbia connection. Maybe, maybe it was just more bullshit. But it feels like he'd have played it with roots in truth. Just like you said about the accent. So he went there, or worked there, or knows someone who did. Alternatively he scoped it out, maybe—what is it— monitored classes. Got the feel so he could talk about it to her. Maybe he faked his name, but he probably picked something that felt natural to him, or meant something to him. He's not going to give her too much truth, but those roots again."

"With a school that size, even with the security, it's not difficult to get on campus, study the layout, gather particulars. Names of instructors, times of classes. He could get most of the information online or simply by requesting it."

It was more, she thought. Something more.

"He studied her, so he knew she had a friend who went there. It was, I'm dead sure, one of his angles. One of the ways he used to get her to talk to him. In those first stages, she's got no motivation to keep it all secret. So she might say to Jamie how she met this guy who goes there."

"Ah." Following her lead, Roarke nodded. "And if he'd been studying her, he would know her friend Jamie's interest in e-work, police work. Wouldn't he want to cover himself there, if Jamie got it into his head to check out this boy who put stars in the eyes of his good friend?"

"If he had a brain he would. Maybe, once they're established and he's got her hooked, he doesn't know teenage girls well enough to realize she's *got* to tell someone. A peer, a pal. So he's not worried about us digging there. But he had to worry about Jamie checking or her— cop's daughter—checking, even just to satisfy her curiosity. He had to show student ID at the vids and so on to get the discount, or wouldn't she wonder why he didn't? Where did he get it?"

"Stolen or forged."

"Maybe both, because if someone checked—and he's got to cover that—he needs to show up on the roster."

"We know he has some e-skills. It wouldn't be hard to do. And," Roarke added, "if he had a brain, he'd have already wiped himself off that roster."

"High probability on that. So tomorrow I'm going to start pushing somebody at the college to get me a list of students reporting a stolen ID, then start wading through that."

"Why tomorrow?"

"Because it's freaking and increasingly annoying Peace Day, and it's late anyway, and nobody's in Administration or whatever."

"I can take care of that."

Narrowing her eyes, she pointed a warning finger at him. "I just told you we have to be careful. I can't have you hacking into Columbia's student files."

"Which is a shame as I'd enjoy that. But I can take care of this with a 'link call."

"To who?"

"Why don't we just start at the top, with the president of the university?"

She squinted. "You know the president of Columbia University?"

"I do, yes. Roarke Industries sponsors a scholarship, and has donated lab equipment from time to time. Plus, I spoke with her at length regarding Jamie."

"So you can just pick up the 'link, give her a tag, no problem?"

"Well, we won't know till we try, will we?"

He pulled his 'link out of his pocket,

tapped his fingers on the screen to do a search. "She's an interesting woman, with a nearly terrifying radar for bullshit. You'd like her." He smiled as the call went through. "Peach. I'm sorry to interrupt your evening."

Across the table, Eve heard the muted response, but not the words. Whatever it was, Roarke laughed.

"Well then, I'm delighted to be of help. As it happens, I'm about to ask for yours. You're aware my wife is a police officer. Ah, is that so? Yes, indeed, she comes across quite well on screen. She's heading an investigation that may have some connection to a student or former student at Columbia."

He paused, listened, flicked a glance toward Eve. "Yes, that would have been her partner. I know the NYPSD appreciates your cooperation. They need to ask for more. I think it would be best if the lieutenant explains to you directly what she needs. Would you hold one moment?"

He tapped for hold, held out the 'link to Eve.

"Peach?" she said. "A university president named Peach?"

"Doctor Lapkoff."

"Right." Eve took the 'link, opened communications. Her first impression was of ice blue eyes so sharp they looked able to pierce steel. They beamed out of a cool, attractive face topped with short, straight brown hair.

"Lieutenant Dallas." The tone was brisk, as no-nonsense as the do. "How can I help you?"

Within minutes, the bureaucratic wheels were turning. Eve passed the 'link back to Roarke. "She says she'll have the data to me within an hour."

"Then she will."

"So I guess I better go back to work, and get ready for it."

Back in her office, she started a match search with the Columbia list and Mac-Masters's threat file, and a second for matches with his case files for the last five years. It would take time.

She used it to study the video again.

He'd stopped and started, she judged, a number of times. Each time Deena hesitated or went off script. Patience, focus. He had a message, and he wanted it delivered.

Blame the father, even though it was perfectly clear the victim spoke only under duress. He'd needed the words said. Daughter to father? Was that important? Child to parent? An issue or just the luck of the draw?

No, nothing was luck on this. Every choice deliberate. Direct to MacMasters, with no mention of the mother. Dad, Daddy—not the mother.

Never forgive. Hate. Never know why. Must pay.

Sins of the father? she wondered. Eye for an eye?

She sat, put her booted feet on the desk, shut her eyes.

The killer was older by a few years— maybe more—than the victim. Deliberate target, used to punish MacMasters. Blood kin.

Relative? Son?

Unacknowledged child?

Possible.

The cruelty of the act, the planning, the message sent—all pointed to intense offense. Against killer? Against relative or close connection to killer?

Note: Search MacMasters's files for

terminations, or arrests/wits/vics that resulted in death or extreme injuries. Add life sentences on and off planet.

Personal, extremely personal. This wasn't business.

She opened her eyes when her unit signaled an incoming. Straightening, she brought up the data. Peach Lapkoff was a woman of her word.

That was the good part, Eve noted. The bad was just how many students at one freaking college managed to lose their IDs.

She needed more coffee.

With more fuel she began the laborious process of whittling down. Even as her unit reported no match on her initial search, she felt the pop.

"Powders, Darian, age nineteen. Lit major, second year. Replacement ID requested and paid for fifth of January, 2060." She brought up her previous list, eyes narrowed. "And here you are again, Darian, hailing from Savannah. All data on current subject on screen."

She swiveled, studied his ID. "Good looking guy, big, charming smile. You're tailor made."

Eve continued to study and wondered if she could be looking at a killer, or his dupe.

"One way to find out."

She rose, tugged on the jacket she'd tossed over the back of her chair, then buzzed Roarke.

"Hey, I've got an angle I need to check out. I won't be long."

"Check out as in go out?"

"Yeah, I've got a possible. I want to work it now."

"I'll meet you downstairs."

"You don't have to—"

"Waste time, and neither do you. I'll drive."

When he clicked off she blew out a breath.

No point in arguing. And she could do a secondary run on Powders while Roarke played chauffeur.

He beat her downstairs and opened the door under the bitter eye of Galahad just as the vehicle he'd remoted on auto cruised to the front of the house.

"Where are we going and why?"

"Columbia, on-campus housing to interview a possible suspect. More likely a potential dupe. But either way that's not my vehicle."

Roarke glanced at the slick two-seat convertible, top down, in glittering silver. "It's mine, and since I'm driving and it's a very nice evening, I want an appropriate ride."

She frowned all the way to the passenger seat. "I have an appropriate ride, which you gave me."

"Safe, loaded, and deliberately unattractive. Key in the address," he suggested, and gunned it down the drive.

She hated to admit it, but it felt damn good, the night, the air, the speed. Reminding herself it wasn't about fun, she started a deeper run on Darian Powders.

"Kid's from Georgia, requested new ID in January. He's the right age, and he's got a pretty face."

"Isn't school out for the summer? Why would he be on campus in June?"

"He's taking a short summer semester, and interning at Westling Publishing. Lit major. He's completed his second year at the college, carries a 3.4 grade average. No criminal, but his brother—who's still in Georgia—has two illegals pops. Minor shit. He's got an uncle in New York, an editor at the publishing house, who has a son a couple years older than this one who took a harder illegals hit. Did six months, and another three in rehab. Bust was Brooklyn's, so not MacMasters."

"Hardly motive for what was done to that girl."

"It's a start," Eve said, and kept working the run as she enjoyed the ride.

7 Eve flashed her badge at the stern-faced droid riding the desk at the check-in for the dorm. She assumed they'd gone droid to try to avoid any possibility of bribery or human weakness with infractions. But she figured that area would be offset by the ability of probably half the residents in reprogramming or memory erase.

The droid gave Eve's badge both a naked eye study and a red-beam scan.

"Purpose of business?"

"That would be filed under none of yours."

In droid fashion, the machine dubbed "Ms. Sloop" according to its nameplate stared blankly during processing.

"I am responsible for the residents and visitors of this building."

"I'm responsible for the residents and visitors of this city. I win." Eve tapped her badge. "This requires you to answer one simple question: Is Darian Powders on the premises at this time?"

The droid blinked twice, then consulted its comp, though Eve imagined it had the information in its own circuits.

During the process, Eve wondered if the pinched-face, tight-lipped, slicked-back-bun look of the machine was an attempt by whoever was in charge to intimidate the residents into behaving.

Since the stern, disapproving facade reminded her of Summerset, she didn't see how it could work.

"Resident Powders logged in at oh-three-thirty. He has not since logged out."

"Okay then." Eve turned toward the elevator.

"You are required to log in."

Eve didn't bother to glance back. "You scanned my badge. That logs me in."

Stepping on, she ordered the fourth floor. "Why can't they use humans?" she complained to Roarke. "Droids aren't nearly as much fun to screw with."

"I don't know. I found it mildly entertaining. And it did look considerably put out."

"Maybe, but it's already moved on." Hands in pockets, she rocked on her heels. "A person would probably sulk or stew about it for a few minutes anyway. That's more satisfying."

When the doors opened, the noise slammed her eardrums, and made her eyes throb. Music—clashing styles, volumes, lyrics—pumped out of rooms with their doors propped open. Voices mixed with them, some raised in argument or debate, others singing along. People, possibly under the influence of pharmaceuticals and in various stages of dress, wandered the hallways.

A couple twined in deep kiss/grope mode just outside a closed door. Eve wondered why they just didn't go inside and finish the job.

She stepped in front of a girl sporting two nose rings and what might have been a tattoo of a honking goose on her left shoulder.

"Darian Powders? Where do I find him?"

"Dar?" The girl flapped a hand behind her while giving Roarke a long, slow, smoldering study. "Straight back, last on the right. Door's open. I'm over that way," she said to Roarke, "if you're interested."

"That's an offer," Roarke said pleasantly. "But I'll be going this way."

"Bummed."

With a look more of wonder than annoyance, Eve watched the girl stroll off. "She completely eye-fucked you."

"I know. I feel so cheap and used."

"Shit. You got off on it. Men always do."

"True enough, which is why we're so often cheap and used."

She snorted, then heading down the corridor glanced in rooms. She saw a jumble of possessions and people, smelled very old pizza and very fresh Zoner. Peace Day signs lay scattered among snoring bodies and bottles of brew, which were probably as illegal as the Zoner.

"Does anyone actually study around here?"

"The ones with the doors closed, I

imagine." Roarke shrugged. "And it being the end of a holiday weekend, I'd think most are still in the mode." He looked as she did at a couple curled up together on the floor in front of a blasting vid screen. "Or simply unconscious."

Eve could only shake her head. "The droid's useless, and they know it."

She stopped at the open door at the end of the corridor. Inside ten young people sprawled on big colorful floor pillows or slumped on a small red sofa. The source of the music here was a comp game blasting on screen. The two remaining people seemed to be dueling on stage. Their icons, outfitted in the pinnacle of trash rock gear, held guitars while their counterparts played the air version and sang at the top of their lungs.

She considered shouting, but judged it a waste of air and effort. Instead she walked in and shoved her badge in front of one of the sprawlers.

It was just a little disappointing that no one scrambled to conceal or dispose of illegals. The boy she badged, scooped a hank of red and black hair out of his eyes and said, "Whoa! What do?"

"Turn it off."

"The what?"

"Turn the game off."

He gave her saucer eyes. "But it's like the final round, and dead heat. Dar could maybe lose his title."

"Heart bleeds. Turn it off."

"Whoa." He scooped his hair again, then scooted over to the main controller to switch it manually. He used pause, which suited Eve. But the participants, and the audience who hadn't seen the badge, went ballistic.

"What the fuck? The fuck? Who did that?" The boy player—who Eve recognized as Darian—whirled around. He looked ready to bash someone with his invisible guitar. "I was about to take Luce down!"

"Bogus." Luce sniffed, tossing a yard of hair the white-blonde of bleached straw. "I had you. Totally under."

"Not this eon. Jesus, Coby, what?"

"Got cop," Coby said and jerked his head toward Eve.

Slouchers and sprawlers came to attention. Darian shifted toward Eve, goggled a little. "Whoa. Seriously?"

"Seriously. Darian Powders?"

"Yeah, um, me!" He raised his hand. "If we're too loud and like that, so's everybody."

Eve saw, out of the corner of her eye, one of the sprawlers butt-scoot toward the door. She stopped him with a single finger point.

"I'm not campus, I'm NYPSD. I have some questions."

Luce sidestepped to Darian, put her hand in one of his pockets in a way that told Eve they weren't just game rivals, but involved. "You need a lawyer, Dar."

"What? Why? Why?"

"When a cop asks questions, you should have a rep."

"I bet you're a law student."

Luce looked at Eve out of eyes such a pale blue they looked like springwater. "Prelaw."

"Then why don't you rep him on the first question. It's an easy one. Darian, can you account for your whereabouts from six p.m. last night to four a.m. this morning?"

"Well yeah. Come on, Luce, that *is* easy. A bunch of us went down to the Shore yesterday afternoon. What, about two maybe?"

"About." Luce kept those pale eyes on Eve. "We got back about seven."

"And we chowed at McGill's, and hit a party at Gia's. She's got an off-campus group. Gia." He gestured to a tiny brunette.

"Um, I don't know when he left, exactly, but it was pretty late. Or early, I guess," Gia offered. "We started the Rock Your Ass tourney, and we were going till close to three. Close anyway."

"We came back here after and crashed," Darian told Eve. "Time, I don't know, exactly, but the log'll have it below."

"Okay, see? Easy." Eve thought of connections, and Jamie's comment about partying late on Saturday night.

"So . . . I did good?" Darian offered the same blasting smile from his ID shot.

"Yeah. No lawyers necessary," she said to Luce. "Do you know Jamie Lingstrom?"

"Sure. We've had some classes together, hang sometimes. Hey, he was at the party last night for a while. You could ask him. . . Wait. Is he in trouble? He's not trouble. He wants to be a freaking cop. Sorry, I mean, he's studying to be an e-cop."

"He's not in trouble. It happens I know

Jamie, too. You're not in trouble either, but I still have questions. Everybody else, clear out."

Bodies lurched up, scrambled. Luce remained glued to Darian's side, and the boy Coby stayed on the floor.

Eve pointed at Coby, pointed at the door.

"But I live here and all that."

"Find somewhere else to be. And close the door behind you."

When he had, Eve looked at Luce.

"I'm not leaving. I'm within my rights."

"Fine. Sit down, both of you."

Eve showed them Deena's ID photo. "Do you know this girl?"

"No. Wait. No . . . Maybe."

"Pick one," Eve advised Darian.

"I think I've seen her maybe?" He looked at Eve as she imagined he might have looked at one of his professors. Earnestly. "Maybe with Jamie? But not like at the party last night, or for a while. I just think maybe. Luce."

Luce frowned over the image. "Yeah. A couple times with Jamie. Not a girlfriend. I asked because she's younger. He said they'd been buds forever. I didn't really talk to her much or anything, but I saw her a couple of times with Jamie at Perk It— the coffee shop. Why?"

Eve ignored the question. "Darian, you requested a new student ID in January."

"Yeah. I lost mine."

"How'd you lose it?"

"I don't know. If I did, I'd probably find it." He smiled, a little weakly.

"Let's try when did you lose it?"

"It was right after winter break. I know I had it when I got back—I went home for Christmas—because you've got to show it to log back into the dorm and all after a break. I got back early, for New Year's and like that, because, well, who wants to be with the fam for the big Eve. Plus, Luce and I had started . . ."

"We're a unit."

Eve nodded at Luce. "Got that."

"We started uniting last fall, and I wanted to get back. I missed her."

"Aw." Luce cuddled closer.

"And we had a big bash for the Eve here. Major bash. I know I had it on the Eve because I had to show it to get the discount on supplies. Not like brew or anything, being underage." He smiled again, very, very innocently. "So we partied until way into the new, and we didn't go out again until the third—the day classes started. I mean, we cleaned up, dumped trash and all that, but we stuck around. We were all wiped from the party, and it was freaking cold anyway. Then I go to check in for class, and no ID."

"On the third? Why is your replacement for the fifth?"

"Ah . . . Well, you know you report and apply, and . . . crap. Okay, okay, so I slicked on the third. I just figured I'd left it back here or something."

"Slicked?"

"I, ah . . ."

He glanced at Luce for direction, but she was staring hard at Eve. "She doesn't care about that, Dar. She's not going to care about slicking."

"Okay, yeah, well, I got another student to pass me through on his ID. You're not supposed to but, it's not against the law. Is it?"

"Don't worry about it."

"I looked everywhere when I got back.

No go. Then, okay, I slicked my early classes the next day, cut a couple so I could go back to the stores where we bought stuff, in case I left it there. No go again. I reported it, end of day on the fourth, so it got issued on the fifth."

"Where do you keep the ID?"

"In the wallet, or sometimes just in my pocket 'cause it's easier. You show it a lot, so it's handy in the pocket."

"Where was it on the night of the party?"

"I don't know. My pocket? Maybe. Or I maybe tossed it in my room, which is why I tore the place up when I realized it wasn't on me. It costs seventy-five for a reissue, plus the forms. It's a hassle."

"I'll need a list of who was at the party."

"Lady—"

"Lieutenant."

"Whoa, seriously?" Surprised respect goggled in his eyes. "Lieutenant, I couldn't do it if you put me in cuffs and hauled me in. We jammed. People came and went, and I didn't know half of them. Somebody from somewhere brings a friend. You know how it is? We got a corner suite here, so it's the biggest on the floor. We get banged when we party. Jamie was here," he remembered. "You could ask him. We were wall-to-wall and then some, so . . . Shit. I'm stupid. Somebody lifted it that night. Damn it, people suck wind."

"They do," Eve agreed.

"And someone used it to do something illegal," Luce put in as Darian paled. "Something that happened last night. Something between six p.m. and four a.m. It wasn't Darian."

"No, it wasn't Darian. I may need to talk to you again, but for now I appreciate your cooperation."

"Aren't you going to tell us what he did, whoever took it?" Darian asked.

They'd find out soon enough, Eve thought. No point in it now. "I'm not at liberty."

"It's about that girl," Darian murmured. "She did something or something happened to her."

Eve signaled Roarke and started to the door. "Take better care of your ID."

"Lieutenant? Is Jamie all right? Is he okay?"

"Yeah." She glanced back, the dark-haired boy and the pale, pretty girl. "Jamie's all right."

She brooded over it a bit as they drove home. "So, the kid, Darian, throws a party on New Year's Eve, and the killer just happens to walk in and cop the ID? Just too fucking lucky in my world."

"Agreed, though it's not impossible it was a moment of opportunity. More likely, your killer had his eye on Darian, or a few candidates including Darian, then took the opportunity to slip into the party, among the crowd. Not difficult to snag the ID then, whether it was on Darian's person, or left in his room. People in and out, jammed together, undoubtedly alcohol or some illegals in the mix."

"He knows the campus, he blends there. He'd targeted Deena, so he had to know she was tight with Jamie, who goes there."

"You're thinking Jamie knows him, or has at least brushed up against him at some point. A friend of a friend of a friend."

"It fits, doesn't it? He might've even used some names she was vaguely familiar with to make her more comfortable with him right off. Those two kids recognized Deena and put her with Jamie. So the killer mentions their names, or others. She automatically feels safe. He's had the ID for months before he first approaches her. Patient as a fucking spider."

She went back to work to write up the interview with Darian, and to begin the laborious process of studying the results from her search of MacMasters's case files.

It was nearly two in the morning when Roarke found her nodding over the data.

"You can't work in your sleep," he pointed out. "It's time both of us were in bed."

"I've got a handful of possibles." She pressed the heels of her hands to eyes gone fuzzy. "Connections to people Mac-Masters sent over for long stretches, ones who bought it in prison. He's got no terminations in the last five years. I need to go back further, maybe. And I need to talk this through with him."

"Which is for tomorrow."

"Yeah. Yeah, it is." She pushed up. "Why are you still awake?"

"Working on digging out wiped data, which with the system MacMasters has is like trying to find a ghost in a dark room while wearing a blindfold."

Since they were both too tired for the stairs, he called for the elevator. "And running the analysis on the copy of the recording. And that would be a hell of a lot more concise with the bloody original. There's no reflection. He's not in her eyes."

"Would've been too lucky." She yawned her way into the bedroom. "I set up a briefing here for seven hundred, since Peabody and I are going to hit the park. Feeney can take the disc in, log it, start the analysis."

She stripped on the way to the bed. "I'll meet with Mira, she'll have a profile. And I'm going to pick Jamie's memory. This guy will have been around, on the fringe, blending in, but he's been around. He's not a ghost. There'll be tracks." She flopped facedown on the bed. "There are always tracks somewhere."

"You've found some in less than twenty-four hours." He slipped in beside her, wrapped an arm around her to tuck her close. "You'll find more."

"Maybe it was a vic." Her voice slurred. "And he figures MacMasters didn't do enough . . . blame the cop, punish the cop. Maybe . . ."

In the dark, Roarke stroked her back as she went under, as Galahad plopped on the bed at her feet. And he thought, *Here we are, all safe and sound for the night.*

She dreamed of dark rooms, and of tracks dug into the hard streets of her city. Following them as things scrabbled away in the shadows. She dreamed of the young girl watching her with dead eyes.

As she tracked, an animated billboard sprang to life, stories high and filled with the image of the girl weeping, defense-less, bleeding. Her voice filled the dark with pain, with fear.

He was there with her—she felt him behind her, beside her, in front of her. Breathing, waiting, watching while the girl begged and bled and died.

He was there while the image changed to another girl, a girl in a room smeared with red light. There, while the girl Eve had been begged and bled and killed.

So she ripped herself out of the dream

with her heart stuttering and the air trapped in her lungs. She forced the air out. "Lights. Lights on, ten percent."

Her hands shook lightly as she stared at them, turned them over, looking for the blood.

Not there, of course it's not there. Just a dream, and not so bad. Not so bad. Closing her eyes she willed her heartbeat to slow, to steady. But she couldn't will away the cold, and Roarke wasn't there to warm her.

Her teeth wanted to chatter, so she gritted them as she got up, found a robe. She checked the time, saw it was just shy of five-thirty. Going to the house monitor, she cleared her throat.

"Where is Roarke?"

Good morning, darling Eve. Roarke is in his main office.

"What the hell for?" she wondered, and went off to find out.

Stupid, she told herself, just stupid to be too uneasy to go back to bed, catch the half hour she had left. But she couldn't face it, not alone.

She heard him as she neared the office, but the words were strange, jumbled, foreign. She thought longingly of coffee, and thought she needed the zap of it to clear her brain because she'd have sworn Roarke was speaking in Chinese.

She walked, bleary-eyed, to his open office door. Maybe she was still dreaming, she thought, because Roarke damn well was speaking Chinese. Or possibly Korean.

On the wall screen an Asian held his end of the conversation in perfect English. Roarke stood, circling a holo-model of some sort of building. Every so often the structure changed, or opened into an interior view, as if he or the other man made some small adjustment.

Expanses of glass increased, openings that had been angled, arched.

Fascinated, she leaned on the door-jamb and watched him work.

He'd dressed for the day but hadn't bothered, as yet, with a suit jacket or tie. That told her the man on screen was an employee rather than a business partner.

He studied the holo, shifted to pick up a mug of coffee from his desk. As he drank he listened to the other man talk of space and flow, ambient light.

Roarke interrupted with another spate of Chinese, indicated what looked to Eve to be the southeast corner of the building.

Moments later what had been solid became glass. The roof on that sector lifted, changed angles, then relaxed into a kind of soft curve.

And Roarke nodded.

She pushed off the jamb when the conversation ended. The screen went blank, and the holo poofed.

"Since when have you been fluent in Chinese? Or whatever that was."

He turned toward her, surprise flickering over his face. "What are you doing up? You've barely had three hours down."

"Pot, kettle. Was that Chinese?"

"It was. Mandarin. And I don't speak above a handful of basic words. Comp translator, two-way."

Her brow knit even as he crossed to the AutoChef. "I've never seen—heard—a translator that clear. It sounded like you, not comp-generated."

"Something we've been working on for a while, and are selling in a few key markets." He handed her the coffee he'd programmed for her. "It makes it easy to do business when it feels and sounds like a conversation rather than a translation."

"What was the thing? The holo?"

"A complex we're building outside of Beijing." His eyes darkened as he studied her face. "You had a nightmare."

"Sort of. It wasn't bad. It's okay."

But she didn't protest when he drew her in, held her. The warmth finally came back to her bones. "I'm sorry. I had to take care of this."

"At five-thirty in the morning? Or earlier, since you looked to be way into it when I got here."

"It's twelve hours later in Beijing. I'd hoped to be done before you woke up." He drew her back. "No point asking if you'd get a bit more sleep."

"Pot, kettle," she repeated. "I'm going to grab a swim. That and the coffee should set me up."

"All right then. We'll have breakfast when you're done. I've got a few things I can see to."

"It's still shy of six in the morning."

He smiled. "Not in London."

"Huh. That always strikes me weird."

She stepped back. "How much of this stuff do you do when I'm conked?"

"It depends."

"Strikes me weird," she repeated, and used his elevator to ride down to the pool.

By seven, she was fueled, dressed, and ready for the briefing. It didn't surprise her to find a buffet set up in her office. Roarke, she knew, insisted on feeding her and her cops as well. She wondered why, and decided to ask Mira one of these days.

She poked her head in Roarke's office through the adjoining door. "I'm going to close this. You're already up-to-date."

He made some sound of agreement as he scanned his comp screen. "Tell Feeney I should be clear by two, and can give him some time."

"All right."

She shut the door as she heard Peabody, McNab, and Jamie chattering their way down the hall.

"Get what you're going to get," she ordered, "and don't dawdle."

"I smell meat of pig." McNab shot to the buffet like a neon bullet with Jamie on his heels.

Peabody sighed. "I'm on a diet."

"There's a bulletin."

"No, really. We're going to try for the beach next day off. I hate bathing suits. I hate me in bathing suits. And yesterday, there was pizza. I think it's still in my thighs." She sighed. "I hope there's fruit, maybe a few low-calorie twigs."

Peabody shuffled toward temptation as Feeney came in. "Baxter and his boy are right behind me, so I better get over there first. McNab, stop hogging the hog."

"Told you there'd be food," Baxter said, and pointed. "Get your share and mine," he told the young, slightly seasoned Trueheart. Then he crossed to Eve.

As was his habit, Baxter wore a very slick suit. But there was no smart-ass on his handsome face this morning.

"We're up-to-date, or up-to-date on the last data you sent. I didn't know the kid, but I know MacMasters. I worked out of the same squad with him when I was a rook and he was a detective on his way to LT. He's as good as they come. If you hadn't pulled us in, I'd have angled for it. If budget gets to be a problem, we'll kick any OT off the books."

"It won't be a problem, but the offer's noted and appreciated."

"There's not a man in the division who wouldn't do the same. We're going to get the fucker, Dallas."

"That's right. Stuff your faces," she told the room in general, "but kill the chatter. We're nearly twenty-four hours in. We don't have time to waste."

"Where's your man?" Feeney asked her.

"He's got work of his own. After two he'll be your man. Okay, let's round it up. Screen on." She stopped as Whitney stepped into the room. "Sir."

"I'm sorry to interrupt. I'd like to sit in on the morning briefing. And to tell you that Captain MacMasters will be available to you, here, at nine hundred. I felt meeting here would be less complicated for him than Central."

"Yes, sir. Ah . . . if you'd like anything that hasn't already been greedily consumed . . ."

"Coffee would do it, thanks. Please, go ahead."

"You're all aware of the case, and the early steps of the investigation. You're all aware that this is a cop's daughter, and that we believe she was target specific. We believe she knew her killer, and had been set up for the events of Saturday night and early Sunday morning. Other data and other lines of investigation have come to light, which I'll brief you on shortly. Feeney, status on EDD."

"Slow. I know that's not what any of us want to hear. The virus used to wipe and corrupt the hard drive is effective. We're piecing it back together one damn byte at a time, and half of those bytes are useless. None of the D and C units in the residence contain anything useful. As far as we can determine, he never contacted the vic and was never contacted by her on any of the house 'links. He never sent or received any e-mail from her from any of the house comps, including her bedroom comp. The bedroom unit was scanned and searched from twenty-fifteen to twenty-thirty-three. Nothing was deleted during that period."

"He checked it out during one of his breaks," Eve concluded, "and didn't find anything to worry him."

"There is nothing to worry him," McNab commented. "There's no mention of meeting anyone, no allusion to a boyfriend in any of her communications on that unit. Maybe they're in some sort of girl code, but I can't crack it."

"She kept it to her pockets. More personal, more intimate, more secret." Eve nodded. "Even her messages and conversations with her best friend about him, off the main comps and 'links. He had her snowed. Keep the focus on the security for now."

She shifted her gaze to Jamie. "Jamie, I need you to leave the room at this time."

"What for?" He boosted up in his chair. "I'm part of the team."

"A civilian part of the team. I'll tag you when I want you back."

"You can't shut me out. I'm doing the job." He turned to appeal to Feeney. "I'm pulling my weight."

"You don't argue with your lieutenant. That's the job, too."

"I'm asking if the lieutenant has faith in me, believes I can handle myself." He got to his feet. "If not, then I'm a drag not an asset. This is about Deena. So you tell me, Dallas, if I'm not pulling."

"That's for Feeney to say."

"He holds his own," Feeney said.

"And I can't hold my own if I'm shut out of parts of the investigation, don't have pieces of the data. If you're going to say something you don't think I can handle, you're wrong."

"It's not what I'm going to say." Was it wrong to want to protect him for what was coming? Maybe it was, maybe. But she could regret not doing so. "I located a music and video disc in the victim's possession, which I believe was created by the killer. Certainly the last section was his work."

She gave Jamie a last look. "Computer, run disc copy labeled H-23901 from cue."

Acknowledged . . .

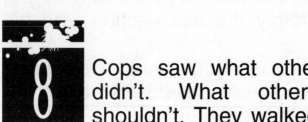

Cops saw what other people didn't. What other people shouldn't. They walked through the worst of the worst, and Eve knew the team she'd assembled could make that walk without flinching.

And still no one spoke. It seemed to her no one breathed as the video played out on screen.

She saw, from where she stood, Jamie drop his gaze, watched his body shudder. And saw Peabody take his hand. The knuckles of his went white—he must have ground Peabody's bone to bone—but she didn't flinch.

And with that connection, the boy lifted his gaze again and watched the rest of his dead friend's nightmare play out.

He'd make a cop, she thought. God help him, he'd *make* a cop.

Even when the screen went blank, and the vicious music silenced, no one spoke. Eve stepped to the front of the room.

"He's going to pay for it." Her tone was iced rage—she needed it; they needed it. "I'm going to say that first, and I want everyone in this room to believe it. To *know* it right down to the gut. He's going to pay for Deena MacMasters.

"She was sixteen. She liked music. She was shy, did well in school and had a small, comfortable circle of friends. She had ideals and hopes, and wanted to help make a difference. She was a virgin, and he stole that from her viciously. He stole her life, her hopes and ideals viciously. Before he did he forced her to tell the father she loved that he was to blame, that she hated him for it. As of now there is no reason for the father to hear that, to see what we've just seen. The contents of this disc are not to be discussed beyond the members of this team until otherwise directed.

"Questions?"

Still the room remained silent.

"Feeney, you and your e-team will analyze the disc, and continue to work on piecing the hard drive back together. I want you to dig out any files, e-mails, notes, anything the victim put on her D and C unit in April. Any searches she made, anything she did around the time she met the UNSUB. She may have since deleted, or put any data pertaining to the meet in some cryptic file. We know the killer found nothing, so deleted nothing. Maybe we'll be luckier."

She picked up her coffee. "Baxter, you and Trueheart repeat the canvass of the neighborhood. It's likely the killer scoped the house, the neighborhood, before Saturday, even before the initial meet. Find me somebody who saw a good-looking boy who could pass for nineteen on that block, frequenting a local cyber café, a twenty-four/seven. I have a list of the vic's favorite haunts. Check them out."

"Yes, sir."

"I'm working on MacMasters's cases, have a few possibles. They don't ring for me, but we'll check them anyway. When you've finished the canvass, you'll wade in there."

She picked up a file with disc attached and handed it to him. "I'll get you some help on that."

"Why don't you let us get started on it, LT. We can tap whoever's got some room for it."

"Fine. I'll leave it to you. Meanwhile, Peabody and I will canvass the area of the park where the vic is reported to have met the killer. After which, we'll meet with MacMasters here, and try to refine the search re his cases.

"Connections," she said. "Connections between MacMasters and the killer, the killer and Deena, the killer and a wit, vic, perp, suspect, or person of interest in MacMasters's files. If the killer isn't in there, someone who matters or mattered to him is. We find the connection."

"If it's the killer," Baxter put in, "it should be easy enough to narrow it by his age. Even if he's got a baby face he's got to be under twenty-six or -seven to pass for nineteen. It might be somebody who did some hard for illegals busts."

Jamie shook his head. "It just doesn't fit. If he'd been on any junk, or a real user, she'd have known and steered away. She knew what to look for there. She'd never hang with a chemi-head."

"I agree with that." Eve nodded at Jamie. "Added to it, someone who's done the hard isn't going to pass for a clean-cut nineteen to a cop's daughter. Still, we check. We don't skim over anything or anyone."

She paused, then pushed the next button. "Jamie, I think you've seen him or met him."

"What? Why? Where?"

"You know Darian Powders."

"Dar, sure." His puzzled face went straight to shock. "You don't think Darian—"

"He's clear," Eve said quickly, "but I believe he's one of the connections. His ID was stolen, most probably during a party in his dorm suite on New Year's Eve. You were there."

"I . . . yeah. Dar and Coby rock a party.

I know them both, did some class time with them. They had a major bash for the Eve." His face hardened, and it seemed to Eve the smudges of sleeplessness smeared under his eyes darkened. "He was there? You're saying the guy who killed Deena was there?"

"Long enough, if I'm right, to steal the ID from Powders."

"But Deena knew Dar—well, sort of. Enough to recognize him. If this guy used his ID and she saw it . . . Cloned it," he said in disgust. "If he's good and has access to the right equipment and programs, he could've cloned the ID, tweaked it just enough, input his own photo and data."

"The basic footprints would need to coordinate." McNab frowned over it. "To clone and counterfeit, you'd need to keep the tweaks minimal."

"The same school, the same birthday," Eve continued. "Probably the same height and build within a reasonable span. He has to know the campus, the routine, maybe he'd gone there, or worked there. The Columbia connection was a good ploy to gain Deena's trust. You go there, Jamie, she's planning to, and she knows Darian a little. His name anyway. He'd need ID to flash when he was with her, going to vids or clubs. You need to think, to go back in your head and start thinking about the party. Before the party, after it. See if you can re-member someone who hung around on the fringes, blended, but didn't do a lot of socializing. He doesn't want to be noticed, doesn't want to leave an impression."

"It was a jam. I didn't know half the people there. I—"

"He wouldn't have stayed long—but I'm betting long enough to watch you, to see if you brought Deena along. This was business for him. It wasn't a party, it was a purpose."

"I'll try. Okay, I'll try."

"He'd have been other places where you'd go. A club, the library, a cyber café, an eatery. Your eyes would pass right over him. He's just one of the crowd. Think back to any time you were with Deena between January and April. Let it simmer in your head, and let me know if you think of anything. Doesn't matter how small or vague."

"Okay."

"Let's get to it," Eve ordered.

As the room cleared, Whitney walked to Eve. "Unless you have objections I'd like to sit in when you talk to MacMasters."

"No, sir, no objections."

"I'll meet you back here then. Meanwhile, give me an assignment."

"Sir?"

"I'm still a cop. I still know how to do a run." He snapped it out, then seemed to catch himself. He gestured the words away and spoke more calmly. "I can do legwork, knock on doors, run probabilities, chase down a lead. You're primary, Lieutenant. Give me an assignment."

"Ah . . ." The juxtaposition threw her off balance. Whitney gave the orders. But it was clear enough he needed to do more than that. He needed to participate. "I have a short list of possibles, gleaned from MacMasters's threat file. To be honest, sir, I don't think we'll hit there."

"But it needs to be followed up on. I'll take it."

"Most if not all can be done riding the desk. If any of them pop, then—"

"I do remember how it's done. I'll find somewhere nearby to work it."

She hesitated, only an instant. "You're welcome to use my office, and my desk here, Commander."

The faintest glint of amusement lighted in his eyes. "I also know the sanctity of an office and desk. Maybe there's another place in this house of yours I can set up."

"Absolutely. I'll see that Summerset takes care of that for you." She took disc files from her desk. "This should be all you need. Peabody and I will be back before nine."

"Good hunting," he said, then turned back to study her murder board.

"We'll split up," Eve told Peabody. "Take it in zones, show the vic's picture to every jogger, dog walker, nanny, flasher, kid, octogenarian, and sidewalk sleeper."

"Somebody's going to remember her because she was a regular. He's another matter," Peabody commented.

"Somebody saw him, and saw them together at the initial meet. He waited two months from then to the murder. People's memories fade. We'll push them back into focus."

She stopped at the base of the stairs where Summerset, bony in black, skull face impassive, waited with the pudgy cat at his feet.

"Commander Whitney needs an office. He'll be working out of here this morning."

"I'll see to it."

That's it? she thought. No smart remark, no sneer? She started to snark at his lack of snark, then realized he'd know what they were working on. The rape, torture, and murder of a young girl, as his young girl had been raped, tortured, and murdered.

There would be no sneers between them for the time being.

"Captain MacMasters is due at nine hundred," she continued in the same even tone. "If I'm not back, you can take him up to my office, and inform the commander."

"Understood. Your vehicle is ready."

She nodded, walked out into the beautiful, balmy morning. If Deena had never met the boy she'd known as David, would she be heading off to the park on this soft, summer morning? Would she already be jogging along the path, feet slapping to the beat of the music playing in her ears?

Breathing in, breathing out, Eve thought, at the start of another ordinary day.

She slid behind the wheel, drove toward the gates.

"How's Jamie holding up?" she asked Peabody. "I need to know if I should throttle back on his duties."

"I think he's riding it out. It's rough for him," Peabody added, "but he's riding it out. He talked a lot about her last night. Good for him, plus it gives me another picture of her to add to my own. Or one of how Jamie saw her, anyway."

"Is it different? His picture from yours?"

"Some, yeah. He didn't really see her as a girl, as especially female. She was a friend, a pal. It makes me wonder if she felt the same, or if that was frustrating for her. It can be a bitch to be the girl the boy thinks of as just a pal."

Peabody shifted, angling toward Eve. "It makes me wonder if that designation wasn't usual for her, that—I mean—she was used to having guys see her that way. So she was maybe resigned to seeing herself that way. Not the girl guys looked at, and wanted to be with."

"Until this guy."

"Yeah. This one *looked* at her, wanted to be with her—or made her think that. And I think she was different with this guy because of it. It's what happens when you go over for a guy, especially at that age, especially the first time. And from everything he said, I think this was her first major crush. Her first serious thing, so she'd be different."

"How?"

"Well, not as shy—not with him. He makes her so damn happy. And a girl, that age, that background, with a college guy making over her? It's all flutters and shudders. She's ready to do what he wants, go where he wants, believe—or at least pretend—that she likes what he likes. She'll make herself into what she thinks he wants. I figure that's one of the ways he got her to keep all this on the down low. So much so she barely told her best friend any real details."

"If you're not already what he wants, why is he making over you?"

"That's logic—and self-confidence, and just doesn't apply to that first rush of romance, especially at sixteen. Just think back to when you were that age."

"I didn't care about any of that when I was sixteen. All I cared about was getting through the system and into the Academy."

"You knew you were going to be a cop when you were sixteen?" The idea struck Peabody as nearly inconceivable. "I was obsessed with music, vid stars, and January Olsen when I was sixteen."

"January Olsen?"

"This really adorable boy I had a crush on." She could sigh over it now, fondly. "I figured we'd cohab, raise two adorable kids, and do important and world-changing social work. If he'd ever actually look at me or speak my name. You didn't have a January Olsen?"

"No—which means it's harder for me to get into her head than it is for you."

"Well . . . I guess on some level Deena and I were kindred spirits. At least when I was sixteen. Kind of shy, awkward around guys, but casual pals with many. I was planning on doing big work. The stuff about her appearance? Her mother and the neighbor noticed she was taking more trouble. That's a sure sign there's a guy."

Peabody began ticking off points on her

fingers. "Updating your do, your wardrobe. That's definitely one. Two, she wasn't hanging with Jamie as much, something he didn't think about until now. He's busy with school and his college friends, so he didn't give it much thought when she made excuses a couple of times when he tagged her to see if she wanted to catch a pizza or a vid. She was eking out her time for the guy, cutting herself off some from her core group.

"That's three," Peabody added. "A break or a little distance from your core. See you want your core group to meet the guy and like the guy, but part of you worries. What if they don't? So keeping him to yourself is a way to avoid the possibility."

"It's awfully damn complicated."

Sagely, Peabody nodded. "Being a teenager is hell and misery and wild delight. Thank God it's only one decade out of all of them."

Her own teenage years hadn't been nearly as hellish or miserable as her first decade. But Eve understood.

"She got sneaky and secretive."

"She was, in a way, having a rebellion. Only she was really quiet about it,"

Peabody added. "I'm also inclined to think Jamie's right about the guy not being on the stuff, or doing any of the hard. She'd have copped to it. And that kind of rebellion wasn't in her. I don't think he's wrong there."

"All this is telling us what kind of mask he wore. Not what's under it. He's taken it off now. No more need for it."

She pulled into an illegal slot, activated her On Duty light.

"It's worse than Coltraine."

Eve got out, said nothing as Peabody walked around to meet her.

"We knew her." Her eyes, dark and troubled, searched Eve's face. "She was one of us. And she was Morris's. I didn't think it would ever hit home as hard as that one, working that one. But this? A cop's kid, a girl like that, done like that? And I knew her. It's worse."

"He knows that," Eve said. "He knows it's worse than anything. He wants it to be, made sure it would be with the video. And he's thinking he got away clean; he's rocking on that. We're going to prove him wrong, and take him down."

"Yeah. Okay." Peabody rolled her shoulders. "I guess that was a pep talk."

"It was a fact. Go north. I'll take south."

A day made for strolling, Eve thought. Cotton-ball clouds dabbed across a sky of perfect and delicate blue. The air held the fragrance of flowers and flowering bushes she couldn't name rioting in swirling islands. Green, green grass rolled like a carpet under tall, majestic trees. The wall of them and the madly flowering shrubs shut out the noise, the pace, the hurry of the city and opened a door to a sedate and verdant world.

The little pond sparkled like a liquid jewel under its pretty arch of bridge with the reflection of the trees and clouds a dreamy blur on its surface.

People sat on benches, drinking from go-cups, talking to each other or on 'links, consulting their PPCs. Business suits, sweats, summer dresses, beggar's rags mixed together in the eclectic array that was New York, even in the green.

Nannies and professional parents took advantage of the weather and pushed kids and babies in strange wheeled devices, or carried them in stranger harnesses. Along the path joggers bowled along with their earbuds, headsets, e-fitness pods tucked on, colorful shorts flapping or skin-suits showing off bodies already viciously toned.

She imagined Deena running along the brown path, her life spread out in front of her like the green, green grass and the brilliant islands of blossoms. Until she stopped to help a boy.

Since they were closer, Eve approached a knot of adults with kids first—warily.

She badged the group at large. "NYPSD. Have you seen this girl?"

She held up Deena's photo.

She got a lot of automatic head shakes. One of the kids—about the age she judged of Mavis's Bella, stared at her with that doll-eyed blankness Eve found creepy while it sucked busily on the plug some-body had stuck in its mouth.

"Maybe if you actually looked at it," Eve said. "She jogged here in the mornings, about this time, several days a week."

One of the women, with a very small, round-headed child strapped to her front, leaned closer. Eve had to force herself not to lean back as the kid waved arms and legs like a human metronome.

"I've been here nearly every Monday and Wednesday morning since May. I haven't noticed her. What did she do?" She lifted her head with an avid, fearful look. "This part of the park's supposed to be a safe zone, at least in the daytime."

"She didn't do anything. Anyone else? She might have jogged here more habitually earlier in the spring. March, April?"

More head shakes, but Eve noticed one of the women taking a harder look.

"You've seen her?"

"I'm not sure. I think maybe. But it wasn't in the park. I don't think."

"Around the neighborhood," Eve prompted, "in a store, on the street. Maybe more than once, if she looks familiar. Or maybe you talked to her." She glanced at the two kids riding tandem in the cart. "She liked kids. Take another look."

"I think . . . Yes. Sure. She's the one who helped me out."

"Helped you out?"

"I had all these errands. The woman I work for, sometimes she doesn't remember I've only got two hands, you know? I had both boys, little Max and Sterling. Sterling's a handful by himself. And I had to pick up a dress for her, and the marketing, and she wanted flowers. Lilies. So I'm loading, and all of a sudden Sterling's screaming like I stabbed him in the ear."

She shifted her gaze to one of the other women and got a smirk of understanding.

"So I'm trying to deal with him, and I'm juggling the stuff I can't stow in the stroller, and this girl—she's the one—she calls out to me and comes scooting up. She had Mister Boos."

"Who?"

"Mister Boos, Sterling's bear. See." She gestured to the boy in the second seat of the tandem stroller. He sat casting looks of suspicion at Eve and clutching a bright blue teddy bear with mangled ears and a shocked expression on its face.

"Mine!" Sterling shouted, and bared his teeth in challenge.

The woman rolled her eyes. "If he can't get to Mister Boos, life isn't worth living.

He'd dropped it, or maybe tossed it, and I hadn't noticed. So she picked it up and brought it over, and about that time Max started wailing because Sterling was. She asked if she could give me a hand, and I said I only needed about six more or something like that. I made Sterling thank her for saving Mister Boos, and told her I only had about another block to go. And she said she was going that way, and she'd carry the market bag if I wanted. It was really nice of her."

"She walked with you."

"Yeah, she—" The woman, who must have had kid radar, whipped her head around and jabbed a warning finger at Sterling seconds before he could follow through and clobber his little brother with Mister Boos.

He subsided, with an angelic smile and a satanic look in his eye. Eve wondered if she'd be hunting him down in about twenty years.

"Sorry, he's getting bored. Where was I? Oh yeah, this girl? She helped me with the bags, walked me right to the building. She was awfully nice, and really polite. A lot of kids that age, they don't even see you, if you know what I mean. She got Sterling to laugh, said how she liked kids. Babysat for a couple of twin boys, I remember she said, so she knew they could take a lot of work."

"When was this?"

"I know exactly because the next day was my birthday. April fifth."

"She was alone?"

"That's right. Walking home from school, she said. She had a backpack, I think. I'm not sure about that, really. But I saw her a few weeks later. Maybe a month, or six weeks. I don't know. It was raining—sky just opened up, and I was rushing to get the kids home. That was over on Second, somewhere between Fiftieth and Fifty-fifth. Because I'd taken the kids to the Children's Museum over there for a program. They had a magic show."

"You spoke to her?"

"No, see I was rushing to get to the bus stop, because the maxi will take the tandem stroller, and it was raining buckets. I didn't want to walk all that way across town in the rain with the kids. But I saw her, and I waved and tried to get her attention. But she and the boy just hopped on an airboard and zipped."

"The boy," Eve repeated and felt the tingle.

"She was with a boy, and they were laughing. She looked really happy. Wet, but happy."

"Did you get a look at him, the boy?"

"Ah . . . Sort of. It was only for a minute."

"Basics. Height, weight, coloring."

"Well, gee, I'm not sure." She pushed at her hair, bit her lip. "Taller than her. I guess we're about the same height, and he was taller. Sure, she was about to his shoulder when they hopped on the board, because she hooked her arms around him like you do, boosted up to put her chin on his shoulder. I thought it was sweet. So, I don't know, about six feet, I guess. Slim. I mean he didn't have any bulk on him. Like I said it was raining so his shirt's all plastered. A white kid. He looked white. Oh yeah, he took off his ball cap and stuck it on her head. That was sweet, too. He had brown hair. Brownish, in a shaggy, to about . . . I don't know." She tapped her hand a couple inches below her ears.

"How about eye color, features?"

"It was really just for a minute. Not even. Oh, he had on shades. Kids do, even when it's raining, for the frosty look. He was cute. I thought, it's nice she's got a cute boyfriend because she really helped me out that day."

"Anything else? His clothes, the airboard? Was he wearing any jewelry?"

"I don't know. It was a minute."

"Would you work with a police artist? You might remember more."

Alarm flashed on her face, and the women around them began to murmur. "I didn't hardly see him, and my boss . . . Plus, I don't want to get her in any trouble. She really helped me out. She's a nice girl."

Eve weighed the options. The media would have the story by the afternoon, if they didn't already. Lid would come off anyway. "You'd be helping her out. She was murdered early Sunday morning."

"Oh come on. No, don't tell me that." As her voice pitched, the kids in the tandem went into dueling wails. "Oh my God."

Immediately the other women closed

in, touching her, gathering their children or charges just a little closer.

"The man you saw her with may have information. It's important I find him."

"I hardly saw him, and it was raining. I don't know. She was a nice girl. She was just a kid."

"What's your name?"

"Marta. Marta Delroy."

"Marta, her name is Deena. Deena helped you out. Now you can help her. I'll fix it with your employer."

"Okay." She pulled a tissue out of one of a dozen pockets. "What do I have to do?"

After Eve made the arrangements, took Marta's employer's information, one of the other women spoke up.

"You said she jogged here in the mornings, about this time? You might want to talk to Lola Merrill. She jogs almost every day now that her daughter started pre-school. She usually comes over to talk after she finishes. Tall blonde, great build. She's probably already on her run this morning."

"Thanks."

She left the women, pulled out her 'link to make arrangements for her favored artist to take Marta, then switched to tag Peabody.

"I was about to tag you," Peabody told her. "I think I have something. A woman who thinks she saw the initial meet."

"Tall blonde, great build?"

"Jesus, do you have super-vision?"

"No, but I got a confirmation and one wit of my own. Get Lola's statement, then I want her to work with Yancy asap. I'll arrange with Yancy. Hold her there a few minutes. I'm heading your way."

She contacted Central, added a second witness for Yancy as she walked toward Peabody's zone. She spotted the blonde, and had to agree the build inside the black running suit with bright blue piping was exceptional.

"Lola Merrill?"

"That's right."

"Lieutenant Dallas, Detective Peabody's partner. We appreciate your help. Tell me what you saw, and when you saw it."

"Some weeks ago, the middle of April, I think, because it was still pretty brisk this time of the morning, and the daffs were just popping. I'd see the girl a couple times a week. She had good form, good stamina. We'd wave or nod, the way you do."

Lola bent into a hamstring stretch. "I never talked to her. That day I saw her with this boy. Nice-looking boy. Off the path, sitting on the grass. He had his shoe off, rubbing his ankle. I didn't stop because it looked like she had it, and they were laughing."

She straightened up, pulled her leg up behind her to stretch the quads. "I kept going, and they were gone when I finished up. First time I'd seen him around, and haven't seen him since. I was telling your partner I haven't seen her around lately either."

"Did you get a good look at him?"

Lola shrugged. "I wasn't paying that much attention. I was just hitting my endorphins. Brown, shaggy hair. Nice looking. Good shoes. I noticed the shoes. It's something I do."

"What kind of shoes."

"Anders Cheetahs—that's top line. White with the navy logo."

"Eye color?"

"Shades. Lots of joggers wear goggles or shades. And a cap. A ball cap. I noticed that. Oh, and he had on a Columbia sweatshirt. I went there myself, so I recognized it."

Eve's gaze shifted to Peabody, saw the same sense of satisfaction there she felt. "Ms. Merrill's happy to work with the police artist," Peabody said.

"It's kind of exciting, but I don't know how much help I'm going to be. I barely glanced at him."

Enough, Eve thought as they finished their circuit of the park, enough to notice his hair, his shoes, his cap, his shirt. Yancy would get the rest, whatever else was buried in the subconscious.

We got lucky," Eve said as they drove away. "Fucking lucky."

"Seriously fucking lucky. Two wits with one sweep, and both willing to work with Yancy."

"Cap, shades—harder to get a solid on his face. He's smart there, but not smart to go with up-end shoes. Probably tried to impress her there. The sweatshirt's his opening, his connection. He can't expect somebody to spot them over on the East Side, like my wit did. And the meet's more than two months before the murder. He's going to figure we'd never put one with the other.

"Sure maybe she'll mention meeting this guy in the park, and helping him out. But after he goes to work on her, it's all secret. He doesn't know girls her age, how she'd have to talk about it with her friend. Now we've got a shadow instead of a ghost."

"About six feet, slim build, brown hair, white, young. Not much of a shadow yet, but more than we had an hour ago."

"Once Yancy's worked them, we'll have more."

She turned in the gates of home. "While I'm talking to MacMasters, start on the shoes. Tap someone in the division to help on that. Whoever's not buried on an active. I'm betting they were pretty new, bought just for that meet. And we'll start canvassing the area where Marta spotted them. See if you can find out what day the East Side Children's Museum had a magic show, and we had a rainstorm. We can pinpoint the day the wit spotted them.

Put someone on that, focus on music venues, vids, gaming parlors, places where teenagers might hang."

"On it."

"Tell Summerset to set you up somewhere." She parked, pushed out of the car. "It's not going to be his neighborhood either. He wouldn't want someone to see him, stop, speak. Not when he was with her. Just the two of them."

She walked in, simply jerked her thumb at Peabody when Summerset appeared.

"Captain MacMasters is waiting in your office. Commander Whitney is with him."

She said nothing, but started up.

"Your gown is ready, and will be delivered today."

"My what?"

"Your gown for Dr. Dimatto's wedding. Leonardo would like to see it on you, in the event it requires any further fitting."

Eve opened her mouth, closed it, and made some growling sound. "It's fine. It'll be fine. Just put it wherever you put those things when it gets here."

Gowns, fittings, weddings. For God's sake. Was she supposed to call Louise, report on the gown?

For God's sake, she thought again.

It would have to wait. Right now she was about to talk to a grieving father about the investigation into his child's murder.

Everything else had to wait.

9 When she stepped to the door-way Eve saw MacMasters standing by the windows. Did he see the green, the color, the bloom, the blue? She doubted it.

He looked diminished, she decided. Worn and lessened by the burden of grief. Could he be a cop now? Think like one, stand like one?

She wasn't sure.

She glanced at the commander, standing beside him. The stance was support, friendship, shared loss.

She would need them both to step back from that loss, to erect a distance of objectivity to give her what she needed.

Or to step away completely.

She walked in. "Commander. Captain."

They both turned. On MacMasters's face she saw that quick spark that was hope. Survivors, she knew, needed answers.

"Is there any progress, Lieutenant?"

"We're pursuing some lines," she told MacMasters. She moved toward her desk, around the murder board she'd deliberately left up. He had to face it, and she'd remembered what Roarke had said when she'd allowed Morris to see the board on Coltraine's investigation.

That he would see she was the center of it. She was the focus.

"I brought the captain up-to-date, from this morning's briefing," Whitney said, his gaze latched onto her face. "It saves you time."

"Yes, sir. We'll go over some of that, but you should know we found two wits this morning who believe they saw Deena with the suspect. Both are willing to work with a police artist. I've arranged for Detective Yancy to meet with them."

"Two?" MacMasters's voice jumped. "Two people saw him?"

"Two independent witnesses believe they saw Deena with a young male. They both gave basic descriptions that match on coloring. Have a seat, Captain."

"I—"

"Please." He wasn't a cop now, she decided. He was a father. She could only try to find the way to speak to both. "I'll tell you what I know, and what we're doing."

She ran through the interviews with the two women from the park. "The timing on Merrill's sighting corresponds to what we believe was the first meet. The timing on Delroy's indicates they continued to meet, and outside what we've established— through your statements, your wife's, Deena's friends—was her usual area. Do you know if she often traveled to the East Side?"

"Not in general. She had her favorite shops and hangouts closer to home. And the locations I gave you near Columbia."

"We can speculate that they met outside those areas to keep their relationship secret. We're working to pinpoint the day Delroy saw them, and I'm sending officers to the location she sighted them. They'll show Deena's photo to merchants, shop clerks, waiters."

She saw the struggle on MacMasters's face, a battle between hope and despair.

"We may find other witnesses to help us identify the suspect. If someone recognizes her," Eve continued, "they may remember him. Merrill, who jogs regularly in that sector of the park, stated she hadn't seen Deena for some time. You and your wife indicated Deena ran in the park regularly."

"Yes. She . . . several mornings a week. She . . ."

"She may have moved to another sector, in order to meet with the suspect."

"Why didn't I notice a change?" MacMasters murmured. "Carol did. But I never . . . If she'd told us. If she'd just . . ."

"Captain, my belief is this man was very persuasive, and very deliberate." Was that comfort? Eve wondered. "He'd studied her, he had a plan, and he played on her youth, her trust. He used the Columbia connection to lower her guard. I feel that's a key. Her friend goes there. She planned to attend. She knew, casually, several other students who are friends of Jamie's."

"Yes. Using Jamie, even a nebulous connection to him, would have engaged her trust. And being in need," MacMasters continued. "Pretending to be hurt or in trouble. She'd instinctively offer help."

"We can see what he did, how he did it, and I'll be meeting with Dr. Mira later today to discuss profile and pathology. But we don't yet know why. We believe she was target specific for a reason. And that you, the work you do, is that reason."

"If you have evidence Deena's murder is connected to one of my cases—"

"I have reason to believe Deena's murder is connected. I don't, at this time, have any specific case or circumstance."

"What reason?" Pain vibrated in his voice, radiated from his eyes. "If this was payback, if this was due to my work, how do you expect me to live with that? How do you expect me to settle for speculation instead of answers?"

Here was the line she had to walk, so

she kept her voice flat and brisk. "I expect you to trust the primary investigator you specifically requested, and the team she's handpicked, to do everything and anything necessary to find those answers. Inside twenty-four hours, we have two potential witnesses who may help identify this man. We have a solid connection to Columbia University, and potentially more witnesses there who may have seen this man. We have a time line of events, and the lack of trace and DNA on scene tell us this was well-planned, not a crime of the moment, of passion or opportunity. Every officer assigned to this case is working vigilantly."

"I don't question that."

Shaky ground, Eve thought. How could the man stand on anything else at this point? "I need to know if you're capable of working through your cases, your memory, your impressions, your gut to help this investigation find a connection. I've been through your case files for the last three years," she continued. "I have a short list, but I don't get a buzz from any of them. You may."

"Give me the names."

"I will. He's not going to be in your threat file."

"How can you be so sure?"

"We'll check out every name in there, believe me," Eve assured him. "But I'm telling you we won't find him there. Anyone who made a threat brings attention. He's been very careful to stay off the chart. How many men between eighteen and twenty-six have threatened you in the last three years?"

"I can weed those out for you quickly. Gang members, illegals dealers, chemi-heads—"

"He's not any of those. She'd have recognized the signs."

She waited, giving him time to deny or confirm.

"Yes." He rubbed the center of his forehead. "Yes. You're right. She knew what to look for. She was careful. She was . . ."

"He's clean," Eve continued, interrupting to give him time to compose himself. "He's smart, and he can be charming. Both wits referred to him as a good-looking boy. Boy, Captain. He's not in your threat file.

Someone connected to him, possibly. You didn't bust this kid. But you may have busted his father, his brother, his best friend, mother, sister. And for this kind of retribution, we're talking serious bust, termination or long-term stretch."

He pushed his hands over his face. "Lieutenant, I've been a boss for some years, and rarely work the streets. Rarely work cases. I supervise them. That was a deliberate choice on my part. I assist, I advise, I coordinate. I've taken primary on an investigation no more than a dozen times in the last six years."

"You're in charge and therefore responsible. That's both reality and perception."

"You're saying this could have come through any of the cases any of my men worked."

"Yes. I believe you had some active part, some visibility or gained some credit. He has not, as far as we know, sought revenge against any of your men. But on you. And the revenge was enacted shortly after your promotion was announced."

Now his face was stricken. "He killed her because I got bars?"

She took the shot, dead-on, unsure if it would shock or revive. "Captain, he was always going to kill her. I'm sorry for it, but that's the reality."

He pushed up, lurched toward the windows to stare out.

"Go on, Lieutenant," Whitney ordered.

"The timing may be important. You were promoted, Captain, and Deena was alone in the house for a period of time. In that part, I do believe he seized an opportunity. I think Dr. Mira's opinions and theories will be valuable, but until I confer with her, we'll approach it this way. We'll go back ten years to start, and begin with terminations and/or arrests and imprisonments resulting in death. Next, arrests or imprisonments resulting in grievous injuries. Then life stretches."

She paused as MacMasters stayed where he was, said nothing. Whitney signaled for her to continue.

"This was no small deal. To murder, to plan, to risk, it had to matter a great deal. We look for a connection to the perpetrator who corresponds with the age zone of our suspect.

"You get me the names," she added,

"I'll run them down. Right now, give me the gut. Who pops out?"

With his back to the room, MacMasters took a breath that shuddered. "Leonard and Gia Wentz. They ran a cookshop, used primarily minors for dealers, to drum up trade around schools and vid dens. I had four detectives on that. We ran an op that busted them in January. Leonard drew down, and there was a brief firefight. Two of my men were injured. He's doing a hard twenty-five, and she's in for fifteen."

"I remember that. Mid-January. It's too close. Nothing this year. He stole the ID New Year's Eve. He was already planning. Go back more."

MacMasters turned from the window to pace. "My men do good work. It's like trying to hold back the tide, but we do good work. We have a solid arrest and conviction rate. Low termination percentage."

"Don't overthink it, Captain. Don't justify it. I'll get us some coffee."

Eve moved into the kitchen. It wasn't going to work, she thought. Not yet in any case. He couldn't pull himself out and think cop. Why should he? How could he?

But she got coffee together, took it out.

"We ruin lives," she said. "If you look at it from the other end, some guy's doing what he does—raping, killing, stealing, dealing, whatever. It's what he does, or what he did this time for whatever reason. We come along and we stop him. More, we do whatever we can to put him in a cage for it. He loses his freedom, his scratch. Could lose his home or family if he's got one. Sometimes if things go south, he loses his life."

She drank coffee, hoping she was getting through. "We ruined it. We're responsible. You're responsible. Think about the lives you've ruined. Think about it that way, not about doing the job, but the results. From the other side."

"Okay." He took the coffee, met her eyes. "Okay. Nattie Simpson. She's an accountant, nice little place on the Upper East, decent income, husband, one kid. On the side Nattie was dealing illegals and cooking the books for a mid-level operation. When we took it down, we took her down with it. She's in Rikers doing the last year of five. They lost the nice little place on the Upper East. The husband divorced her two years ago, got full custody of the kid."

"How old's the kid?"

"He'd be about ten, twelve."

"Too young. Maybe she has a brother, a lover. We'll look at her."

MacMasters dragged a hand over his hair. She could see him grasping, reaching, trying to come back. "Maybe this was a hired hit."

"I don't think so. Give me one more name, off the top."

"Cecil Banks. Bad guy. Dealt Zeus, hunted runaways and kids who ran the streets, got them hooked, pimped them out. Ran an underage sex business. We worked with SVU on that. When we busted the main operation he tried to rabbit. He went out a window, missed the fire escape, and took a header down four stories. A lot of people lost heavy income and access when we took him and his operations out."

"When?"

"Two years ago last September."

"Family?"

"Ah, yeah. Yeah. He had a couple of women, addicts. Both claimed to be his wife. Neither were, legally. He had a brother, younger brother. He did some running for Cecil, but copped a plea down to rehab and community service. Risso. Risso Banks. He'd be about twenty-two, twenty-three."

"They're not in your threat file."

"I was in on the busts, but not as primary. The women made a lot of noise, but nothing that worried me. The kid, the brother? Cried like a baby, which helped him with the plea."

"Good. We'll check it out. That's what I want you to do. Whatever springs, write it down, note the dates, the basic circumstances. We'll take it from there."

"Lieutenant, what is the probability Deena's murder is connected to me, to the job? You'd have run that."

No way to soften it. And to do so insulted him and his child. "At this time, with the data gathered, the probability is ninety-eight point eight."

He sat again, and the mug in his hand trembled slightly. "It's better to know. Better to know. Do I tell her mother? I have to, but how? How do I tell her mother? We're planning her memorial. Thursday. It seems too fast, too soon. Thursday. We just couldn't . . . I'll write it down. But how do I stand it?"

He broke. And watching him shatter twisted her heart, her guts. She stood where she was as Whitney went to him, as her commander gently took the mug of coffee, set it aside, and put his arms around MacMasters.

Whitney looked at her, signaled for her to go.

She left, headed downstairs. She wanted out, just for a moment, just for a breath of air. When Summerset paused on the bottom landing, some of the anger, some of the pity must have shown on her face before she schooled it away.

"The loss of a child goes deeper than any," he said. "It doesn't pass the way other losses may. However the loss came, a parent looks inward. What could I have done, what didn't I do? When the loss comes from violence, there are more questions. Every answer you give him is both pain and comfort, but there can't be any comfort without the pain."

"None of the answers I gave him today lead to comfort."

"Not yet."

When he continued on, Eve simply sat on the steps. She'd take her moment there.

Before she could take the moment, her 'link beeped. "Dallas."

"Lieutenant Dallas, this is Dr. Lapkoff of Columbia University. I spoke with you and your husband last night."

"That's right."

"I'd appreciate a few moments of your time today, regarding this matter."

"This matter is a homicide investigation."

"I'm aware." Lapkoff's face remained cool and set. "As portions of that investigation cross my milieu, I'd like to discuss it. This institution will cooperate with you as much as possible. I would appreciate the same from you and your department."

"Are you on campus now?"

"I am."

"Twenty minutes," Eve said and clicked off.

She took out her communicator to contact Peabody. "Status?"

"More of those shoes have been sold in the past six months than you'd think.

I'm concentrating on New York venues and online sources."

"Keep at it then. I'm going to meet with the president of Columbia, then with Mira. After, we're going to check out a couple of possibles. I'll swing back and get you, or tell you where to meet me."

She clicked off, contacted Mira's admin. "I need the doctor to meet me rather than come into her office. I'm going to be in the field."

"Dr. Mira is—"

"An essential member of this investigative team. The commander has given this investigation top priority. I need her to meet me at the building housing the offices of the president of Columbia University in an hour."

"She can't make it in an hour. Ninety minutes."

"Ninety minutes," Eve confirmed.

She drove to Morningside Heights, and to the beauty and the age, the dignity of Columbia. She parked as close as she could manage to Administration, ordered her On Duty light and security on.

Any campus dick who tried to cite it or

move it would be shut down, quick and fast.

Summer students lolled on the greens, sat near the fountains or strolled along the paths from building to building. Ages ranged from shy of twenty to nearing the century mark. Some of those older were staff, she assumed, but some would be students as well. Furthering their education, going for advanced degrees, taking a short course like a hobby.

Dress also ranged, she noted, from slick suits to maxicargos, jeans to microskirts. Plenty of ball caps, plenty of University tees and sweats.

The UNSUB could have blended here so easily, on a campus that sprawled and spread with dignified greens and stately old buildings. Like Central Park, she thought, it was a world within a world where a strange face wouldn't cause a single lifted eyebrow. Particularly if he looked as if he belonged.

Know where you're going and go there. Sit on the grass or a bench and take in the air, or do a little outdoor studying.

Observing. He'd have observed, even as she was now. The look, the rhythm, the feel.

She made her way into Administration, offered her badge for scanning. "I have an appointment with Dr. Lapkoff."

The guard nodded, read the scan. "She put you on the log, cleared you through."

He shifted, gave her quick, concise directions to the office of the president.

Rarified, Eve thought as she took the stairs. The air, the architecture. The Urban Wars had missed defiling or destroying most of the older buildings here. She imagined there were contemporary touches—cams, security, alarms, animated guides. But they'd tucked them away, out of view so the ambiance was age and tradition.

Before she'd reached the offices, a man of about thirty in one of those slick suits crossed the wide marble floor and waylaid her.

"Lieutenant Dallas?" His smile was as slick as his suit, his accent faintly, very faintly, Italian. "I'm Dr. Lapkoff's administrative assistant. She'd like me to bring you right in."

Good-looking guy, she noted, but he'd never pass for nineteen again. And his mocha skin couldn't be mistaken for white.

Too bad, the admin of the president would've been an excellent possibility.

"How many people work in this building, administratively?"

"In the summer?"

"No, fall through spring."

"I can certainly get you that information. Dr. Lapkoff has an administrative assistant, an executive secretary, and a personal assistant. Each of us also has an assistant. Then, of course, there's the provost and his staff, the vice presidents and theirs. Right this way."

He led her through a reception area and straight into the president's domain.

She'd thought it would be more posh and intimidating. Instead, despite its grand scale and dignified antiques, it looked like the office of a very busy woman. It boasted an excellent view of the campus and a stingy seating area comprised of worn furniture and upholstery faded by time and sun.

Still, the wall of photographs and degrees could project the intimidating. As could the woman who rose from behind a big, cluttered desk.

Her height and build earned her the

term *statuesque*, and the strong features vied for dominance with the laser blue eyes.

Eve imagined that piercing look had given recalcitrant students, faculty, and donors alike a good chill.

"Lieutenant, thank you for coming, and for being so prompt." She strode around the desk with the gait of a woman who got where she was going with minimum detours and shook Eve's hand briskly. "Harry, let's get Lieutenant Dallas some coffee."

"No, thanks."

"No? You can go Harry. Lieutenant." She gestured to a chair, then circled behind her desk again. The position of power. "I understand you paid a visit to one of our dorms last night."

"Correct."

"I asked Darian about it this morning. He's afraid he might be in trouble, and is considerably upset about the circumstances."

"He's not in trouble with me. The circumstances are upsetting."

"They are. Darian is an excellent student with only a few minor infractions. I vetted his record thoroughly and personally this morning. I'm concerned that one of our students was used to commit a crime, and one of this nature. We've provided you with the data you requested."

"Appreciated."

Lapkoff sat back, smiled a little. The smile softened her face, but the eyes remained bold and sharp. "You're annoyed with being summoned here, so to speak. I understand. We're women of position and authority, and being *summoned* grates."

"Murder grates, Dr. Lapkoff, a hell of a lot more."

"Yes, it does. I didn't ask you to come just to satisfy my curiosity. Though I admit I wanted a look at Roarke's cop. And Jamie Lingstrom's. I've taken an interest in Jamie, as he brought us Roarke."

Those piercing blue eyes sparked with amusement for a moment. "Again, so to speak."

"Roarke's taken a personal interest in Jamie."

"So I'm told. And I understand from Darian Jamie's also connected to this girl." She angled her head. "Another thing I imagine we share is an ability to interrogate and elicit information." She waited a moment. "And to keep information to ourselves. I appreciated your discretion, Lieutenant, but—"

She leaned forward again. "This isn't just my job. This university and all that goes with it are my responsibility. And my passion. The obvious conclusion is this university may be connected to Deena MacMasters's death. That disturbs me."

She paused, shook her head as if impatient. "No, that's not accurate. It pisses me off. If the person who killed that girl is associated with Columbia, you can believe I want to find out. I want to offer any assistance I can."

"I appreciate your cooperation."

"My paternal grandfather was a cop."

Eve's eyebrows lifted. "Is that so?"

"In St. Paul. His stories fascinated me as a child. He retired a Detective-Inspector. We were very proud of him. Lieutenant." Peach folded her hands on the desk. "I believe in law and in order— and in a very dry martini. I also believe in this university, what it stands for. Darian and Jamie are what it stands for. Darian is sick with guilt and worry. Jamie, though I haven't spoken to him, is probably sick with grief. You, Lieutenant, have a reputation for getting things done, and kicking whatever ass needs to be kicked to do it. So do I. This office, and any office or facility at this university are at your disposal."

"That's quite an offer."

Now Peach edged forward and those eyes were frosted glass. "I saw the morning reports on the murder."

"So it's out."

"They didn't have much, but enough. They showed her photo."

"I hope to have an artist's rendering of the suspect by end of day. That may lead to a name and location, but unless he's in the system already, something like that can take a great deal of time. Do you have imaging programs?"

"We do."

"It's possible he was a student here at one time, or employed here. It's possible that if you ran that artist's rendition through imaging with your database of student and staff IDs, you could match him before we do."

"I'll arrange it."

"It can't be done by anyone on staff. I

need a cop to do it. That would take a warrant without your permission and approval on record."

"You'll have both."

"That certainly cuts through the bullshit."

This time Peach flashed a brilliant grin. "One of my best skills and favorite occupations."

"Well then, when we have the sketch I'll have an EDD man report here for that duty."

"I'll clear it."

"I believe the suspect hacked into your student files in April, added his data, or the data he wished, so that any check would show him as a student here. He would have removed that data on or about the day of the murder. A good e-man might be able to find those hacks, and trace."

Peach blew out a breath. "All right. It will be a lot of tedious work, I imagine."

"That's a good portion of what we do. Tedium."

"Understood. Not so different from what I do. I suppose I was hoping for something more immediate and exciting."

"Then you didn't listen to your grandfather's stories very closely."

She smiled again. "I suspect he juiced them up. Still you get juice. I'm looking forward to reading Nadine Furst's book on the Icove case."

"Hmm." Eve got to her feet.

"Lieutenant. While I do believe in law and order, in education and in that dry martini, I also believe in youth—its potential and its brevity, its marvelous thirst. I'm very sorry about Deena MacMasters, very sorry that youth was taken, and that potential ended."

"So are we all."

Peach handed Eve a card. "My contact information, including my personal 'link. Please use it if you need anything."

"Thank you, Dr. Lapkoff."

"Call me Peach."

10 As she crossed the green Eve reached for her pocket 'link to check if Mira was on site or close, then spotted her. The police psychiatrist and top profiler sat in the white stream of sunlight on the wide ledge of a grand fountain. She wore shades with bold pink frames. Eve wasn't sure she'd ever seen the elegant Mira in shades, much less any so frivolously female. Her face tipped up to the sun, her hair scooped back to wave at her nape and expose the multi-colored dangles at her ears, Mira looked absolutely relaxed and perfectly at home with the casual summer pace of the campus.

A faint smile softened a face lovely in repose while the water spilled musically from stone tier to stone tier behind her. Her excellent legs were crossed, exposed by the knee-length skirt of a suit the color of vanilla cream. Sassy open-toed shoes in the same tone boasted needle-thin heels. Beside her sat a petal pink handbag large enough to swallow a toddler.

Eve wondered if Mira slept, and if she should poke her or clear her throat. Then the smile spread, and Mira sighed deeply.

"God! What a gorgeous day. I so rarely get to take advantage of a spectacular morning like this." Mira lifted her shoulders, then let them fall in a kind of happy shrug. "I have to thank you for pulling me outside."

"Well, I'm glad there's an upside. I didn't have time to go downtown and back. We're pushing hard on this."

"Understood. The age of the victim and the connection to a police officer make it a priority. Can we speak here?"

"Yeah." Eve sat beside her. "You read the file."

"Yes." Mira touched her hand briefly to Eve's, a gesture they both knew acknowledged the painful memories of Eve's childhood. "Would you have taken this case if MacMasters hadn't asked for you specifically?"

"I don't cherry-pick assignments." The sharp tone, the defensiveness in it, caught Eve off guard. She shook it off. "If I can't handle what comes to me," she said, "I don't deserve the badge. That's that."

"For you, yes, I agree. Not with the philosophy, but with your belief in it. She's lucky to have you—Deena—because you understand what she faced in those last hours of her life."

"It's not the same."

"No, it's never the same. And, conversely, it's precisely the same. I need to ask before we discuss the case, about your nightmares and flashbacks. I need to ask," Mira repeated, gently, when Eve's face went blank. "If this case exacerbates them—"

"It's not. It won't. They're not as bad." Dragging a hand through her hair, Eve struggled to put annoyance at the personal queries aside. Mira was right, she admitted, the question needed to be asked. "I still have them, but they're not as . . . severe," she decided. "They're not as frequent or as intense. I think I've come to a place—I don't know—it happened, and nothing can change what he did to me. But I stopped him. If I go back, in the nightmares, I can stop him again if I have to. He doesn't have the power anymore. I do."

"Yes." Mira's smile was as brilliant as the sunlight, and again she laid her hand over Eve's. "You do."

"I can't stop the nightmares, but I can handle them better now. They're not a dance in a meadow, which I don't get anyway. Why is dancing in a meadow with all that tall grass hiding whatever's slinking around under it, and the bugs flying around your head such a fun deal?"

"Hmm" was the best Mira could think of.

"What I mean is I don't look forward to getting jerked around by my subconscious, but it doesn't kick my ass nightly, not anymore."

"I'm glad to hear it. Very glad."

"I had a few moments, looking at Deena,

at what was done to her, that had me a little shaky. But I got through it. It won't affect my ability to lead the investigation."

"I'd worry about your ability to lead the investigation if you weren't touched in some way by what was done to her."

Eve said nothing for a few moments. "And you brought this up, pushed it, so I could get it out. So I wouldn't have it sneaking around in the back of my mind."

Mira gave Eve's hand a quick pat. "Did it work?"

"Apparently."

"Well, good for me. And you. And Deena."

"Okay." Done, Eve thought. For now. "Did you review the video?"

"Yes. Particularly cruel, isn't it? To force the girl to say those things, to intend the father to hear them, to show, graphically to the father the result."

"No question it was a message to Mac-Masters."

"No, none. It was all a message. The location, the use of police restraints, the method, and even the length of time the killer spent. Hours."

"He enjoyed it," Eve commented. "He enjoyed stretching it out."

"Undoubtedly. But more, it's a form of bragging. An in-your-face gesture. I did this to what you loved, in your own home, and I took my time."

"He made her suffer, wanted MacMasters to know she'd suffered, that he'd had total power over her."

"The rapes are another form of that power, and that message. I violated her, hurt her, humiliated her, terrified her, took her innocence before I took her life." Mira shifted, angling toward Eve. "And he did so by first charming and dazzling her, making her feel something for him, believe he felt something for her."

"It hurts more that way." Eve studied the students strolling or jogging by. "Hurts her more when she understands he felt nothing."

"It adds to it, to that power. He deceived her first, developed a relationship with her that took effort and time—and again he took his time. He enjoyed the planning, the deceit, her romantic entanglement with him as much as the killing itself."

"He's young. If he passed for nineteen, he can't be past thirty." She watched the people walking by, calculated their age on looks, skin tone, movement, gestures, wardrobe. "And I'd say younger than that. Mid-twenties. But he's organized, controlled, focused. He doesn't have a young mind, doesn't give in to impulse— or certainly, not with this. He stalked and studied and researched his target. He knew exactly how to approach her."

"Sociopathic tendencies, with a purpose," Mira confirmed. "It's a dangerous combination. While the video wasn't an impulse, it was indulgent. He needed MacMasters to understand: This is your fault. Even the cruelty, the rape, the killing wasn't enough unless MacMasters understood he was to blame for it. He didn't want the father just shattered, he wanted him to understand this was a result of some prior act or offense."

"We're going through his cases. I've got a couple of lines to tug."

"He'll be buried there." Mira shook her head. "Nothing and no one obvious. While it's hard to believe this is his first kill, it may be. It was a purpose, so may very well have driven him for some time. All the evidence you've gathered indicates to me he knows how to acclimate, to blend, to behave in a fashion society considers normal or acceptable."

"He's spent time on this campus, and he has e-skills."

"He has education. Your victim was a bright student, and she'd expect him to have education as he posed as a college student. He would do what's expected, therefore acclimate. He has a job or a source of income. But I believe he deals with people. He would need to, to observe them, to ply his trade of being what's expected. He probably lives alone and is considered by his neighbors, his coworkers, to be a nice young man. Friendly, helpful. He detests authority, but would be careful not to show it. Does what he's told, and if necessary, finds a way to pay back any slight or offense.

"The police are the enemy," Mira continued, "but it's unlikely he'll have a sheet. Minor stuff, perhaps, before he fully developed control and focus. More than that, *this* cop is the enemy, someone to be crushed. But not directly. He understands it's more painful to take away a loved one."

"Like MacMasters took away one of his."

"I believe so. Yes, that would be my conclusion. If it was MacMasters and him, the punishment would have been more direct. But this punishment—it's your fault—indicates a specific sort of payment. You took mine, I take yours."

But who? Eve wondered, frustrated. Or what? "MacMasters has ridden a desk for a long time. He doesn't work the streets. He's got a rep for closing cases, or supervising cops who do. But he's methodical, not flashy. He's a straight arrow, and he doesn't have any terminations. He's never taken down a suspect on the job."

"There are other ways to take away a loved one besides death."

"Yeah, and I've thought of that. But, do you rape and kill, go through all that led up to it, because a cop had a part in sending your brother, your father, whatever, to a cage? It's eye for eye. Death for death. It's purpose, like you said."

"I'm inclined to agree, but people die in prison, are killed or self-terminate. Or come out and do the same. Witnesses are murdered to prevent them from testifying, and the police work to convince them to testify. Victims are not always given justice."

"Yeah, been there, too. How do we find this bastard's loved one—who died, was killed, went in, got whacked—in the case files of a cop with more than twenty years on the job?"

"He'll believe or have convinced himself that this person was or is innocent. As Deena was innocent. You might consider that this connection to the killer was abused, injured, raped, killed in or out of prison. Or one who self-terminated after release, or after an attack. I'd start looking for someone who was strangled or smothered. The method was another message. He could have beaten her to death, used a knife, given her an overdose. There are any number of ways to kill a helpless girl. He chose the method."

"That's right, that's exactly right." Eve narrowed her eyes as she turned it over. "Every detail was planned. Of course he planned the method. Not just because he wanted to see her when he killed her, not just because he wanted to use his hands. Because he had to, to make his point. It's a good angle. We can narrow it down with that, push on that."

She thought it through. "They're having Deena's memorial on Thursday."

"There can't be anything more painful. How is MacMasters holding up?"

"Barely. He's ready to take the blame, even without knowing about the vid. The killer wasted time there. He asked me how he was supposed to stand it, and I didn't have an answer. I don't know what it's like to have a kid, but I know when the vic's a kid it's harder. We all feel that. I don't know how anyone stands it when it's their kid."

"Most rely on the natural order. Children bury their parents, not the other way around. Those of us who do what we do know murder, even death, has no respect for the natural order. This is a burden MacMasters and his wife will never lay down. In time, they'll live, work, play, make love, laugh, but they won't ever lay this down."

"Yeah." She thought of what Summerset had told her. "That's what I hear. In any case, the memorial. I think he'll find a way to be there. I think he'll need to see the results of his work. He'll need to see MacMasters grieve and suffer. He'd have to be absolutely sure, wouldn't he, that he'd done the job? However focused he is, he's still young. What's the point of screwing with someone if you don't see them squirm?"

"I agree. There's a very high probability that he'll find a way to attend, or at least find a way to observe MacMasters. The girl was the weapon. MacMasters was the goal."

"That's what I think. Thanks for meeting me."

"I only regret I can't find an excuse to work right here the rest of the day. It's a lovely campus. I've given some lectures here, and attended a couple of performances, but—"

"Wait. Lectures. Performances—like theater?"

"Yes, they have an excellent theater."

"And the public can attend this stuff?"

"Of course. They—"

"Wait." She snapped it this time, and yanked out her 'link. "Dr. Lapkoff."

"That was very quick."

"I need a list of every performance, concert, lecture, vid, live, holo—open to the public from April to this past Saturday. Send it to this contact." She read off the data for her unit at Central.

"I'll arrange it."

"Thanks."

"You know Peach?" Mira asked when Eve clicked off and keyed in another code.

"Huh? Well, sort of. You know her?"

"Yes. Dennis and I are patrons of the university. He taught here for years."

"He—really? Mr. Mira taught here?"

"You know he was a professor."

Eve thought of Dennis Mira and his comfortable, misbuttoned cardigans, his kind eyes, charmingly vague demeanor. "Yeah, I guess I never . . ."

"He still gives the occasional course and often lectures. We're very friendly with Peach and her family."

"Small world. Jamie." She turned back to the 'link. "Have you gone to any of the concerts, plays, lectures, whatever at Columbia since April?"

"What?" He had the glassy-eyed look

of an e-geek deep in chips. "Yeah, I went to a lecture on e-crime."

"No, not that. Something Deena would have been into."

"You mean like singing and dancing and shit?" He gave her a look that could only come from the young and the pained. "Why would I?"

"What I thought." She cut him off, tagged Peabody. "I want you to go to the scene, get any playbills, posters, souvenirs, whatever the hell pertaining to any concert, performance, lecture at Columbia from the time of the meet until the day of the murder. Bring them to Central. Toss in any of the same from anywhere during the same time frame."

"Can do. On the shoes? I thought about what you said. Upper East wasn't his spot. Probably Deena's area isn't either if he didn't want any chance of getting spotted. So I'm focusing on downtown vendors. Just a hunch."

"Not bad. We'll work that first. Get the stuff, head to the house. I'll be there inside an hour."

Eve shoved the 'link away, rose. "Thanks. Good angle. I have to book."

"If you're heading back to Central, maybe I could catch a ride."

"I have to go see a guy about his dead brother."

Mira gathered up her big pink bag. "Won't that be interesting? May I?"

"I guess. He's a potential. Not high on the list, but . . . Well, if he gives us any trouble, you could hit him with that bag and do some damage."

Mira stroked a loving hand over the pastel leather. "We all have our weapons."

When they reached her vehicle, Eve did a run on Risso Banks, obtained his home and work addresses.

"White male, age twenty-four. He's kept his nose clean since his brother's bust and unfortunate demise, and has gainful employment. Which fits the profile. Unmarried, no cohab on record. Also fits. And it doesn't. His brother goes down—literally, as in four stories to splat. MacMasters is the boss, but not the primary, and it's a shared bust with SVU. Cecil, the brother, worked the illegals and pedophile trades."

"A charmer."

"Apparently. He wasn't raped, kicked around, smothered, or strangled. He took a header out a window while trying to avoid arrest. Still, not far out of the way."

"A lot of it's eliminating, isn't it? Legwork, 'link work, details." Obviously content, Mira settled back. "What an interesting vehicle. It looks so ordinary from the outside, but it has more hardware than my office inside. And it's very comfortable—smooth, too," she added as Eve wove through traffic.

"It moves like a turbo, and verticals like a jet-copter. Armored and blast proof. It was . . . sort of a favor-slash-present from Roarke."

"A present so you wouldn't have to continually knock heads with Requisitions. I heard about the last wreck."

Before she could stop herself, Eve hunched her shoulders. "It wasn't my fault."

"No, but . . . And the favor so you'd be able to accept it, and he'd be able to feel you were as safe as possible."

"I guess bull's-eyes like that are why you have all the initials after your name."

"That, and I like to think knowing you and Roarke fairly well. It's an excellent favor-slash-present. Tell me, since we have a little time, is everyone ready for the wedding? We're looking forward to it."

"I guess, probably." The word *wedding* had a little ember of guilt and unease burning in Eve's gut. "I'm supposed to tag Louise—people tell me—and offer to do matron-of-honor stuff. I don't know what that is. We did the shower thing, and the dress I'm supposed to wear's being delivered today. What else is there?"

"Is that a rhetorical question?"

"Shit."

"I'd advise to contact Louise when you have a few free moments, and ask her if she needs anything. Very likely she won't need anything but to talk or vent for a bit. She's an efficient sort who knows what she wants and has certainly arranged it. But there are invariably little glitches and headaches at the last minute. All you really need to do is listen."

Eve cut her gaze, full of cautious hope, toward Mira. "Really?"

"I'd give that an eighty-eight-point-three probability."

Eve mulled it, relieved. "That's decent."

"I went by their new home last week, to

take a look at Charles's office. He's nervous and excited, and has set up a very
good area there. Of course I got a tour of
the whole house. It's coming along beau-
tifully, I think. Urban, classic, eclectic—
very them. They're going to make a nice
life there."

"It's good. They're good. It's all good. I
just want to get through this wedding
thing."

"Don't tell me you're nervous."

"No. Well, yeah." Nervous about being
nervous had Eve shifting in her seat.
"What if the case is running hot, or I'm
about to close it, or any of the shit that
comes down on the job comes down on
the day? What do you do? With Roarke, I
don't have to worry. He gets it. If I have to
cancel something or I'm late, whatever,
he gets it. He's extremely frosty in that
area. And I still feel guilty sometimes. But
this is other. I get that this is, like, The
Day. It's major for Louise. I don't want to
screw it up."

"You can only do what you can do, Eve.
Louise understands emergencies, priori-
ties, the demands of a vocation. She's a
doctor."

Eve frowned over it a moment. "That's right. She's a doctor. If she's got her hands in somebody's body cavity, she's not going to pull them out and walk off to put on a fancy dress. She'd finish first."

"I certainly hope so."

"Okay. That's better. It's okay."

"What are you wearing?"

"A yellow thing."

Mira smiled. "Eyes straight, don't look at me, and tell me what I'm wearing."

"Did you forget?"

"Indulge me."

"A suit, knee-length skirt, three-button jacket—off-white. Kind of vanilla. Square, silver buttons, lacy top. Shoes, light pink, cut-out toes, ankle-breaker heels about the width of a needle. Multicolored stone earrings, dangle style, silver, and a silver three-strand neck chain with some little stones set at various points. Humongo pink handbag, and fairly iced pink-framed sunshades—both of which match the paint on your toenails. Wedding band, fancy silver wrist unit with sparkly bracelet.

"How do you remember to stick on all that," Eve wondered, "the sparkly things?"

"It's called vanity," Mira told her. "I enjoy

mine. And it's so interesting you can only recall your dress for the wedding being a yellow thing, and can describe what I'm wearing down to the width of my heels. Which, yes, are miserably uncomfortable, but so pretty."

Mira turned her ankles to admire them. "And now that I've seen your closet first-hand, I don't know how you resist decking yourself out in all those beautiful clothes every day."

"Maybe I'm like the vehicle," Eve decided. "Keep it ordinary on the outside, so nobody notices all the hardware inside."

"Very good." Mira laughed. "Very good."

"It's what he does," Eve murmured.

"And we've circled back."

"Keep it ordinary, every day, unobtrusive on the outside. Nobody sees what's inside. Nobody sees a monster. When he goes to get a slice or buy shoes, nobody notices him. Or, if he wants them to, they see a nice kid, good-looking young guy. Not spectacular, that they'd remember. Just good-looking, polite, barely stirs the air. We've got two wits who saw him with Deena, and that's all they gave me, nearly all. We'll do better because Yancy's good at digging out the details, but they didn't think about him, didn't check him out especially. Wouldn't have noted him at all, most likely, except he was with her. They knew her, so they noticed him."

She snagged a second-level spot a half block from Risso's work address, then glanced at Mira's heels. "It's a short hike. Can you handle that?"

"I'm a professional."

Halfway down, Eve cursed, sighed, then vaulted over the safety rail to the sidewalk. "Be right back," she called out as Mira gaped at her.

She'd seen the snatch, and really the mark deserved it. Bopping along, gawking at storefronts with his back pocket bulging. Or it had been until the street thief plucked out the wallet with the classic bump and grab.

The thief continued on, unhurried, with the wallet already inside the right front pocket of his pants, under the bulk of his baggy hoodie.

Eve sprinted a quarter block to close the distance, then dropped down to a brisk New Yorker's pace. She tapped the thief on the shoulder. "Sorry, can you help me?"

He gave her a round-eyed innocent look, just another guy on the street. "What with?"

"Well, I've got other stuff to do, really pressed for time, so you could help me out and just hand me the wallet you just lifted. It's in here." She slapped her hand on his pocket. "Oh, and any other property you've lifted today, too. Then we can both be about our business."

"Don't know what you're talking about. Piss it." She felt him gather to run, grabbed his shoulder.

"You could really make this quick and simple for both of us. I don't want to take time to— Hey!"

He ducked, pivoted, squirmed like a snake shedding skin, and left her holding an empty hoodie.

He had a squat torso on squat legs. It really wasn't even a challenge. Despite the fact she had to dodge pedestrians when the thief was content to shove, bull, and burst through them, she caught him before the end of the block.

"Help, help!" He barked it out when she pushed him face-first into the nearest building. "Police!"

"Come on, you moron, you know I'm the police." She cuffed his hands behind his back, kneed his legs apart to make him spread them. "If you make me chase you again, you're going to be eating sidewalk."

She patted him down, found no weapons and six wallets.

"Any one of these yours, asshole?"

"I found those." Darting eyes replaced wide eyes. "I was going to find a cop and turn them in. Sweartagod."

"Uh-huh. I saw you find this one in that guy's back pocket. I'm sure he's going to be really grateful."

"I called for uniforms." Mira hurried up on her ice-pick heels.

"Good, saves me." She tapped the thief on the back of the head. "See? See? You just couldn't help me out. Now we've both got to go through the deal. You!" She pointed at the mark who was currently one of the lookie-loos staring at the scene.

"Me? Me? I didn't do anything."

"Got ID?"

"Yes. Sure. I got . . ." He reached for his back pocket. "My wallet! My wallet's gone!"

"Isn't that a coincidence? I've got it right here." Keeping one elbow in the small of the thief's back, she held up the wallet. "It's like magic, isn't it? To get it back you'll need to wait here for the uniformed officers and file a report with them."

"I was having a good day," the thief muttered. "A really good day."

"It's in the toilet now." She held up her badge to flash the two uniforms hustling their way.

It took time she didn't want to spend, but in the end, she supposed, justice was served.

"You gave me such a start," Mira said. "One second you're there, the next you're jumping over the rail and running."

"Yet another reason not to wear fancy duds and ankle breakers."

"You have a point."

They backtracked to the store where Risso was employed.

A lot of gadgetry, she noted, all under the banner: *20% Off! This Week Only!*

that had probably been draped there for years.

She made Risso Banks from his ID shot, and saw him make her for a cop. He strolled over, with a redwood-sized chip on his shoulder.

"Saw you take down that mug. He didn't have any speed."

"He had six wallets that weren't his."

"Crime's everywhere."

He was a good-looking guy—a bit on the smirky side—with a short centurion cut that looked fresh. Dark hair, sulky brown eyes. The right height and build, but she didn't get a buzz off him.

"Do you want to talk here, Risso, or somewhere more private?"

"If you've got something to say, say it. The boss knows I had some trouble a while back. I haven't had any since. He knows that, too. I did the terms of my deal."

"Your brother got a harder deal."

He shrugged, then head jerked her toward the rear of the shop. "He screwed me up. Fed me illegals before I'm ten, got me hooked. I worked for him, sure. What else was there? And when it came down, he ran, and he left me for the cops. He ran, trying to save his own ass, and didn't do anything to help me. So he got what was coming to him, as far as I can see. And I'm not shedding any tears over it. I got straight, I got work. Cops like to come around giving me the fish eye, fine. I'm clean."

"If you give me the right answer to one question, I walk out. No harm, no foul."

"Depends on the question."

"You got attitude, Risso. I have to admire that. Saturday from six p.m. to Sunday, three a.m."

"We close at six on Saturday. Me and the boss closed up, left about quarter after. You can ask him."

"And after?"

He gave a jerky shrug that she interpreted as annoyance rather than nerves. "Went home, got cleaned up some. Eight o'clock me, the boss, and three other guys played cards like we do Saturday night, once a month. Game was at my place this round." He grinned, with that hint of smirk. "Friendly stakes."

"I'm not worried about the stakes. Is

that your boss?" She gestured toward the potbellied man trying to sell a customer a new PPC.

"Yeah. And the guy in the back, Carmine, he was at the game."

"Hold on a minute."

She crossed to the potbelly, held up her badge. "Quick one. Who closed with you Saturday night, and at what time?"

"Risso, he's over there. We closed it up about six."

"When did you see him next?"

"At his place, a couple hours later. We had a card game. Is there a problem?"

"No, no problem. Thanks."

"He's a good boy," the man said as Eve started to turn away. "He comes in on time, does the work, and doesn't complain. I gave him a raise last week 'cause he earned it."

Eve nodded. "He's not in any trouble."

She walked back to Risso, handed him her card. "Cops come in giving you the fish eye, let me know."

He stared at the card. "Why?"

"Because I asked a question and you gave me the right answer. Because you're not your brother."

Eve walked out while he continued to stare at the card.

"That was well done," Mira told her.

"Elimination. Just crossing the lines."

"That's not what I meant."

Eve shrugged and walked with Mira back to the car.

**II** Karlene Robins punched in her code, swiped her realty ID in the slot. She hummed to herself as security recognized both. A perfect day, she thought, shaking back her curling mane of glossy black hair. She had hopes to make it spectacular by closing the sale on the very frosty loft with her very young and well-heeled client.

It was just what he was after. She could hardly believe her luck, and the timing. The property had fallen into her lap, just the night before, when the previous buyers broke contract.

Their loss, and she really hoped her gain.

She stepped inside the tiny lobby area, coded in for the elevator.

The commission would be a whopper, and couldn't come at a better time. She was getting married on Saturday, and thinking of it, she did a little spin into the elevator.

She could close this deal, have all the paperwork in order in a snap, snap, snap. When she and Tony got back from their honeymoon, they'd go to settlement, she'd present the happy new loft owner with a big-ass gift basket full of fancy wines and eats—and most important—collect her big, beautiful commission.

She scanned the little elevator car, nodded approval. Good security, smooth ride, privacy. And the openwork iron doors, she thought when she reached the loft, added that funky retro touch.

They opened soundlessly into a high-ceilinged space with wide, wide windows and a double trio of skylights.

The original wood floors—and how often did you find *that*—were stylishly distressed. The walls, neutral tones chosen to sell, were fully soundproofed. Kitchen, she mused, wandering through, totally up-to-date. Compact, shining appliances with the fun and funky zebra-striped counters configured for maximum use of space.

The client probably wouldn't cook for himself. He was from money, and currently trying to make a name for himself as an artist. He'd entertain though, and this was a fine space for that.

Add two bedrooms—one that would stand in very well as studio space with more skylights, more windows—and southern exposure—and what she considered a dream bathroom with jet tub, jet shower, drying tube, smoked glass walls—and he'd never do better.

The place said—no cheered, she corrected—it cheered young, fun, hip, and well-off.

She fluffed her hair, turned to check herself out in the mirror. Appearance mattered. She'd dressed carefully, groomed carefully to suit the client and the location.

He wanted SoHo, arty, a hot spot amid plenty of galleries, restaurants, clubs. And this was it. Karlene figured his real estate agent should reflect the same at a showing. She'd chosen the short black skirt, the high leopard-print heels, and the bold red top with its silver beading rather than a more sedate suit very deliberately.

It transmitted young and frost—which she was, she thought with a laugh—but for some clients you wanted to project maturity, stability, sobriety.

This guy was younger than she was.

Must be nice, she thought as she glanced at her wrist unit, and continued to wander, to fluff some of the wildly patterned pillows on the furniture staged in the living area. Barely twenty-two and able to afford a prime SoHo loft.

She and Tony had a nice place, she reminded herself. And with her eye for decorating and bargains she'd squeezed plenty of juice in it. But one day—and with commissions like this one—they'd be able to afford a big, sunny loft.

She dug into her bag, took out the scent tube she'd chosen. In the kitchen again, she crouched to plug it into the air system. In moments, the loft would smell, subtly, of sugar cookies. A good choice, she felt, for a younger client.

She crossed to the living area's mood

screen, switched it on to a lively, energetic mix of colors and shapes, then ordered the music system on—not too loud.

"Set the tone," she said, turning in a circle to take it all in, "make it home."

She considered opening the wall panel to display the security monitors, then decided against it. He was too young to worry overmuch there—and she'd make a point of showing him when they did the tour. Instead she walked to the wide front windows, stood looking out on what she hoped—for herself and her client—would soon be Drew Pittering's neighborhood.

Like the kitchen, the people walking below were up-to-date. Neo-Bohemian was the tone here, the pace. Artists displaying their wares on the sidewalk, people sipping coffee drinks and having intense conversations outside of cafés and bistros. Too-iced-to-care boutiques squeezed in beside edgy little galleries.

It suited him so well. Commission aside, she worked hard to suit the client to the property, and vice versa. Before she hit thirty, she intended to have her own business. She'd already chosen the name. Urban Views.

Four years left in her goal, she mused. And she just *knew* she'd make it.

If Drew took the bite here, she'd be on her way.

He was running a little late, she realized. But then, client was king. She took a breath, then pulled out her 'link. She was going to be optimistic, think positive—and make reservations for her and Tony at their favorite restaurant to celebrate the sale.

It wasn't jinxing it, she told herself. It was anticipating it. Visualizing it. Tonight, they were going to drink champagne and toast the future.

Once done, she ran back through her appointment book to make certain she had the rest of her week—her last week as a single woman—in order. Final fitting, final consult with the caterer and planner, the full day of spa and salon treatments for herself and her wedding party.

Check, check, check.

When her 'link beeped, she checked the display and had one moment of concern. "Please don't be calling to cancel," she muttered, then answered with a cheerful tone. "Hello, Drew! I'm standing here looking out your front window. It's a very frosty view."

"Sorry, sorry, I'm running late. I got caught up with the work and lost track. But I'm nearly there. Heading down the block now."

"That's mag." Relief had her barely resisting a dance. "I'll clear you in so you can come right up. You have the address."

"Right here. I love this neighborhood, Karlene. It's just what I want."

"Wait until you see the space." She walked over to shut down security for him. "I swear, if you don't snap this up, I'm buying it myself."

"Just tell me nobody else is looking at it yet. I've got a good feeling."

"I contacted you first, as promised. Nobody's due to see it until tomorrow as I told you. We've got a jump on it."

"Perfect. I'm on my way up. Hey, love the elevator. Ten seconds."

She laughed, closed the 'link. And greeted him with a stunning smile.

"Really sorry I kept you waiting," he said as he came in. "But I brought a makeup gift." He offered her one of the two go-cups of coffee he had in a takeout bag.

"You're forgiven." She toasted him with the cup. "Where should we start?"

"Let me just stand here a minute." He shifted the bag on his shoulder, looked around the open living area. "This is . . . look at the light in here."

"That's what made me think of you, straight off. So much natural light. Tailor-made for an artist. You could use this whole space for your work. But if you actually wanted to use it for living, for entertaining, the second bedroom has the same exposure, and skylights."

"Privacy screens? I don't like to feel anyone watching me while I work."

"Of course." She held up a finger. "Computer, engage privacy screens, all windows."

With a quiet hum, the clear screens lowered. "As you can see, they're top-grade. They don't affect the light. You can darken them if you want to cut the sun."

"Perfect." He smiled at her. Young, charming, attractive. "Absolutely perfect. How's the coffee?"

"The same." She took another sip. "To move to location for a minute, you've got it all. Restaurants, galleries, clubs—and

mag coffee shops as you've already discovered."

"It's where I want to be." He stepped
away from the elevators, wandering now
behind the screened windows.

"The furniture's staged to give you a
feeling, an idea of one use of the space.
The fact is, Drew, you could do anything
with this area. Work, play, a combination.
I know you said you didn't cook, but you
have to see the kitchen. It's perfect, ultra
and efficient. Maybe a girlfriend would
enjoy using it."

He grinned, wagged his finger.

"I know, no girls right now," she said
with a laugh. "Art first. But artists can entertain like minds, right? And have to eat.
You can zap leftover takeout, stock the
AutoChef, and there's a built-in D and
C—for checking out takeout spots, deliveries, menus."

"Now that works for me."

"Oh, and the security system. You can
take a look at the camera zones."

He waved that off. "Let's see the rest
first."

"We'll take the master bedroom then.
It's staged, too, so you'll have an idea how

it could be used. And the advantage of being on the top floor? Skylights there, too."

She took a few steps, weaved a little.

"Okay?"

"Wow. A little light-headed."

Concern shone in his eyes. "Why don't we sit down a while?"

"No, I'm fine. I'm good. Just putting in a lot of late hours, trying to get everything done."

"Right. Big day Saturday."

"The biggest. And since we're taking off on Monday for Honeymoon-Extraordinaire, I want to get everything cleaned up. Just need another jolt." She took a deep swallow of coffee.

"There's a little half bath off the second bedroom—or what I see as your studio. That would be handy for you, but the master? It's rocking-A."

She walked in, then swayed as her knees buckled.

"Hey, hey." He took her arm, her weight, walked her toward the bed. "Let's sit down."

"Sorry. I'm so sorry." She all but floated down to the bed. "I feel . . . wrong. I'll be okay in a minute."

"I don't really think so. Here, finish this up." He held the coffee to her lips, poured it down her throat as her eyes glazed.

"Wait."

"Oh, don't worry. I'm going to take my time. We've got all day."

His face blurred, but for an instant, the look of it, his teeth bared in a horrible smile, she felt fear. She felt fear, then nothing.

Since he'd sealed up in the elevator, he opened his bag for the cord.

"Safety first," he murmured, and bound her hands behind her back.

As the sellers had provided very nice high-end sheets, he used them to secure her legs by the ankles to the bright silver knobs of the footboard.

He took out the rest of his tools before he stripped, and stowed his neatly folded clothes in the bag.

He studied Karlene as he finished off his own, undoctored coffee, decided she looked peaceful. That wouldn't last long.

The loft was soundproofed, he'd verified that. Just as he'd verified that the other two tenants in the building were at work.

Naked, he walked over to the controls

to change the music to some hard, grinding thrash, bumped up the volume a bit. Satisfied, he went back to the main security controls, checked the cameras, checked all locks.

Later, he thought, when he'd sufficiently . . . softened her up, she'd give him her security number. She'd beg to give it to him. He'd log her out, shut down the cameras, and upload the virus.

But before that, well before that, he'd give her pain, and give her fear. And he'd talk to her, intimately, about her bitch of a mother. And why Jaynie Robins was responsible for her daughter's ugly death.

He set the doctored go-cup—a ploy as he'd purchased the actual coffee blocks uptown, then transferred it—on the kitchen counter.

He went back to the bedroom, checked his to-do list to make certain he'd forgotten nothing.

When she moaned, stirred, he smiled.

Time to go to work.

Eve strode into the Homicide bullpen with a purpose. Several conversations stopped. Baxter got to his feet.

"LT—"

"Ten minutes, conference room, full briefing." She kept going, straight into her office. She needed five of those ten to clear her head, organize her thoughts. She got coffee, turned to check the incoming on her comp.

"Media, media, media. Screw that. Talk to the liaison." She brought up the list—Peach Lapkoff moved fast—and skimmed the performances, the dates.

"Computer, start search. Victims of rape/murder through suffocation and/or strangulation within penal system. On and off planet, including halfway houses, home detention, local, federal, global. Add factor of connection to MacMasters, Captain Jonah, as part of investigative, administrative, or arresting team."

Acknowledged . . . length of search?

Brother, son, lover. Could be any. Could be none. "Twenty-five years."

Warning . . . Search for data of this nature twenty years or more will delay results.

"Then you'd better get started. Command given."

Acknowledged . . . Working . . .

"Computer, send results, year by year, to both my office and home units."

Warning . . . Extracting data by year will delay results.

"Can't be helped. Command given."

She topped off her coffee and left for the conference room while the computer worked.

She'd hoped Peabody would be back so she could palm off the setup on her partner. Instead, she loaded the data in the room comp, began updating the board.

She muscled out a second board and began to write.

Crime mirrors previous event?

Connection—MacMasters to killer—killer to person unknown killed by same MO. Search in progress.

UNSUB—organized, focused, ability to acclimate.

She continued, listed the salients of Mira's profile.

Two wits with possible sightings of UNSUB currently working with Detective Yancy.

Columbia connection. Student and staff files accessed.

Shoes ID'd by wit, Columbia sweat-shirt, long shots.

Attendance with vic, Columbia public performances and/or lectures, long shot.

She was still writing when Baxter and Trueheart came in.

"Report."

"Neighborhood canvass, zip. If we get a sketch, I think we'd have better luck. We hit her known haunts, got zip there. Kids in and out, who pays attention? Plenty who recognized her, but nobody who put her with a guy who matches what we know."

He passed to Trueheart. "Well, we didn't really do any better with the canvass of the area your wit states she spotted them. We had a couple people who thought maybe they'd seen her, but wouldn't commit. We had one who thought he'd seen her and with a boy around twenty. But he couldn't give us any more than that. Not even coloring, build, clothing. Just maybe. We have his name and data, when we get the sketch."

"We've started going through MacMasters's cases, working from current back,"

Baxter added. "Anything that even squeaks, we're running."

"Split it, work from each end and meet in the middle," Eve ordered. "We're stalled on the more currents, so let's start hitting further back, all the way back and working forward."

"Back to files from about a quarter century ago?" Baxter rubbed his nose. "You're the boss."

"That's right." She glanced over when Peabody came in carrying a large box. Trueheart hurried over to take it from her.

"My boy's a real gentleman," Baxter commented.

"More than the cops on the elevator when I had to squeeze in with that sucker. Have to be fifty playbills," Peabody continued. "And programs and posters. Saw where you were going and went through her things, added show and concert tees and other memorabilia."

"Good. I got the list from Dr. Lapkoff, detailing performances and lectures at the university since April. Odds are if the vic attended, the killer went with her. We match the paraphernalia to the list."

She turned to the murder board where

she'd put up a map. "Red pins show the three locations we know they were together. The park, the Second Avenue location, and her home. We're going to keep digging until we add more."

She checked her wrist unit. "Where the hell is EDD?"

"I tagged McNab on my way in. He said they'd be here." Peabody scanned the conference table. "No food, no beverage. Anybody want? Stupid question," she said before anyone answered. "Be right back."

"Well, while your refreshments are being arranged," Eve began, breaking off when Feeney and McNab walked in. "Nice you could make it."

Feeney shot a finger at her. "Neck-deep. Gonna need a transfusion for the blood I lost leaking out of my freaking eyes."

He sat, circled his neck. Eve heard the pops and cracks from across the room.

"Son of a bitch used some new virus. Nothing like we've seen before. I've got men working on identifying it, piecing together the elements."

"New viruses pop up every day," Eve

said. "Comps are supposed to be shielded anyway. CompuGuard's supposedly on that."

"They're busy trying to regulate, screwing around with privacy issues, unregistered. The new shit crops up every few weeks, really good new shit every year or two. This is really good new shit."

Eve considered. "How long would it take you to come up with really good new shit?"

He put on a sober face. "I'm an officer of the law."

"Yeah, and?"

He shrugged. "Depends on how much time I've got to work it, how much damage I want to do."

"Something like this?" McNab put in. "You'd have to have a good hundred-fifty dedicated hours in it. More if you're a hobbyist and not cued in. Plus you'd have to do it shielded. CompuGuard's got spotters. They don't catch everything, that's for frigging sure, but if they slap you, you're slapped hard."

She started to speak, but he anticipated her. "We started a run on CG's known infractions and fines. The trouble is they don't like to share, so we have to get an official go every time we hit a flag."

She thought of Roarke's skills, and his unregistered equipment. There, she considered, she might be willing to blur the line if necessary.

She turned back to the board, wrote: *New comp virus, possible e-education or employment.*

"Yeah." Feeney nodded. "It's an angle."

"Mira's profile, which I'll cover, includes his having employment, or an income source. It includes education, skill, focus. All required for e-work."

"Bet your ass," McNab agreed, then grinned as Peabody came in hauling another box. "Hey, She-Body, let me give you a hand."

"See, my guy's a gentleman, too." Peabody added a flutter of eyelashes.

"He scented food," Baxter said.

"Sandwiches, soy chips, Energy bars." Peabody snagged a sandwich herself. "Water, fizzies, Pepsi."

"Brain drain," Jamie said, "need fizzy."

"Current." Eve grabbed a tube of Pepsi, cracked it, then briefed the team on the morning's progress and avenues.

"Method as mirror." Feeney shoved the last of the mystery meat and processed cheese in his mouth. "That's a good one. He didn't take her out that way for the hell of it."

"On the other hand, using a blade, bat, pipe, something of that nature," McNab speculated. "It's messier."

"He had drugs. ODing her's not messy, but he didn't go with that. Even a blade," Baxter continued, "in a heart jab—and he had plenty of time to aim, isn't going to give you spatter. Bare-handed strangulation. That takes time, effort, and yeah, that purpose again."

"Hurting her was the thing, right?" Jamie stared down at the fizzy in his hand. "That was the score."

"He didn't really mess her up." Trueheart cleared his throat when eyes turned to him. "Her face. If he was working off rage, he would have. I think. Maybe he didn't want to use his fists, mess up his hands. But there were plenty of weapons in the house. Objects he could have used as either blunt or sharp instruments. And he choked her more than once, so . . .

that's what he wanted. That's the way he wanted to kill her. I think."

Baxter beamed. "Boy gets an A."

"To pursue this angle, I'm running searches on like rape-murders within the penal system, with victims who connect to MacMasters and his investigations or the investigations by officers under his command."

"That's going to take a hell of a while," Feeney calculated. "But it's a good angle."

"Meanwhile, as Detective Yancy is not here, he's still working with one or both of our wits. We'll get that status after the briefing. Baxter and Trueheart have goose egg thus far on the canvass. They will recanvass when we have a sketch.

"We're also tugging lines with Columbia. We'll do searches on students and staff—again—" she said before anyone commented. "Widen it to include all Southern states, and go back another five years. We'll also cross-reference the articles brought from the vic's room pertaining to theater and lectures with any given at the university since April. If he took her or accompanied her, we'll have another location, and more potential wits. Peabody. Shoes."

"Shoes. Okay, the wit from the park made the suspect's shoes. Anders Cheetahs, navy on white. These are high-end, geared for running shoes. As the wit's opinion was they were new, or fairly new, I've been doing a search for vendors with sales of this model starting in January. Let me just say a hell of a lot of people fork out a hell of a lot of scratch for a shoe you're supposed to run in. I've split that into various categories. Online, Skymall, New Jersey, and New York sectors. As the locations where the suspect is known or believed to have been with the vic, I flipped to concentrate below Fortieth, online, and outside Manhattan."

She paused to slug down water. "And still, a lot of shoes. Given his reputed height, I've focused on average sizes for males of six feet, and slender build, according to the highest probability. And still—"

"We get it, Peabody," Eve snapped.

"Sorry. I've kept the search on Auto on my PPC. But I had some thinking time riding the subway back to Central. School's sprung, and there were a lot of teens and twenties in the car. I thought about how they were dressed, you know? And that started me thinking. We're going on the theory he blends, acclimates. I agree. But I started to wonder about that first meet. He had it planned out. The Columbia sweatshirt—it was like a costume for his character, something she'd relate to. And the shoes? She was a runner, so she'd have probably recognized he was wearing high-end running shoes."

"Dressed the part," Eve agreed.

"Yeah. And he plans, right? Thinks things out in advance. So why wouldn't he plan out his costume? When I'm buying something important to wear—like, say, for an important event, I want to coordinate, be sure everything goes together. If I can I buy it all—dress, shoes, bag, all that, in one place. If I just can't, I take one of the pieces I have, or even a picture of it when I'm hunting for the rest."

"A picture?" Eve asked, sincerely astonished.

"Sure. You don't want your bag to clash with your shoes, or your shoes to look crappy with your dress. You want to look good. And even if you've got a squeeze . . ." She sent McNab a flirty look. "Even then, you want to make an impression."

McNab sent Peabody a gooey smile. "You always look good to me."

"Stop before I'm sick," Eve ordered.

"Maybe he bought the shoes, the pants, the running pants together. In the same place, I mean," Peabody continued, but snuck her hand between the chairs to wiggle fingers with McNab. "An outfit. It was, in a really twisted way, like a first date. First-date wardrobe is major. He wanted her to see him in a certain way, to give off a certain impression."

"I get it," Eve murmured. "Girl gets an A."

"Really?" Peabody puffed out. "Because I've started another search for venues that sell college gear, running gear, and Anders shoes. There's a lot, but not as many as just the shoes."

"Shades," Eve said. "He had on shades, and a cap."

"I'll plug it in. The other thing is, if he did buy all this from one vendor, he probably didn't go with cash. Not if he didn't want to stand out. It has to be near a grand, or more. He'd use credit or debit. He'd leave a trail."

"Why would he worry about that?" Eve nodded. "Nobody's going to notice, think twice. Push it."

"All over it."

"Baxter, Trueheart, keep working the files. When and if I have any results from my like-crimes search, we'll factor it. I'll give you a pint of my own blood," she told Feeney, "if you get me something off that hard drive."

"Your man contacted, should be in on it later this afternoon. He's got some tricks."

No question about it, Eve thought. "The vic's memorial is scheduled for Thursday. I want a team—any of you who can be spared, as well as uniforms in soft clothes, any detectives I can get to attend. He's going to want to be there, want to reap the benefits of his work. Whatever we have re the sketch by that time, every man on the team will have a copy. Let's go, keep the hammer down."

Eve waited, and tried to ignore the quick lip-lock and ass-grab Peabody and McNab exchanged by the door.

"That was good thinking," she said, "the buying angle."

"Shopping is a vital part of my life, unlike yours. Still, it feels like we've got lots of angles but no shape. He's still a ghost."

"Let's hope Yancy can bring him to life."

12 She knew better than to push yancy when it came to renderings. But she thought she could try a single, firm nudge. When she didn't find him at his workstation, she did a quick search of the trio of private conference rooms.

She interrupted two other police artists, but didn't find Yancy.

She tracked him down in the break room.

He stood, leaning against the short counter, munching on dried fruit from a bag, eyes closed, headset on.

His mop of hair curled appealingly

around his striking face. He wore his sleeves rolled up, his shirt unbuttoned at the collar, and a pair of well-worn jeans.

It occurred to her he probably looked more like a college kid than a police detective.

Could pass for twenty-two or -three, she thought. Younger if he worked at it.

Then his eyes opened, and she added on another five years. The eyes knew too much for barely two decades.

"How old are you?"

His brows lifted. "Twenty-eight. Why?"

"Just figuring something."

He munched another handful of fruit. "You're thinking of the suspect. He skews young, but may be older."

"Something like that." She glanced at the bag he offered. "No, thanks. Why do you eat that?"

"I wish I knew. I finished with Marta."

"Delroy, nanny from the park. What do you have?"

He shook his head. "She didn't get a good look. She was game, and she worked at it, but it comes down to a quick glimpse, and in the rain. She's pretty solid on height and build, coloring, hair length. I walked her through it, and it's coming out that she saw his profile. I got what feels like real on what he was wearing, and a pretty good idea of the style airboard. But his face is mostly impression. Young, good-looking."

"Why don't you show me?"

He puffed out a breath. "You're not going to be happy."

But he led her out, wound around to his workstation. Standing, he called up the sketch on the computer, then laid out the drawing he'd done.

"Shit. It could be anybody. It could be female."

Yancy lifted a finger as a point. "Yeah, and the second part might be an advantage. It was a male, she's sure of that, but she used terms like cute, and once, pretty. It may be he's got androgenous features. Young girls feel safe, and are often attracted to boys with androgenous features. They're not as threatening."

"So, we may or may not have a pretty boy who may or may not be nineteen."

"I've got your second wit coming in. She's due in about a half hour. I did a quick 'link warm-up with her. She's more decisive than Marta, brisker, comes off more confident. I may do better with her. And what I get from her I can use with what I've got here. I'll show the finished to both wits, and see if it rings."

"Tell me about the airboard."

"Black, silver racing stripes. Metallic silver, she thinks, because it glinted, and it was raining so no sun. That's pretty simple for an airboard design. So I did a search. Two manufacturers make one that basic design. Go-Scoot and Anders Street Sport."

"Anders."

"Yeah, how about that? Wasn't that long ago you were investigating his murder."

"Small world, even for the dead, I guess. But it's interesting as the second wit ID'd his shoes as an Anders brand. Could be brand loyalty. Get me what you can get me as soon as you get it."

"You got it," he said and grinned.

Back in her office she did a run on Nattie Simpson, the husband, the kid. As MacMasters had told her, Nattie was doing her time at Rikers. The husband—now ex—had relocated to East Washington, with the kid. He was thirty-five, and couldn't pass for a teenager. The kid was ten, and couldn't pass either.

Still, she followed through with a call to Rikers for an overview of Nattie before she crossed that angle off her list.

No connection, no pop, she thought when she'd finished.

Dead end.

She checked the search results on like crimes, and found nothing to connect to MacMasters in the last five years.

She considered adding in victims and witnesses, then decided her office unit would probably implode from that much activity. She'd do it at home.

Earmarking that for later, she began cross-referencing Deena's box of souvenirs with the list from Lapkoff.

There, she hit fast.

"Spring musical, *Shake It Up*, May 15–18."

She skimmed through it, scanning photographs, play summary, the cast and crew lists, the ads, in case Deena had made any notations.

Though she found none, she logged the playbill into evidence, bagged it.

She continued through, making ordered

piles—plays, concerts, dance theater, performance art. And frowned when she came on a second playbill for *Shake It Up*, same dates.

"Did you take his, too, Deena? Shit, shit." She grabbed Seal-It from her desk, coated her hands. She paged through the second book, and found a small notation inside a heart above the summary.

D&D
5/16/60

"One's his, one's got to be." She logged and bagged the second playbill, then placed a 'link call to Jo Jennings.

Her mother answered. Not frazzled this time, Eve thought. Weary.

"Ms. Jennings, I need to speak with Jo."

"Lieutenant, my girl's wrecked. Just . . . devastated. Do you know she's blaming herself? Blaming herself for not telling anyone Deena was seeing a boy? All she did was keep her word to her best friend, but she's crushed with guilt for it now."

"It may help her if she can do something to help. I just want confirmation on something, if she can give it to me. And it could be extremely important to the investigation."

"All right. All right." Ms. Jennings rubbed her forehead. "She's in her room. She's barely come out since you came and . . . She may be sleeping. I'm not going to wake her if she's sleeping."

The 'link cut to holding blue. Eve used her comp to e-mail a priority message to Berenski at the lab.

Have a possibility for prints re the MacMasters homicide. Will hand-deliver asap. This is priority. Don't give me any shit.

"Lieutenant. Jo's here. I'm going to stay with her."

"That's fine. Jo, I need to know if Deena went with the boy she was seeing secretly to a musical production at Columbia University. On May sixteenth."

"I dunno."

"Would she have told you? I know she enjoyed theater, got excited about theater. She saved playbills. She had a large collection of them."

"He was supposed to take her that night and he killed her." Tears sprang and spilled.

"But it wasn't the first time they were supposed to go see a play together, was it?"

"She said he really liked theater, too. He's just a liar."

She said it fiercely, bitterly. "Just a liar."

"Lieutenant, that's enough."

"Hold on. May sixteenth, Jo. They'd been seeing each other for about four weeks then. It was a musical about college students performed by college students. I bet she enjoyed it."

"Shake It Up."

"That's right. Did she go with him?"

"It was like an anniversary. A month. She met him for dinner, then they went to the play. He gave her a little stuffed dog."

Eve remembered the collection of animals. "What kind of dog?"

"A little brown and white one. If you rub its ears it says *I love you.* Mom."

"Okay, baby, okay. That's all, Lieutenant."

"Jo, you helped me a lot. You helped Deena by talking to me, by remembering."

"I did?"

"Yes, you did. Thank you."

Jo turned her face into her mother's

breast. Ms. Jennings nodded at Eve, then clicked off.

Eve grabbed the evidence bag, strode out, swung by Peabody's desk. "I may have something. Two playbills for a Columbia performance, one the best friend confirms Deena attended with the UNSUB, on May sixteen."

"Two? She kept his."

"Seems logical. I'm taking them to the lab now, personally. I've got more I want to input in the searches, but this unit won't deal with it. I'm working from home after the lab."

"Roarke's up in EDD."

"Shit. Well, I'll see him at home later. I also need to go by the scene. He gave Deena one of the stuffed toys. Could get lucky there, too. I'll run it, get that to the lab first thing in the morning."

"If I hit anything in the meantime, you'll be the first."

"Right, do a secondary, adding in an Anders airboard. Black with silver racing stripes. Street Sport. He may have purchased that along with the shoes."

"Got it."

Eve dragged out her 'link as she headed down to the garage.

"Lieutenant," Roarke said.

"I've got some field work, then I'm going to work from home. I'm heading out now. Just, ah, fyi."

His eyebrow raised. "Then I suppose I'll have to get myself home."

"Sorry. When you do . . . we'll talk about that then."

"If you say so. I'll be there . . . eventually. Eat something, and don't wait for me," he ordered and broke transmission.

She frowned at the blank screen. She knew annoyed when she heard it. He shouldn't have poked into the cop work if he was going to get annoyed she couldn't hang around to give him a damn ride home.

She stewed about it all the way to the lab, and was primed to chew out Dickhead's heart if he gave her any grief.

"What is it?" he barked at her. "It's frigging end of shift for me since you got me in here . . ." He trailed off, paling a little as he scooted to a safe distance on his rolly stool. "Jesus, Dallas, did you just growl?"

"I'll do more than growl. I'll rip out your liver with my bare hands and eat it." She slapped the two sealed playbills down. "One of these is going to have his prints. I want his goddamn prints and fuck your end of shift."

"Hey, hey, hey. You used to at least offer me a decent bribe. Not that I'd take one, under the circumstances," he added hurriedly. "Just saying."

Shoulders hunched, he drew one of the playbills out with tongs, set it on a sterile pad. He ran a scanner over the front, keyed in something on his comp. Blew out a long-suffering breath.

"Got smears, and lots of them, some partials, a couple of decents—and that's just the cover of one. Do you know how many people handle this kind of thing? You got the people who put them to-gether, pack 'em, ship 'em, unpack 'em, divvy them up, pass them out."

"I want every print, and smudge, on both of them—inside and out—analyzed and ID'd."

"It's not a fucking snap. We'll do it, we'll get it done, but it's not a fucking snap with this many hands on them."

"Just get me the prints. I'll do the eliminating."

"Damn right you will." He pointed at her, stood—or sat—his ground. "We got you what you needed this morning. I worked this myself, and put two of my best on it. We did our job, and we'll do this one, too. So don't jump down my throat."

Because she respected his annoyance and pride a lot more than his whining and bullshit, she nodded. "The bastard who killed Deena MacMasters handled one of these. Had to. I don't have a face, I don't have a name. I've got lines and avenues and angles, but I don't have a single viable suspect. We're going to hit the end of the first forty-eight, and I've got no suspect."

"We'll get you what you need."

She stepped back, hands in her pockets. "Two boxed seats, third base side, Yankees, first home game in July."

He bared his teeth in a smile. "That's more like it."

What the hell, she thought as she trudged back to her car. He'd have earned it.

She started to head back uptown, toward home, then realized she wasn't all that far, not really, from Louise's new place in the West Village. A quick detour, and she could do her duty.

Probably Louise wasn't even home. Probably. And if Charles was, she could just make noises about stopping in on the way home to see if there was anything she could do for Saturday.

She'd be off the hook, and it wouldn't take more than thirty minutes.

Excellent plan. She called up the address, which she couldn't remember, on her in-dash, and began weaving and dodging her way toward the more trendy sector.

Shady trees, old brownstone and brick, tidy little front courtyards gave this slice of the West Village a neighborhood appeal. Flowers bloomed, little dogs pranced on the ends of leashes held by people who could afford to stroll on a weekday afternoon. Vehicles, of the smart and shiny variety, lined the curbs. She snagged a spot two blocks from her destination and used the walking time to run probabilities.

Mira's profile said he worked, and since he had better-than-average e-skills, maybe he worked in that field. The computer gave the idea some merit with a seventy-two-point-one probability.

Going with that, she thought, if he'd attended Columbia, he'd have taken e-courses. More, certainly, than were required for any degree. Possibly, he majored in some e-field.

Tap the source there, she thought, and refined her search request to Peach Lapkoff to include students from Southern states who'd majored in or had a strong focus in e-degrees.

Immersed, she might have walked by if Louise hadn't hailed her.

"Dallas! You have to be the last person I expected to see walking by."

Distracted, Eve stopped, glanced over. And there was the bride-to-be, with her sunny hair under a pink ball cap, wearing a dirt-smeared T-shirt and a pair of baggy cotton pants. The doctor held some sort of little shovel in her hand while flowers burst into bloom at her feet.

"I was in the neighborhood. Sort of. Did you actually do that?" Eve gestured to the flowers spreading and climbing behind a pretty iron gate.

"I did. Who knew?" Laughing, Louise pulled off gloves the same color as her cap. "I was going to get someone to do it, then I thought, for God's sake, I can dig into someone's abdomen, I ought to be able to dig in some dirt. It's fun!"

"Okay." She wasn't sure about that part, but the results were fairly mag. "It looks great."

"I wanted to get it all in before the wedding. Some of the out-of-town guests are coming for dinner tomorrow night. I have to be insane adding a dinner party to the list, but I can't stop myself. Come in! You have to see the house."

"I'm just swinging by," Eve said when Louise opened the gate. "On my way home. To work. But I thought I'd see if there's anything you need, or that I should—could do to help you out before the deal."

"I think everything's right on schedule, which is helped by the fact I'm ridiculously hyper and out of my mind. I had no idea I'd be such a lunatic about every tiny detail." She led the way up the path through the flowers to the main front door. "I have lists of lists. And I'm enjoying every minute of it."

"It shows. You look stupid happy. In a good way."

"I am, exactly. We are. Charles is down in his office with clients. He'll be another hour at least."

"How's that going for him?"

"It's going great, and it's so much what he wants now. This is all so much what we want." She opened the door, gestured Eve into the foyer.

Smooth, Eve would have said, with walls in warm, subtle color accented with stream-lined mirrors and bold art. A sleek table held slim, sinuous bottles in various sizes and sharp colors.

The theme continued with that mix of bold and quiet when Louise grabbed her hand to pull her into a living area with more sleek in the lines of the sofa, a hint of curve in the shape of chairs.

The impression was what she sup-posed would be upscale urban chic, with the personal touches of photos, flowers, and bits and pieces she remembered seeing in their individual apartments.

"This place was empty when you bought it, right?"

"Yes." Pleasure sparkled Louise's eyes

to silver. "We've had the best time furnishing and decorating it. We still need the finishing touches, but—"

"It looks finished."

"Oh, not yet, but it's evolving. Let me show you the rest."

Impossible to say no, so Eve trailed through the house, and tried to make appropriate comments or noises when Louise rhapsodized about how she'd fallen in love with a particular lamp or chair. Throughout, the ambience was style, slick, and somehow calm.

"Charles isn't allowed in here yet." Louise opened a door. "This is bridal mania."

Eve wouldn't have called it mania, but more organized chaos. In what she assumed would serve as a guest room, Louise had set up her wedding HQ. Two open, partially packed suitcases sat on a bed while gift and shipping boxes were tidily stacked or arranged in a corner. Wedding gifts, Eve supposed, that hadn't yet found their place. On a desk beside a mini D and C sat a stack of discs, with a pile of notecards.

In the center of the room sat a large,

two-sided board covered with bits of material, photographs of flowers, outfits, hairstyles, food, charts and time lines.

Eyes narrowed, Eve circled it, only mildly surprised to see a comp-generated image of herself in the yellow gown.

"It's like a murder board," she murmured, then winced. "Sorry, bad comparison."

"Not entirely. It's the same principle. Everything that applies is on there, right down to the olive picks for the reception. I'm obsessed."

She laughed a little desperately as she pressed her hands to her heart. "I've got charts and spreadsheets on the computer to keep track of gifts, responses, seating, wardrobe, including the honeymoon. It's like a drug."

"You don't need me."

"Not for the details, but boy, otherwise." Louise grabbed Eve's hand again, then released it to wrap her arms around herself. The quick, jerky movements were completely out of character.

"Maybe you need a drug," Eve suggested.

"Hah. I'm nervous, and I never expected

to be. We're changing our lives for each other, making a life with each other. It's what I want, and I want it more every day I'm with him."

"That's good."

"It's so good. But I'm nervous because I want the wedding—that one day—to be so perfect, so exact I'm making myself nervous about all the things that can go wrong. Silly. I'm caught up in the fairy tale of the day."

"Because you're not nervous or worried about what comes after it. The two of you already changed your lives, made your life. It's right here in this house."

To Eve's concern Louise's eyes went damp. "Oh God, I *do* need you." She threw her arms around Eve. "That's right, you're exactly right. We did, we have. I'm not."

Flummoxed, Eve patted Louise's back. "Okay."

"I can worry about the limo being late picking me up at the hotel, or the flowers being off a shade, or what size flutes for the champagne because marrying Charles doesn't make me nervous at all. It makes me happy and settled and content. *Thank* you."

"No problem."

"Let's get out of here. We'll go down and have some coffee."

"I really can't. I've got to get back to work."

Louise stepped back, her gray eyes going somber. "It's that young girl, isn't it? The one who was raped and murdered in her own bedroom. I heard the report, and they said you were leading the investigation."

"Yeah."

"I hope you find him quickly," Louise said as they walked back downstairs. "Her parents must be devastated."

"We're working some angles."

"Then I won't keep you, even though I wish you could stay. I'm so glad you came by. Now I can be nervous without being nervous about why I'm nervous."

"So you say." Eve paused at the door as something clicked. "What hotel?"

"Sorry?"

"Why do you need a car to pick you up at a hotel?"

Louise shrugged, and her expression turned sheepish. "More obsession. I don't want Charles to see me before the wedding because of the ridiculous bad-luck myth. But maybe it's not a myth so, why take the chance? And since I'm going to need all day to get ready and deal with details, I decided I'd stay in a hotel the night before, get my spa services there, have Trina come in to do my nails, hair, makeup, that sort of thing."

Here, Eve realized, was something she could do, should do as matron of honor. "Cancel that. You can't stay in a hotel room, alone, the night before the deal. You can stay at the house, where it's all happening anyway." And she thought, here was the major sacrifice for friendship. "Trina can do whatever you need there. Maybe you want a couple of women friends with you. It's a ritual thing, right?"

Face glowing, stunned, Louise shot out her hands to grip Eve's. "That would be absolutely amazing. Absolutely perfect. It would mean a lot to me."

"Then it's done."

"Thank you." Louise hugged Eve again. "Thank you."

"Go log it on your board. I'll see you Friday night."

"Five o'clock rehearsal," Louise called out.

"Sure." Did she know that, Eve wondered. Rehearsal? Jesus, they had to do it all twice? She pushed a hand through her hair as she walked back to the car. They'd probably have more charts and time lines, and . . .

"Shit!" Ignoring the insulted look from the pair of women she passed, Eve snatched out her communicator. "Feeney, check back on the security. See if there's another glitch, a lag, any anomaly previous to the night of the murder. Not too close," she added. "He wouldn't rehearse it, time it, too close to the actual murder."

"You want me to pull off this to wade through weeks?"

"What if he'd been in the house before? Cased it? Wait. Let me talk to MacMasters first, see if he noted any blip."

She cut Feeney off, tried MacMasters as she quickened her pace to the car. "Captain, can you tell me if you experienced any problems with your security system over the past six months. Even minor glitches?"

"No." His eyes seemed to have sunken into his skull. "I run a system check weekly as a precaution. The upgrades added a few months ago claim that's unnecessary, but—"

"What upgrades?" She got behind the wheel.

"The maintenance company automatically informs us if and when upgrades are available."

"When did you last upgrade?"

"I'm not sure, I think . . . Sometime in March. I coordinated it with our annual maintenance check."

"Does the company do the upgrades and the check in house or on site?"

"Both."

"I need the name of your maintenance company."

"Security Plus. We've used them for years. They're top-rated. Do you think someone there—"

"I'm going to cover that angle, Captain. We're going to cover them all. I'll get back to you."

She pushed her way uptown while she hit Feeney again. "Start in March," she told him. "MacMasters got an upgrade on the system in March, and his maintenance company came in to add it. Company's Security Plus, and I'll run that down."

"It would take balls to walk right into the house that way—and brains. He'd get a firsthand look at the system. Where it is, how it works, right on site. But we've already checked out the company. It's what we do. I've got the upgrade, and the tech who plugged it in. He's clean, and he's twenty years too old to fit our guy. Worked for the company fifteen years."

"Damn it. Maybe this guy's connected. Maybe he's got the same system, and got the same upgrade. He'd get the same notice. Maybe he doesn't rehearse on site, but he damn well practiced. Run it anyway. I'll run down other clients with the same system, the same upgrades."

"Save yourself the time. I'll get a man to run that down. It'll be quicker."

"Get back to me. Wait, shit, wait. Does this company have more than one location?"

"They've got a dozen in the metro area, counting New Jersey."

"He could still work for them. Work for

them, be a client—or both." It felt right. "Let's push this. I'm in the field, then I'm working at home. Send me everything you get."

"You asked for it," Feeney muttered and clicked off.

 To save time, Eve assigned two of her detectives to retrieve the stuffed toy from the crime scene and hand-deliver it to the lab. She wanted to push on the possible connection to the security company.

When she walked into the house, she gave Summerset one brief glance. "Why don't you just outfit a droid in one of those funeral director suits and have it lurk in the foyer? It'd be livelier."

"Then I would miss your daily attempts at wit."

"I only need to attempt as the target comes in at half." She bounded up the steps, pleased. Half-wit, she thought. Pretty good one.

She went straight to her office, shedding her jacket on the way to her desk to check her incomings.

The lengthy list of names from Peach Lapkoff proved the woman fast and efficient. Eve wished she had her on the payroll. Peabody had come through with a list of vendors within the city that carried all the items in question, and added a memo that she'd be in the field checking them.

She read over the list of Security Plus locations in Manhattan, the data on the tech who'd worked at MacMasters's, and fought impatience when there was nothing incoming from Yancy before she got coffee.

With it, she circled her board. "One connection, just one solid link, that's all I need. If you couldn't access the house and the system prior to the night of the murder, you'd still want to walk it through, wouldn't you? You're so careful, so precise. Working for the company you could access the data without sending up any flag. Or maybe you're good enough to hack into it from outside."

She turned and circled back.

"I don't think so. I don't think so. Outside poses too many variables. But maybe you don't have to do that because the vic's given you enough data about the layout. That's not as precise, not as detailed, but it would be enough."

She stopped, drinking coffee, rolling up to her toes, back to her heels. "Maybe there's no glitch for us to find because you could test that on your own. Solid e-skills, but not genius. If you were stellar you could have found a way to bypass the cameras without setting up a flag with a remote before you went in, but you had to do it from the inside, input the virus to corrupt the hard drive. The system's too good for your skill set."

She angled her head as she continued to study the board. "I wonder, I wonder . . . Does it piss you off that you're good, but not brilliant? Not exceptional enough to bypass the security cams? Not exceptional enough to get past MacMasters's— the enemy's—security block. Does that get under your skin? I bet, yeah, I bet that's a pisser for you. Because he's rich enough, smart enough, careful enough to have the very best, and you can't quite slither through the very best."

She worked to try to fit some of the new pieces together, then sat, feet up, eyes closed to try to think them together.

Client's the smartest way, the safest way, she thought. But the systems are high-dollar—extreme high. And require a private home for install.

But it doesn't have to be your home. A friend's, a relative's, a client's. She thought of fresh questions and sat up to nag Feeney again. Incoming signaled and presented her with the list of employees and clients, with a negative cross-reference already done—from Roarke.

She cross-checked both lists with the fresh data from Columbia, and hit another negative.

Annoyed she pushed up the pace. "You're there, you're in there, you bastard."

She circled, paced, sat, worked it a dozen different ways from a dozen different launch points.

And while she worked, Karlene Robins died.

In the loft, he checked and rechecked details. He'd logged her out of the building hours before, and had sent her fiancé a very sweet text so she wouldn't be missed. He dressed, then placed his tools as well as her 'link, her PPC, and her memo book in his bag. Once again, he shut down the cameras, uploaded his virus.

He walked out of the building and headed home.

Cop work, Roarke thought, was bloody tedious. He had no doubt he'd be doing considerable more of it very shortly. But when he walked into the house, he was determined he'd be doing none of it until he'd had a decent meal and an hour to clear the buggering e-junk out of his head.

"This is a change," Summerset commented. "You coming home late for dinner without notice, and looking annoyed and tired."

"Then don't tempt me to insult you as Eve does."

"She's in her office, and has been since she got home. Is there any progress?"

"Not nearly enough, considering."

He continued up and found her where he'd thought he would, at her desk hunched over data and coffee.

She pushed to her feet when he came in, but he pointed a finger to stop her before she spoke. "We're having a meal since all you've had is coffee and a candy bar."

She blinked, then noted she'd neglected to dispose of the wrapper. "I need to know if—"

"I'll tell you what there is to tell you, but I damn well want some food."

"Okay." It occurred to her that he'd had less sleep than she had, and was juggling his work with hers. "I'll get it."

His brows lifted. "Will you now?"

"Yeah. How about a steak? We can probably both use the boost."

"I damn well could." He reached out as she walked by, stroked her hair. "Thanks for that."

While she went into the kitchen, he opened a bottle of wine. Deliberately, he turned his back on her murder board to keep it out of his head for a few minutes. A little clearing-out time, he thought as he sipped.

His brows rose again when she rolled out the dinner for two on a table when he'd assumed they'd eat at her desk.

"Let's eat by the windows," she said and nodded to the wine as she pushed the table toward them. "I could use a glass of that."

He poured a second glass, then went to her, tapped the shallow dent in her chin, kissed her. "Hello, Lieutenant."

"Hi, Civilian. Let's take a breather."

"I could use one nearly as much as I can use that red meat."

"Okay." She sat, stabbed her fork into one of the salads she'd programmed with him in mind. "I went by to see Louise at her new place."

Now his brows winged up. "Aren't you full of surprises?"

"I was almost there anyway, and . . . Okay, I figured she wouldn't be there so I could just leave a note and get, you know, friend credit."

Looking at her, listening to her, he

laughed for the first time in hours. "Never change."

"Well, it should've worked, but she was there. Planting flowers, which who would expect?"

"Astonishing."

"I don't have to eat sarcasm to recognize the flavor. Anyway, I had to go in and go through the place. Have to say it looks like them. Smooth and sophisticated and now. She's whacked with happy, which kind of infects anyone within a ten-foot radius." She stuffed salad in her mouth to get it over with. "Like an airborne virus."

"God, you romantic fool. No wonder I adore you."

She offered a smirk. "So, while I was infected, she's talking about how she's going to stay in a hotel the night before the wedding because she doesn't want Charles to see her on the day of, and she's got to get rubbed and polished and painted. I said she should stay here."

"She should, of course."

"And then I said how she'd probably want her women friends with her. I don't know where that came from. It just came out of the whacky-happy infection. It wasn't until I had some distance, and it was too damn late, that I realized one of those women will be Trina. Has to be. So now I've opened it all up to a bunch of women with wedding mania, one of whom will come at me—oh yes, she will—with gunk and goo."

Her heart, Roarke thought, would always win out over her sense of self-preservation when it came to those who mattered to her.

"But think of the friend credit you'll accumulate."

"I don't know if it's worth it. Plus . . ."

"Murder," he said when she trailed off. "You've already given me a breather, and red meat. You don't have to stop yourself from talking about it."

"You looked tired and irritable, and you almost never do. That's my job."

He thought of Summerset's "annoyed and tired" and felt the scowl take hold before he could stop it. "I was both."

"I'm better at it."

He laughed again. "Got me there. I enjoy e-work as a rule, particularly when there's a challenge involved. But this is like trying to unravel a ball of string one thread at a time."

"Maybe we won't need it. I have other threads, and I'm tying them together. Yancy's working on his face. I've got various contact points, and when I pin him on one, there'll be others. I think he may be in the e-business, or he can afford a lot of toys. Including the same security system involved. It's your system. You update it regularly."

"As technology emerges, refinements, options, yes. A customer would be given the option to add any or all of the new features or refinements."

"Which MacMasters did, in March. The timing's too damn good. A couple of weeks later, Deena meets her killer. I can't connect the killer or MacMasters to the tech who did the updates, but there's going to be one, to him or to the company. Security Plus."

"It's not mine. We bid out service and maintenance to companies, and customers have the option of choosing from them, or at their risk, using an independent. Security Plus is a solid organization, and a service center for most top-of-the-line systems."

"But you upgraded the system in March."

"I can check."

"While you're at it, can you find out who bought the same system as MacMasters within the last six months? Year," she corrected. "A year, and had the same upgrades done in March. He's spent a lot of time on this project. He'd get the upgrades, too. He'd get every one of them."

"I'll warn you it sells very well to a certain level of clientele, and most will spring for the upgrades."

"Something's going to cross eventually. The system, his employment, his education, his face, his motive. It's going to cross." It damn well *had* to cross. "Then it's going to cross again and again. Then we're going to take that ball of string and shove it down his throat."

"I look forward to helping with that. For the girl, her parents, for you. And for the very selfish reason the fucker compromised my system."

"All good reasons."

"I'll get the data for you. It might take a bit."

She indulged in another sip of wine. "Why don't you set up a run and search, and we'll finish the breather with a swim."

He angled his head. "A swim? Would that be a euphemism?"

"Maybe."

"I'll set it up."

She wanted the water, a good, strong swim—both literally and euphemistically. She needed the physical to offset the hours and hours of thinking. Maybe if she stopped thinking for just a little while, she'd go back to it with more clarity.

Too many threads, she decided. She needed to find one, get a good grip on it. When she pulled, the rest would unravel.

And, she admitted, she was still thinking.

She didn't bother with a suit, and instead stripped down in the moist, fragrant heat, and dived into the deep blue water. She felt him spear in beside her, and as she surfaced began to cut through the water. She knew him, and his competitive nature. He'd match her pace, push himself—as they were matched in speed and ability in the water.

They hit the wall at the same time, flipped, and raced back. The rhythm, fast, hard—beat striking beat—did its job. Impossible to think when every muscle worked to its full potential, when the heart began to pound from the exertion.

At five laps they were still stroke for stroke, kick for kick.

She pushed, a little more, and a little more yet, slicing through the deep, dreamy blue, stretching for another inch while the water flew up from the power of scissoring legs. A little faster, a little harder, digging down for the speed and the power, she caught the blur of his face as she tipped hers up to grab air.

Again, she thought, again, and curled her body, pumped her legs to drive herself off the wall. Beside him, true as a shadow, she struck out through the clear, the cool, the blue.

She lost track of the number of laps, of time, of everything but the motion, the pace, the sheer physical push and pleasure of spurring herself, and him.

Challenge and motion, skin and water, speed and need.

And when he caught her, slick, wet

body to slick, wet body, in mid-stroke, she was ready for him.

Searching, their mouths came together, cool from the water, hot from hunger. With quick, frantic bites she answered the urgency of the kiss while her racing heart pressed to his. She wrapped her legs around his waist, too desperate to care if they sank like stones.

"Now." She'd go mad if it wasn't now.

She captured him even as he gripped her hips, and those hips plunged, demanding more, taking more. When he gave her more, shoving her back to the wall, bracing her, her head fell back on a single choked cry.

Strong, sleek, he thought as he ravaged her neck. And always so much his. Love and lust, need and pleasure swirled inside him as water fumed up in the storm of their mating.

With him, again with him, beat for beat, demand for demand, in this last frantic lap of the race. She chained herself to him, arms and legs locked like shackles as her mouth fused to his once more.

And strong and sleek, she quivered for him as he drove them both to the finish.

He lowered his brow to her shoulder, then managed to grip the edge when she started to slide. "Have a care." He could barely murmur it. "Or they'll find us both floating facedown in the morning."

"Okay." But she curled into him. "Need a minute."

"You're not alone. I had no idea swimming laps made such intense foreplay."

"My idea."

"There, you've collected sex credit and friend credits in the same day."

The sound she made was half laugh, half sigh. "Louise is all nervous about the wedding, about all the details being perfect. She has charts and time lines and told me how she's a wreck of nerves and didn't expect to be."

"It's an exceptionally important day."

"Yeah, but I said she's nervous about the minutiae because she's not nervous about the marriage, about Charles, what they're doing and why."

He brushed his cheek to hers as he drew back to study her. "Aren't you the wise one?"

"I wasn't nervous about the details of

the wedding stuff when we got married. I barely paid attention to them, dumped it on you."

"You did." He kissed the tip of her nose. "But then you were distracted by a serial killer."

"No, that's not it. I mean, yeah, that was a factor." She brushed his hair, wet black silk, away from his face. "But I figured out I wasn't nervous about the minutiae because I was nervous about the rest. About marriage, you, what we were doing and why. I thought that was the crazy part of it—you, me, marriage." She cupped his face in her hands, looked into his eyes. "I'm really happy I was wrong. I'm really happy."

It surged through him, everything she was to him. "There, too, you're not alone."

She brought her lips to his again, softer now, sweeter. Then eased back. "That's enough of that. Breather's over."

She wiggled free, pushed to the head of the pool to climb out. When he stepped out, she tossed him a towel.

"As breathers go, it was exceptional."

"Yeah, well, anything worth doing. He'd think that."

Roarke wrapped a towel around his waist. "And our transition is complete."

"Well, my head's cleared. I think he's good at what he does—careful. Doesn't want too much attention. But he's the reliable guy, the one who gets it done without the fanfare. People would say, oh yeah, Murdering Bastard's reliable. I bet he hates that."

"Why so?"

Tossing on a robe she walked to the elevator. She'd change into soft clothes for the rest of the night's work. "Because he's better than that. Better than they are. He's young, he's good-looking, charming, efficient, smart, and skilled enough to come up with, or get someone else to come up with this e-virus that's got all you geeks stumped."

"We're not stumped," Roarke corrected with some annoyance as they rode to the bedroom. "The bleeding investigation is ongoing and we're pursuing all shagging avenues."

While it amused her to hear him quote the usual departmental line—with the addition of the Irish—she shrugged. "Point's the same. He's not going to be in management, not even middle management unless it requires wearing a name tag. He'll be the clerk or tech or laborer who never bitches about getting work or OT dumped on him. Who plods through the work, gets it done, but doesn't object when his boss or coworker or supervisor takes all or most of the credit."

In the bedroom she pulled on a support tank, underwear. "And he'd hate it, the way he'd hate not being able to beat Mac-Masters's security from the outside."

"You think so?"

"I know so, because I'm looking at you. You're pissed off because he's done something e-wise you haven't been able to figure out. Yet," she added, not bothering to disguise a grin when those blue eyes fired. "It's frustrating."

"You're making it more so," Roarke muttered.

"You'll deal. But the point is, the average guy is a shell, a suit he has to wear that probably doesn't fit very well. The little things oppose a good fit. Leaving the glass, making the vid, spending hours on the kill, and doing it inside the house. Easier ways, safer ways, but he's got to show off a little."

Intrigued, Roarke continued to dress. "And what does all this tell you?"

"Well, adding in he's young, and that's going to factor even with his sense of patience and control, he's going to make more mistakes. Maybe just little ones, show-offy ones, but he'll make them. And I'll be able to use his need to shed that ordinary suit when I have him in interview. He'll want to tell me."

"And for now?" She scooped a hand through her damp hair. "It tells me if he works for Security Plus, he'll be one of the geeks. Wherever he works, he takes home a decent salary, but damn it, not enough to afford that system. He has to be a geek for either the manufacturer or a service company."

"I had Caro get me the names of every male under thirty who works for that arm." He spoke of his redoubtable admin. "The rest of the geeks and I have been running them throughout the day. None of them are standing out, and none have made a tidy fit with your profile."

"Profiles can be off. That was good work, getting the data, taking it into EDD."

"Perhaps I'll ask for a raise."

"I just gave you one." She shot him a grin as they walked out of the bedroom. "I like a service company better. It's more in keeping. Service, don't create. No splash."

"I just serviced you, and I distinctly recall splashing."

"Okay now we're even on the sex jokes."

"It's only fair. Eve, he could be an independent consultant, a brain trust, a troubleshooter. The field is wide and open. He may not work for any one company."

"Shit. Shit." She had to pace. "That would be even better for him, wouldn't it? Someone who comes in, fixes things, or gives advice, but doesn't actually do the day-to-day. It's perfect. Damn it. I'm going to work through it all again, piece by piece. Add in the data you get me, shuffle it with the Columbia data. Then—"

"One thing you haven't considered," Roarke interrupted. "He's young, smart, skilled, and he has no scruples. There are other ways for someone like that to make money, enough to buy a top-flight system and the residence to put it. You steal it."

"Steal it?"

"In the grand old e-tradition. Hack into accounts, siphon funds off. Keep that mid-level, too—nothing too big. He knows how to use someone else's ID to get what he wants. Identity theft's a profitable business if you're talented."

She rubbed her hands together as the idea took on weight. "You risk getting caught, but he's willing to risk. He's careful and keeps the risk low. Why work, or work very hard, when you can just take. It's an angle. It's a good one."

Her desk 'link signaled even as they walked into her office. She charged for it, scanned the readout quickly. "Yancy, give me something good."

"I had a second session with each of the wits. I had to give them, and me, a break between, but I know we need to push. I think I've got something, or something close. Lola's more sure than Marta, but—"

"Show me."

"Hold on. Neither of them saw his eyes, because of the shades. Those and the cap hid part of his face. I've projected the most likely, probability eighty-seven and change, for those features. Eyes, eye-brows, forehead. Marta got a glimpse of the forehead, the upper face when he pulled off the cap, but—"

"Show me," Eve demanded.

"Coming through, on screen and hard copy, projected, and with cap and shades."

She leaned over her unit, studied the images that popped in split screen. Roarke walked to the printouts sliding out its slot.

Young, she thought. Early to mid-twenties by her cop gauge. Caucasian male, with even, attractive, somewhat feminine features. Small, straight nose, full lips, soft eyes, a bit heavy-lidded. The face was oval, almost classically so, and the hair dark, shaggy, trendy.

She studied the image with it, where the features were obscured by the cap and shades. And nodded.

"You gave me good, Yancy."

"If you're confident with it, we can send it out."

"No media. Team members only for now. He's going to come to the vic's memorial, odds are. I don't want to alert him, scare him off. Get this to the other members, with a lock on it. I'm going to start an image search, see if I can ID the bastard."

"Good luck."

"You gave me more than luck. This could make the difference. Send it out, Yancy, and go home."

"You can count on it."

When Yancy signed off, Eve considered her options, then contacted Jamie.

"Hey, Dallas."

"You're going to have an image coming through," she said without preamble. "Take it and get over to Columbia. I'm going to set it up for you. I want you to start using their imaging program, see if you can get me a match."

"It's him."

"It's what we've got. This is locked, Jamie. Nobody but you, or McNab if you need him. It doesn't go to any of your e-pals."

"I get it. I know. I'll work it, Dallas."

"I'll get you cleared. Work good," she said, then blew out a breath and once again contacted Peach Lapkoff.

"Well, Lieutenant, we're getting to be best friends."

"I apologize for interrupting your evening. We have an image, and I'm sending Jamie over to the university, as an expert consultant, civilian, to work with your imaging program."

"Now?"

"Now. I need you to clear this, Dr. Lapkoff, and to keep it confidential. I can't afford a leak."

"I'll take care of it personally."

"You're making my job easier."

"My grandfather would expect no less."

"She's okay," Eve mumbled as she broke transmission. "So." She nodded at the images on screen. "There you are, fucker. Now who are you? Computer, initiate search and match, all data on individual in current images, begin with New York City residents."

Acknowledged. Initiating . . .

"Auxiliary search, same images, same directive, for match with students listed in File Lapkoff-Columbia-C."

Acknowledged. Initiating Auxiliary search . . .

"Could get lucky there, find him on the short list before Jamie's halfway to Morningside Heights. Okay. Now when I get the data you're running, I can add that into the mix and—"

He nudged her aside, tapped a quick series of keys. "It's finished, a few minutes ago. And yes, we did an upgrade on that system the third week in March. You want a third search, with this data, I take it."

"Affirmative."

He ordered the task himself. "I'd say it's time for more coffee, and I should take myself off to the lab to have mine."

"We may not need—"

"That's not the point, is it? I'm not going to let that git beat me. Carry on, Lieutenant, and so will I."

She got her own coffee, then added both sketches to her board. As her computer worked, she circled the board and considered Roarke's theory. Hacking or ID theft. A boy had to hone his craft, didn't he? And a younger version of the man on her board might have made a couple of mistakes. Slipped a little as he learned all the ins and outs.

A little smudge on his juvenile record, she mused. We can add that in, yes, we can. We can add that possibility. Maybe back home, wherever the hell home was.

Sticks close to the truth, she recalled. He'd told Deena he'd had a little brush with the law over illegals. Maybe he'd had them with cyber crimes instead.

She let the computer continue its search and sat with her PPC to run criminal, focus on juvenile offenses, with the data she'd accrued from Roarke and Columbia.

It didn't surprise her to find so many. The cop in her was more surprised when anyone got through life without a smudge or a bump or a bust.

She began the laborious process of scanning, eliminating, separating into possibles. Once again, she lost track of time, and nearly bobbled her third mug of coffee when her 'link signaled.

"Dallas." Jamie's face told her what she wanted to hear. "I've got him. I think I've got him. It's a ninety-seven-point-three probability match. It's from five years back, and he only had a semester and a half in but—"

"Send him to me. On screen, now," she ordered when the transmission hummed." She stared at the ID photo. "Good work, Jamie. Shut everything down there, wipe the search."

"It's him, isn't it? It's the bastard who killed Deena."

She looked into Jamie's tired and furious eyes. "You did good work," she repeated. "We'll brief in the morning. Go home. Get some sleep."

She knew he wanted to argue, it was clear on his face. But he pulled it in. "Yes, sir."

She cut transmission then turned back to the screen to study another young, attractive face.

"Hello, Darrin Pauley. You son of a bitch."

In the lab, Roarke finessed, twisted, prodded. He'd grabbed the amorphous tail of the ghost and was fighting to hold it. "Do you see it?" he demanded.

On a wall screen, Feeney's eyes were narrowed to slits. "I've got eyes, don't I? You need to recalibrate the bypass, then—"

"I'm bloody well doing that." Roarke swiveled to another comp, keyed in another code.

"I can box it from here." On another screen, McNab paced. "If we ride the back end from here—"

"Keep working the enhance," Feeney snapped. "I've got it."

"Roarke."

"Not now!" the order shot out at Eve from Roarke, and from the two males on the wall screens.

"Jesus, wall of geek," she muttered. Then saw the other image, a shadow on shadows.

"You're pulling him out."

"We've got him, but by our bleeding fingernails. Quiet. If we can't lock this, we'll have to do it all again."

As she watched, the screen began to blur with white dots. She heard McNab say, "No! Damn it, no! It's another strain. Jesus."

"Not this time," Roarke snapped. "The pattern's there. Reverse the code, every other sequence."

Eve could see the light sheen of sweat on Feeney's face, hear the steely determination in Roarke's voice.

The dots on screen faded.

"We did it!" McNab cried out.

"Not quite yet," Roarke's voice eased slightly. "But we bloody well will."

She didn't know what they were doing,

but the shadow on screen shimmered so she feared it would vanish. Then it steadied, stilled.

"Locked!" McNab called. "We locked the bastard. Rocking-freaking-A." He leaped up into a victory dance.

"Christ." Roarke leaned back. "I could use a pint."

"I'm damn well having one. Good work, every damn one of us," Feeney said.

"Ah . . . is that it?" As Eve gestured to the shadow, every eye, on screen or in the room, turned a jaundiced look on her.

"We broke through the virus," Roarke told her. "We pieced together this image from distorted pixels. We performed a bloody miracle. And no, that's not it. That's it for now."

"We'll start enhancing, defining, cleaning it up," Feeney told her, then took a long pull from a bottle of brew. "It's going to take hours, maybe a day, but it's there, and we can pull it out. And while we're doing that, we've got the sequence and coding locked down to get the rest of it. We'll be able to give you the little son of a bitch walking right in the door."

"That'll be a cap on it. Meanwhile,

thanks to Jamie, I've got a name, and a point of origin. Darrin Pauley, age twenty-three. Data claims he lives in Sundown, Alabama, south of Mobile, with his father, Vincent Pauley. I've got no connection to either Pauley with MacMasters—yet, but he fits right down to his shy smile."

"He's no more in Alabama than my ass is," Feeney put in.

"No, but his father is. I ran him, and he's gainfully employed, living with his wife and twelve-year-old daughter, in Sundown."

"Could be a blind," Feeney suggested.

"Could, but the family resemblance is striking. He needs to be interviewed, now, and face-to-face."

Roarke glanced at the equipment he'd begun to enjoy again. "I suppose we're going to Alabama this evening."

"You suppose correctly."

14 She had to appreciate being married to a man who could call up one of his own private jets in a fingersnap and pilot it if he had a mind to.

In this case, he did, which was a big advantage. She could sit, continue doing runs, argue with Peabody, bounce theories off her personal pilot, and basically ignore the view out the windscreen.

"I'd've been ready in five minutes," Peabody complained. Her face sulked on screen while in the background McNab continued his e-work in incomprehensible geek.

"It would've taken you thirty minimum to get to the transpo. He's not going to be there, Peabody. You're not going to miss the collar, for Christ's sake. And I need you right where you are, digging down to find a New York address or contact for Darrin Pauley. Employment, driver's license, criminal, finances, medical. Each and every fucking thing."

"I could do that while—"

"You can have a plane ride another time."

Peabody's pout perked, just a little. "When?"

"God. Dig. Now."

"I will. Am."

"And work the shoes and the outfit angle. Check to see if he has a credit or debit under that name. If not, we're going to cross the data you have with males with the initials DP. He used Darian Powders's ID. Stick with the familiar, so maybe he has other aliases with those initials."

"That's good. I'll—"

"That's it. Bank a few hours' sleep because we're briefing a full team at seven hundred. Book the conference room. I'm out," Eve said and broke transmission.

"While I find myself, as always, excited by your commanding demeanor," Roarke said, "this member of the team isn't available at seven tomorrow."

She suppressed the urge to swear, because damn it, she could've used him. "Civilians get a pass."

"I can reorder a few things if Feeney can use me, and be available to him about the same time I managed it today."

"If it works for you. He's not going to be in Alabama. He needs the payoff of seeing, firsthand, MacMasters devastated. And he's been in New York for some time. Maybe not for five years, maybe not the whole time since his stint at Columbia, but for a while now. Keeping an eye on things, spinning his web. He's going to come to the memorial, so I can't release the sketch to the media and tip him off. Which I may do by pushing at his father."

"Then why are you? Wait until after the memorial."

"Calculated risk." She wanted to stand up, pace, but the size of the plane, the expanse of the night, the emptiness outside the windshield kept her in place. "Off chance he *is* there. Very off chance, but it can't be ignored. Better chance, his father knows where he is, and I can get it out of him. Then shut the father's communications down until we take the bastard down. The other end of it is, I get nothing, the father tips Pauley off, and he's in the wind. But . . ."

"You don't think so."

"Family man, long marriage, another kid. No criminal other than a minor bust for disturbing the peace when he was in his twenties. Solid employment record, mid-level salary, small house in the 'burbs, mortgage. Is this guy going to risk his wife and daughter, that little house, the job, the life, to dodge a police investigation into the rape-murder of a girl? Risk charges of obstruction, accessory after the fact, and anything else I can use to pressure him?"

"Depends, I'd say, on how much he loves his son, and how far he'd go to protect him."

"I wouldn't understand that kind of love, the kind that shields monsters. I don't think it is love. If he does love this sick, son of a bitch, I'll use that. He needs help. Help us to help him. If I don't find him, someone else might. He killed a cop's kid, and someone else might put that above the law."

She drummed her fingers on her thigh, tried to ignore the shimmy of the plane as they started to descend. "I've got to take another risk." She tagged Baxter at home. "Take the sketch," she ordered without preamble. "Get Trueheart and canvass the coffeehouses, clubs, hangouts around the university, and on campus."

"Now?"

"No, gee, whenever you feel like it. Jamie worked an imaging program at Columbia. Check in with him, let him know you're in the field. And, if it isn't too much trouble, if it doesn't interfere with your plans for the evening—"

"Jesus, Dallas, bust my balls."

"Your balls have never interested me, Baxter."

"Again, ouch."

"Take the sketch around MacMasters's neighborhood. Anything pops, tag me. Otherwise, briefing at seven hundred, Central, conference room."

"Fine. fine. Where the hell are you?"

"I'm about to be in Alabama." Her stomach flipped. "I hope, sincerely, in one piece. Peabody has the details if you need them. Move it, Baxter."

"Moving it."

Lieutenant Dallas, who would charge through a firefight to do the job, closed her eyes with her stomach quivering as they dipped toward touchdown.

She was better when they were zipping along the roads in some spiffy, topless rental with the heavy Southern air whipping around her head.

"A little late for a cop call to a family man," she said. "Good, it gives us another advantage."

"It's not that late. We're on Central time," he told her. "We're an hour earlier here."

She pressed her fingers to her eyes. "So we're here before we left. How does anyone keep their brain from frizzing over stuff like this?"

Unable to resist, Roarke gave her a poke and a grin. "And when we go back, we'll lose an hour."

"See? It's senseless. How can you lose an hour? Where does it go? Can someone else find it? Does it get reported to the Lost Time Division?"

"Darling Eve, I have to inform you the world is not flat, nor is New York its center."

"The first part, okay, but the second? Maybe it should be. Things would be simpler."

He slowed, sliding onto a suburban street where the trees were plentiful and the houses jammed so close Eve wondered why the occupants didn't just live in apartments. They'd probably have more privacy.

Tiny yards spread until the wash of street and security lights, and the scent of grass along with something deep and sweet, wound through the air.

Following the vehicle's navigational assistant, Roarke turned left at a corner, then stopped at a house—much like all the other houses—in the middle of the block.

Eve frowned at the house. Had she become spoiled and jaded living in the enormity of what Roarke had built, or was the house the size of your average shoe box? Two little cars sat, nose to butt, in the narrow driveway. Low-growing flowers crawled along its verge.

Lights beamed against the window glass. In their glow, she saw a bike parked beside the front stoop.

"These people couldn't afford to send a kid to Columbia. Unless he bagged a scholarship—and that's out of profile— how could they pay that kind of freight?"

"Well, the wise and foresighted often begin saving and investing for college educations while the child is still in the womb. Even then, yes, it would take considerable."

She got out, started toward the house. Stopped dead with her hand resting on the butt of her weapon. "Do you hear that?" she demanded as she cocked her head at the repetitive basso belch that rose into the steamy air.

"Of course I hear it. I'm standing right here."

"What the hell is it?"

"I'm not entirely sure, but I think it may be some sort of frog."

"Frog? Seriously? The green hopping things?" She scanned the dark and the streams of streetlights. "It sounds really big. Like alien-frog big."

"I don't have much personal experience

with frogs, but I don't believe they have alien frogs in Alabama. At least not the sort that require stunning with a police-issue."

"We'll see about that." Just in case, she kept her hand on her weapon.

Through the front window she saw the movement on the entertainment screen, and the man kicked back in a recliner, the woman with her feet curled up on the sofa.

"Quiet evening at home in front of the screen," Eve murmured. "Could they, would they, if they had any part in . . . what's she doing? The woman? What's she doing with those sticks and the fuzzy thread?"

"I have no idea. Why should I have the answers to these things?"

"Because," she said and made him laugh.

"Well, at a guess again, it appears to be some sort of . . . craft."

She continued toward the door, studying the sticks, the yarn, the woman. It popped out of some file of buried facts. "Knitting!" Eve punched Roarke's shoulder. "I got one. She's knitting."

"If you say so."

"I saw that stuff—the sticks, the thread,

somewhere, some case. She's knitting, he's watching the screen and having a beer, and the girl's bike is parked by the door—and not chained down. These aren't master criminals who helped plan the murder of a teenager, and if they're involved in hacking or identity fraud, I'll take up knitting."

"All that from a glance through the living room window?"

"Security? Minimal, and right now it's not even activated. No curtains drawn, nothing to hide here." She stepped to the door, knocked. In a moment, the woman opened the door, without checking and asking who was there.

Her easy smile shifted to surprise, but didn't lose any of its welcome. "Well, hi, what can I do for y'all?"

The voice was as warm and sweet as the air. She brushed back at her honey blonde hair the way some women did when caught unawares.

"We're looking for Darrin Pauley."

"Oh goodness, I think he lives up in Chicago or something. We haven't seen him in—"

"Who is it, Mimi?"

"They're looking for Darrin, honey. I don't mean to have you standing here in the doorway, but—"

Eve pulled out her badge, watched Mimi's eyes widen on it even as Vincent Pauley stepped to the door. "What's all this about? Police? New York police? He's in trouble? Darrin's in trouble? Well, hell." He said it on a sigh, something resigned, sad, unsurprised all at once. "We'd better talk inside."

He gestured them in while his wife rubbed his arm in comfort. "Why don't I get us all some tea? It's a warm night, and I bet you could use something cold."

"Mama?" A little girl looked down over the banister from the top of the stairs to the right.

"You go on back to bed, Jennie. It's just some people to talk to Daddy. Go on now, you've got a big day tomorrow."

The girl blinked sleepy eyes at Eve, then slipped back upstairs.

"We're all going to Play World tomorrow, along with Jennie's best friend and her parents. Two days of amusement and water parks. Lord help us. And I'm babbling. Let me get that tea."

She scooted away. Eve wondered if her hurry was to get away, or to get back quickly. Either case, she and Roarke were left with Vincent Pauley of the handsome face and sorrowful eyes.

"Let's have a seat. Screen off," he ordered, and the comedy chuckling away shut down. "I guess I always wondered if I'd get police at the door sometime or other about Darrin. It's been years since I even laid eyes on him. I can't tell you where he is. He doesn't keep in touch."

"When did you last see your son, Mr. Pauley?"

He smiled, but there was bitter around the edges. "I don't know that he is my son." He rubbed his eyes. "God, some things never stop coming up behind you, do they? I was with his mother when he was born, and had been with her for months before. I put my name on the records. I thought he was mine. But I didn't know she'd been with someone else before she was with me, while she was with me. I wasn't yet twenty, green as grass and dirt stupid with it."

"Don't say that, Vinnie!" Mimi came in

carrying a tray with a big pitcher, several glasses full of half-moon slices of ice.

Roarke rose. "Let me help you with that, Mrs. Pauley."

"Oh, thank you. Don't you have a nice accent. Are you from England?"

"Ireland, a long while ago."

"My grandmother's grandmother, on my father's side, she was from Ireland. From somewhere called Ennis."

She pronounced it wrong, with a long I at the start, but Roarke smiled. "A lovely little town. I have people not far from there."

"And you came all the way to America to be a policeman."

"He's a consultant," Eve said, firmly, as Roarke smothered a laugh. "Darrin's mother is listed as Inga Sorenson, deceased."

"That's the name she was using when I was with her, and I left it that way on the records. I don't know if it was her name. I don't know if she's alive or dead. I'm told she's dead, but . . ."

"Why don't you tell me when you last saw him or spoke with him?"

"I guess maybe six years ago, or seven."

"Seven," Mimi confirmed. "Early spring because I was putting in the bedding plants out back, and Jennie was in kindergarten. Vinnie was at work, and I was alone here. I was afraid to let them in so I called Vinnie and he came right home."

"Them?" Eve repeated, and saw Mimi slide her gaze toward her husband.

"Darrin, and the man who may be his father," Vinnie said. "The man he considers his father, and the one Inga was with before me, and maybe during me for all I know. My brother."

"There's no brother listed on your records, Mr. Pauley."

"No. I had him taken off. It cost me a lot of money, and it's illegal, I guess, but I needed to do it. I needed it before I could ask Mimi to marry me."

"He's a bad man. A very bad man. Vinnie's nothing like him, Officer."

"Lieutenant. Dallas. How is he a bad man?" Eve asked.

"He does what he wants, takes what he wants, hurts who he wants," Vinnie told her. "He always did, even when we were kids. He took off when we were sixteen."

"We were?" Roarke repeated. "You're twins then?"

"Fraternal, not identical." The distinction seemed an important point for Vinnie. "But we look a lot alike."

"I'd never mistake them. There's something scary in his eyes." Mimi shivered. "Something mean, just not right in them. And I'm sorry, Vinnie, it's in that boy's eyes, too. No matter how sweet he smiles or how polite he talks, it's in his eyes."

"Maybe it is. Anyway, they weren't here long. They wanted to stay a few days. God knows why, or what they'd done they needed to put up here. I said Darrin could stay, but Vance had to go. He wouldn't stay without Vance. I asked him about his mother, why wasn't his mother with him. He's the one who said she was dead. He said she'd been dead for years. Murdered he said."

"How?"

"He didn't tell me. I was shocked, and I asked him, how, when, who? All he said was he knew who was responsible. And he had plans. Mimi's right. Something not right in his eyes, when he said that I could see it. He had plans. I wanted them both away from my family."

Vinnie glanced toward the stairs. "I wanted them away from Mimi and Jennie. Even if he's mine, I didn't want him near my girls. That's the hard part, you know? Even if he's mine."

"We're yours," Mimi whispered. "That's what matters."

Vinnie nodded, took a long drink from the frosty glass. "I wasn't twenty when Inga . . . she was beautiful. Sorry, sweetie."

"That's all right." Mimi took his hand, gave it a hard squeeze. "So am I."

He brought their joined hands to his lips, pressed them hard to her knuckles. "You sure are. You sure are."

"Go on and tell them about it," Mimi prompted. "Stop worrying yourself and tell them."

"All right. I fell for her, for Inga. For who I thought she was. I don't know if she'd run away from my brother, or if they planned it all together, to dupe me, to use me so she'd have somewhere safe to stay while she was nesting. It was hard not knowing. Not so much anymore, but back then, when it happened, it was hard. And so I paid to have Vance's name taken off my data."

"Nobody's going to give you grief over that, Mr. Pauley," Eve assured him.

He nodded. "Well, that's good to know. Anyways, Inga left when Darrin was a couple months old. Took whatever wasn't nailed down in my place, my car, cleaned out the savings I had, even the little account I started for the boy before he was even born. All there was was this video cube from my brother, laughing, telling me thanks for filling in for him. I found out he'd been arrested near to a year before. For some kind of fraud or something. I guess maybe he sent Inga to me, so I'd . . . fill in. And when he got out, he took them. Just like that.

"I never saw her again, never saw Vance or the boy again until that day Mimi called me home. I hired a private investigator to try to find them, but I couldn't afford him for very long. Never came to nothing, but I wanted to try. I don't know if he was mine, the boy, but back then, he felt like mine."

"You did the best you could."

He smiled at Mimi, but his eyes were damp. "It felt like giving up. I guess it was. I was mad a long time, and then, well, I met Mimi. I put it behind me, until they showed up here a few years back. And I don't know where they went from here. We got an e-mail from Darrin about three years ago. He said he was in college, in Chicago. How he was making something of himself, studying hard. He sounded . . ."

"Sincere," Mimi put in.

"I guess he did," Vinnie said with a sigh. "He asked if we could maybe help him out a little. Money. Knowing Vance, I checked it out. And he was registered at the college like he said. So I sent him a thousand dollars."

"And never heard a word back," Mimi finished. "But right after that? Somebody accessed our bank account. That was just our emergency account, thank the Lord, where Vinnie got the money he sent Darrin. It only had another five thousand in it. He took four of it. He did it, Vinnie," she said when her husband looked ready to protest.

He sighed, nodded. "Yeah, I expect he did."

"Vinnie wouldn't report it to the police."

"If he's mine, he's entitled to something. And I could be finished there. It's all he's entitled to. I tried to contact him through the college, but they said he wasn't registered. They had no record of him. I argued, because they damn well had two weeks before. But I didn't get anywhere."

How much were they entitled to? Eve wondered. "We believe the man you know as Darrin Pauley is and has been in New York. We believe he has committed various cyber crimes and engaged in forms of identity theft."

Vinnie lowered his head to his hands. "Like Vance. Just like Vance. What do I tell my parents? Do I tell them?"

"Mr. Pauley, there's more. There's harder, and within the next forty-eight hours it's going to be in the media." He lifted his face to meet her eyes, and his were full of fear. "The man you know as Darrin Pauley is the primary suspect in the rape-murder of a sixteen-year-old girl. The daughter of a decorated police officer."

"No. No. No. Mimi."

She put her arms around him, and though her face registered shock and horror, it didn't show disbelief. Her eyes met Eve's as she held her husband, and she nodded. "I was afraid of him. When he looked at me, I was afraid. That girl, we heard about it. We heard about it this morning on the bedroom screen when we were getting dressed. They said your name. Lieutenant Dallas. I'd forgotten."

"I need anything you can remember, any detail you can give me on Darrin, your brother, Inga Sorenson."

"I think they may have hit my parents up for money a few times." Vinnie rubbed his eyes again. "We don't talk about it, or them, but it's hard to say no to your own."

"Let's find out."

"Let me do that. Let me talk to them, explain . . . somehow. I'll just use the other room. Is that all right?"

"Go ahead."

"What do we do now?" Mimi asked. "What should we do? If he comes here—"

"I don't believe he will. You've got nothing he wants. But I'll talk to your local police. If he contacts you, you should stay calm, behave naturally. And contact your local police, and me immediately."

"We're going on vacation tomorrow."

"And you should," Eve told her. "Go exactly as you planned. Get out of this."

"Enjoy your daughter," Roarke added. "You have a good family. This isn't part of it."

On the drive back to transpo, Eve stared up at the sky. "Just more victims."

"She's a sensitive. At least she has a whiff of it," he added when Eve turned her head to study him. "Just a sense I got from her, and one I think could explain why she saw what's inside that boy. Maybe he wasn't as adept at hiding it, but I think she saw inside, and it frightened her."

"She was right to be." Settling down, she started a standard run on Vance Pauley. "And she was right when she said Vance was a bad man. Lots of trouble here. The juvie's unsealed, so somebody beat me to that along the way. He had trouble starting at nine. Truancy, theft, destruction of private property, cyber bullying, hacking, assault, battery."

"At bloody nine?"

"I'm moving through. Twelve on the first assault. It was the ID fraud that had him in during the Inga period. Then he drops off, just like that. He's got a mile-long sheet from childhood to the age of twenty-one, then nothing."

"Got smarter."

"Or Inga was smarter, and ran the games, taught him. And I've got nothing on her, nothing on that name that corresponds to the age, the description Pauley gave me, the location she lived when she was with him. She's listed on Darrin's records as his mother, DOD, May sixteen, 2041. He'd have been four. But there is no death record corresponding."

"She'll be in MacMasters's files. Not under that name, necessarily, but she's the motive. The reason for the plan he had even seven years ago."

"Yeah. And I'll find her."

She pulled out her 'link when it signaled. "Dallas."

"Are you seriously in Alabama?" Baxter demanded.

"I'm on my way to transpo, and will be heading back."

"Could you pick up some barbecue? There's nothing like Southern barbecue."

"Baxter, it's your ass getting barbecued if you're tagging me for nothing."

"Can I have barbecue if I've got something? Jesus, Dallas, you're going to scare my appetite away with that face. Okay, we got a hit. Girl working the bar at a club that caters to barely legal college types. She made the sketch. She says she had some classes with this guy. He really did go to Columbia. Better yet, she's a grad student, working her way through her master's, and says she saw him—you're going to love it—at a party on New Year's freaking Eve."

"At Powders's."

"At Powders's. Tells us she was there solo, and hey, why not, so she put a little hit on him. He wasn't into it. Believe me, a man would be crazy not to be. Right, Trueheart?"

"She's very pretty."

"Hot. Steaming, finger-burning hot." He sighed the sigh of a patient tutor. "My work is never done with this boy."

"Write it up."

"That's where the boy's work is never done. So we hied ourselves—"

"What yourselves?"

"Hied ourselves over to Powders's, and got confirmation. He, his roommate, and his unfortunately underage twist all recognized him. Just somebody they'd see around now and then. But the girl noticed him party night. She said she always notices frosty guys—and gave our own Trueheart a little flutter."

"Sir, she did not—"

"You need to be more observant, my young apprentice. So we've got wits put him in Powders's on the night the ID was lifted. It's good."

"It's good."

"Dallas, it's too damn late to go knocking on doors at MacMasters's."

"It's only . . . shit." An hour gained, an hour lost. She just hated it. "You'll hit it after the briefing tomorrow."

"We've got a couple more maybes here and there. Shilly's the solid."

"Shilly."

"I know, she even has a steaming, finger-burning name. About that barbecue."

She cut him off.

"The PA's going to be pleased with that when we take him down," she said to Roarke. "It's nice case-building. If you manage to clean up that hard drive, get me that picture of him going in the door—"

"And we will."

"We'll put him away. But we have to find him first. Got his face," she mumbled. "Got a name. Not the one he's using now, no, not the one he used with Deena. That was David. But a name. Got his connection, got his kinship."

She noted they were about to enter the transpo station. "I can start the search for Inga—whatever name she was using—on the way home."

"I could find her faster, I'd wager. If you'd like to pilot."

"Ha-ha."

"You'd enjoy flying more if you'd learn the controls."

"I'd rather pretend I'm on the ground."

Roarke sent her a quick smile. "And how many vehicles have you wrecked, had blown up, or destroyed in the last, oh, two years?"

"Think about that, then imagine it happening when I'm at the wheel at thirty thousand feet."

"Good point. I'll do the flying."

"Do that, ace."

He parked. "They had something, the Pauleys. A solid base, a strong connection to each other. Each of them solid in their own right, from my perception, and more yet together."

"I wouldn't argue. He feels responsible, and feels a kind of grief over Darrin. Even though it's very unlikely he's the father."

"Blood still, either way. Blood's a strong tie. Kinship, as you said. And a good man like that, he'd feel it regardless."

"A bad man can feel it, too," she said and got out of the car to fly home.

I5 She'd been Irene Schultz—at least in June of 2039 when a young Jonah MacMasters had collared her for fraud, possession of illegal substances, and soliciting sex without a license.

Her male companion, one Victor Patterson, had been questioned and released though MacMasters's case notes indicated his complicity. Lack of evidence against him, and the woman's confession made it impossible to hold and charge him.

A male child, Damien Patterson, had

been removed by child services into foster care during the investigation, and subsequently returned to his father. Schultz had taken a deal, and had done eighteen months.

Case closed.

"It has to be her," Eve said as she and Roarke walked back into the house. "Everything fits. Two months after her release, she poofs, and so do Patterson and the kid. Vanish, no further data on record."

"Picked up new identities."

"That's the pattern." She headed up the stairs. "Change ID, move locations, start a new game. But here's a new angle. From the case notes, it's clear MacMasters believed Patterson—or Pauley—was part of the fraud. He let her take the rap, and she let him. She went down for it. More, Vinnie said nothing about illegals. His brother's got no illegals bumps on his record. That's new. Where'd it come from?"

It didn't fit, it didn't play, Eve thought.

"And the solicitation? Those are stupid risks for these kind of grifters. Stupid, and it doesn't come off she'd been stupid. The woman played Vinnie for a year. She knows—knew—how to run a game, long and short. Then, boom, she goes down not just for fraud, but possession and so-licitation? It's off."

"Sex and drugs are quick money if you need it," Roarke commented. "And big money if you know how to play them. That's telling."

Eve paused on the stairs, considered. Quick and big. "It might fit Pauley. Greed, impatience. It might."

"And it's telling," Roarke added, "that when she made this deal for the eighteen, she didn't roll on Pauley. It would be SOP, wouldn't it, to offer her a still lighter sentence if she implicated her partner?"

"Yeah, it would. And there would have been some sympathy for her. Young mother, clean record—or so it appeared. She went with a public defender." She moved into her office, straight to her com-puter. "I've got the name, and the name of the APA from MacMasters's case notes. But he wouldn't have the negotiations in here. I need his memory on this."

"She didn't die in prison."

"No, she didn't die in prison. Why is MacMasters to blame for her death, whenever and wherever and however it happened? It's illogical, and in his twisted way, he's logical."

She paced to the board, around it. "Something not in the case files, the notes, something not on record? But he's a kid, hell almost a baby really, right? So how does he know what happened, how does he know MacMasters has to pay?"

She pinned up Irene's mug shot.

"Because Pauley tells him," she concluded, studying the photograph, the harsh and weary eyes of the woman. "Pauley tells him how it went down, from his point of view anyway. Or how he wants it to play. It can't be, yeah, I let your mother take the full rap while I walked. No, it can't be that."

As she circled, spoke, talked it out, Roarke eased a hip onto the corner of her desk. He loved watching her work, watching her re-create, dig down.

"What kind of man lets the mother of his child take the hit? How can you stand back, let her fall while you walk?"

She thought of Risso Banks. "I looked at this guy, had to check him out. Young guy. His older brother made him an addict, played him into the sex game, then when the bust came, left the kid and tried to save himself. And that's how he remembers his brother, leaving him and trying to save his own ass."

"Darrin Pauley would have been too young to remember."

"Yeah." Eve nodded. "Yeah, so Vance Pauley can write the story however he wants. They worked together, no question, but she goes down alone. He can't let it come off like that to his son, or he's a coward, a user. MacMasters railroaded her? You can make that play, you can always make it play that the cops screwed with you. And still . . ."

"A year and a half in prison against the rape and murder of the cop's child twenty years later?" Roarke looked at the photos, the stark differences, on her board. "Very imbalanced."

"Symbols. Mira said it was all symbolic. So there's more, has to be. Something between her release and her death, something that Pauley can point back to? Something about her arrest, her time in that led to her death?"

She pushed at her hair, tried to put herself in Darrin Pauley's place. "If Darrin told Vinnie the truth about when she died—and why lie about that—it was about two years after the arrest, about six months after her release. What happened during that six months? I need to find her dead, that's what I need to find, and track back from there."

"You have considerably more data on her now. You'd be able to streamline the search you've already done."

"Exactly."

"Allow me. Computer access results of search of female victims of rape-murder by strangulation and suffocation and refine with DOD 2041. Victims with initials I, S."

Acknowledged . . .

"Computer," Eve added, "input victim's age as between twenty and twenty-eight, and as having given birth to at least one child."

"Right you are," Roarke commented.

She had to smile at him. "You did okay, for a civilian."

Acknowledged . . . File accessed, search commenced. Working . . .

"No," Roarke said when she turned

toward the kitchen. "No more coffee, not at this hour. You'll never sleep. And while the answers you hope to get with this search are vital, they won't help you catch your man tonight."

It was hard to argue, even though she wanted the damn coffee.

She stuck her hands in her pockets. It wasn't just the comp that could give her answers. "He's got to have another ID, has to be using one. Why isn't it popping? Why do we only get Darrin Pauley?"

"Change your hair and eye color, even skin tone, some features. All perfectly legal, and even fashionable. While he may have elected to use the same basic look for the student ID he used with Deena and his Darrin Pauley ID, he's likely to have a half-dozen others, with enough variation to slip by a search. More hair, or less, a variance of coloring and some subtle shift in features to pass for mixed race. And with some skill, and some money, it's very easy to keep an ID off the grid entirely."

"If he works, he has to have one that would pass, and would be on the grid. At least initially. It's routine to do a quick background check before hiring."

"Depends who's hiring, but yes, most routinely. But one doesn't have to stick with the same. Once hired, how often is an employee's ID run through the grid? Especially if, as you've theorized, he keeps out of trouble, stays steady."

"So he uses one look for his time at Columbia, possibly another for his approach to Deena, and maybe varies it otherwise. Different looks and personalities for different marks. Mavis worked that way back when."

She *itched* for coffee, but hooked her thumbs in her front pockets and focused on the job. "Mira's profile suggests he lives alone. Maybe so, maybe. But maybe he's still hooked with his old man. A partnership like that, it would continually reinforce the mission, wouldn't it? And it would help him maintain that control, that patience, because he'd always have someone to talk to about it, to share his success with, to brag to."

"Someone to cheer him on," Roarke added. "To help with the legwork, the research, the income."

"Maybe he doesn't work at all, the income source is the grift. They're good at it, and it teaches him how to blend, to acclimate, how to get along. That fits profile."

Task complete, the computer announced. *One result from search. Display?*

"On wall screen one," Eve ordered. "Illya Schooner, age twenty-five, born in North Dakota, parents deceased, no sibs."

"Easier if you eliminate any family, as their data would need to be generated."

"Yeah, yeah, but she's got the kid on record. David Pruit this time, and lists Val Pruit as husband and next-of-kin, as father of the boy. She looks different from the ID and mug shots taken as Irene Schultz. Longer hair, lighter hair, curly, change of eye color, fuller lips, sharper cheeks, the mole beside her top lip. She's shaved off a year on her age, the neck's longer, the eyebrows thicker and higher."

"Much of which can be done by some e-tweaking, if the subject doesn't want to deal with more permanent facial adjustments. Who really notices some of the more subtle differences, except a cop? And much of it's just put down to whim. She changed her hair, wanted green eyes instead of blue."

"She died with this face, or a close proximity, in Chicago, where she had her address at the time, in May of 2041. Rape-murder by strangulation. I need more than that. I need the case file, the investigator."

"Eve, it's too late to push Chicago PD to search for a file for a murder nineteen years ago. You'd have better luck in the morning."

"I can get some data through IRCCA now. And . . . Computer, search for David Pruit, DOB October six, 2037, mother Schooner, Illya, father Pruit, Val. Second search for Val Pruit, same data."

Acknowledged. Working . . .

"They won't be in the database."

"No, but I want to confirm that. At some point, wouldn't they repeat an ID? You've gone through all that time, trouble, expense. Why not update it? Reuse it."

"An excellent point."

"And meanwhile, I can tap IRCCA, and put through an official request for the case file."

"All right then, but you have to be done for the night."

With coffee, she could probably push

through another hour, maybe two. And would be doing little more than accessing data that could be done while she gave it a rest.

"How hard would it be to set up a search for minor variations like this?" She brought up Inga's ID photo, splitting the screen. "Adding in a five-year age span, the initials."

"Setting it up, easy enough. The results? They'll be all over the bloody place. She's a very attractive woman in her early to mid-twenties with a certain set of initials, and features with a slight variance. Have you any idea how many there might be in the world who fit that basic description?"

"Stick with the U.S. And I'm thinking him. Darrin/David/Damien."

"And still."

"I'll wade through the results. All you have to do is get them."

"I'll set it up, then we're going to bed."

"That's a deal."

She woke just after five to the blessed scent of coffee. Opening one eye, she saw Roarke by the AutoChef, sipping a tall mug and watching her.

"I thought the timing worked," he said as he lifted a second mug and brought it to her.

"Thanks. Have you already started today's quest for world economic domination?"

"That's not scheduled till six, which I calculated was about the time you'd start today's quest for truth, justice, and ass-kicking."

"Sounds about right. I've got a good feeling. With what we've got, what we're getting, we may be able to pin him down today. I can put together enough to haul him in. If EDD gets me the image of him walking into the house, I've got more. Motive, means, opportunity. It's all there. Circumstantial, but strong."

"I like an optimistic cop."

She felt more so after she'd showered, dressed, had a second cup of coffee and a waffle.

In her office, she checked for incoming on the wild hope that someone on the graveyard shift at Chicago PD decided to do a good deed. No luck there, she noted, but she'd push that again and soon. She checked the results of the search Roarke had run at her request, and felt that optimism drop several notches.

"Three hundred and thirty-three thousand possibles? Shit." She noted he'd run a secondary search adding a current New York address. That cut it down to slightly more than thirteen thousand.

And he'd run those results against people who'd purchased the security system. The man thought like a cop, she decided, even if the result came up goose egg.

There had to be another angle, another way to whittle down those possibles. Back burner, she decided, until she'd updated her reports and prepped for the briefing.

It took her most of the hour, and restored most of her earlier optimism. Just before seven, she contacted Whitney.

"Commander, I've just sent you an updated report."

"Yes, it's coming in now. Highlight it."

She did so, smothering the urge to get to her feet, to stand as she preferred when giving orals.

"I feel," she continued, "we're stacking the building blocks of a solid case, and refining our search for the suspect. It's my belief Captain MacMasters may be able to provide more details, and more insights into the matter of the arrest, interrogation, and sentencing of Irene Schultz, and that will further assist us in apprehending Darrin Pauley."

"When do you brief your team?"

"They're arriving now, sir." She signaled Peabody, McNab, and Jamie to silence as they came in chattering.

"I'll have the captain in my office at nine. He's agreed to issue a short statement to the media at noon. We'll need to do the same, and to stand with him. He will not take questions, but you will. Five-minute duration."

Crap. Crap. Crap, she thought. "Yes, sir."

"Brief your team, Lieutenant. I'll contact Chicago from here, give them a push on the information you need."

"Thank you, Commander."

She ended the conversation just as Summerset wheeled in a long buffet table, and Trueheart came through the door pushing the other end.

"God, doesn't anybody think about any-thing but food?" she demanded.

"Thinking is often clearer when the body is properly attended." Summerset stepped ably out of the way of the stam-pede. Eve saw his gaze track to the mur-der board, and knew it lingered on the crime scene photos of Deena. He looked back at Eve. "I wish you all the clearest of thoughts."

When he left the room, she rose, got cof-fee. "Settle down, people. This is a briefing not a stuff-your-face contest. Screens on," she ordered. "This is our suspect," she be-gan. "Born Darrin Pauley, age twenty-three. And this is what we know or believe we know about him."

She moved from the suspect to the man believed to be his father, and from there to the woman who'd been his mother.

"She's the key in his lock," Eve said. "Whitney is reinforcing my overnight re-quest to Chicago for the files on her murder, and the request to speak directly with the primary and other investigators on that case."

"I can get media reports," Jamie suggested. "It's, like, twenty years back, but I could dig up any media coverage of the murder."

"All right. The data from IRCCA states she was both raped and sodomized repeatedly, possibly by more than one attacker. She was not bound, which explains why this didn't pop on like crimes. She was beaten, more severely than our vic, and also showed signs of illegals use."

She gestured to the board where she'd noted the similarities between the murders of Deena MacMasters and Illya Schooner. "Evidence indicates she was partially smothered with a pillow found on scene, and was strangled with the bedsheets. She was found in a mid-level LC flop by maid service, and had been dead according to the report for eight hours. No witnesses came forward, none who were interviewed gave the police any salient information."

"Shock and amazement," Baxter muttered.

"She was not a licensed companion," Eve continued. "However, when interviewed, Victor Patterson stated that they were experiencing some family difficulties as she had begun to prostitute herself to finance a growing drug problem. He was alibied for the time in question."

"He could've had it done," Baxter speculated. "If she'd gone on the junk, was a liability to the game, he might have wanted to get rid of her."

"Possible, but unlikely. Look at the background." She brought his sheet up on screen. "Bust, bust, trouble, trouble, right up until he got out of prison and ran off with her. Then nothing. He's skimmed under the surface since. And on her? Nothing, not a damn thing before she took the fall for the fraud. Did he get that smart in prison? My money says she was the brains, she was the smarts. But something changed once she did the time. That's the turn. Peabody, get data from her stretch in Rikers, find somebody who remembers her."

"Can do. Maybe it was just the time in itself," Peabody suggested. "It's like you said, she had nothing prior. Free as a bird, doing things her way. Then bam, she's in a cage for a year and a half."

"Soured her," Eve considered. "Shook her confidence. And if she'd gotten a taste for illegals on the outside, that could be fed inside. Expanded, exploited."

"She's not the same person coming out as she was going in." Peabody studied the mug shot. "She looks pretty rough on the going in."

"Yeah, she does. Not the beautiful, vibrant type Vinnie Pauley remembered just a couple years before."

"The wrong guy." Trueheart blinked when all eyes shifted to him. "Um. I mean to say, the, ah, longer-term exposure to Pauley, the wrong guy. His influence maybe started her on a downturn."

"It could fit. The timing, the changes. What we know," Eve added, "is between the Inga Vinnie Pauley knew and the Illya who died bad in a Chicago sex flop, there was a big slide. And it would appear that for a chunk of that, and for years after, Vance Pauley had influence over Darrin Pauley. How about the security imaging on the victim's house?"

"I've got that." McNab rose, held up a disc. "Okay if I plug it in?"

"Go ahead."

He went to her desk. "Display, screen three. You can see there's more definition," he began.

"I can?"

"It's slow. It's not like a routine clean and enhance, and can't work at that pace. We were able to capture and lock the image, but it's severely corrupted. The pixels have to be repaired every level, every step. Feeney and I captured and locked two more last night, using the same procedure we worked out. And we've got those in process. I think that's all we're going to retrieve."

"We're going to work on a way to speed the process," Feeney put in. "We're on that, but no promises."

"I'm meeting with Whitney and Mac-Masters at nine, and hope to pick through MacMasters's memory of the arrest of Irene Schultz, any other data he might have. Peabody will pursue the shoes/wardrobe angle. Baxter and Trueheart will recanvass the area around the crime scene with the sketch. At noon MacMasters will issue a statement to the media, as will I. I will briefly take questions. I've initiated another search, with the current results over thirteen thousand possibles."

When she explained it, Trueheart cleared his throat. "Maybe, if they own the security system, the father bought it. Used one of his aliases."

"Good thought. Run that. We brief at Central at sixteen hundred, at which time I'll have selected the other members of the team to cover the memorial. We'll rebrief— unless we have this fucker by then—at seven hundred tomorrow, full team. Now get out there and find this bastard. Baxter, one minute."

She walked into the kitchen, came back with a bag, which she tossed to him.

When he looked inside his face beamed like the sun. "Holy shit, we got us some Alabama barbecue. I love this woman."

"Save the love for Roarke. He dealt with it. Move out. Peabody, with me."

Peabody waited until they were out of the house, in the car, and Eve sped down toward the gates. "Okay, I know we're in deep investigative mode, and we have a lot of threads to tug, then tie together. But everyone has their specific thread or threads. I'll be all over the retail outlets *asap*."

"And?"

"And so, I thought we could take just a few minutes to talk about the wedding."

"Louise has a handle on that. I know because I went by and talked to her about it. I did that duty."

"You really did, and more. She filled me in, totally," Peabody said with a happy gleam in her eyes. "Inviting her to stay Friday night, and have the rest of us was abso mag of you, Dallas."

"It was a moment of weakness." One Eve prayed she wouldn't regret as she swung downtown. "What is, exactly, 'the rest'?"

"You know, the usual. Me, Mavis, Nadine, Trina. Maybe Reo if she can make it," she added, thinking of the APA. "And, ah, Trina's bringing another consultant so we'll all get beautified. But the best part is, we'll all be there for Louise. With her. So I was wondering if we could set up a kind of bridal suite for her."

"What does that mean? I'm not going to

have her camp on the lawn. She'll have a room. A suite. Whatever."

"Yeah, yeah, but can we sort of bride it up? Flowers, champagne, candles—I've got some my cousin made that are really soothing—girl food, music. Set the mood."

Eve said nothing for a moment. "I should have thought of that, right?"

"No. That's what I'm here for. It's all going to be mag, and this is just like a bonus round for her."

"It's fine. All fine."

"Okay! I thought we could—"

"No, that was the few minutes. I want Jenkinson and Reineke on the memorial detail. Make sure they get the details on the time and place of the briefings. I'm going to ask MacMasters for recommendations on two of his detectives for that duty as well. And we'll want half a dozen uniforms, at least half of them from MacMasters's division."

"Getting cops from MacMasters's division's a good move."

"Any cop who can make it will be there anyway. I want that place covered, but we need to keep the watch for the suspect tight. The more cops who know his face, the better chance one of them will try for him, tip him off, or scare him off."

"He has to know the place will be packed with cops there to pay respects. That might scare him off anyway."

"I don't think so." Eve wormed through a gap between a maxibus and a Rapid Cab. "He'll like it. Like the idea of being able to walk right in. Another needle in the eye. As far as he knows, we've got nothing."

"After the media conference today . . ."

"He'll still think we've got nothing." Eve intended to make sure of it.

The minute she walked into Homicide, Eve smelled doughnuts. And thought: Nadine.

She gave the detectives and uniforms in the bullpen one long, steely stare, then strode to her office. As she expected, the star reporter sat in the visitor's chair. Nadine sipped coffee, no doubt caged from Eve's own AutoChef. She shot Eve a fluttery look out of amused green eyes, and fluffed her streaky blonde, always camera-ready hair.

"Nearly nine o'clock," Nadine said, "late for you to be checking in."

"Not too late for me to boot you out."

"Come on, Dallas, I've laid back off the MacMasters story." Amusement faded. "I've reported it, respectfully, and stuck with the statements from the department liaison. I know MacMasters. I work the crime beat. I'd hoped, for a lot of reasons, you'd be able to close this one quickly. That's not happening."

Eve stepped over to get coffee for herself. "There's a media conference scheduled for noon."

"I'm aware, and I'll be there. Give me a jump."

"I can't do it. Can't and won't," she added before Nadine could speak.

"You've got something. I know you, and you've got something." Eyes narrowed, Nadine jabbed a finger toward Eve. "Do you have a suspect? How close are you to making an arrest?"

"And you know me well enough to know I'm not going to answer any of that."

"Off the record." Nadine held up her hands to signal no recorder. "I might be able to help."

She had in the past, no question. But here, Eve thought, it couldn't be done.

"You're going to say no. Before you do let me tell you that when you've worked the crime beat the way I have, you get to see how cops work—the good, the bad, the indifferent. You see what it is to do the job you're doing. Now this kid, this cop's kid is murdered this way, and it comes practically on the heels of Detective Coltraine's murder. It's hard to stand back from that. I can be objective, Dallas, because that's my job. But it matters."

Eve contemplated her coffee. "Maybe you'd want to do a segment on your show on high-end security systems."

"Isn't that odd? I was just considering doing a segment on *Now!* on high-end home security systems."

"Spooky." Eve cocked her hip, slid a hand into her pocket as she drank. "A lot of experts feel the Interface Total Home 5500 is one of the best, if you can afford it. You know, as a cop, I have to wonder: Do people shell out for something like that because they want to be secure, or because they have something to hide?"

Nadine gave her slow, feline smile. "That's an interesting angle."

"Maybe. You know, thousands of people in New York bought that system, and pay for the regular updates and maintenance—Security Plus being a big and trusted service agent. Probably most of them are just careful law-abiding types. Then again, it only takes one."

"It would be hard to find that one who bought it for reasons other than law-abiding ones."

"A long, tedious process," Eve agreed easily. "Even if you, say, decided to check out those customers with certain initials. Like D.P. or even V.P. That would narrow it down some, but odds are you'd have to wade through hundreds."

"True, but reporters and their research staffs are hardwired to wade through the tedious."

"Yeah. Cops wouldn't know anything about that." Eve smiled thinly. "Go away, Nadine. I have a meeting."

"I'll see you at noon." Nadine rose, started for the door. "And I'm looking forward to the upcoming wedding festivities, including the slumber party."

"Shut up."

With a laugh, Nadine sauntered out, and finishing her coffee Eve thought at least she'd come up with a possible way to cut down on those possibles.

16 Eve walked into Whitney's office to find both men standing. Though MacMasters still looked pale, and there were lines dug deep around his eyes and mouth that hadn't been there even at their last meeting, he seemed . . . straighter, she thought.

And the cold, hard look in his eyes told her he was ready.

"Detective Peabody is handling some assignments, and about to pursue a lead," Eve began. "I thought it better for her to stay on top of that than to attend this meeting."

"Jack told me you . . . The commander informs me you have a possible lead that connects to an old case of mine."

"I do. We were able to identify an individual through image matching with the sketch Detective Yancy composited from the two witnesses. He's identified as Darrin Pauley, with a residence listed in Alabama."

"Alabama."

"Captain, we believe this identification is falsified, and that this subject may be involved in fraud, cyber crime, and identity theft. I spoke with Vincent Pauley, who is listed as the subject's father on this identification."

She ran through it briefly, watched Mac-Masters struggle to pinpoint the names, the details, the case.

"Twenty years ago?"

"I believe it was twenty-one years. We are accessing all data on the investigation, the individuals involved. You got the collar, Captain. You worked with a detective named Frisco, who went down in the line six years later."

"Frisco trained me. He was a good man, solid cop."

"I have a copy of the file. Looking through it might jump your memory."

"Use my desk," Whitney told him, and plugged in the disc Eve offered. "Meanwhile, Lieutenant." He gestured her a few feet away. "You'll have the file on the Illya Schooner murder this morning. A Lieutenant Pulliti, retired, was primary on that investigation. He'll contact you. I have the name and contact data for a Kim Sung, who was a guard assigned to Irene Schultz's cell block during her incarceration."

"Thank you, sir. The information should be helpful."

"I remember a few tricks."

"I know this," MacMasters murmured. "I remember this. I was still in uniform, hadn't taken the detective's exam yet. Frisco let me take the lead on it. We got a tip from one of our weasels on this woman running scams. She'd solicit a john, then she'd copy his ID, his credit card. Next thing he knew, he'd have all these bogus charges, or he'd find his bank account lighter by a few thousand. A lot of marks don't report that, especially if they're married or involved, or have something more to lose."

MacMasters studied the screen, nodding slowly. "Yeah, I remember this. I remember her. She had, apparently, been targeting the type least likely to make noise. But she scammed the weasel's brother, and that rolled it out to us. Frisco and I set up a sting. I posed as the mark and we trolled the area where she was known to work."

"And she bit," Eve prompted when Mac-Masters fell silent.

"Sorry, it takes me back. Before Deena was born, when Carol and I were just beginning, when Frisco was alive. He was a tough bastard. Sorry," he repeated, bringing himself back. "Yes, she bit the second night. It was clean and simple. We busted her on the solicitation without a license, found illegals on her, and a cloner."

His eyes narrowed as if he worked to see clearly back through two decades. "Yeah, that little cloner. It was slick, I remember that, too. Barely the size of her palm. Pretty damn slick considering it was twenty years back. She had my ID on her, too. I'd never felt her lift it. She was stoned, and she still pulled the civilian ID

I'd put in my pocket without me feeling the grab, even though I'd been waiting for it."

"She'd been using?" Eve asked.

"Yeah. She didn't have the look of a longtimer, of the street, but she was high. She had ups and Exotica on her, and both in her system. Maybe she needed them to have sex with the marks."

"How'd she play it?" Eve asked him. "Did she try to barter, work a deal, bitch, cry?"

"No, none of the usual. She—the impression I'm remembering is she seemed shaken, a little scared. That's what I'm remembering, and that she wanted her call right off. You see that here in the notes. She wouldn't say anything about anything until she'd made her call. But she didn't call a lawyer, like we figured she would. She cried then. That's right," he mumbled. "She started crying during the call. I could see her through the glass, the tears running down her face, and I felt . . ."

"Go ahead," Eve prompted.

"It's not important, not relevant. I remember I felt bad for her, sitting there, crying, looking so tired and defeated. I guess

I said something like it to Frisco, and he told me to toughen up. In more colorful language."

MacMasters smiled, very faintly. "He could be a hard-ass. We stood by, and when she finished, she asked for a court-appointed."

"You went to see the man going by Patterson."

"She wouldn't talk until she'd talked to the lawyer, and it was late, middle of the night by then, so we didn't think we'd get a go with her until morning. And we figured she'd contacted this guy, the one listed as her husband, as her kid's father."

"Contacting him so he'd have time to get rid of or conceal anything incriminating."

"Had to be," MacMasters agreed. "What the hell did the guy think she was doing all night? Playing bridge? So while she was in the tank, we went over to her residence. You could see, ten seconds in you could see he was wrong. He was wrong, Patterson. But the apartment was clean. No illegals, no evidence of fraud. Child services took the kid, and we took him in for questioning."

"That night?" Eve prompted.

"Yeah. Frisco and I both wanted to get him in the box, push him. But he played it innocent, and he never came off that. He claimed to believe she worked nights at some dive off Broad. He was sweating," MacMasters added as he looked back. "I can still see the sweat rolling down his face, like the tears had with hers. Maybe if we'd had more time to work him. But her lawyer told us to get the APA, her client wanted to deal."

He took a breath, working it out in his head. "We figured she was going to roll on the husband, implicate him to deal down. We pulled off him, went in to talk to her. She confessed."

"Just like that?"

"Just like that. Her lawyer wasn't happy, you could see that. The APA hadn't even gotten there yet, but she insisted she wanted to get it done. Claimed an addiction to Exotica, and that it had caused her to prostitute. Took the full rap. Claimed she bought the cloner on the black market. She wouldn't flip on Patterson. We pushed there, and when the APA got into it, he offered her a better deal if she pulled the husband in. But she wouldn't. They dealt her eighteen months, and he walked. They gave him back the kid.

"Frisco used to say, 'Sometimes slime slides.' This was one of those times."

"Was she afraid of him?"

"Hell, no." MacMasters let out a half-laugh. "She loved him. It was all over her. She loved the son of a bitch, and he knew it. He let her take the fall. More we figured, when Frisco and I talked about it, we figured during that call, when she started crying, the bastard talked her into taking the fall."

"It fits," Eve said quietly. "It runs true."

"You can know something without being able to prove it, without being able to make a case." Even now, twenty years later, the frustration flashed clearly on MacMasters's face. "We made the case on her, we closed the case. She did the time, and she earned it, but . . ."

MacMasters shook his head. "It was the law, but it wasn't right. Not through to the core of it. Patterson let her go down, alone, and he played the shocked husband, the desperate father. We did their financials, you can see here in the file.

They didn't have much more than two months' rent in their account. Where did the thousands she'd scammed go? She said to her illegals habit and gambling, but she couldn't tell us where she'd gambled it away. It was bullshit. They had it squirreled, but she never shook off that stand. She stuck firm that she'd spent the money, and he hadn't been any part of it. Hadn't known. And he comes to her sentencing with tears in his eyes, holding the little boy, with the boy crying for his mother. It was—"

He broke off, got slowly to his feet. In place of frustration, a cop's memory of a case that hadn't gone down quite right, came shock. "The boy. It's the boy you think killed Deena?"

"It's leaning that way, yes."

"But, for God's sake, he would do that, he would do that to an innocent girl because I once arrested his mother? Because she did less than two years?"

"Irene Schultz aka Illya Schooner was beaten, raped, and murdered by strangulation in Chicago in May of 2041."

He slid back into the chair as if his legs dissolved. "Patterson?"

"No, he was alibied. I'll have the full file later this morning, and will reach out to the primary on the investigation, but he looks clear on it."

"How could he blame me? How could he blame me for that, and kill my child?"

"I don't have the answer for you. Captain, did Pauley—Patterson—did he threaten you in any way?"

"No, just the opposite. He cooperated fully on the surface. Played the 'there must be some mistake, please can I see my wife.' He never asked for a lawyer. When I pushed the illegals, the cloner in his face, he put on the shock, the disbelief, then the shame. He played it like a symphony."

"You said it was the middle of the night when you pulled him in. But she didn't try to stall, try to get her PD to push for a bail hearing?"

"No. We stalled some, let them stew and caught a couple hours of sleep in the crib. The APA wasn't coming in until morning anyway. It didn't make any difference in her statement. I felt for her. Goddamn it, goddamn it, I felt for her. She protected him, and he let her. I felt for her, and that little boy. The little boy crying for her. Now my daughter's dead."

Sometimes, Eve thought, having the answers didn't ease the pain. Even as she went down to her office to search for more answers, she felt the weight of that on the back of her neck.

She found the Chicago file in her incoming, and sat down to read it through. She'd given it a first pass when Lieutenant Pulliti contacted her via 'link.

"I appreciate you reaching out, Lieutenant."

"Happy to. Just because I took my thirty a couple years ago doesn't mean I'm sailing on Lake Michigan. Cap said this was about an old homicide. Illya Schooner."

"That's right." He'd retired young, Eve thought. He couldn't have been more than sixty-five, with a full head of dark hair, clear brown eyes. Either the job hadn't put the years on his face, or he'd spent a chunk of his pension getting face treatments.

"Rape-murder," she said. "Vic was female, mid-twenties."

"I remember," he interrupted. "I was working the South Side back then. It was rough, hadn't come back far from the Urbans. Scary time."

"I bet."

"They'd worked her pretty good. Cap said he sent you the file."

"That's right."

"So, you can see, they worked on her. Took some time to mess her up that bad."

"You say 'they.' The ME reports state it appeared she was struck by both a left- and a right-handed attacker. But it's not conclusive."

"The Stallions worked in pairs back then."

Eve scrolled down to his notes. "The gang that held sway on that area held the illegals and sex trade."

"The Stallions *were* the illegals and sex trade on the South Side. They held it more than a decade. She infringed. For them, it was business. Somebody tries to cut into your business, you take them out. Hard."

"But you looked at the husband."

"Yeah, we looked hard, too. Seemed overkill even for the Stallions, unless she was cutting big. And if she was cutting big, where was the cut? Rules of play, they'd've warned her off first, or if she was any good maybe give her a chance to work for them."

Pulliti tapped the side of his nose. "It didn't smell right."

"You couldn't tie him in, the husband?"

"Alibied right and tight. Had the kid at home. About the time she was getting the shit raped out of her, he was knocking on a neighbor's door to ask for help since the kid was sick, and his wife was—he said— at work. Neighbor verified."

"Yeah, I see that."

"But it didn't smell right. We're knocking on doors and everybody says how he keeps to himself, hardly says boo, stays with the kid at night, takes him off during the day while the woman sleeps, or goes off on his own. But that night, the night he needs an alibi, he knocks on somebody's door. Sure was convenient."

"You think he set her up?"

"Thought it, felt it. See, the Stallions, back then, they'd initiate a member, or a business partner. Beat-down or gangbang, take your choice. You take the beating or the banging, then you give them their cut of your business."

Sex and drugs, she thought. Quick money, big money.

"You think she went with them for that voluntarily?"

"Maybe, or maybe he gave her over. They'd take a trade, especially a woman. I'll tell you, that's the way it smelled to me, but there wasn't one shred of evidence pointing that way. She was the meal ticket from what I can find, not that they had anything much to show for it."

"Just a couple months' rent in the financials," Eve interrupted. "Not hefty chunks."

"That's right. Not a hand-to-mouth kind of thing, but not your caviar and bubble wine either."

"Under the radar," Eve voiced.

"You could say. So, maybe he gave her over to the Stallions, and things got out of hand. I don't know, but it was just too damn pat with him. He comes up with the line about how they were having marital problems, and she was having trouble with illegals. But the neighbors said they never heard them fighting. And they looked like a nice little family any time they went out together, except the woman looked kinda worn down."

As she talked to him, Eve made her own notes, formed her own theories.

"This address, where she and the man and boy lived. What kind of neighborhood was that?"

"Solid middle. Working families, a lot of kids. They had a good apartment in a nice building. Nothing flashy, but nice. The husband, he had some flash."

"Did he?"

"Expensive wrist unit, shoes. The boy had plenty of trendy toys. They had up-market electronics. He was working in e-repair, consulting sort of deal, and she was—according to him—a professional mother. But he hardly put in any time on the job, and did most of the looking after the kid, according to the neighbors. I asked him about the wrist unit. Said it was a birthday present from his wife."

"He was off," Pulliti said. "My gut said he was off, but the evidence said he was clean."

When Chicago had given her all it could, Eve sat back, closed her eyes.

He was off, but came away clean. There was a pattern.

He let the woman take the fall for him—just as he'd let the woman sleep with, live with his own brother, and like he may have let her scoop up johns and marks in gang territory.

Sex, she thought. Did he like her to use sex to scam? Was that part of a thrill?

When had the illegals come into it? When had she started using?

MacMasters said she might have needed them to have sex with her marks.

Maybe so. Not with the brother. It's kinship in a twisted way. They'd looked alike, and she'd lived the con of making a family.

She pushed up, paced to the window and back. Paced to her board and away.

No, he hadn't knocked on a neighbor's door out of sheer coincidence the night of her murder. No way in hell. But it wouldn't have been just a cover for the cops. Couldn't be. They'd never have put him at the scene of the murder.

Covering though. Covering his own ass while she was being raped.

He knew something was going to happen to her, something bad. Something that could involve the cops coming to the door. A deal. A setup. A trade.

But the boy grows up and goes after MacMasters, mirroring the crime against his mother on MacMasters's daughter. Why? Because MacMasters was the arresting officer, in another city, two full years before his mother's murder?

What kind of sense did that make, even for a sociopath? It didn't follow . . .

She stopped, turned to stare at the board again. Unless . . .

"Dallas, I might have a line on—"

"Who's the biggest influence in your life?" Eve interrupted. "I mean, who would you say gave you the foundation for what you are, how you think, what you believe?"

Peabody frowned over the question. "Well, I like to think I think for myself, and there are a variety of factors in my life experience—"

"Cut the crap."

"Okay, at the base? My parents. Not that I go along with everything there, or I'd be in a commune raising goats or weaving flax, but—"

"The base is there. You're a cop, but with Free-Ager tendencies." She tapped Yancy's sketch as Peabody's frown deepened over the analysis.

"So, who most influenced this one? His mother's murdered when he's about four. Who'd be the biggest influence on what he believes, how he views the world?" She jabbed her finger into Pauley's ID print. "This one. He's a con artist, an operator. He taps his parents for money time and again, even though they know better. He's grease, he slides. His own brother has to pretend he doesn't exist to barricade himself. A smart and devious woman falls for him to the extent she takes an eighteen-month rap so he can skate—and she gets into prossing and illegals *after* they're hooked. Not before, after."

"The wrong guy," Peabody offered. "Like Trueheart said."

"Yeah, a really wrong guy. And if he tells the kid how his mother was lost, murdered, because the cops screwed with her, why wouldn't he believe it?"

"Because they didn't?"

"That doesn't matter. The kid's already predisposed to believe it. He's lived his whole life believing it, and wanting to even the score. He's lived his whole life targeting marks, taking what he wants, living on the other side. And liking it. Planning out the ultimate con. Pauley let the woman take the fall for him, but that's not what the kid hears. Pauley covered his ass on the night she was killed, but *that's* not what the kid hears. When you keep hearing the same thing from the person who has the power—and Pauley had the power for years—you believe."

Her father had held the power, Eve thought. He'd told her she was nothing, told her the police would put her in a dark hole and leave her there to rot. And for a long time, she'd believed him to the extent she was as terrified of the police, of anyone in the system as she was of the man who beat and raped her.

"Dallas?"

"It's classic," Eve concluded. "If you want to create something, someone, to obey, to believe, to become, you repeat, repeat. Punish or reward, that depends on your style, but you drill the message home. They killed your mother. They're to blame. They need to pay."

It struck like a hammer in the gut. "They, not he. It has to be *they*. The system, everyone who had a part in it. It's the system he hates. Oh, goddamn it. We need a run, now, on every official connected to Irene Schultz's arrest and incarceration. Her lawyer, the APA, the judge, the warden, the CS rep who removed the kid, the head of CS at the time, the foster home. We need whereabouts, family, family whereabouts."

Peabody's dark eyes went huge. "He's going after someone else."

"One cop isn't enough." Eve launched herself at her unit, ordered an immediate run. "He started it, but others are complicit. It's their fault his mother went away, their fault she was murdered. Took her away from him, so he's going to take something away from them. Frisco, the other cop, he went down. He's out of play. Can't punish the dead, can't make the dead suffer."

Peabody, already working it on her PPC, nodded. "Her lawyer's still in the city, a partner in a law firm downtown. Divorced, one child. Male, age fifteen."

"We inform, and get them covered. The

APA's in Denver now, married, two minor children. We contact, inform, inform local authorities."

As she started down the line, her desk 'link signaled. She glanced, impatient, at the readout. Then her stomach sank.

"Dallas."

Dispatch, Dallas, Lieutenant Eve.

Too late, Eve thought as she pulled up outside the SoHo loft. I'm too late. With Peabody she walked past the officers outside the building, and into the elevator.

"We'll want all security, want to knock on all the doors. Contact Morris."

"Already done. Dallas, I informed Whitney. He's moved your media conference to sixteen hundred, and will keep a lid on this as long as possible."

Eve stepped out of the elevator, into the living area. Upmarket, she thought. Wealthy bohemian. "Who owns it?"

"Delongi, Eric, and Stuben, Samuel. Mid-divorce. The loft is on the market, and currently untenanted."

"Lieutenant." One of the officers stepped to her. "No visible sign of break-in, no visible sign of struggle or theft.

She's in the bedroom. A real estate agent found her. He was showing the apartment to a couple of clients. My partner's got them in the second bedroom."

"Keep them sequestered. We'll work the scene first." She stopped at the kitchen, studied the single go-cup of coffee on the counter. "Was that here when you arrived?"

"Yes, sir."

"Record and bag, Peabody."

She moved on, stopped at the bedroom doorway.

Not a child this time, she thought as she studied the body. But young. Early twenties. Whose daughter was she?

"Victim is female," she began for the record. "Early to mid-twenties. Privacy screens are engaged here, and throughout the living area." She scanned the room. "There's no sign of struggle. Victim appears to be fully dressed."

With her hands and feet sealed, Eve entered to examine the body. "Ligature marks on ankles, facial bruising, bruising around the neck consistent with manual strangulation. ME to confirm."

She crouched, angled herself to see

the victim's wrists. She expected to see police restraints, as with Deena, but this victim's wrists were bound with some sort of colorful cord.

"Cording around wrists, deviation from Deena MacMasters's homicide. Get the ID, TOD, Peabody."

Blood on the sheets, she noted, consistent with violent rape. She hadn't been a virgin, not likely, but she'd suffered the same pain and terror.

"Bruising on thighs and around genital area. No underwear. She'll have been sodomized, too, and smothered, repeatedly. It's not a fucking copycat. Why did he use cord instead of cuffs?

"Not a cop's kid," she concluded. "The cuffs were another symbol. What's the cord symbolize?"

"Victim is identified as Karlene Robins," Peabody stated, "age twenty-six, Lower West Side address, with cohab Hampton, Anthony, employed by City Choice Realty. TOD is sixteen-thirty-eight, yesterday."

Peabody looked over at Eve. "That's before we had the sketch, before we had a name, before—"

She broke off when Eve held up a hand. "Irrelevant. Look for her bag, her 'link, appointment book. You won't find them, but look. Flag for ME," she continued for the record. "Tox screen priority.

"She's Jaynie Robins's daughter, the child services agent who removed Darrin Pauley into foster care during the Irene Schultz investigation. She came to show the apartment. He poses as a client, and all he needs to do is be ready when the right property comes up. Not a college student this time. That wouldn't do the job. No, this sort of property? Young exec, or trust-fund baby. Arty type, for this neighborhood, I'd say. Likes music, or the arts, the scene. He brings her coffee. Nice gesture. Hey, I picked some up for you, too. Takes her out, sets her up, just like Deena. Except for the restraints."

"It plays for me. Dallas, there's no bag, no purse, nothing of hers. They've got a couple of comps, but they're for show. The security station's locked. I mastered it, and the cams are shut down, the discs removed, the drive's been corrupted."

"There's building security on a place like this, too. We're going to roll her, then

I want you to check that out. I'll start on the wits when I'm done here."

When they rolled the body over, Eve bent down to examine the cords. "Some kind of bungee cord?"

"For kids." Peabody blew out a breath. "You use it to hang stuff from their cribs or strollers so they can pull. Bright, primary colors and designs usually. Stimulate the eye."

"Child services. Symbolic, like the cuffs." He'd had fun with this, she thought. The little jabs and pokes. "Check out building security, and make sure EDD's on the way."

She moved to the second bedroom, signaled the officer on duty to step out. All three people began to speak at once. Eve simply held up a hand, then pointed at the man sitting alone.

"You. You'd be the real estate agent. I'm Lieutenant Dallas. Name, please."

"Chip Wayne. I work for Astoria Real Estate." He took out a card, passed it to Eve. "I had an appointment this morning with Mr. and Mrs. Gordon, to show them this loft. It's just gone back on the market, and—"

She held up a hand again. "How do you gain access?"

"It's a code. All listing agents are given a code for access, and have to input their own ID code. I just—"

"What time did you arrive?"

"We met outside just after eleven. We had an eleven o'clock showing. We—we came up together, and began with the living area. Ah, Mrs. Gordon wandered off to look at the bedrooms. We encourage clients to look around, and then she—"

Eve stopped him again. "The place is furnished, but the records show it's been untenanted for three months."

"It's staging. Rented by the owners. To, ah, give the prospective buyers a better feel for how it looks, lived in. I don't know how that woman . . . I don't know how she can be here. The log says the agent from City Choice showed it yesterday, and logged out at twelve-thirty."

"Is that so?"

"The building is well secured." He looked almost pleadingly toward the couple huddled together in a chair. "It's prime property. Quiet, safe."

"Yeah, safe." Eve looked over at the

woman. Not much older than the victim, she judged. Shaking, teary. "You found the body."

"I—I wanted to see the bedrooms. Especially the master. We want a large master, with a view if we can get it. So I . . . And she was there, on the bed. Dead. She looked dead. I screamed for Brent, and I ran away from the—from her."

"Did you go into the room? Any of you?"

"Nobody went in. I play a cop on screen." Gordon smiled weakly. "*City Force*, maybe you've caught it."

"Sorry."

"Doesn't matter. Brash young detective, maverick. Anyway, a lot of it's bullshit, I guess, but you get how you have to secure a crime scene. So we didn't go in, or touch anything after Posey found the woman. We called nine-one-one."

"Okay. Mr. Wayne, how far in advance do you make these appointments for showings?"

"It depends. In a case like this one, fast as you can. There was a contract on it, but it fell through. We heard about it yesterday, but City got the jump on us. They must have somebody on the inside, some-body at the lending company who gave them the head's up. I contacted the Gor-dons as soon as I got word, but we couldn't make it in until this morning."

"Why them, particularly?"

"It's just what they're looking for. The location, the property, the price range. It's exactly what you've been looking for."

Gordon gave him a look of quiet disbe-lief. "Chip, you've got to be kidding."

"The owners are bound to be willing to renegotiate the price, considering. We can—"

"Brent, I want to go. Can't we leave? Please."

"Give me your contact information," Eve told them, "and you're free to go. We may need to talk to you again."

Eve walked the loft again, made notes, ran it through her head while the sweep-ers began their part of the job.

"Cams off on building security, too, and the virus . . . it looks like it infected that system. They're linked up with the individ-ual security. It's not the same system as the first murder," Peabody continued, "but it's the same brand. A commercial model.

Also, the other residents aren't home. Word is everybody works days. The building is typically empty from around nine in the morning to around five in the afternoon, weekdays. I started a background on the other residents. I'm not getting anything that clicks."

"He scoped it out. He wouldn't have had much time, but he did his homework. He was waiting for the opportunity, and knows how to take advantage of it. She should have a record of the appointment on her office comp, something there. We'll get his name. Whatever name he used. Where's the cohab this time of day?"

"He works from home primarily. Research consultant. Their place is only a few blocks from the real estate agency."

"We'll take him first. The parents, they're in Brooklyn, right?"

"Yeah. The mother works as a family counselor now."

Eve nodded, took a last look before calling the elevator. "It's all about family, isn't it?"

**17** Anthony Hampton wore casual office wear, a trim goatee, and high-end skids. He greeted Eve and Peabody with a quick smile, and a harried look in green eyes that sparked against warm brown skin.

"Ladies. What can I do for you today?"

"Anthony Hampton?"

"Yeah, that's me."

"I'm Lieutenant Dallas, NYPSD, with my partner Detective Peabody."

"Cops?" His smile turned to a grin as he studied the badges. "That's a first. Is there a problem in the building?"

"No, sir. We'd like to come in."

"Okay, sure, but . . ." He glanced behind him. "We're kind of in mid-chaos around here. Getting married on Saturday."

Eve felt the clench in her gut, but stepped inside. The hard, she realized, just became brutal. And brutal should always be done quickly. "Mr. Hampton, I regret to inform you that your cohab, Karlene Robins, is dead."

"What? Jesus, that's not funny. If this is one of Chad's sick jokes—"

"Mr. Hampton, the body of Ms. Robins was found this morning. She's been officially identified. I'm very sorry for your loss."

"Come on, come on, that's fucking *bullshit*." The anger slapped out as he grabbed Eve's arm, shoved her toward the door. "Get the hell out of here."

"Mr. Hampton." Eve countered the grip, muscled the man into a chair. "Karlene was murdered in a loft in SoHo, where we believe she took a client for a showing. Did she take a client on a showing yesterday?"

"That's what she does. That's what she's doing right now." He dragged out his pocket 'link. "Right now." He punched a single key. And shoved at his hair as a musical voice informed him Karlene was unavailable. "Karlene, I need to talk to you. Goddamn it, Karlene, now. Whatever you're doing, I need to talk to you now."

"Anthony." Peabody crouched down, laid a hand over his. "We're very sorry."

"She'll tag back. She will." His breathing began to heave and hitch. "She's just busy. It's a crazy week."

"When did you last speak with her?"

"I . . . Yesterday, when she left for work. But, we texted a few times."

"She lives here, but she didn't come home last night?"

"She had some work, a client on the hook. And then she was going to Tip's to do some wedding stuff. She stayed with Tip last night. Tip. I'll get ahold of Tip, and then . . ."

Eve let him play it out, let him call the friend, listen to her tell him she hadn't seen or heard from Karlene. She watched anger and disbelief take its horrible slide into grief.

"She—she's at work. She's at work. I can contact her boss, and she'll—"

"Anthony." Peabody repeated his name, in that same gentle way.

His eyes changed, filled with desperate pain. "But she can't be dead. That can't be true."

"When did she text you?"

"I don't remember, exactly. Here." He shoved the 'link at Peabody. "It's logged. It's right in there."

As Peabody took the 'link, stepped away to check its log, Eve pulled a chair over to face him, sat. "Mr. Hampton, look at me now. Detective Peabody and I need your help. Karlene needs you to help us find who hurt her."

"How is she dead? How is she dead?"

"We believe whoever she took to the loft killed her. Do you know who the client was?"

"That can't be. This is all . . . not real."

"Who was the client?" Eve repeated.

"It was some rich guy. Some wannabe artist from a rich family. Young guy."

"Have you met him?"

"No. But—"

"Do you know his name?"

"She probably told me. I don't know."

"She'd have a memo book here, an appointment book."

"She keeps one here, one in her bag, one at work. Anal. In the office." He stared hard at Eve's face, intensely, as if he had to focus on her to form each word. "We share the office here. I work at home. I work at home, and sometimes she does. We're getting married on Saturday."

"Can we get her book, take her book?"

"I don't care."

Eve signaled Peabody. "Do you know how this man, the one she was with yesterday became her client?"

"I'm not sure. She's been looking for the right place for him for a few weeks. Big fish. She said big fish. The SoHo loft. That just popped up again. She was so excited. It was just the right property for him, she said. Exactly what he wanted, and the commission would be extreme. She had to move fast.

"Where's Karlene?"

"We're going to take care of her now."

Slowly, he shook his head side-to-side. "She doesn't like to be taken care of. She takes care of herself. Are you sure? Are you really sure?"

"Yes."

He buried his face in his hands, began to rock, began to weep. Eve rose, moved quietly away to where Peabody waited.

"A text came in to his 'link at fourteen-ten, and another at eighteen-oh-three."

"She was bound and raped by the time the first went out, dead before the second."

"He had the friend's name, gave the word, spending the night and so on, the way Hampton stated. The memo book lists an appointment with D.P. for yesterday at nine-thirty a.m., the SoHo address. I went back through it, and there are a couple others. And one, the initial one from the looks of it, that lists an appointment with Drew Pittering."

Eve went back to Anthony to ask for permission to search through Karlene's things, and to take both his 'link and the memo book.

"Who can we call for you, Anthony?" Peabody asked him when they'd done all they could. "Let me call someone for you."

"My—my family. They're in town for the

wedding. They're here, in the hotel. They're here for the wedding."

When they walked back outside, Peabody pressed the heels of her hands to her eyes. "I know it's never easy, and notification just doesn't get to be routine. But that? It had to be one of the worst. All the wedding stuff lying around. It killed me."

Eve pushed it aside, viciously, as she had inside the apartment. "Hampton didn't recognize the sketch. But Darrin wouldn't need to stalk her here. Cohab works at home. Makes it too hard to take her there. But her line of work, that makes it easy to take her in a locked, empty space. You pose as a rich guy, young, attractive—and I bet charming sticks in there. She'd check it out, that's routine. Check out his ID, but he'd have covered that."

"I ran the name, along with the image, and his age—and I got nothing."

"He's already wiped it. But she'd have checked him out. Maybe there's something on her comps here or at work. It's not going to have his real address, but it's another pin in the map."

"You're cutting it close to the media conference."

"Fucking media." Eve raked at her hair. "I need you to go by her office, get whatever you can."

"What about notifying her parents? Oh, Jesus, Dallas, don't make me do that solo."

"Take a grief counselor with you. And get the parents into Central. I want to talk to the mother." She considered the fact Peabody would have to get to Brooklyn and back. "You take the vehicle. I'll catch the subway back to the house."

"Okay. Dallas, we couldn't have stopped this. We couldn't," Peabody insisted. "We had nothing to connect Karlene to Deena. Nothing."

"He knew that. He counted on that. Maybe he's counting on us not being able to make the connection between the two of them yet. It's a big leap without the springboard. I'm going to give him more reason to count on that."

On her way to the subway, Eve tagged Nadine. Sometimes the media had its uses.

As usual, the media liaison tried to prepare Eve, and as usual, Eve threatened bodily harm.

She walked into the media room at Central, and took her position between Commander Whitney and Captain Mac-Masters. The liaison stepped forward to outline the procedure, the rules, then asked the captain to give his statement.

In full dress blues, MacMasters took the podium. He stood like a cop, straight, with his eyes level.

But he'd aged, Eve thought. Years in a matter of days. He'd gone from lanky to gaunt, from steady to brittle.

"Early Sunday morning my daughter Deena was brutally murdered in her own home. In her own room. In her own bed. She was sixteen years old, a beautiful, bright, loving young woman who had never in her short life caused harm. She was our only child. She loved music and shopping and spending time with her friends. Deena was a normal teenager, with hopes and dreams—and those hopes and dreams as they often are for the young—were to change the world."

His smile was heartbreaking.

"She was a little shy, and still passionate about her desire to help others. Family and friends who have come or called to comfort my wife and myself speak first, almost always, of Deena's sweet nature. It's a testament to her.

"I have been a police officer half my life. I believe the police will bring Deena's killer to justice. I ask you, as a police officer who has sworn to serve and protect, and as a father who was unable to protect his only child, to contact the NYPSD if you have any information on the person who murdered Deena."

Questions rang out, of course, as he stepped away despite the instructions of the liaison. Eve ignored them as she stepped to the podium. She stood, silent, stony-eyed, until they faded away.

"I'm Lieutenant Dallas, and the primary investigator in the matter of the murder of Deena MacMasters. A full team of investigators, from Homicide, EDD, and support services, is working this case. We are pursuing all leads, and will continue to do so until the individual who murdered Deena MacMasters is identified, apprehended, and charged. We believe Deena MacMasters knew her killer. We believe she admitted him into the house on the Saturday evening, at which time her killer incapacitated her with a drug added to her soft drink. He then bound and raped her repeatedly over a period of several hours before strangling her. The investigative team will work diligently until we are able to exact justice for Deena MacMasters."

The questions rained again.

"Why do you think she knew her killer?"

"From statements given by her family, her neighbors, and her friends, we don't believe Deena would have opened the door to a stranger, especially when she was alone in the house. Evidence leads us to conclude the attack occurred inside the house, and that Deena was unconscious and unable to defend herself or attempt to defend herself prior to being bound."

"What evidence?"

"I will not discuss specific evidence on an ongoing investigation."

She continued, answering questions, dismissing others, circling more.

"Lieutenant! Nadine Furst with *Now!* and Channel Seventy-five. How is the rape-murder of Karlene Robins, whose body was discovered this morning in SoHo, connected to Deena MacMasters?"

It was a perfectly timed bomb. Reporters scrambled, shouting, checking 'links and PPCs.

"I'm here to answer questions pertaining to the investigation of the Deena Mac-Masters homicide."

"And I just gave you one." Nadine pushed forward. "Isn't it true that the body of another victim was found only this morning? That she, too, was bound, raped, murdered by strangulation?"

Eve's stare might have bored through steel. "We have not determined if the two cases are connected."

"But there are very specific parallels."

"And there are specific differences."

"What differences?"

Eve allowed the leading edge of anger to snap out. "I cannot and will not discuss the details of either of these investigations."

"Do you believe these two women were victims of a serial sexual predator?"

The bomb shot shrapnel throughout the room. Eve shouted over the chaos. "We have drawn no such conclusion. We have drawn no conclusion at this time that these cases are related."

"But you don't discount the possibility of serial. Or copycat."

"I will not speculate. I will not feed you—any of you—speculation or conclusions so you can bump your ratings. Two women—one barely old enough to qualify for the term—are dead. That should be enough to spin your current media cycle."

She strode away, fury in every step.

"Lieutenant!" Whitney's sharp command stopped her. "With me. Now."

"Yes, sir."

She followed him into the media ready room, where he closed the door.

"Well. Your performance was exceptional. I hope to God it generates exceptional results."

"We couldn't keep a lid on the Robins homicide for long. Bringing it out like this, it makes it look like we're caught flat-footed, like we're still a dozen steps behind. If he thinks we're looking at serial or copycat, he'll feel smug. We have a chance at the memorial tomorrow. And we may be able to get a line on him through the connections. One or more members of the connected families may have been approached by him in some way. If he thinks he's still got room, he may try for the next on his list, and soon."

"Work it. Brief your team. And consider yourself thoroughly dressed down for allowing a media leak of this nature to get through."

"Yes, sir."

She headed straight to her office, putting what she hoped was enough restrained fury on her face, in her stride, to ward off any cops who might approach her to offer support, or to wheedle information.

Roarke turned from the AutoChef as she slammed her office door to punctuate the moment. He held out a mug of coffee.

"Victor, spoils," he said.

"Huh?"

"Just a little reward for your part in that well-timed duet. I think it should play very well, and be lapped up by most. On the other hand, I know you, and Nadine. She wouldn't have ambushed you that way, and you'd have taken her down harder if she had."

"Let's hope the intended audience does some of the lapping. I don't like using Karlene Robins that way."

"It doesn't diminish the truth, or what you'll do."

"A day late for her, and a hell of a lot more than a dollar short."

She would think that way, he knew. It made her what she was. "I hear—as the grapevine climbs quickly—that you were already taking steps to inform and protect those connected to this old MacMasters arrest when you were called to the scene of this second murder."

"I knew it was connected to MacMasters, something on the job. I knew it was personal, and I believed it was a mirror of another crime. But it took me two days to find it."

"Eve, don't do this. The data wasn't there to be found. There was no Irene Schultz to show up on your search of rape-murder victims. The very nature of who these people are—were—may be tomorrow— makes it tricky and time-consuming to find them. Consider the fact you found this connection at all, and will save the lives of other targets."

"I know you can't save them all. I know it. But when you have to swallow that hours would have made the difference, it doesn't go down easy. She was getting married on Saturday. Robins."

"Ah. Well." Following instinct he put his hands on her shoulders, drew her in.

"I'm standing in that apartment where she lived with the man she was marrying in a couple days, and I'm seeing all that wedding junk. Like at Louise's. Goddamn it, Roarke."

He said nothing. There was nothing to be said.

"I know you can't save them all," she repeated. "I know you can't catch them all, and even some you catch will slither through the system. But this one's not going to. Sick, smug son of a bitch."

"All right then. What's next?"

She stepped away. "We interview all those involved in the Irene Schultz matter, and we find out if he's made contact with anyone's daughter, son, sister, brother, mother, father, second cousin twice removed. We set up for tomorrow's memorial. We work the case. We push on the electronics. And why aren't you huddled with your EDD pals?"

"We'll discuss that at the briefing."

"Then let's get started."

In the conference room, Eve gave a brief overview of the investigation for the benefit of the members she'd added to the team. She followed it with a report on the early steps of the Robins case.

"Peabody."

"After the notification to Hampton, I went to City Choice. I spoke with the vic's supervisor and two of her coworkers. None of them could identify the suspect by the pictures we have. It's not unusual for a client not to come in to the offices, and in fact, more usual for the real estate agent to meet same at a property or another location."

"Handy for him."

"All three individuals I spoke with recall the vic speaking of a Drew Pittering, and one, specifically recalls the vic telling her she'd tapped a new client when he contacted her. Her office log lists a contact from Pittering on May fifteenth, with the note he was looking most specifically for space in SoHo, and his preferences for same. It also lists meeting him at two properties in that sector, and providing him with two virtual tours of other locations. Finally, it lists her appointment with him at the SoHo loft for nine-thirty a.m., yesterday."

"Reineke, Jenkinson, you'll follow up with the other properties, knock on doors, show the photo. Peabody," she repeated.

"EDD has all the electronics from her home and her work space, as well as those from the crime scene. With a grief counselor I notified the victim's parents." She let out a breath. "Um. When questioned, Jaynie Robins did not immediately recall Irene Schultz or the case. She agreed to come into Central today to speak with the lieutenant, and stated she would look through her archive of case notes and files to try to refresh herself on the matter. The fact is, she was pretty shaken up, and I'm not sure she was taking in any of the details on this old case. I left them with the grief counselor, and they'll be escorted in shortly."

"Okay. Good work. Feeney, progress?"

"I'm going to pass this to the civilian."

When Eve looked toward Roarke, Feeney shook his head. "Wrong civilian. Brief the lieutenant, Jamie."

"McNab and I have been putting in some long hours on this, and back with Feeney and Roarke and a couple of the others upstairs. But we just couldn't figure any way to speed the cleaning process. Not with the extent of the corruption. Then Roarke said something about trying to split another matrix clone on a second JPL and merge texels with the corrupted pixels and stir up the ppi to defuck the bitmapping."

"Did you say defuck?" Eve asked. "Is that a technical term?"

"Ah, it just sort of expresses the procedure. See, for this particular application, the regions are made up of supixels, and when infected the standard triad—"

"Stop the madness." She resisted, barely, just slapping her hands over her ears. "I'm begging you."

"Well, it's frosty max if you get how it works and why. When Roarke talked about the clone and merge, I started thinking maybe we could go rad and do a merge and ramp, input an HIP to counteract, then extrapolate, do the clone, and restart the defuck from that point."

"Makes me proud," Feeney said as Eve pressed her fingers to her eyes.

"Will somebody just give me the progress. In English?"

"Picture's worth a thousand. Put it up, Jamie," Feeney ordered.

"Roger that." Using a remote, Jamie displayed an image on screen.

Eve shifted, stepped back. There, on screen, Darrin Pauley was captured in midstep as he climbed the stairs to the victim's front door. He wore a cap, which she identified as from Columbia, shades, and a shy smile. Deena, young, pretty, beaming, stood in the open doorway, her hand held out for his.

"Excellent," Eve murmured.

"Bloody brilliant," Roarke stated.

"I wouldn't've thought of it if you hadn't started the ball." Jamie nodded toward Roarke. "And you were the one who actually did the conversion and—"

Roarke shot a finger at Jamie. "Bloody brilliant."

"Well." Though he shrugged, pleasure shone on Jamie's face. "Yeah."

"The PA will have to be a complete

screwup not to cage this bastard for First Degree. But we have to catch him first. Can you do the same with the SoHo security?"

"Now that we've identified the virus, have the process?" Feeney bared his teeth in a smile. "We'll have all of the Mac-Masters and the SoHo vids for you before end of shift."

"Nice work, all of you. Damn nice work. He's wearing a backpack, handy for holding his supplies. The same shoes the wit ID'd from the park."

"That brings me to retail," Peabody put in. "I've got a strong lead on the shoes, and the rest. An outlet right on campus, which unfortunately screwed my downtown hunch. The shoes, the sweatshirt, sweatpants, cap, shades, backpack, airboard, several T-shirts, and a windbreaker were purchased there by a Donald Petrie, on March thirty-first."

"Address?"

"The address that came up is in Ohio, and actually is the home of one Donal Petri, age sixty-eight, who was pretty steamed when he got the charges for a bunch of stuff from a college outlet in New

York. He reported the fraud in mid-April upon getting the bill. I've got the name of the clerk whose ID number was on the sale. I haven't yet been able to contact. She's a student at the university."

"We'll run it down. Tomorrow's memorial," Eve continued and outlined the plan.

Toward the end of the briefing, Eve received word the Robinses were being escorted into Central. Because she wanted privacy, she directed them to be taken to Interview A. She gathered the case file on Irene Schultz and the mug shot.

She found them sitting together at the table, hands linked. She supposed the best term for the way they looked would be shell-shocked.

"Mr. and Mrs. Robins, I'm Lieutenant Dallas. You remember Detective Peabody. We want to thank you for coming in like this, and to offer our sincere sympathy for your loss."

"I talked to her yesterday morning." Jaynie's voice quavered. "When she was on her way to . . . that appointment. I wanted to tell her my sister and her family were getting in this morning. My niece, her cousin, is one of the bridesmaids. We were going to have a get-together tonight. She was so excited. About the wedding, and she was so confident she'd make this sale. She was so happy."

"She talked to you about this man?"

"Not really. She just said it was the perfect client for the perfect property, and the sale would be the perfect wedding gift. I have her dress, her wedding dress." Disbelief swirled with the grief in Jaynie's eyes. "I'm keeping it because she doesn't want Tony to see it. It's in the closet in her bedroom at home."

Peabody put a cup of water on the table, laid a hand on Jaynie's shoulder before taking her seat across the table.

"He didn't care about her, Mrs. Robins. But I do." Eve waited until the woman looked at her again, focused on her. "I care about Karlene, and with your help I'm going to find the person responsible and see that he pays for what he did to her."

"She didn't do anything to *him*." Owen Robins stared out of shattered eyes. "She never hurt anyone."

"He doesn't care," Eve repeated. "Not about Karlene, not about sixteen-year-old

Deena MacMasters. He cares about what he sees as payback. He cares about hurting everyone he believes took something from him. Irene Schultz. That's all he cares about."

Eve took the photo from the file, laid it on the table. "I need you to try to remember her."

"I looked back at my archives. It was so long ago. I believed in the work, believed in putting the welfare and best interest of the child above all. Still, it was never easy to remove a child from the home, even when it was best. I lasted almost ten years. A long time. Then we moved to Brooklyn, and I counsel families. I try to help. I always did."

"I understand."

"I don't really remember her, this woman. Not clearly, I'm sorry. There were so many. Too many. My notes, I brought them. You can have them. I made note that the living conditions seemed very good, and the child well-cared for. Temporary removal was based on the mother's arrest, and the suspicion that the father was complicit. There were no friends or relatives, so the boy was placed with a foster family. And he was returned to the father within forty-eight hours. I don't understand how he could take my child's life because I put him in a safe place for two days. He wasn't harmed."

"Do you remember anything about the father?"

"I have in my notes he was upset, but polite. That he appeared to relate well to the child, showed concern for him. He packed toys and clothes for the child himself, and soothed the boy when he said good-bye. I would have testified to that in court, had it become necessary."

Her lips trembled until she had to press them hard together to still them. "It's important to make note of the relationship, the environment. I have in my notes that in the initial observation he appeared to be a good parent. As he was cleared of any knowledge of his wife's illegal activities, the child was returned to him. There were no follow-ups, and the case was closed."

"All right. Thank you."

"It's no help. None of it helps Karlene."

"I think your notes and impressions will be a great help. I'm going to have you taken back home. I have to ask you not to speak to the media. They'll come, they'll push. For the sake of other children he may have targeted, I'm going to ask you to say nothing to anyone about this conversation. For the best interest of the child, Mrs. Robins."

"You'll keep us informed about . . . you'll tell us?"

"You have my word." Rising, she went to the door, signaled the uniforms waiting. "These officers will take you back home."

"We need to go to Tony."

"They'll take you there. They'll take you wherever you need to go."

Peabody watched them go. "It was good of you to tell them they helped. They really didn't."

"We can't know what might help."

"It breaks my heart, Dallas. Instead of going to their daughter's wedding, they'll go to her funeral."

"Then let's make damn sure it's the last funeral he's responsible for."

18

When Eve found Roarke in her office again, she frowned. "Why are you still here?"

"They don't need me in EDD at this point. I can deal with some of my own work as easily from here as anywhere, with the benefit of being with my wife."

"I'm going back in the field. I have to go by the morgue, then track down the student who sold the suspect his gear."

"I've nothing more interesting to do."

She considered it. She could leave Peabody to write and file the reports, nag the lab, run the probabilities on which target might be next.

"Fine. You're with me."

"My favorite place."

With the work dumped on Peabody, Eve took the morgue first.

"You don't need to go in. I don't expect any surprises here, no revelations. It's just procedure."

"In any case." He continued down the white tunnel with her. "I remember when we brought Nixie here," he said, speaking of the little girl whose family had been slaughtered in a home invasion. "Brutal. But then, I suppose, it always is. She's doing well with Elizabeth and Richard, and young Kevin. They're making a family. I think she's able to do that because you gave her resolution."

"She's tough. She'll make it okay." She paused outside the doors to Morris's suite. "The one who's responsible for what's in there? He didn't have to crawl through his mother's blood like Nixie did, he didn't have his entire family slaughtered in their own beds. He doesn't have half Nixie's spine. He's weak, and

I'm going to give him one hell of a resolution."

There, Roarke thought, there she was. She could feel the blame, and the pain—perhaps she needed to—but she could and would always come back to purpose.

Morris wore mourning black today, with a shirt of deep red. Music wove quietly through the air as he closed the Y-cut on Karlene with sure strokes.

"You're done with her?"

"I started on her immediately. Hello, Roarke."

"Morris. How are you?"

"Better than I was. I hoped I wouldn't see either of you until the wedding, and under much happier circumstances. I pushed the tox screen," he told Eve. "And found the same combination, though I might have missed it if I hadn't been specifically looking. She'd been dosed approximately six and a half hours prior to death, and in a lesser amount than our first."

"He realized he didn't need her to be out as long," Eve concluded. "And he didn't have as much time to work on her. Or didn't want to take as much time."

"Other than that, and the use of elasticized cord rather than police restraints, his method remains the same. Bound, ankles and wrists. Ankle restraints removed and reapplied. Multiple rapes, vaginal and anal, an almost casual beating considering the violence of the rapes. Sporadic smothering and choking. COD manual strangulation. She fought. As evidenced by the abrasions, lacerations, contusions on her wrists and ankles."

"He varies in small ways to suit the circumstances, but sticks with the overall method."

"There's one other variation," Morris said. "She was pregnant."

"Shit." It punched straight through her. "Goddamn it."

"Under a week along. She may not have known."

Eve shoved at her hair. She didn't bother to curse again. "Her people are going to come in. Her parents, her cohab. They were getting married Saturday."

Morris released a long sigh. "Fate's a cruel bastard."

"Fuck fate, people are cruel bastards. There's no need to tell her people about the pregnancy, unless they ask. Not yet anyway."

"No, there's not." He stepped back. "First the virgin, now the bride."

"What?" Eve's head came up, her eyes sharpened. "Wait. What comes after?"

"After?"

"Virgin, bride—what's next? If it's a kind of progression. Logical, organized. What's after bride?"

"Newlywed," Morris suggested.

"Wife. For some . . ." Roarke looked down at Karlene with pity. "Pregnancy, motherhood. A cynic might say divorce often fits in there at some point."

"It might be a way of selecting the order, even the specific vic. You drive. I want to work it. Thanks, Morris."

She had her PPC out even as she strode back down the tunnel.

"It would be monumentally fortunate from his point of view," Roarke said, "for him to be able to find the proper victims for the sort of progression you're proposing."

"I don't think so. They don't have to be female—though I imagine he prefers. Newlywed—either sex. Then you could say husband instead of wife, expectant father, and so on. He's got kids, grand-kids, siblings, parents—maybe extended family—to choose from."

She slid into the car. "I told Peabody to work probability on stage of contact. Mac-Masters, then the CS supervisor, the CS rep, the PD. Maybe he's picking them in order of appearance. Or maybe this way. But there has to be some sort of selection process. A timetable, for trolling them, re-searching them, arranging the meet, de-veloping the relationship. And there's overlap. He contacted Karlene while he was working Deena. Started the second round before finishing the first."

"So, by that criteria, he's started round three."

"Yeah, and maybe beyond that. I fig-ured the PD most likely, and we're on her, but she doesn't have anyone who fits this other progression." Eve shook her head as she scanned the data. "She's been di-vorced six years, no kids. She has a sis-ter, married over twenty-five years—that's no newlywed. A niece and a nephew, nei-ther married."

"You don't have to be married to be

pregnant, or to have a relationship that results in a pregnancy."

"Good point. Could be one of them for that stage if so, could be the sister for the wife—the long-term kind. We'll keep them covered, but I don't think they're next."

"Speaking of next, where am I going?"

"Hmm? Columbia. I need to find the clerk. She lists a dorm as her address, and the retail place as her employment. She hasn't answered her 'link and hasn't returned any of Peabody's requests for contact. I just want to tie that one up."

"Then why not go to the orchard?"

"Trees?"

"And pick a Peach." He used the in-dash 'link to do it himself.

Dressed in a power-red suit and shoes that emphasized her height—and made Eve's ankles throb when she noted them—Peach Lapkoff waited outside the administration building. Those razor-sharp eyes took on a sultry hue as she held out both hands to Roarke.

"It's wonderful to see you."

Eve stood by, brows raised as they bussed cheeks. "And you," Roarke said. "You look brilliant."

"I'm off to reach into the deep pockets of some alumni shortly. It's best to look the part. Lieutenant." She offered Eve her hand. "I've found Fiona. She's been in a two-day retreat. No communication devices allowed. I've had her pulled out, as it seemed important enough to interrupt. She'll be brought here. I wasn't sure if you'd require my office, or some other area."

"It's not necessary. It shouldn't take long."

"I heard the reports that there'd been another murder. Another young woman raped and murdered."

"We can't confirm the cases are connected."

"The media doesn't have a problem throwing out speculations about a serial killer, targeting young women. We have a lot of young women on campus. There's serious concern."

"I'd advise your students and staff to take sensible precautions. But the media's claims or speculations have no confirmation from the NYPSD."

Peach continued to stare at Eve as if trying to X-ray her brain. "I was worried when you requested Fiona Wallace be located. That you might have reason to believe she's in some danger."

"Absolutely not. It pertains to a sale she made last March in Sports Center that may connect to the investigation."

"I'm relieved." Peach's gaze shifted over Eve's head. "Here she comes."

"Do you recognize all your students on sight, Dr. Lapkoff?"

"Peach," she said. "No, I don't, but I looked her up when you requested I locate her. Miss Wallace."

"Dr. Lapkoff." The girl was no more than twenty with skin pale as the moon and what looked to be several pounds of red hair piled on top of her head. She was slightly out of breath from, Eve concluded, the trip across campus and fear at being summoned by the president.

"You're not in any trouble." The power female took on a faint maternal tone. "And you won't be penalized for the time out of the retreat. This is Lieutenant Dallas, with the NYPSD. She hopes you can help her."

"Help?"

"Yes. Would you like me to step away, Lieutenant?"

"It's not necessary. You work at Sports Center."

"Yes, ma'am. I'm a year-round student, and I work there to help with living expenses. I've worked there for over a year now."

"You were working there on March thirty-first."

"Ah. I'm not sure. Maybe."

"You sold several items to this man." Eve drew out the sketch. "Do you remember him?"

"I'm not sure. Exactly. It's over two months ago, and we're a really popular store. It can get really busy."

"I have a list of what he bought. It might help you remember." Eve started down the list, saw Fiona blink when she got to the shoes. "You remember?"

"I do. It was a really big sale, and the shoes are really high. I remember because I told him they were going on sale, for one day, in just another week. Ten percent, and that's a lot when they go for three and a half bills, you know? But he wanted them right then. He looked a little different from this picture. That's why I didn't recognize him right away."

"How so?"

"His hair was a lot longer, and wavy. He had mag hair. He was really cute. I guess I flirted with him a little, the way you do, asked if he lived on campus, and what his major was. I think he said he was living off campus. He was nice, but he didn't flirt back, so I figured he was seeing someone or I didn't push the buzzer for him. I made some joke about him hitting the jackpot or something because he was buying so much. I remember he smiled, because, wow, killer smile. And he said—because I thought it was funny—clothes make the man. It seemed like a weird thing to say when he's buying sweatshirts and that kind of thing. I bagged it all up, and he left."

"Have you seen him since?"

"No, I don't think so."

"Okay, Fiona. Thanks."

"Did he do something illegal?"

"We're interested in talking to him. If you do see him, do me a favor. Don't approach him, and contact me." Eve handed her a card.

"Sure. Should I go back to the retreat now?"

"Yes," Peach told her. "Straight back."

"Yes, ma'am."

"Did that help?" Peach asked as Fiona hurried off.

"It confirms some information, continues to establish pattern, and tells me he's got smug going up against careful, and sometimes smug wins. Yeah, that's helpful. As you've been. Thank you."

"I'm happy I could help, and I hope the media reports, very soon, that you've arrested this man."

"So do I."

When they reached the car, Roarke asked, "What next?"

"I need to go back over the list of names and data of those connected with the Irene Schultz arrest. I need to talk to them, all of them, and try to figure out his next target."

"They don't all live in New York."

"No." She got into the car. "But he's got, apparently, an endless supply of IDs, and credit to go with them. Maybe his next target's in New York, maybe not. I need to interview all the connections to possible targets to try to work it out."

"Not all the connections live in New York either, or in the city. You could, of course, shuttle around to and from, or conduct the interviews via 'link."

"I'd rather a face-to-face, but it's not practical, so most of it will have to be by 'link. The problem is people expand. They get married and/or have kids. The kids do the same. Or they have sibs who do it. In twenty-odd years, you've got a horde spiraling out of one person."

"People and their propensity for progeny." Amused at her, Roarke shook his head. "What can be done?"

"What I'd like to do is get them all into Central, take them one at a time, then if necessary, pool them altogether, to see if one person's answers jogs something salient from another."

"I can arrange that."

She slanted him a bland look as he drove them home. "What? You'll have everyone transported to Central—from wherever they happen to be? Not only impractical, but plenty of them won't go for it. Another problem with people is they have lives, and can get fussy when asked to put them on hold to aid in a police investigation they may or may not believe really involves them."

"There's transporting," he said, "and there's transporting."

"Well, sure, your transports are all slick and shiny, but—"

"Eve, while I often have to travel for business, or have someone brought in, how much more often do I conduct business halfway around the world, even off planet, without leaving New York?"

"Yeah, but you've got . . ." She had a sudden memory of walking into his office unannounced while he conducted a meeting. A holographic meeting. "It could work," she considered. "We don't use holo for interviews generally because if you're dealing with a suspect, even witnesses in some cases, the defense will try to get anything gathered by that method tossed. It's tricky because it can be manipulated. You want to make it solid, you need a confession or hard evidence face-to-face, on record. But this . . ."

"You're not looking for a confession, not interviewing suspects, or even people of interest."

"Yeah, it could work. I'll want to run it by an APA, make sure there's no procedural angle I need to cover. If any information I get leads to an arrest, we don't want some slick lawyer trying to claim the information was tainted, therefore, blah, blah. But I think we can do this."

"You used holo on Ricker."

"Yeah, and he's already doing life without possibility of parole. They can try to dance around the method for slapping him with conspiracy on Coltraine. But you order a cop's murder, from the inside of an off-planet penal colony where holo-visitations and legal consultations are allowed? It's going to be hard for anyone to argue the method, and I cleared it first. Cleo wasn't part of the holo, and she was allowed to view it. I didn't use any evidence, per se, from the holo in drawing her confession, and I, again, cleared it first. The judge already tossed her lawyer's petition to dismiss on that one."

"I'm glad to hear it."

"I think we can use this, if the parties agree. I'd save hours of time, and have the next-best to face-to-face. I just need to make sure our ass is covered on it."

"You cover the asses, and I'll set it up."

"How long to set it up?"

"The basic program, twenty minutes at

most. Then I'd need the coordinates of those you want to bring in. It would take a few minutes to triangulate each holo."

"It bears repeating. You're handy to have around." She took out her 'link and contacted APA Cher Reo.

There was, as expected, some legal jumbo. But even with it, she would save considerable time. She continued to consult with Reo as she walked into the house, and thought one advantage to legal crap was the opportunity to totally ignore Summerset.

Once she got the nod, she began making the contacts and arrangements. She'd hit the halfway point when Roarke beeped through. "The program's set, in the holoroom. I need those coordinates."

"I'll bring them to you. Peabody can make the rest of the contacts. Five minutes."

She routed the rest to her partner, then gathered what she needed. She used the elevator, and stepped out into a larger and somehow swankier version of her home office.

"Hmm."

"Appearances can count. One of these

days, you might consider replacing that desk of yours with a workstation like this one."

She frowned at the dark, shiny surface of the U-shaped console, its built-in D and C unit and sleek control panel.

"I like my desk."

"Yes, I know." He kissed her lightly, then pointed to a table at the rear of the room. "Have a sandwich."

"We have sandwiches?"

"Eat. You can station yourself at the desk, if you like. Knowing you, I assume you'll be on your feet most of the time. Your interview subject can be placed at any chair, or the sofa. The unit here, and the wall screen are both fully operational should you need them."

Slick, she thought. Very slick. "It has to be recorded."

"It will be."

Because he pointed at the table again, she picked up a sandwich. "Let's bring Peabody in first."

He nodded, used his own 'link.

"Peabody." Peabody's face went glowy at the sight of Roarke. "Oh, hey. Hi!"

"Hi. The lieutenant would like you to join us."

"Okay. Wow. I've never holo'd before."

"I'll be gentle," he said and made her giggle. "There. I have you. Initiating."

Little dots of lights swirled, then the swirl became Peabody.

"Oh. Gee. That was easy. It didn't feel weird." She looked around, blinking. "It is weird, but it didn't feel weird. What's that?"

"What? It's a sandwich."

"Oh, it's a panini. It really looks good."

"There's more over there. Help yourself."

"Thanks." Peabody turned to the table, reached out, and her hand passed straight through sandwich and tray. "That was just mean. I can't help myself because I'm not really here. But I am here. I don't understand holo-science. Every time McNab tries to explain it to me, my brain goes to sleep."

"Let's leave that to the geeks and be cops. Finish the contacts, get the waivers. I'll connect with the PD again, then we'll bring her in."

It was weird, Eve admitted, but it was

also smooth and efficient. In moments, she had the former public defender sitting in her programmed office.

"I appreciate the time, Ms. Drobski."

"It's no problem. I'd like to get this business resolved as soon as possible. It's unnerving."

"I'm sure it is. Your safety, and the safety of your family is a priority."

"You have viable evidence that I—or my family—is being targeted? Evidence that substantially links this jeopardy to a defendant I represented more than twenty years ago?"

"You're thinking like a lawyer. I'm thinking like a cop. Which one do you want to trust your life to, and the lives of your family?"

The woman shifted either in discomfort or annoyance. "I'm here, aren't I?"

"You were shown an artist rendering of the suspect. Are you still certain you've never seen this man before? On screen image, Darrin Pauley."

Drobski studied the screen. "I haven't, not to my knowledge."

"You have a brother."

"Yes, Lyle. As I told you, he's a financial consultant. I spoke with him, and he's been shown the sketch, as has his wife, and their son. I'm concerned enough that I've been through this with my parents, and they live in Arizona. None of them recognize this man."

"Who are you closest to?"

"I'm sorry?"

"In your family. Who are you closest to?"

"That's very difficult to . . . my father, I suppose. He's the reason I became a lawyer. I can promise you, Lieutenant, he's not naive or gullible enough to allow himself or my mother to be put in danger. And he's targeting women, isn't he?"

"We don't rule out a change to male target. Who else is there?"

"I don't have any other family."

"Who else are you close to? Family isn't always blood."

"Oh. God." For the first time, Drobski looked shaken. "Lincoln, Lincoln Matters. We've been involved for over a year now, and my partner, Elysse Wagman. We're very close, have been since college. She . . . she's like a sister."

"Peabody."

"On it."

"You think he might go after Lincoln or Elysse? I need to tell them—"

"We're taking care of it right now. Is Elysse married, cohabbing?"

"No. In fact she just came out the other side of a difficult divorce. She has a daughter, my goddaughter, Renny. She's only eleven."

"We'll take care of them." She saw Peabody give her the nod out of the corner of her eye. "Police officers are on their way to her residence right now, and to Lincoln's. When we've finished, I'll contact both of them myself, and explain everything."

"You really think it could be—"

"I'm not going to take any chances. I want you to tell me everything you remember about the Irene Schultz case."

"I remember it very well. I hadn't been a PD long, and I was still idealistic. Green. I felt, since she didn't have any priors, she had a young child, I could make a good deal for her. I figured I'd get them to kick the illegals charge, the solicitation, maybe plead it down to a year, and mandatory rehab. Maybe get part of the year in a halfway. Then even before I talked to her, I got the whiff that they wanted her husband, and maybe I could get her straight into halfway and rehab with no cage time if she flipped on him."

"But she didn't."

"Wouldn't. She insisted, even to me, he had no part in what she'd done, no knowledge of it. I explained, tried to nudge her some, but she wouldn't budge. I tried the mom card. I really wanted to help her. She wouldn't be able to take care of her little boy if she was in prison. But, she stuck. Worse, when the APA came in the next morning to deal, she insisted on taking the first round. I could've dealt it down to a year, but she wouldn't let me. I felt like a failure."

"Did you speak with the husband?"

"Yeah. He was angry. Outraged when I told him she'd taken the eighteen. He said she shouldn't do more than a year inside. I agreed with him, but he blamed me. When I told him she wouldn't let me try to deal, he calmed down some, even apologized. When we went into court, he brought the baby. A really beautiful baby."

Her gaze went back to the wall screen.

"God. I held him. I held that baby while Irene and her husband had a minute. I actually held him. I felt sick when he cried for his mother. Sick that I hadn't been able to do more. You get over that after a while, after being buried under the work, the system. That's when you have to get out, when you get over being sick you couldn't do more."

When Eve felt she'd gotten everything she could, she brought in Elysse Wagman, keeping Drobski in place as both of them requested.

The woman absorbed the information Eve gave her, took it all in without a flinch. "I'm going to send my daughter to Colorado, to my mother. Tonight."

"Lissy, you should go, too. You should—"

"Ms. Wagman." Eve interrupted Drobski's worry. "I understand your concern for your daughter's safety. The officers will assist you in any way they can with the arrangements for her transportation to your mother. I can't order you to stay, but I will ask you. If you have been targeted, any change in routine may tip him off. We can and will protect you."

"For how long?"

"As long as necessary. Would you please take another look at the image on screen? A closer look."

"I'm just not sure, either way."

"He may have longer hair, or shorter. He could look just a little older."

"Longer hair," she murmured. "It could be . . . Jesus, it could be. Longer hair and a beard. Dom Patrelli."

Bingo, Eve thought. Even as she turned to order Peabody to run it, her partner was working her PPC. "How do you know him?"

"I do pro bono work out of a legal-aid clinic, Lower East Side. About three weeks ago, when I was leaving this— he—came running up. Out of breath. Asked if I was Elysse Wagman. He said he was a journalist, and doing a spec piece on women in law with an emphasis on domestic cases. It's my specialty. He said he'd run behind, had tried to get there before the clinic closed, asked if he could just walk with me, ask me some questions. I didn't see the harm. He was charming and earnest, and so interested in the work we're doing."

"He gave you his name, his credentials."

"Yes. I guess it was kind of quick, he was a bit fumbly. But we were right on the street. He just walked with me for a few blocks, asked the right sort of questions. He'd done some good background on the clinic. I was impressed, and pleased. We can use some positive exposure. He bought me a cup of coffee from a glide-cart, and asked if he could contact me if he had any follow-ups."

"And did he?"

"The next week, he was waiting outside the clinic when I closed up, with coffee. I had some time, so we walked over to the park, sat on a bench, drank coffee while we did his follow-up. He was . . . he was a little flirty, nothing over the top or offensive. I was flattered. He's twenty years younger, easily, and I . . . I'm an idiot."

"No. He's very good at what he does."

"We talked, that's all, and it came out he's a fan of Zapoto's films."

"Jesus," Drobski murmured.

"I know. I'm a rabid fan, and we got into that, debating, dissecting. There was a mini-festival in Tribeca that weekend."

"You went out with him."

Elysse moistened her lips, pushed at her hair.

Nervous, Eve thought, but equal parts embarrassed.

"I met him there Saturday night. We had drinks after, a little dinner. God, I actually told him I couldn't ask him back to my place because of my daughter, which was an obvious way of saying let's go to his. And he said his roommate's mother was visiting, and it would be awkward. Then he kissed me and put me in a cab. He kissed me," she repeated, pressing her hand to her lips.

"We went out again the next week— just lunch, soy dogs down on the wharf. He made me feel young, sexy—and eager," she confessed, "because he said he wanted me to have a little more time. I'd told him about the divorce, and my daughter. I told him about my girl. He wanted me to have more time because he wanted me to be sure."

"When are you seeing him again?"

"A week from Friday. He's working this weekend."

Not if I can help it, Eve thought.

19 "She's not the next in line," Eve said. "He's playing her along, stringing it out. Divorced—that's a couple steps further along. He plays her perfectly. Changes his look, his image. Young, but not too young, flirtatious, but not too, interested in what interests her—knowledgeable about those interests."

"She doesn't tell anybody about him because it's early days yet," Peabody put in. "And she feels a little foolish contemplating an affair with someone twenty years younger."

"He doesn't have a house 'link, he tells

her, his pocket's broken. He hasn't gotten around to replacing it. He doesn't want her contacting him yet. He needs to keep her anxious and off balance. He's got the power. But she's not next."

"Somebody else is." Concern covered Peabody's face as she studied the images of possible targets Eve had displayed on the rear wall screen. "And probably this weekend."

"He doesn't get another one. Let's take the child services supervisor, then the APA."

She downed coffee between interviews and gave Peabody a twenty-minute break to grab a sandwich of her own.

She began to see the steps, the stages, the story that took place twenty years before, and thought she understood the players, their roles, their choices.

"She went down for him," Roarke concluded. "He conned her into it, or convinced her in that call she made after the bust. 'We can't both go down, baby, who'll take care of the boy?'"

"That, maybe," Eve agreed, "but he'd already been in once. Prints on file. They'd bust him hard on the ID fraud if she admitted he'd been involved, and he'd do more than the eighteen months for the second offense. He'd use that. 'You'll do a year, sugar, and I'll be there for you. If they look at me, it's five to seven.'"

"You got that right. He had more on the line than she did."

"And he'd need her to go down quick and clean, make it easy for the cops and the PA. No fuss, no muss, no looking too hard at him."

"And more, I think more, if they both went down, there'd be no one to maintain their identities. He could push that. The center wouldn't hold, and they'd be exposed for what they were. A lot more than a year and a half at stake. And she's the one who got caught, wasn't she? She's the one who got careless. Why should they lose it all when she could suck it up?"

"That's my take," Eve agreed. "He'd already gone in once, and he wasn't going back. Some time, some dealing, some pleading hardship, she could've gotten off with the year, and part of that, maybe most, in a halfway, mandatory rehab. But that would've made it risky for him. The quicker she goes down, the quicker he's clear. But it's more, I think."

Sliding her hands into her pockets, she wandered the room so familiar—an illusion, but familiar. And remembered.

"With my mother, I'm vague. It's blurry with only a few clear flashes. But I know— I knew—she hated the . . . fact of me. But she had me, and she stayed at least long enough for me to have a few pictures in my head, to remember specific events."

"As Darrin Pauley does?"

"Whatever he remembers, or has been taught to remember is different. I know I wasn't a child to either of them. I was a commodity. A potential income. But did they come up with that together, or did one convince the other? That's a question I'll never have the answer to, and isn't important."

She wouldn't let it be important.

"But in this case, maybe it is."

"Why she chose, or they chose to have the boy," Roarke continued.

"She's the player, the brains, the front man. He's the manipulator who likes the flash and she taught him what she knew.

The sex, the drugs, that's cheap money, and lacks finesse. Quick and greedy, like you said. She had to have finesse to play Pauley for a year. And the kid? He should've been baggage, she should have shucked that off. She didn't. So she either wanted the kid or she wanted Pauley—maybe both. The kid wasn't a commodity. Maybe a cover, but even that's a stretch."

"Easier to move, to blend, to work the grift without an infant to tend to," Roarke agreed.

"When Pauley got out, they could've left the kid with Vinnie. Poofed."

"Taking them both, the woman Vinnie loved, the child he thought was his? It's cruel."

"Fits the pattern. She was clean and healthy, and they had a decent stake—one they stole from Vinnie—and in a couple of years, she's using and soliciting. And it shapes up that he was running the show."

"Easy money," Roarke concurred, "with her doing the work."

"It's Pauley, he was her weakness. She whored for him, and dealt for him—and somewhere along the line he started running the show, looking for easier money, more flash, more cash. By the time she did her eighteen and they shifted to Chicago, he was in full charge."

She took a breath. "That's the way it was, that's the way I remember it. The way it felt to me when I remember them together, or get those flashes of events. She was a junkie and a whore—and he ran the show. So maybe I'm projecting."

"I don't think so."

She shook her head. "That's for later, maybe it'll be useful. We have to deal with the now. Let's get Peabody back and take the judge."

He went to her first, took her face in his hands. "Whatever you remember, or feel, you need to know that whatever they were they did one worthwhile thing in their miserable lives. And that was you. Whatever they were, they couldn't destroy that. They couldn't stop you from becoming."

Judge Serenity Mimoto, a trim and tiny woman, studied the sketch of Darrin Pauley on screen. "He looks like his father."

"You remember the father?"

Mimoto cut intense eyes to Eve. Their

striking azure color radiated against smooth hazelnut skin. "I refreshed myself on the matter, and those involved, when your office contacted me earlier. I'm familiar with the details of the case. The defendant, through her attorney, had reached an agreement with the prosecutor. She pled guilty to all charges, with the APA recommending a sentence of eighteen months. Taking into account the nonviolent nature of the crimes, the lack of previous criminal record, the defendant's cooperation and plea, I so ordered. She was remanded to the Minimum Security facility at Rikers."

Mimoto nodded toward the screen again. "And I remember him, the baby in his father's arms, crying for his mother. I allowed them a moment to say good-bye. She took the boy briefly, very briefly, then passed him to her attorney and embraced the man. I thought, so she has no comfort to give her son, but needs to take it from the father."

"You haven't seen him, the father or the son, since that day in court?"

"No, I don't believe I have. If this young man's case comes before me, when

you've arrested him, I'll be forced to re-
cuse myself due to this conversation, and
the previous connection. So I'll ask you,
Lieutenant, do you have enough for an arrest?"

"I believe we do, and will have more."

Mimoto inclined her head. "You hope I
can provide you with some of that more."

"Yes, I do, and by doing so prevent him
from harming someone close to you. You
pronounced the sentence that put his
mother in prison. Six months after her release, when she, her son, and her partner
were going by different names, and I believe continuing the confidence games
and illegal activities that resulted in her
arrest and incarceration, she was raped
and murdered in a manner nearly identical to that of my two victims."

"And you believe this is the man responsible for two murders, because he
somehow blames his mother's death on
her arrest and incarceration?"

Eve appreciated Mimoto's calm demeanor as much as her quick understanding. "Yes, and I believe he's been
indoctrinated to make that connection
throughout his life."

Mimoto lifted a sharp black eyebrow. "That's for the psychiatrists and lawyers to sort out. He won't come after me. That's a pity as it wouldn't be the first time I've been threatened or targeted in my twenty-six years on the bench. Someone in my family. I have a very large family, Lieutenant."

"Yes, Your Honor, you do. Four siblings, all currently married, three children, also all currently married. Eight grandchildren."

"And another on the way."

"Ma'am. Your oldest granddaughter is also married."

"And made me a great-grandmother only yesterday."

"Oh." That one hadn't made the data records yet, Eve thought. How did *anyone* keep track? "Congratulations."

"A boy. Spiro Clayton, seven pounds, eight ounces."

"Um. Nice." She supposed. "Your husband, who has four siblings and so on. Your parents, and all four of your grandparents."

"Along with various aunts, uncles, cousins, nieces, nephews, and the prog-

eny thereof. We are, one could say, le-
gion."

Exactly, Eve thought. Where to begin?

"I've found a pattern, Your Honor. A
way he chooses his targets. From the . . .
breadth of your family, I don't doubt there
would be a member who fit any of his criteria. However, I have established contact with three other potential targets, so
fining down the remaining pattern to two
of his requirements. I'm looking for someone you're close to—in that family or
someone you consider as family—who is
recently married or who has recently lost
a spouse through death."

"A beginning and an end."

"The probability is extremely high these
are the two parameters left. I should add,
it's possible he hasn't yet made contact
with the widow or widower. While this is,
by pattern established, the last target, the
newlywed will almost certainly be next,
and may be targeted for this coming
weekend."

For the first time the enigmatic face
showed a frisson of fear. "So soon. Lieutenant, we are, fortunately, long-lived in

my family. We have suffered loss, of course. An aunt who was dear to me passed only a year ago."

"I'll take the information, but I believe the target will be female. Both his victims and the three targets we've established have been women."

"Ah . . . a cousin a few months ago. His wife—" She pressed a finger to her temple. "I'll have to check. She lives in Prague. My mother would have all the information. She's a family database."

"Someone closer. He doesn't want to hurt you, but devastate you."

"None of my children or grandchildren are recently married. Two of the grandchildren are engaged. I have a niece who was married last summer, another who'll be married this fall. And . . ." She trailed off, shaking her head. "Let me take an hour or so on this. I'll contact my mother. She'll know. In fact, she'll have a list of everyone and their current address from the renewal ceremony invitations."

"Renewal?"

"Yes, yes, my parents decided to renew their wedding vows on Valentine's Day. She decided after seventy years they'd earned a booster shot, a massive party, and a second honeymoon."

"A second honeymoon. Like newly-weds."

"Yes. They're eighty-nine and ninety-three and . . ." Mimoto's face went blank with horror. "Oh my God. My mother? He's targeted my mother?"

"It's possible. I want to bring her in. Sit tight, Your Honor. Peabody."

"I'm pulling up the number now."

"Put it on speaker when you have her 'linked, in case she wants to verify with her daughter. Then have two officers in plainclothes report to her residence to ensure her safety. We've got her," she assured Mimoto. "She'll be covered."

Within minutes, the holo-image of Charity Mimoto sat beside her daughter. For someone looking square-eyed at ninety, Eve thought, the woman looked damn good.

She was long where her daughter was petite, rawboned while the judge was delicate, and her skin tone several shades deeper. But the eyes, intelligent and azure, were all but identical.

Charity took one look at the wall screen.

"Why it's Denny. He's shaved his little beard and fiddled with his hair, but sure, that's Denny all right."

"Do you have his full name, Mrs. Mimoto?"

"Of course, I do. Dennis—but he goes by Denny—Plimpton. He's that nice young boy I've been teaching to play piano. I teach piano a little to earn my mad money. He's taking lessons on the sly to surprise his mama. It's so sweet."

"Oh dear Jesus. Are the police there yet? Mama, don't you or Daddy answer the door unless it's the police. Make them show—"

"Seri, your grandma didn't raise a fool." With admirable aplomb, Charity crossed her long legs and got comfortable. "What's this boy done, Lieutenant Dallas? Because it's hard for me to believe he's done anything to cause all this commotion. He couldn't be sweeter or more well-mannered."

"He's the prime suspect in two homicides."

"Murders? This boy?" She started to laugh it off, then narrowed her eyes at Eve's face. "Wait just one minute. I know you. Of course, I do. I'm so fuddled up about all this business and beaming around like old *Star Trek* episodes I didn't see it. I've seen you on the news, and I saw you on it just today. About that little girl, and the other one. You think this boy did that?"

Eve started to give the departmental line, then decided to cut through it. "I know he did. How long have you been giving him lessons?"

Charity held up both hands, pushing them out as if to thrust the words back. "Just a minute. A minute here. I've always been a good judge of character. Passed it on to you, didn't I, Serenity? I never saw any bad in that boy. But I'm looking right at you, Lieutenant, and I guess I can judge that. I've given him five lessons so far, Wednesday afternoons, though he had to switch one to a Thursday evening a couple back."

"Daddy plays golf Wednesday afternoons. You've been alone with this monster."

"Why did he switch the one lesson?" Eve asked.

"He said he got called into work. He's a

computer programmer, and there was some glitch or other he had to take care of. It was raining that day," she added. "My Deke doesn't play golf when it rains, so he was home all day. And once a month, Thursday evenings, he goes and plays poker with some of the boys. He wasn't home the Thursday evening this one came."

Those soft blue eyes sharpened. "That was smart, wasn't it? Smart to know all that, to make sure I'm the only one who's seen him. Why, he's a fucker, isn't he?"

"Yes, ma'am, he is. Has he ever come to your home on a weekend?"

"No, but he asked to switch this week's lesson to Friday afternoon."

"Lieutenant, my father, my husband, brothers, the grandsons, they're all going on a camping trip this weekend. They're leaving Friday. My mother would be home alone until Sunday. He must know."

"Sure he knows, didn't I tell him myself?" Charity slapped a hand to her own thigh. "I must've said something a couple weeks back about how glad I was going to be to have the house to myself for a couple days, and damned if I didn't tell him all about it. He asked where they camped, how long they'd be away. It was smooth, when I think about it, all how he'd never gone camping, wasn't sure he'd like it. And last Wednesday, he brought it up, making sure, I see now, that it was still on."

She gave a grimace of disgust. "He's planning on coming here to kill me. I'll kick that little bastard's ass to next week."

"I bet you could," Eve said. "But you're going to have to leave that part to me."

Charity drew a deep breath, then gave Eve a look of approval. "You look like you can handle it. What do you want us to do?"

It took time to lay it out, reassure, and to bring in the last name on her list, find the target, interview, and again reassure.

At the end of it, a tired Peabody sighed. "We'll get him tomorrow, at the memorial. We'll get him then, and all the rest will just be precaution and backup. Because, well, we want him but . . . Louise's wedding."

"Don't. Don't even start." Tired herself, Eve scrubbed her hands over her face. "Briefing tomorrow as scheduled. We'll bring the rest of the team up to speed. I'll write it up. Go ahead and fill in McNab and Jamie since you're going to do that anyway. Then shut down. You need to be on full charge tomorrow."

"I will. Because we have to take him tomorrow. For the sake of law and justice. And true love."

"Roarke. Please."

He smiled. "Good night, Peabody," he said, and discharged the holo.

"Okay, and peace reigns across the land. For a minute. I need the recording so I can—"

"Disc copy." He offered it. "And another is already transmitting to your unit. Now, come with me."

"I have to—"

"Yes, I know you do." He took her hand, drew her to the elevator. "If there was enough time—or I thought I could browbeat you into it—I'd see you took a hot bath and a relaxation session, but rather than argue for the next many minutes . . ."

He drew her into the bedroom.

"I don't have time for that either."

"Dear God, sex, sex, sex. It's all you think about." He turned her toward the sitting area.

There was candlelight, two glasses of wine, and—

"Is that cake?"

"It is."

"I get cake?"

He pulled her back before she could pounce. "It depends." He pulled a small case out of his pocket, watched her happy surprise turn to annoyed scowl.

"I don't need a blocker."

"You do if you want cake. I know you have a headache—overwork, stress—overthinking—it shows. Take the blocker like a good girl, and you'll have cake."

"It better be really good cake." She popped the blocker, then immediately grabbed the plate. One bite had her closing her eyes. "Okay, it is. Really good. Worth it. Ten minutes for cake."

"Seems only fair." He tugged her down to sit.

"We found them all." She closed her eyes again, not in pleasure but relief. "All five."

"Saved them all."

"No, not all."

"There are five women, and their families, who think differently."

"If we can take him tomorrow." She let it ride a moment, took another bite of cake. "The judge's mother? Something."

"Indeed she is."

"Do the math. Seventy years into the marriage deal, and she's ninety. Twenty when she stepped into the deal, started popping out kids. Seven decades later, and it's still there. It's what Pauley wants to destroy. Not just the person, but the connection. Strangle them with their own family ties."

A slow sip of wine went down smoothly. "If we don't take him tomorrow, she'll hold up. She'll stand to it.

"I don't want to screw up the wedding," she said suddenly. "I don't want to mess this up, but if—"

"One step at a time."

She let out a huff of breath. "Yeah. One step at a time."

In the morning, Eve stood in the conference room outlining positioning and strategy for her team. Using a remote, she highlighted specific areas of the blueprint on screen.

"The ten-story building holds bereavement facilities on floors one through three, offices and counseling centers for same, four and five, ah, showrooms and retail spaces on six and seven. Eight through ten are hotel facilities offered to families and other attendants of the memorials and funerals held on site."

"One-stop shopping," Baxter commented.

"Yeah." And, well, creepy to her mind. "Moreover, their preparation facilities in the basement comprise over four thousand square feet, and two outside entrances. There are four banks of elevators for a total of twelve cars, a glide between the hotel floors and the retail areas. Stairs, here, here, here, and here." She highlighted. "Serving all floors."

"Lots of ins, lots of outs," Feeney added.

"Plus, you have the main doors here, facing south, additional entrances west and east, and two egresses north. Both the size and the position of the building add complexity. The MacMasters memorial is being held on level two, southwest corner, which includes a large, open terrace facing the park, as do all rooms on the west side. Three other memorials and two viewings overlap the time frame of the MacMasterses. Twenty of the twenty-two hotel rooms are occupied. All offices, chapels, counseling centers, and retail markets will be open."

"Place'll be jammed," McNab pointed out. "That could give him an advantage."

"We weren't able to persuade the owners or various managers to cooperate, and have no authority to compel them to do so. We'll focus on entrances and egresses, concentrating on the memorial areas. They consist of this room where the formal memorial will take place, and these two smaller parlors, all with access to the terrace and the corridor."

She switched to a view of the memorial areas, with points already highlighted and numbered. "We cover the exits, as assigned here, with rovers continually sweeping point to point. If and when he's spotted, we close off the exits, box him in. Those positioned at exits remain at their stations while those roving move in. I want him taken fast and clean."

"Lieutenant." One of the uniforms from MacMasters's squad signaled. "The place is going to be jammed, but the memorial's going to be jammed with cops. That's an advantage for us, if we get the suspect's picture out, put the full blue on it."

"Making the picture department-wide gives us more eyes, and no control or focus. I want this tight, and I don't want the suspect tipped off because a cop gives him the hard eye. He's been on the grift all his life. He'll know what to look for. I don't want it there for him to find. Feeney."

"We have an e-team monitoring the security cams. The building has cameras at every entrance, on all elevators, and in their retail areas. Any sighting'll be relayed."

"If and when that happens, everyone is to remain at post," Eve continued. "We want to lure him in, not scare him off. Now, any questions about the overview?" She waited, scanned the room. "All right, specific assignments."

When she'd dismissed the team, Eve continued to study the screen, searching for flaws. "A lot of ins and outs," she said, echoing Feeney.

"We'll have them all covered." Still Peabody studied the screen as well. "It's a good point about all the cops that'll be there, at some time during the two hours.

If we broadcast the sketch through the department, it would be like a rabbit walking into the wolf den."

"Too many opportunities for leaks and hotheads and mistakes. I thought rabbits hopped."

"Well, yeah."

"And if we're going to use that kind of analogy, bringing the department in would be like all those cooks burning the pie or whatever it is."

"I think it's spoiling the broth."

"Who eats broth?"

"Sick people, maybe."

"Burning the pie makes more sense, because then nobody can eat it, sick or healthy. A small, tight team," she continued while Peabody puzzled over pie. "Then when he's in, we box and close. He's got no reason to be worried. He thinks we're chasing our tails."

"Yeah, we're getting hammered by the media. Even knowing it's for the good of the cause, it's an ouch."

"Suck it up," Eve ordered. "He can walk right in, go right up to MacMasters, look him in the eye, and see the result of his work. Then that task is complete. Multitasking, that's what he does. He figures he'll have the third on his list, the judge's mother, Friday or Saturday, and the Robins memorial Monday. He's free to move on to the next."

She shut down the comp and screen, gathered the discs.

"Let's head over there now. I want to go through the place, top to bottom, before the team assembles."

Not for the first time Eve wished the Mac-Masterses had chosen a smaller, less complex venue for their daughter's memorial. She stood in the large entrance foyer, all but smothered by the scent of lilies, and studied the various escape routes.

Up, down, in, out, sideways, she thought. The place was a hive, and the staff a swarm of quiet bees in black suits. She crossed the slick marble floor toward the first bank of elevators.

"Excuse me. Is there any way I might help you?"

Eve looked at the sober face of the woman who stepped toward her.

"Security detail for the MacMasters family." Eve pulled out her badge.

"Of course." The woman consulted a mini e-board. "The MacMasters memorial service will be held in Suite two hundred. That's the second floor. Would you like me to escort you?"

"I think we can find the second floor."

"Of course." Sarcasm slid off her well-oiled composure, as her eyes, her voice, continued to radiate an oddly efficient sympathy. "Nicholas Cates is managing that program. I'll notify him of your arrival. Is there anything else I might help you with today?"

"No."

Eve stepped into the elevator, called for the second floor.

"She was just creepy," Peabody decided. "I know she's supposed to be comforting or reassuring, but creepy is what she is with that whispering-in-the-graveyard voice. So's this whole place creepy. It's like the upscale death hotel."

Considering, Eve pursed her lips. "I was thinking it's more like an exclusive spa of death. They give corpses manicures in the basement."

"Eeww."

"Don't say 'eeww.' It's wussy."

"Places like this make me feel wussy, especially now that I'm picturing some chatty death tech painting a DB's fingernails."

"Maybe Trina should work here."

They stepped off into another wide corridor, with more rivers of marble, more elaborate banks of flowers. As they walked, Eve glanced into open doorways to see respectfully black-suited staff already setting up for services.

More flowers, she noted, wall screens activated to do test runs of vids or photos the family of the dead chose.

"Lieutenant Dallas." A man with golden hair and an angelic face hurried toward her. He boasted the male version of the whispering-in-the-graveyard voice Peabody had coined. "I'm Nicholas Cates. My supervisor told me to expect you. I'm sorry I wasn't downstairs to greet you. What can I do to help?"

"You can cancel the other services and viewings this morning, and keep everyone not directly connected to the Mac-Masters memorial off this floor."

He smiled, sadly. "I'm afraid that's just not possible."

"So I'm told."

"While we want to cooperate to the best of our ability, there are others, the departed and their loved ones, who must be considered."

"Right. You've verified your internal security, and all staff members on site?"

"Of course. Everyone's accounted for. We've accommodated your electronics teams. They'll have use of my offices for the day."

She moved past him, into the main room of the suite. As with the others, preparations had begun. She ignored the flowers, the laughing young face of the dead on the wall screen, in images on easels, the glossy white coffin draped in pink and purple flowers—bold blossoms on ice.

She checked the terraces, the parlors, the stairways, the restrooms, and the small meditation room across the corridor.

All exits would be covered by electronic eyes and warm bodies. She and Peabody had completed runs of every staff member, and secondary runs on every staff member assigned to duty that day. She would have plainclothes officers, including herself, mingling with the mourners. And all of them would be wired.

Every cop under her command had been briefed and rebriefed on operation procedure.

Nothing to do, she thought, but to do it.

 **20** Thirty minutes before the memorial, the team in place, Eve watched the MacMasterses and a small group of others file off the elevator. She moved aside as Cates led them toward the suite for their private viewing.

But Carol MacMasters shook off her husband's supporting arm and whirled on her.

"Why are you here?" she demanded. "Why aren't you out there doing your *job*? Do you think we want you here, want your condolences? My baby is dead, and the monster who killed her is still out there. What good are you to us? What good are you?"

"Carol, stop. Stop now."

"I won't stop. I'll never stop. It's just another case to you, isn't it? Just another file. What good are you? It's all over the media that you have nothing. Nothing. What good are you?"

As she began to weep, the older man beside her pulled her to him. "Come on now, Carol, come on now. You need to sit down, you need to come with me."

When he led her away, the others followed while MacMasters looked helplessly after them. "I apologize, Lieutenant."

"Don't."

"She wouldn't take a soother. She wouldn't take anything to help her get through. I didn't know she'd been watching the media reports until it was too late to stop her, and she's too . . . too upset to understand. It's partially my fault. In trying to comfort her I told her you'd have him before today. I know better. I hoped you would, but I . . ." He shook his head, turned into the room.

A moment later, Cates closed the double doors. Carol's weeping battered against them like fists.

"She was wrong, Dallas," Peabody said. "She was unfair."

"Wrong maybe. Unfair's a different thing."

"But—"

"Focus on why we're here." She walked away from the door and the sound of weeping. "Feeney? Eyes on?"

"Eyes on," he said through her earpiece. "Peabody's right, you're wrong. That's all on that. Your man's coming in. Whitney and his missus, the commissioner, some brass from Illegals. We're getting deliveries, north side, pretty regular. Flowers, messengers, what I take are blowups of dead people. Couple stiffs carted into the basement."

"Copy that. Keep me updated." She waited until the elevator opened. "Commissioner Tibble, Commander, Mrs. Whitney. The MacMasterses are inside the suite for the family viewing."

"We'll wait." Dark eyes hard, Tibble nodded. "Anything to report?"

"Not at this time, sir."

"I hope your strategy justifies the beating we're taking in the media." He looked toward the closed doors. "And results in some closure for the captain and his wife."

"We'll take him if he shows, Commissioner, and I believe he will. Alternate plans are being formulated to apprehend him tomorrow if—"

"I don't want to hear about alternate plans, Lieutenant. Your suspect is in custody this afternoon or the sketch is released."

He turned and walked to the window at the end of the corridor.

"Your plan to make the investigation appear stalled has worked better than we could have anticipated," Whitney told her. "We're under a lot of pressure, Lieutenant."

"Understood, sir."

Whitney and his wife stepped away to speak to other arrivals.

"That's not—"

Eve cut Peabody's mutter off with a look. "Don't say it's unfair. I'm primary. I take the knock if there's a knock coming. Check in with the rest of the team. We're going to start filling up out here soon. I didn't expect you to make it for this," she said to Roarke.

"I adjusted a few things." He glanced toward her commander, and the city's top cop. "I'm glad I did, and might have some part in helping you finish this."

"He'll show. The probabilities say it, Mira says it, my gut says it. He'll show, and we'll box him in, take him down. Then while the department takes a short round of applause from the media god, I'll have him in *my* box. And then . . ."

She stopped, took a couple of quiet breaths. "Okay. Okay. I'm a little pissed off."

Roarke trailed a hand down her arm. "It looks good on you."

"No room for that. No room. One set of prints on the playbill, no match in any database. We get him, we'll match them, but it doesn't help us get him." She jammed her hands into the pockets of her black jacket. "Nadine and her amazing research team haven't hit on any likelies on the security system clients."

"I've got some ideas there I'm still working," Roarke told her.

"Time's running. It needs to be today." She spotted Cates coming out of the adjoining parlor to speak to Whitney and his wife, then lead them, along with Tibble, inside.

"We're green," she announced.

She'd expected a large crowd—a lot of cops stopping to pay respects, and neighbors, Deena's school friends, their families. But there were more than she'd anticipated.

She saw Jo Jennings and her family, the neighbor she'd spoken to on the morning of Deena's murder. She saw cops she recognized, and many more she didn't, but simply made as cops. Young, old, all in between. Dozens of teenagers mingled among the dress blues, the soft clothes.

More than one burst into tears and had to be led away while images of Deena played over the wall screen. Eve exchanged a look with Nadine across the room, but kept her distance.

She circled the room, again and again, studying faces, builds from different angles.

"Got another group approaching the

main entrance," Feeney said in her ear. "Eight—no nine—mixed male, female, age range about sixteen to eighteen. Hold on, hold on, another one's moving in with them. Male, ball cap, shades, dark hair, right build. It's . . . No, it's not him."

Whitney moved up beside her. "Students from Deena's school were given permission to attend." He answered Eve's frustrated look with one of his own. "Jonah wasn't aware Carol had arranged for it."

"He hasn't come in any of the entrances. We'd have made him. We're only into the first hour."

She watched Mira come in, then make her way through the crowd toward the grieving parents.

Too many cops, she thought, too many kids. She tracked staff as they offered little cups of water, thimble-sized cups of coffee or tea, or brought in yet more flowers.

The air in the room was overripe, a garden of grief.

People spilled onto the terrace, into both parlors, and their voices ebbed and flowed into a sea of sound. Through it she listened to team members report status through her earbud.

She started toward the terrace as much for some air as to do another sweep.

As she reached the doorway a crash had her whirling around. Screams, shouts exploded as the sea of sound became a sea of panic. She pushed, shoved her way through, shouting for status, status, and yanked out her communicator. In front of her, people went down in an avalanche of flailing bodies. A shove from behind pitched her violently forward, slamming her down to her hands and knees. The communicator shot out of her fingers on impact, crunched under stampeding feet as she swore.

She took a blow to the eye, to the nose as she went down, another to the small of the back as she fought her way back to her feet in a tidal wave of people rushing for the exits.

Through the gaps she saw a couple of uniforms muscling a male to the floor. The ball cap he wore fell off, and his shaggy brown hair flopped forward.

Swiping blood off her face, she pushed forward again.

And she saw him, standing at the edge of the chaos, looking across the tumult of panic to the glossy white coffin blanketed with pink and purple flowers. She saw the man who'd put Deena MacMasters in that cold white coffin smile as he stared at the man who held his weeping wife beside it.

In seconds, the wall of people surged again, blocking both her view and her forward progress.

"Second-floor suite entrance. Main. Confirmed sighting." A woman fell into her. Eve simply pushed her aside, plowed on. "Suspect is wearing a black suit, white shirt, staff ID. Goddamn it, goddamn it, move in."

Only static sounded through her earpiece. And ahead of her, the doorway filled with fleeing people, forming a human barricade that cut her off.

She pushed, dragged, bulled while behind her she heard Whitney's commanding voice demand order. Too late, she thought, too fucking late. When she made the corridor, she searched right, left, spotted Trueheart helping an elderly woman into a chair.

She reached over, grabbed him. "Suspect is wearing a black suit, white shirt, black tie, staff ID. Hair's short, medium blond. Send it out. Now. Now. I want this building shut down. Nobody out."

"Yes, sir."

She rushed for the stairs, all but leaping down them, bursting into the foyer.

"Oh, your nose is bleeding, let me—"

"Did a male, early twenties, short hair, medium blond, staff suit and ID, come through here?"

The woman who'd greeted her on arrival stared at the blood on Eve's face. "Ah, yes, I believe I just saw one of our assistants just—"

"Where did he go?"

"He just left. He looked as if he was in a hurry."

Eve charged outside, scanned in every direction. She caught sight of the two cops she'd assigned to the main doors giving chase. Cursing, she leaped down to the sidewalk, kicking into a full-out sprint as she yanked out her 'link, patched through to Dispatch.

"Dallas, Lieutenant Eve, in foot pursuit of murder suspect heading north on Fifth at Fifty-eighth. White male, twenty-three, slim build, blond hair, wearing black suit, white shirt, black tie."

She couldn't see him, not through the wide stream of pedestrians flooding the sidewalk. She dodged, wove, eating up one block, then a second.

Even as she gained ground on the two cops, she knew it was fruitless. When she caught them at the cross street she didn't need to hear their report. It was clear on their faces.

"We lost him, Lieutenant. He had a solid block on us when we got the alert, and he was moving fast. We barely caught sight of him. He just poofed in the crowd."

"How'd he get by you?" she demanded. "How the hell did he get by you?"

"Lieutenant, we were on watch for incomings. Wired into the EDD guys keeping us up on any possibles heading in. This guy walked out with a small group of staff. We'd just gotten an alert there was a ruckus upstairs, that we'd taken the suspect down. There was a lag between that and the notification the suspect was posing as staff and on the loose. We pursued as soon as we got it. We were lucky to even catch sight of him before—"

She cut it off with a lift of her hand. "We'll debrief this clusterfuck at Central. Report back to your unit and await orders."

She clipped back, furious, her face throbbing, and only shook her head when she saw Roarke moving quickly north toward her.

"We lost him. Goddamn it."

Roarke took a handkerchief out of his pocket, handed it to her. "Your nose is bleeding."

"I got clocked twice, maybe more in that riot. Knocked out my com, trampled my communicator. And he walks right out, right under the noses of two cops. He did exactly what he'd come to do, and had the extra benefit of watching us act like morons. What the fuck happened?"

"I don't know." He took her elbow to steer her through the Fifth Avenue throng. "I saw you go down, but by the time I was able to get through that mass of panic, you were gone. I came after you when Trueheart said you'd gone in pursuit."

"A lot of good it did me. He was lost before I hit the sidewalk."

As she approached the building, arrowing through the people congregating on the sidewalk, Peabody came down the main stairs.

"Gone," Eve said.

"Damn it." Peabody hissed out a breath, then winced at Eve's face. "I thought I took a knock," she said, tapping ginger fingers to the bruise on her cheek. "You took harder."

"Let's go clean this mess up. What do you know?" Eve demanded as they went back in.

"The best I can get is some hair-trigger tackled some kid, and another cop helped him wrestle the kid to the ground and restrain him. Panic ensued. We've got all parties in one of the private parlors upstairs. Baxter's riding herd there. Whitney's with the MacMasterses, and is to be advised when you're back on site. We had to call in MTs. People got bruised and bloodied. We've got a really big mess, Dallas."

"Clean up what you can on the periphery, and inform Whitney I'm talking to the officers and the civilian involved. My communicator's toast."

"Why don't I speak to whoever manages this place," Roarke suggested. "Smooth over what I can."

"Couldn't hurt. But I'm going to *speak* to him later. Son of a bitch." Eve squared her shoulders and went up to the second level.

The scent of lilies and roses was stronger now, probably because so many of them lay trampled. She skirted around broken glass, puddles of water, to where Trueheart stood outside a door.

"We got the word on the suspect, Lieutenant. Sorry. Ah, Baxter has the two officers involved here, and the kid. We brought in an MT to look at the kid. He's got some bruises."

"Perfect. Just perfect."

She stepped inside, closed the door at her back.

A male of about eighteen sat in a blinding-white chair while a grizzled MT checked his pupils.

"I'm okay," the boy said. "Mostly just got the shit and the wind knocked out of me. I'm okay."

"I get called to take a look atcha, I take a look atcha."

The MT ran a wand over the bruise on the boy's jaw.

Eve spared a glance toward the two cops slumped on a sofa of the same blinding white, flicked one to Baxter who rolled his eyes heavenward.

Yeah, she thought, *call on that higher power. We're going to need it.*

"I'm Lieutenant Dallas," she told the boy.

"Ah, yeah, hi. I'm Zach. Can I just get out of here now? I need to find Kelly. I came with Kelly. She went to school with the dead girl. I just came with Kelly because she was freaked about seeing the dead girl."

"What's Kelly's full name?"

"Kelly Nims. Everything went whacked in there, and I don't know if she's okay."

"Detective Baxter, have someone find Ms. Nims."

"Yes, sir, right away."

"Thanks. I'll feel better once I know she's frosted. We're tight, and like I said, she was already freaked."

He bore a surface resemblance to Pauley, she noted. The basic build, coloring, the shaggy hair. She noted the ball cap in his lap.

"Zach, I'd like to apologize for the unfortunate occurrences, and any inconvenience you've experienced. And also to assure you, I'll look into this thoroughly and personally."

"I was just standing there, then it's like I got hit by a maxibus and I'm chewing carpet, and everybody's yelling and running. I think somebody stepped on me. These guys, they put cuffs on me, and I could hear Kelly screaming. But the air's knocked out of me, you know? I couldn't do anything. It was weird, but . . ." He smiled a little. "Kind of iced, too. They said stuff about my rights and all. Am I supposed to call a lawyer?"

She hoped to hell he didn't. Any lawyer worth a single billable hour would snatch him for a client and sue the department up the ass and out again.

"You're not in any trouble, Zach. It was a mistake, a very regrettable one. Again, I hope you'll accept my personal apology."

"Sure. No big really."

Baxter slipped back in. "Kelly's fine, Zach. She's waiting for you right outside."

"Straight. So, can I go?"

"Is he clear?" Eve asked the MT.

"Got a couple knocks, that's all." The MT turned his gimlet eye on Eve. "You got worse."

"If you'd give Detective Baxter your full name and contact information," Eve told Zach, "the officer on the door will take you down to Kelly. If you have any questions, or any problems, you can reach me at Cop Central."

"That's a major." He put his cap back on, rose. "It's all been totally Dali."

"At least. Baxter, lend me your recorder. Mine was damaged." She took his, pinned it on.

"Want me to take a look at that face?" the MT asked.

"Not now."

"Well." He pulled a cold wrap out of his case, tossed it to her. "Get that on there anyway."

She waited until both Zach and the MT left, then turned to the two cops.

"Engage recorder. Dallas, Lieutenant Eve, in interview with two hotheaded fuckups who have managed to completely undermine a precisely organized operation and allow a murder suspect to stroll away."

"Lieutenant—"

"You do not speak until so ordered." Deliberately, she turned to the one who'd kept silent. "Name, rank, house, division."

"Officer Glen Harrison, out of the One-Two-Five, assigned to Illegals under Captain MacMasters."

"You, same data."

"Officer Kyle Cunningham, out of the One-Two-Five, assigned to Illegals under Captain MacMasters."

"And you two clowns decided to do my job for me today?"

"We came to pay our respects, offer our support to the captain and his wife. It's all over how the investigation's stalled."

"Is it?" Eve said pleasantly while Harrison shut his eyes at his companion's comment.

"That's the word," Cunningham said.

"And you decided to give the investigation a little momentum by manhandling a civilian, disrupting a memorial service, and causing general panic. During which time the actual suspect was able to elude those of us who are actually working the investigation."

"The kid looked like him."

Her eyes went to slits. "And how do you know that, Officer Cunningham? Just how have you come by any descriptive data on the suspect?"

"Word gets around."

"So, on one hand word gets around that the investigation is stalled, and on the other word gets around that we have a description of a suspect. You decide to join those hands together and fuck up my op. A man who's killed two people is now in the wind due to your actions. The investigation is compromised, the department is now vulnerable to a civil suit not only from a kid you tossed to the ground, but from this establishment, and any other individuals who may have been injured or just decide to claim emotional hardship. You assholes."

"Look, I don't have to take this." Cunningham surged up. "I got a look at the sketch, and the kid looked like him, even dressed like he did. I acted, which is more than Homicide's been doing since the captain's girl got raped and murdered Sunday."

Eve stepped forward. "Sit your fat ass down or I'll put it down."

"Like to see you try."

"Cunningham, for Christ's sake, for Christ's sake." Still on the sofa, Harrison rubbed a hand over his face.

"Officer Cunningham, you've earned yourself a thirty-day rip for insubordination. Further determination of your status will be determined. You will sit when I tell you to sit, or you'll be looking at sixty days right off the top."

"The captain's my boss," he said, but he sat.

"And I am your superior—in so many ways. But yeah, the captain's your boss. Your actions today have destroyed an operation that could have—damn well would have—seen to it that the man who raped and murdered Deena MacMasters was in custody right fucking now. Who showed you the sketch?"

Cunningham jutted up his chin. "I don't say nothing more until I have my rep."

"Your choice." She looked at Harrison. "You?"

"I didn't see the sketch, LT. I heard about it, but I didn't see it. Cunningham took the kid down, shouted out he had the bastard and needed assistance. I assisted."

"Write it up, call your reps. Get out of my sight."

When they filed out, Baxter came over, took the cold wrap, twisted to activate. "Use it. Your eye's going black."

She twisted, imagining for one happy moment the cold wrap was Cunningham's neck. "Jesus Christ, Baxter."

"We're in the soup, and goddamn. I'd kick Cunningham's ass, but it's a waste of time. For what it's worth, I got a decent view on how it went—and it went quick. Harrison's telling it straight. He moved in to assist another officer. I can't see hanging him for it."

"That won't be up to me."

"I'd just caught sight of the bastard. Pauley. Just made him, then the place went up like somebody yelled 'bomb.' I couldn't get to him, got pushed back, trapped in a corner. Trueheart carried some old woman out of it. She got knocked cold. We had him, Dallas. We'd've had him."

"Means jack now." She dragged her hand through her hair. "And now I have to go get my ass fried like I just fried Cunningham's."

"It's not right. Not fucking right."

"My op. My soup."

Peabody was waiting when Eve stepped out. "The commander's in the meditation room, this level. We can go over now."

"I'll go over. Inform the team we'll debrief at the conference room in one hour."

"I'll inform the team, and we'll go over. You're rank, but we're partners. I'm in this, too."

"No point in both of us getting our asses kicked over it."

"There is to me."

"Fine. It's your ass."

"Every square inch. Trueheart! Inform the team we debrief in one hour at Central, conference room. It's heady to outrank someone," Peabody said as they continued on. "At least I outrank him for the moment."

"Whitney's not going to bust you down to uniform. One of us leaked the sketch, and my money's on a uniform there. So, after we're roasted, we do some roasting ourselves. Either way, it comes down to a FUBAR on this op."

She stopped outside of the meditation room. "Last chance."

"No. I'm in." Peabody opened the door herself.

Jonah and Carol MacMasters sat together on a small sofa. From her chair, Anna Whitney leaned forward and poured tea from a delicate pot into delicate cups. Whitney turned from the window.

"We'll speak elsewhere," he said, but before he could move away from the window, Carol sprang up.

"How could you let this happen? How could you? At Deena's memorial?"

"Carol, stop. Stop." MacMasters got to his feet.

"It's a disgrace."

"Yes, it is." He took his wife by the shoulders. "And it was my men who caused it, not the lieutenant's. It was my men."

"Regardless of that, this was my operation," Eve said, "and my responsibility. I have no excuse, Mrs. MacMasters, and my apologies are hardly adequate."

"Is that supposed to mean something

to me?" Her eyes burned with a fury Eve imagined hurt less than grief. "You take responsibility?"

"No, but it's all I have. I should be standing here telling you I have the man who killed your daughter in custody, and I'm not. Nothing I say can mean anything to you."

"Carol." Anna put the teapot down. "You've been a cop's wife too long to do this. You've been a cop's wife long enough to know everything that can be done is being done, and that lashing out at the lieutenant doesn't help Deena." She stood. "Now, come with me. We'll go sit with Deena while this is sorted out."

She led Carol out, closed the door quietly behind her.

"Lieutenant," Whitney said coolly, "report."

She did so just as coolly and in careful detail. When she spoke of Harrison and Cunningham, MacMasters rested his head in his hands.

"Who leaked it?" Whitney demanded.

"I'll debrief within the hour, sir. I will have that information within an hour and five."

"I expect you to have better control of your team, Lieutenant. I expect you to have the judgment and control to prevent this sort of leak in an operation under your command."

"Yes, sir."

"Jack." MacMasters spoke wearily. "They were my men."

"And as the lieutenant correctly stated, this was her op, and her responsibility." Whitney turned his gaze pointedly to Eve. "Lieutenant, I'll need a full evaluation and written report, tonight."

"Yes, sir. I'll refine the team according to that evaluation, and present you with a detailed overview of the alternate operation to apprehend the suspect tomorrow with the Mimotos's cooperation."

"If you expect me to sell not releasing Darrin Pauley's sketch and some salient information to the public via the media to the commissioner, you'd better sell it to me."

"If we release the sketch, let him know we're close, he'll be in the wind." He could already be in the wind, she thought. And that was a hard, hot ball in her belly.

"He's young," she continued, calmly,

firmly, "and he's patient. He can afford to wait, a year, five years before moving on another target if he goes rabbit now. He may select another. He'll alter his looks—which he was cautious enough to modify today—use his skill in ID fraud to take another identity, or series of them, and settle back until Deena and Karlene Robins are forgotten, until the other known targets are no longer protected."

"She's right, Jack." MacMasters held up a hand, let it fall. "Dallas was right about him coming here today. She's right about this. If I have any weight here, I want you and the commissioner to know I agree with the lieutenant."

Eve took MacMasters's weight and pushed with more of her own. "Commander, if we release the sketch, we'll have morons like Cunningham flooding the tip line with sightings of teenagers and twenty-somethings in ball caps while Pauley closes shop here and moves on to wait his chance.

"If we release the sketch, he wins. If we let this play out, and frankly, Commander, it burns my ass, but if we allow the media to portray this fiasco today as a monumental screwup, and we control that feed, he'll be only more confident, and he'll move on Mrs. Mimoto tomorrow, as planned. Release it, and we lose the chance."

"We'd have had him today, sir." When Peabody spoke up, Eve glanced at her with a combination of surprise and annoyance. "That's not an excuse, it's a fact. We will need to interview staff members here, and access their security as it's obvious Darrin Pauley gained access much earlier, and was in the building prior to the memorial. But even with that, we'd have had him."

Whitney lifted his eyebrows. "You're confident of that, Detective?"

Eve was pretty sure she heard Peabody gulp, but her partner continued in what passed for confidence. "Yes, sir. Detective Baxter made him, just as the lieutenant did. His communication to me was delayed due to the chaos Cunningham and Harrison created, the same chaos that injured Dallas and damaged her coms. Instead of entering the room where we could and would have boxed him, he slipped away rather than engage in the confusion, and risk being interviewed as we are now interviewing a number of participants. That's his caution, sir, just as profiled. He behaved exactly as anticipated. He will behave as we anticipate tomorrow."

"And you're willing to risk lives on that?"

"Commander—"

"No," Peabody interrupted Eve. "He asked me. I would risk mine on the lieutenant's judgment. It's easier to say so since, in this case, mine runs the same path. I wouldn't risk lives, even my own, to save the department's face. That's what we'd be doing to publicize Pauley's face now. Risking lives to save face. That's my judgment, sir."

"Jack, again if it matters, that's my judgment as well."

Whitney glanced at MacMasters. "And mine, but it still has to be sold. I'll be speaking, very shortly, with Officers Harrison and Cunningham. They are your men, Jonah, but the fact remains the operation and the results are Dallas's responsibility."

"Yes, sir, they are," Eve agreed.

"You have thirty hours. I can hold the information for thirty hours. If the suspect isn't in custody at that time, we go public.

Damn the leak, Lieutenant, and get it done."

"Yes, sir. Captain, my sincere regrets."

"I want in." MacMasters pushed to his feet. "The leak will cost you at least one man. I want to take his place."

There were times, Eve thought, you had to go with the gut. "With the commander's permission, we could use you."

"Your call. I'll have Anna take Carol and your family home."

I'll drive," Roarke said when they prepared to head to Central. With a shrug Eve slid in, and gave herself the luxury of closing her eyes.

She opened them again when something landed in her lap. She lifted her eyes at the candy bar. "First cake, now candy."

"You look like you could use a lift."

"It could've been worse." Her head ached, her face throbbed, and her suspect was probably having a cold brew and a good laugh. "I don't know how at this very minute, but it could've been worse. There could have been locusts," she decided, and tore the wrapping off the chocolate. "That would've been worse."

"On a happier note, I don't believe the department will be troubled by a lawsuit from the bereavement company."

She bit in, savored. "What did you do, buy the place?"

"An interesting solution, but no. It was simply pointed out that the company held the lion's share of liability as it was their security who allowed an intruder, which I assumed was a wiser term than suspect."

She took another bite, sneered a little. "You got that."

"That they allowed the intruder access to their facilities, into a memorial for a murdered minor where several people, including police officers were injured. I believe those in charge now understand the ramifications, and the possible consequences—and publicity—of a countersuit."

"That's why you wheel the deals."

"It is, yes. How's my favorite face?"

She turned to study him. "You look okay."

"And as fond as I am of what I see in the mirror, I like your face even more."

"It hurts." She allowed herself a momentary sulk. "I'm glad it hurts because it reminds me I fucked up."

"Oh well, it's pity party time. Go on then, you're among friends."

"I should've anticipated him infiltrating the staff."

"Why?" Roarke glanced at her, tried not to smile when he watched her scowl over the next bite of candy. "From where I'm sitting it's more trouble than it was worth—or should've been."

"Because he's careful. It gave him better cover. Who looks at all those black suits and sees anything but another black suit? It gave him more access, let him choose his time, which was at peak."

"And added to the risk of being tapped by the senior staff members and managers who know the people assigned to each suite or memorial. I'll tell you why he went that way—took an unnecessary risk—if you want my view on it."

"I'll take your view on it."

"He could get a look at his work, close-up, another pat on the back from himself to himself." Adjusting his speed, Roarke snuck through a light on the yellow. "He delivers some flowers, gives her a study. And I'll wager hoped to take himself some photos that he'd look back on fondly."

"Goddamn it. Goddamn it, that's exactly what he'd do." She dragged a hand through her hair, pulled. "I missed it."

"Easy to see it from this side, analyzing the whys after the fact. His youth is part of it—caution and impulse—and it's most likely she's his first kill. This is his mission, and he'd be careful not to risk it. Now, he's got the makings for a nice scrapbook."

"Let's keep this between us, for now. I let MacMasters on the team. He doesn't need to hear this."

"Is that wise, letting him on?"

"I'm going to find out."

She took her time getting to the conference room. She wanted everyone assembled when she arrived. She moved in briskly, walking to the front of the room, waiting while Roarke took his seat.

"Captain MacMasters is joining this team, as of now. I'll be taking individual reports and analyses. Before I do, I want the individual who shared the sketch of the suspect with Detective Cunningham, and possibly others, to identify himself."

She didn't need a raised hand, a confession, not when she saw Officer Flang's eyes cut away.

"Flang, explain yourself."

"Lieutenant, I was just trying to help. It was getting really crowded in there, and the more eyes we had—"

"Did I or did I not give a direct order regarding this, Officer, when you brought up the issue in the pre-op briefing?"

"Yes, sir, but—"

"I have to assume, Officer, that you considered yourself more capable of leading today's operation than me, that you believe your judgment superior to mine."

"No, sir, I just thought—"

"You thought it was acceptable to disobey a direct order from a superior officer. You're mistaken. You're on report, Officer Flang, and you are dismissed."

"Lieutenant—"

"Don't speak." Her order chilled the room as Flang visibly withered under her stare. "Further, if one more drop—a single drop—of this leak slides out of the pipe, I will see to it that you're charged with obstruction of justice. I want a list of every name with whom you shared this information on my desk inside fifteen minutes. Now, I repeat, Officer, you are dismissed."

The room was silent as a tomb as Flang left.

"If anyone else believes their judgment is better than mine, or that following orders is optional, there's the door." She waited two beats, let the silence hum. "Now, we're going to go over every step of this clusterfuck from every angle, then we'll outline, streamline, refine and re-refine the op for tomorrow.

"Feeney. Security."

21 Well into the evening, with every possible contingency addressed, dissected, and readdressed, Eve walked through the doors of home with Roarke.

Summerset, looming as usual, cocked an eyebrow. "I see you've had your monthly facial, Lieutenant."

"Trina will be here tomorrow. Maybe she can decorpse yours."

Eve scowled her way up the steps. "Damn it, that was weak. His was better. His was good. Just one more thing to be pissed about."

"I'm surprised you have the energy to bicker. I want an hour in the whirlpool."

She rolled her tense shoulders, and winced as the movement sent something new throbbing. "That sounds good. I've got aches making themselves known all over."

"Start the tub, why don't you, and we'll both have a whirl. I'm getting us both a very big glass of wine."

"We covered it all." She went into the bathroom to order on the water, the temperature. As the wide scoop of tub began to fill, she went over the steps and stages of tomorrow's operation.

"I can't think of anything we left out. It's a smaller space, more controlled. No excess civilians. As long as Mrs. Mimoto holds her own, just long enough to get him inside . . . Better, better for the case if he drops the mickey, but we can take him before that if she looks shaky. We have enough."

Today's botch, he thought, had shaken her confidence, had her second-guessing. "Put it aside for a bit. You'll overthink it." He came in with two glasses of wine— very large.

"The contingency op was always the

better scenario. I wanted to take him to-day, shut him down, but . . ." Her mouth dropped open when Roarke shed his shirt. "Holy shit. I didn't know you got hit."

"Mmm." He glanced at the mirror, and the symphony of bruises along his ribs. "My second favorite face avoided any violent contact, but a good deal of the rest of me feels like it's been ten rounds with the champ, and the worse for it. It was a bloody madhouse in there."

"We're lucky nobody had to make use of the facilities." She stripped off her own shirt, and Roarke traced his fingertips over her bruises.

"Ouch."

"That's exactly right." After peeling off the rest of her clothes, she sank into the hot water. "Oh God. Thank you, Jesus."

"When we're done with this, we'll play doctor." He stepped in, cursed. "Bloody hell, Eve, it's hot enough to flay the skin."

She opened one eye to peer up at him. "It'll feel good when you're all the way in. Jets on. Oh, mama!"

He had to laugh as he slid in the wide tub beside her. Maybe losing a few layers

of skin—especially the bruised and battered layers—wasn't such a bad idea. In
any case, sharing a tub of hot (next to
bloody boiling) churning water with his
wife at the end of the day made up for
quite a bit.

He picked up his wine, took a long sip.
"I might feel next to human once I finish
this."

"Come on, tough guy. Dublin street rat.
You've had your ribs pounded before."

"Older now, aren't I?" He closed his
eyes, let the hot water beat and froth over
the aches.

"But not softer." To prove it, she trailed
her hand down his chest, found him,
stroked him. "Nope, not softer."

His lips curved. "So, you're wanting to
stir up more than some hot water."

"Figure I owe you." She shifted positions until she straddled him, watched
amusement and lust light in his eyes.
"How many times do you figure I've gotten you bruised or bloody since we met?"

"I stopped counting long ago." His
hands stroked down her back as she
opened, took him in. "Ah, there now. Bet-

ter than the wine for making me forget my troubles."

She took the wine from him, sipping even as she rose and fell, rose and fell. "It's all for medicinal purposes."

"I'm an excellent patient."

She brought the glass to his lips, tipped before setting it aside, before laying her lips to his. "It's good," she murmured against his mouth. "It's good."

Slow and fluid, with the water swirling and lapping, the steam from the heat rising, they moved together. Here, with as much comfort as passion, she laid her head on his shoulder, let her body rock them both to pleasure.

The crest, a long, liquid shimmer, brought a quiet sigh.

"It's good to be home," she told him.

"Always."

"Now that we're feeling human, let's just stay in here and wallow."

He wrapped his arms around her, closed his eyes again, and wallowed.

Easy sex and a long soak soothed the aches. Still, he wouldn't let her dress until he'd run a wand over the bruises to help them heal, and gotten another cold wrap for her face.

"Give me the wand," she ordered. "Your bruises are worse than mine."

He gave her the wand, but turned her so she could see herself in the mirror.

"Oh crap." She poked at her purpling eye. "Crap. Even with the wand and the cold pack, that's not going to be gone by Saturday."

"It won't be your first wedding with a shiner. You had one for ours. Trina will cover the worst of it."

"Don't remind me. Damn it, do I have to call Louise, say anything about tomorrow?"

"Summerset's taken care of it. It's all managed."

"There was a rehearsal thing."

Roarke kissed her lightly. "Managed."

"Well, hell, now he has something else to sniff at me about. I want to check in with Baxter and Trueheart, just make sure everything's in place at the Mimotos."

"Do that if it helps you relax. I have a couple things to check on myself. Then I want a meal."

They retreated to opposite ends of the

bedroom with pocket 'links. When he'd finished, Eve was sitting down, frowning into space.

"Problem?"

"No, they're in, the house is secured. They'll take shifts through the night, just in case. Baxter said Mrs. Mimoto, and her husband, are okay about it. More than okay. They want to do it. They're revved to do it."

"You spoke with them both yourself just a few hours ago."

"I know, and they agreed. They're solid. It's just I expected some nerves, more questions from them, a need for more assurances. Instead, they cooked dinner. Like with ingredients, right there in the kitchen. Baxter said they went out and bought stuff especially after I talked to them so they could make this big home-cooked meal for him and Trueheart."

Appreciation lit Roarke's face. "What did they have?"

"Roast chicken—a real clucker—mashed potatoes and gravy, green beans. The real deal, too. It must've cost them. And they had lemon meringue pie for dessert. They did all that for a couple of cops. Baxter's in love with her, by the way. She's going to open the door of her house tomorrow to a man she knows wants to kill her, intends to rape her, brutalize her, and kill her. And she baked a pie for a couple of cops."

"It's more surprising for you to be treated with courtesy and kindness."

"They made up a guest room so the one off shift can catch some sleep. Yeah, it's more surprising. He wants to snuff that out. He wants to end the kind of person who would do that, would think of those things. And that doesn't surprise me. I was sitting here asking myself if that's a good thing or a bad thing."

"It makes you a good cop, and the fact that you'd ask yourself the question makes you a better one." He leaned down to kiss her bruised eye. "Why don't we see if there's any roast chicken to be had around here?"

Deke and Charity Mimoto lived in a pleasant single-family home in White Plains. The old, established neighborhood had weathered the years well, and benefited from the updates and influxes of wealthy young suburbanites. Big, leafy trees and pretty gardens dotted a landscape where the lawns were trimmed, the sidewalks even, and the paint was fresh.

"We've been here fifty-three years," Charity told Eve. "We wanted to put down roots when we started our family, and in a neighborhood where kids had yards to play in. My Deke's handy, so he's done a lot of fixing up over the years. A man who can fix a leaky toilet's as good as a billion-aire from where I sit. Is your man handy around the house?" she asked, wagging a finger at Eve's wedding ring.

She decided it was probably the first time, and the last, she'd actively wonder if Roarke had ever fixed a toilet. "In his way."

"Deke built the sunroom with his own two hands, and finished off the down-stairs so we have a nice, big family room. I've lost track of the times he remodeled the kitchen, or one of the baths. We like to keep up."

"It's a very nice house, Mrs. Mimoto." But Eve was more interested in the layout than new countertops.

"A good place to raise children, and a

good place when the grands came along, and the greats. We haven't said anything about all this to the family. Usually most of us know what's going on with the rest of us, so this isn't our way."

"I appreciate your cooperation, Mrs. Mimoto. Our concerns are to keep you safe, and to apprehend this man. We're going to do both today, then get out of your way."

"Oh now, you haven't been in our way." Charity made waving gestures with her hands. "We enjoyed having David and Troy," she added, obviously pleased to be on a first-name basis with Baxter and Trueheart. "Such nice young men. Have a muffin," she invited, holding out a cloth-lined bowl to Eve. "I baked them fresh this morning."

"I—"

"Go on, go on. You could use some meat on your bones."

"Thank you. Mrs. Mimoto, I'd like to go over with you what we need you to do, and say, where officers will be posted. Your safety is the first priority."

"You sit right down here. I'll get us some coffee, and we'll talk."

Eve ate the muffin—truly exceptional—

drank the coffee—not half bad, considering how spoiled she was—and carefully went over every step of the plan.

With the talk of leaky toilets and baked goods, Eve had concerns the woman didn't fully understand the risk, the seriousness. The tabletop discussion served the dual purpose of fully informing her bait, and relieving Eve's mind.

The woman asked the right questions, gave the right answers. However homey she appeared in her shiny kitchen with its display board crammed with children's drawings, she owned a shrewd mind and a steel spine.

"Do you have any other questions? Is there anything you're uncomfortable with or uneasy about?"

"You need to stop worrying." Charity patted Eve's hand. "You're a worrier like my Serenity. I can see it. Worrying gives you tension headaches and bad digestion."

"Mrs. Mimoto, I have to ask you. Aren't you afraid?"

"Why should I be afraid when I've got the police all through the house?" Those soothing and exotic eyes peered out of the old face. "Are you going to let him hurt me?"

"No, ma'am, I promise you he won't hurt you. But we are asking you to open your door to a murderer. And I also have to tell you, again, we could take him outside. We have enough for an arrest."

"But it's going to help slam-dunk your case down the road if you take him *inside*, and after he tries to drug me. I've got a judge for a daughter, and plenty of lawyers in the family. Cops, too. I know what's what." She leaned forward. "Do you know what I want, honey? I want you to take that little fucker down, and take him hard, and I want a piece of it."

Eve's lips twitched at the sound of the expletive in the pretty suburban kitchen.

"That's what we'll do."

"Good. How about another muffin?"

"No, really." Eve pushed back from the table just as MacMasters came in.

"Sorry to interrupt. Mrs. Mimoto, your husband wondered if you could give him a hand with something when you had a minute."

"Can't find his lucky socks." She shook her head as she got to her feet. "Seventy years, and he can never put his hand on them. You help yourself to that coffee." As she walked by MacMasters, she patted a hand on his arm. "We'll get him today, and your girl can rest easy."

MacMasters's face tightened as he stared at the floor.

"That's part of it," Eve said as she crossed to him. "It's what we do. The best we can do. I need to ask you something, Jonah, and I need to hear the truth. Is getting him going to be enough?"

MacMasters brought his gaze back to Eve's. "You need to know if you can trust me."

"I need to know if I can trust you. I'm not in your position, but that doesn't mean I don't understand the conflict."

"I've thought about killing him, how easy it would be. You know I've thought of it."

"If you said you hadn't I wouldn't believe you." She couldn't read his face, his eyes. He was too good a cop to show what was in his mind. "I like to think you'd have weighed the satisfaction of it against the consequences. Leaving your wife alone when she needs you most. There are plenty of other consequences, but they're not going to weigh real heavy for you right now."

"I want to kill him. I want him to suffer. I wish I could say the badge, what it stands for, what it is to me would stop me from killing him. I wish I could say knowing you'd take me down for it, and I'd leave Carol alone would stop me."

"What will?"

"I want him to suffer. I think I'll wake up every morning of my life, and my first thought will be my girl's gone." He took a breath, slow in, slow out. "I want to wake up every morning for the rest of my life with the second thought of knowing he's still paying for it. Every day, every hour for the rest of my life I'll know that. So will my wife. I need to be here when that suffering begins. You can trust me. And if that's not enough—"

He reached for the weapon on his hip, offered it.

"You gave me the answer," she told him.

Nodding, he holstered his weapon.

Eve went upstairs as the Mimoto men loaded up a pair of ATs for their camping trip. She, along with Feeney, watched the outside activity from the EDD setup in Deke Mimoto's den. Photographs and sports paraphernalia crowded the room. An enormous recliner faced an entertainment screen flanked by shelves jammed with more photographs and countless trophies.

"The old man played baseball back in high school, through college and into Double A. Got picked up by the Yankees, played a season—hit three-fifty-two."

Intrigued, Eve gave the memorabilia a closer study. "What position?"

"Catcher. Then he bunged up his knee, and that was that. Went into teaching, and coached high school ball. Moved up to principal, then to county administrator, some politicking. Worked construction most summers. Hell of a guy," Feeney added with obvious admiration. "He was up here quizzing me on the equipment. Hope I'm half as sharp at his age."

She turned from the shelves. "Am I doing the right thing, Feeney? Letting Mac-Masters in on this?"

He leaned back in his chair. "Does it feel like the right thing?"

"Yeah. Yeah, it does."

"Then you've got to go with it."

Moving back to the screen, Eve watched the Mimotos. Charity stood, hands on her hips, giving orders while her men loaded. Just another morning, from the looks of it, Eve thought. Another summer morning in the suburbs. Family calling out to one another, laughing, ribbing each other.

She watched Mr. Mimoto give his wife an enthusiastic hug, saw his lips move as he whispered in her ear.

"Is he worried?"

Feeney shook his head. "You'd think he would be. I asked, thinking I'd give him the pep talk. But he said his Charry can handle herself. He was proud of it. I have to say, I'm half inclined to think she'd take this bastard down without us."

"Maybe so." Eve laid a hand on Feeney's shoulder. "But let's do it for her. There they go," she mumbled, as the last of the men piled in an AT.

Charity stood, blithely waving good-bye. Then turned, strolled back toward the house, pausing to stoop and pull a few weeds out of a flower bed on the way.

In moments, Eve heard the sound of piano music drifting up the stairs.

"Nice," Feeney commented after a few bars. "Nice to hear a classic, and hear it played with some style."

"Yeah, I guess." Eve stepped to the privacy-screened window to scan the street from another viewpoint. "What is it, Beethoven or something?"

"Kid." Feeney let out a windy sigh. "I don't know where I went wrong with you. You got no culture. That's Springsteen. That's The Boss."

"Boss of who?"

Feeney shook his head in disgust. "Hopeless. Get out of here and send Jamie in. We're on the clock now. And besides, he can be educated about classic music."

"Fine. Check the eyes and ears one more time," she told him as she walked out. "Let's make sure they're a go everywhere we need them."

She did another walk-through of the house, checking on the position of her men, running checks on all coms. No mistakes, she thought, not this time.

She joined Peabody in what Charity

called her sitting room just off the living area.

"The music's nice," Peabody commented.

"Yeah, so I'm told. He'll tag her first, on her pocket 'link, so she'll be ready for him, quick to open the door. And it's a way of making sure she's alone, that the house is empty. It's the same pattern as Deena. Good neighborhood, most of the residents at work. She's set out something to drink, to eat. That's her habit, her way. He knows it."

"It's nearly time," Peabody added. "And she just keeps playing the piano."

"She'd make a good cop." Eve glanced at the miniscreen that gave her a full view of the living area.

She had men posted inside and out, some of them—like herself and Peabody—literally steps away from Charity Mimoto.

No, Eve wouldn't let him hurt her.

But she needed him inside. He wouldn't hear the cage door slam down, she thought. Wouldn't know he'd walked into the trap.

"We got him," Jenkinson said in her ear. "Heading east on foot, two blocks. Navy shirt, brown pants, ball cap, black shades. He's wearing a black backpack and carrying some flowers."

Eve thought of the flowers he'd brought to Deena. "Roger that. Hold your position. All positions hold. Teams A and B, wait until he's in the box, inside the box, then move to secondary position. Sound it off."

She waited until she'd received an acknowledgment from each team leader. "Mrs. Mimoto?"

"Yes, dear?"

"He's on his way. Just a couple blocks away. Are you okay?"

"I'm just fine. How are you?"

Eve shook her head at the woman's unshakable aplomb. "We're good. He's bringing you flowers. I want you to do everything we rehearsed, but then you're going to want to put those flowers in water. You excuse yourself, and go to the kitchen."

"That's when he'll drug my lemonade, won't he?"

"That's likely. You stay in the kitchen. We've got you, Mrs. Mimoto."

"I'm sure you do, but let's get him." Her pocket 'link beeped. "I bet we know who that is. Don't worry. Hello?"

On screen, Eve watched Charity smile at the 'link. She angled it, just as she'd been instructed, so Eve could see his face on the 'link display from her screen.

There you are, you bastard, she thought. *Keep coming. Just keep on coming.*

"Hello, Denny. I was just thinking about you!"

"Hi, Mrs. M. I'm running a couple minutes late, just wanted you to know, and to make sure we're still on, that your husband and all got off okay."

"Of course we're still on. I've got us a nice pitcher of lemonade and some muffins. My men are on their way to the wilds!" She laughed, easily. "It'll be nice to have a little company before I settle into my solitude."

"Aw, you didn't have to go to all that trouble, Mrs. M. But if those are your muffins, I'm walking faster! I'll be there in one minute."

Yeah, come on, Eve thought as various teams relayed his progress through her earpiece. *Come right on in, you son of a bitch.*

"Well, I'll pour that lemonade," Charity said cheerfully. "See you in a minute."

Charity shut down the 'link, set it on top of the piano. "How'd I do?"

"Perfect," Eve said.

"I believe I might've missed my calling," she said as she rose to pour the drinks. "I could've been a screen star."

Eve watched her eyes go fierce, saw her take a long, deep breath before her face turned harmlessly pleasant again.

"Here we go," Charity murmured and started toward the door.

"Turning up the walk," Feeney told her.

"Hold positions. We do this by the numbers. No chatter. Wait for my go."

She watched Charity open the front door, and the quick, charming grin on Darrin Pauley's face.

"You look real nice today, Mrs. M."

"Oh, listen to you. Come on in here! Oh, look at those daisies. Aren't they pretty?"

"I just wanted to thank you for letting me take my lesson today."

"That's the sweetest thing." Charity sniffed at the flowers. "Take a minute to sit down, have some lemonade. I bet the walk made you thirsty."

"I guess it did."

"A young man like you's always hungry. You have a muffin."

"Thanks." He shrugged off his backpack, set it beside a chair before removing his cap, his shades.

Charity stood where she was, smiling at him. "How's your mama doing?"

"Oh, she's fine. I wish she didn't work so hard. Wish I could do more for her."

"I bet you're doing more than she'd ever think to ask," Charity said, and Eve hoped she was the only one who heard the underlying ice in the tone. "And won't she be surprised when you play for her? I don't know another boy your age who'd go to so much trouble to please his mama."

"I owe her everything. I bet your family feels the same about you. Especially your kids. Are you sure you're going to be all right here on your own? Alone until Sunday, didn't you say?"

"Oh, I'll be fine, and happy to have the place to myself until Deke and the boys get back Sunday. Now you have a muffin while I go put these pretty daisies in water. I won't be a minute."

"Okay."

Charity strolled out of the room, didn't break stride even when she sent one fiercely satisfied glance in Eve's direction.

As her footsteps echoed away, Darrin took a small vial out of his pocket, tipped the contents into her glass.

"Go. All positions, go."

Weapon drawn, Eve rushed the room only seconds before a half-dozen cops did the same.

"Hello, Darrin," Eve said. She smiled as he stared at her. "Hands behind your head. Now. On your knees."

"What's this about?" He obeyed, but turned his head side-to-side, with the perfect mix of fear and confusion on his face. "My-my name's Denny, Denny Plimpton. I have identification."

"I bet you do. Darrin Pauley, aka Denny Plimpton, among others, you're under arrest for murder, two counts." Eve gripped his wrist, yanked his arm behind his back.

She looked up and into MacMasters's eyes. "Captain, would you read this son of a bitch his rights?"

"I . . ." MacMasters cleared the rust from his voice. He looked down at the weapon in his hand, then slowly holstered it. "You have the right to remain silent," he began as she secured Darrin's wrists in restraints.

"Thought you were playing her, didn't you, Darrin?" Eve hauled him to his feet. "Playing an old woman. But she played you. She played you like a piano. This time? You're the mark."

The frightened boy fell away, and he smiled. And when he smiled, turning his face toward MacMasters, the shadow of the monster slouched behind his eyes. "Maybe you'll get intent to rob, but that's all you'll get."

Eve jerked him around so he faced her. "Keep telling yourself that, Darrin."

"Look what I found." Baxter held up a pair of the cutaway restraints bailiffs carried in courtrooms. "There's a recorder here, too, a can of Seal-It, and hmmm." He held up another vial and a small package of pills. "I bet these contain illegal substances."

"Bag it, log it, bring it. And the contents of Mrs. Mimoto's glass. Transport this thing into Central, book him. I'll be in real soon, we'll chat.

"Get him out." She shoved Darrin toward Jenkinson, then walked up to Mac-Masters. "You did the job. You maintained. We've got him now. You should go home, tell your wife we've got him now. Be with her."

"I'd like to observe your interview." His face was like stone, pale and sharply carved.

"We'll let him sweat a while. You've got time to go home, tell your wife. She needs to hear this from you."

"Yes, you're right." He held out his hand. "Thank you, Lieutenant."

"Captain."

He started for the door, stopped, turned. "I thought about it, even after what we talked about. I could have taken him out. Clean line, one stream. I could have done it. Now I have to think about that."

"Bastard did his job there," Eve murmured. "Cracked the foundation of a damn good cop."

"I think, with some time, the foundation's going to prove solid. He did the job, like you said," Peabody pointed out. "It was good, you having him read the bastard his rights."

"Yeah. Contact the judge, assure her

that her mother's safe, and it's done. We can contact her father, but I assume she'll want to do that herself."

She turned away. "All right, boys and girls, good work. Let's close it down."

At Central, Eve formally notified her commander, the PA's office, contacted Mira with a request she observe. She wrote her report.

She sat, her boots on her desk, and drank a cup of coffee.

Peabody tapped on the doorjamb. "He's been booked and processed, and he's been sitting in Interview for an hour."

"Mmm-hmm."

"Reo and the commander are here, MacMasters just came in, and Mira's on her way."

"I'm up on that."

"Don't you think we ought to start working him?"

"Feeling twitchy?"

"No. Yes. Well, Nadine's chomping to break the story."

"Not yet. Nothing yet."

"Well . . . we're supposed to be back, you know, with the rehearsal. I know they're using stand-ins, but if we wrapped this, we could still . . ."

Eve merely turned her head, stared.

"And ah . . . We should talk about how we're going at him," Peabody decided on the spot. "And if we leave him sitting too long, he might start thinking lawyer."

"He's not going to lawyer. What name is he going to use? What address? His ID's bogus. Besides, what good did a lawyer do his mother? That's what he's thinking. Fuck lawyers, fuck all of us. He's too smart to go down. Or, if we get lucky, he'll go down a hero in his own mind."

"Well, how do we work him? Oh, let me guess." Peabody rolled her eyes. "I'm good cop."

"No good cop."

A quick, almost childish delight bloomed on Peabody's face. "I don't have to be good? I can be bad?"

"We hit, hit hard. Getting the confession isn't the tricky part."

"It's not?"

"He'll want to confess after he understands we've got him cold. He'll want the hero badge. The tricky part? Getting him to flip on his father." She dropped her feet to the floor. "Let's do it."

Eve walked into Interview, dropped her file on the table, took a seat. Peabody took the chair beside her.

"Record on," she said and read in all the data, including every known alias she'd discovered.

She noted the quick jump of a muscle in Darrin's jaw, and knew the depth of her knowledge caught him off guard.

"Legally, I'm covered using the name on your birth records," she said conversationally, "but I like to be thorough, seeing as you've used so many names, including the two used when you murdered Deena MacMasters and Karlene Robins. So, which name do you want me to use in this interview? Your choice."

"Fuck you."

"For the record, would fuck be your first name or your last? Never mind. The courts frown on my using that sort of profanity to address interview subjects. Though, personally, I think it fits."

"To the ground," Peabody agreed.

"I'll stick with Darrin. We've got you cold, Darrin. You're a smart guy, so you know this. Well, maybe not so smart as you were set up and knocked down by a ninety-year-old woman. One you intended to incapacitate with an illegal substance, bind, beat, rape, sodomize, and murder."

"Give me a break." His sneer struck her as both young and arrogant. "She's old. I couldn't even get wood up to do some dried-up old woman. Makes me want to puke to think about it."

"The stiffie pills in your backpack would've helped with that, but you'd have gotten it up, Darrin. Even though I suspect you've got a twig in your pants instead of a decent bat. Because it's all about the hurting for you, the torment, the fear, the pain. That's what turns sick fucks—oops, I said fuck—like you on."

"How are you going to prove that?" He leaned back in the chair, relaxed. Looked around the room as if bored. "Yeah, I figured I'd lay her out. She's got a lot of valuables in that place. I was going to rob her and walk away."

"I see. So with Deena and Karlene,

your intention to rob just went a little too far. Resulting in . . ." Eve opened the file, tossed the two file shots on the table.

This time his facial muscles twitched into the smallest of smiles.

"You are a sick fuck." Peabody shoved back her chair as she sprang to her feet. She leaned over the table until she was nose to nose with Darrin. "It pisses me off we're wasting time with you, that we have to go through this routine. We've got witnesses, you asshole. We've got security recordings of you walking into Deena MacMasters's house the night you killed her. Of you entering the building the day you killed Karlene Robins."

"Bullshit. That's bullshit, because I was never anywhere near those places."

"Bullshit? I'll show you bullshit. Wall screen on!" She caught herself, glanced toward Eve.

"Go ahead, you've already spoiled my surprise."

"Display image 1-A," Peabody ordered.

The screen filled with a clear shot of Darrin climbing the steps of the MacMasters's home toward a smiling Deena. The time stamp pulsed in the bottom corner as the recording continued with him reaching her, offering her the flowers, easing into the doorway, into the house.

"She told her friends about you— David," Eve added as he stared at the screen. "She told them all about her secret boyfriend from Columbia University. The shy guy she met in the park."

"We've got eyewitnesses who saw the meet," Peabody continued. "We've had your face for days, picking up other witnesses who saw you together."

"She kept souvenirs—like the program from the musical you took her to at the college. Your prints are on it." Eve tossed another paper from the file on the table. "We got a match once you were printed downstairs."

Face blank, he nodded. "So, you got lucky."

"You keep thinking that, too. Now, let's discuss details."

22

"Luck?" Eve tipped back in her chair, meeting his smirk with one of her own. "Luck that EDD killed your virus? Or that we know what you were wearing on New Year's Eve when you lifted Darian Powders's ID? I know where you bought the shoes you're wearing, Darrin, and how much you paid for them. The backpack, too, and the Columbia sweatshirt you had on when you lured Deena into the first meet in Central Park."

Now she smirked, deliberately, leaning back in a way that transmitted casual derision. "I know what kind of airboard you ride, and exactly where you rode it, with Deena, on a rainy afternoon in May."

"That's bullshit."

He didn't look afraid, not yet, Eve thought. But he looked puzzled, and just a bit defiant.

"You keep thinking that, asshole." Peabody all but growled the words, and made Eve think she'd have to teach her new "bad" cop to tune it back.

"I knew what you looked like when I set you up at the media conference, the day after you raped and strangled Karlene Robins. *Drew.* I know your name, where you were born, oh, and the name you were using when your mother bought it in Chicago."

There, Eve thought, that hit the mark. Rage boiled out of his eyes. He turned it back, quickly, she'd give him that. But she'd seen it and the trigger she needed.

"We're just smarter than you, Darrin. You got lucky at the memorial, no question. But, gee, looks like your luck ran out. Like your mother's did in that prossy flop in Chicago."

"You're going to want to be careful."

"About what? You're nailed. You've got

some skills with electronics, but they're average. You couldn't find a way to jam the cameras or the lock, you couldn't by-pass the system without being inside. The virus?"

She rolled her shoulders, stretched lazily. "It was a good try, kept our e-team entertained for a while. But the fact is, an e-rookie has more chops than you. But then, you learned most of them from your father."

"Well, that depends." Peabody shrugged. "We're not sure if Vincent or Vance Pauley is his father. His mother let both of them have the bangs."

"Right, right." Eve waved agreement as Darrin's jaw clenched. "I wonder if your mother knew, since she fucked both of them. But, hey, it could've been someone else altogether. Since she was a whore."

"Shut your fucking mouth."

"Want to shut it for me, Darrin? The way you shut Deena's, Karlene's, when you held a pillow over their faces after you raped them? I wonder, when you were raping them, looking at their faces when you pounded and tore into them, did you see your mother? Is that how you got it up, Darrin? Thinking about Mom, and how you really wanted to fuck her?"

She didn't blink when he lurched up. His hands balled into fists as the lead of his restraints clanged against the bolt.

"Want to take a shot at me? It's a pisser not to be able to fight back, isn't it? I guess you know how Deena and Karlene felt. You must be disappointed that you won't be able to watch Judge Mimoto's mother struggle, hear her scream. Or Elysse Wagman," she said and looking into his eyes recited the names of his other targets.

"We found them all," Peabody said, piling on scorn. "That's how *lucky* we are."

"Now you won't be able to finish your sick homage to your whore of a mother."

He got his hands under the table, tried to lift it, heave it, but Eve and Peabody simply counterweighted the other side.

"Frustrating, isn't it?" Eve commented. "To be helpless. To be controlled."

His muscles trembled with the effort, but he pulled back, sat again. "If you've got me nailed, why are we wasting time with all this?"

"That's what they pay us for. So, if you're

in a hurry, why don't you lay it out for the record?" Eve prompted. "You know you want to. It has to be satisfying to brag about what you did manage to pull off. I can give you a little springboard. You've been stalking your targets for months, researching them, planning. Hell, you've been thinking about it for years. All your life, basically. I have to figure you picked Deena to start as she was the easiest. Just a kid, a shy girl—the virgin—easily dazzled by attention, excited by the idea of a secret boyfriend. You used the Columbia connection. You'd gone there, so you knew the campus. And since her friend Jamie Lingstrom goes there, a little fieldwork and you could toss out some names she'd recognize. Lower her defenses."

He shrugged.

"If you think we're going to offer you a deal, like your mother got when she was caught using and whoring twenty years ago, think again."

Darrin bared his teeth in a vicious smile. "You can tell MacMasters his precious daughter was the whore. I've been fucking her for weeks."

Eve glanced at Peabody. "Did we actually think this moron had some smarts?"

"We did. He's sure proving us wrong since we know, conclusively, the only way he could get his pathetic dick into Deena was to drug her, restrain her, and rape her."

"All you had to do with his mother was pay her."

"Shut the fuck up. You don't know anything."

"Enlighten me. Explain to me why the people involved in your mother's bust in New York twenty-one years ago are responsible for her death in Chicago nineteen years ago? Help me make that leap, Darrin."

"It was that fucking cop who ruined her. Set her up."

"MacMasters set her up?"

"Planted the illegals on her, blackmailed her into having sex with him, the same as rape. Then he covers it up, says she's whoring. My mother was the best shifter on the grift there was."

Eve changed her tone, put a touch of admiration into it. "She had the ID skills."

"She could be anybody she wanted to

be, take anything she wanted to take. And so what? Nobody got hurt."

"How about the people she swindled? How about Vincent Pauley?"

"Marks." He shrugged again. "They're lame enough to get taken, they get taken. Vinnie? He's always been a dick, always been jealous of my father, always came in second best to him. My mother needed somewhere to stay when she was pregnant with me and my father got railroaded into prison. She only slept with that asshole for my sake."

"Is that what she told you?"

"She never talked about it, any of it. What happened to her ruined her. Took the life out of her before those cops set her up with the Stallions in Chicago. Before they killed her."

"Interesting." Eve furrowed her brow, flipped through the papers in the file on the table. "None of that's in my file. Where did you get this information?"

"My father told me everything. How they tore the life out of her before they killed her, how they ripped our family apart because the cops blackmailed her into trying to get the goods on them."

"So . . . the Chicago cops blackmailed your mother to infiltrate the Stallions."

"MacMasters set it up. She was worn out when she got out of prison, and he used that. He had an in with that crooked judge, and made her weasel for him or he'd send her back in."

"But she was killed in Chicago."

"She tried to get away, take me away, but he tracked her, and set her up with the Chicago cops."

"He must've been pretty obsessed with her to go to all that trouble."

"That's the way it was."

"Your father gave you all this information."

"He had to raise me on his own, because they killed her. They humiliated her, locked her away, raped her. She was beautiful, and they killed her."

"And she loved you," Peabody said, with a hint of sympathy. "She sacrificed for you."

"She lived for me. We had a good life. We didn't have to play by anyone else's rules." Darrin balled his hands into fists on the table. "She was free, and beautiful. That's why MacMasters wanted her, why he forced her. Then he had to cover it up. They had that bitch take me away."

"Jaynie Robins."

"In MacMasters's pocket, like the rest of them. They tried to keep me from my father, but he fought to get me back. He promised my mother he'd take care of me."

"And Robins's supervisor, the APA, the judge, the rest?"

His face went cold again, blank again. "They were all responsible, one way or the other."

"So you and your father worked out how you'd avenge your mother, how you'd make those who'd hurt her pay."

"Why should they get away with it? Why should they have their lives, their families?"

"So your father—Vance—picked the order. He picked Deena as the first target, the first kill."

"We decided together. We're a team, we've always been a team."

"So he could do some of the research, the stalking on one target while you worked another. Very efficient."

"We're a team," Darrin repeated. "We've always been a team."

"Plus he could go to Colorado to research the APA while you stayed here to work Deena. How did he decide you'd plan to kill the sister there, and not the mother, for instance?"

"For Christ's sake, the sister's in New Jersey. It's basic geography."

"He did the preliminary stalking there then, right? Until the contact."

"Didn't I say we're a team? He'd start the field- and e-work, gather the data, then I . . ." His face tightened. "I'm not saying anything else about my father."

"Fine. Protect him like your mother did. You go down, he walks. There's déjà vu. Only you don't go away for a year and a half like she did. You're going away for two life terms, no possibility of parole, with the extra twenty-five for intent on Mrs. Mimoto."

"Long time," Peabody commented, "when you go in this young. You know, Dallas, I bet Vance had alibis set up for himself each time the kid here went on a kill. That's his pattern."

"Doesn't matter, the old man's got no balls. We've got the big fish here, and he can flop and gasp on the shore alone."

"If you think I'll turn on my father, you're crazy. And you'll never find him."

"Couldn't care less. You're all I need, Darrin. You're young, and that just makes me want to sing and dance. Because that means you'll be in a cage on a rock off planet for about a century. You're going to have a really, really long time to think, to figure out how you've been screwed with."

"You think you scare me? It was worth it, just to see MacMasters standing there, and his dead daughter in a box. It's better, even better, because now he knows why. He'll know why, every day he sucks in air, that he killed his own daughter the day he killed my mother."

"I'll give you the bonus. Make him suffer even more. Walk us through what you did to Deena."

His lips twitched into a smile. "You were right. She was easy."

It made her sick, turned her stomach into a raw, churning mass of revulsion. She'd seen it, most of it, in her head already. But now he spoke for the record, relaying every detail. Not reveling in it, Eve noted. Somehow his pragmatic step-by-step was worse than glee.

He'd done what he had to do. What, she believed, he'd been created to do.

When he'd finished relating the murders of Deena and Karlene, his framework and intentions for murdering the others, he sat back, eyeing Eve quietly.

"Is that enough for you?"

"We're done. You'll be taken back to a cell. The court will appoint counsel for you if you don't select an attorney of your own."

"I don't need a lawyer. I don't need a trial. Your laws mean nothing to me. I'm young, like you said. Eventually I'll find my way out, my way back. And I'll finish what I started."

"Sure you will." Eve rose. "Record off. Peabody, get someone to take Darrin back to his cage."

She waited until Peabody stepped out. "He set you up, Darrin, this man you worship. He twisted your mind from the time you were a baby, so he could cover his own actions, maybe his own guilt. He set you up, like he set your mother up, his brother up. He set your mother up, here in New York, and again in Chicago. Because he wanted quick money. Because he wanted her to do the work. Because he was, is, a coward."

"You're a lying cunt." He spat at her, with that vicious smile in place.

"Why would I lie? You'll ask yourself that eventually. Vance Pauley? He's a user."

"You don't know shit."

"More than you can imagine," she said, thinking of the first eight years of her life. "The reason I'm telling you this is because sometime in the long, long decades you're in that concrete cage, you're going to think about it. You're going to think, and wonder, and maybe realize the truth. I really hope you realize the truth. Because it'll make you suffer. Your father killed your mother."

"You're a liar."

She only shook her head. "No gain in it for me. I've closed this case, and you're finished. You'll have a long time to think about that." She turned to the door, nodded to the pair of uniforms who stepped in. "Take this worthless shit back to his cage."

Eve stood where she was, pressed her hands to her face. Rubbed hard as if to scrub away a film of ugly memories.

She turned to MacMasters when he came to the door. "I'm sorry you had to hear that."

"Don't be. She was mine, and I needed to know . . . everything. I needed to know. You're going after the father now."

"Yes, I am."

He nodded. "This is enough for me, has to be. I'm taking a leave of absence. My wife and I need time. She asked me to apologize to you."

"There's no need."

His face was unbearably sad, unbearably weary. "There is, for her. Please accept."

"Then I do."

He nodded again. "Good-bye, Lieutenant."

"Good-bye, Captain."

She made a copy of the recording, gathered her files. When she walked into her office, Roarke turned from her window.

"This is getting to be a habit. I didn't know you were here."

"I haven't been here long. Long enough to have heard the last of that." He came to her, stroked her cheek. "Difficult for you.

Hideous to hear him go step-by-step on what he did to that girl, and to that young woman."

"There'll be worse. There's always worse." For a moment she felt inside her what she'd seen in MacMasters's eyes. Unbearable sadness. Unbearable weariness. "Something like that, like him? It makes you realize there's never a limit on cruel."

"Dallas?" Peabody hesitated at the door. "I just wanted to tell you I'd write this up. Mira was in Observation as requested, and she'll write up her findings."

"Good. Don't worry about the paperwork. Go. I've got a few things left to deal with. Do me a favor and go take care of the Louise thing. Whatever's left of the rehearsal, the rest of it."

"We can be late. She'll get it."

"Yeah, she will. But there's no point. Go. If you're handling it I don't have to feel guilty for being late."

"Okay. It'll be good to shake this off, just shake all this off and do something . . . bright."

"Yeah. I'll be another hour or two." She let out a long breath when Peabody's footsteps echoed away. "Bright. I'm not in the mood for bright. Computer, display map of Manhattan, Lower West."

"Why?" Roarke asked when the computer acknowledged.

"You weren't there for the whole thing. He gave me the old man. Gave me conspiracy to murder, conspiracy to attempted. I'm not sure he realized it. He didn't give me where the nest is. Not directly. But he said he walked home. After he killed Robins, he walked home."

She rubbed the rocks of tension in the back of her neck. "And the coffee. The go-cup. Those Hotz Cafés are all over the place. But figuring he didn't walk from one side of the island to the other, he picked up the coffee between his nest and the scene. Probably closer to his nest. And the nest is going to be within reasonable walking distance of the loft."

Roarke stepped behind her, gave her neck and shoulders a good, hard rub. "Then you're going to like the data I brought you."

"What data?"

"On the security system. No, try to relax for one damn minute," he ordered. "Let's get a couple of these boulders out of here. I've been running various data streams on that, adding some Nadine's research team came up with. And I'd refined it to about a dozen most likelies, which I assumed you'd want to check out."

"That's good. Excellent. The data," she added. "The shoulder rub's not so bad either."

"Just doing my job. There now, that's a little better." Stepping back, he took out his PPC. "If we add the geographical element to the data I have . . . We have not a dozen, but . . . one."

Her eyes lit with purpose. "Give me that."

"This is my job, too." He held it out of reach. "A Peredyne Company in the West Village."

"Not an individual, not the usual initials. Just the P, which could be why I kept missing it."

"It may also be because Peredyne's listed as an arm of Iris Sommer Memorial."

"I.S. Clever. Well, you're more clever since you found it. I need to run it to make sure it's not—"

"Already doing it," he told her. "And . . . there's no listing in New York for either of those companies. It's a shell within a shell."

She turned, rushed out to the bullpen. "Baxter."

"Nice job, Dallas." He gave her a wink, a salute. "I love going off the roll on the upside."

"You're not going off the roll. Conference room, five minutes. Trueheart, with Baxter."

"But—"

She simply turned and pulled her new communicator out of her pocket as she got moving. "Feeney," she said. "We found the bastard's hole. Conference room. Now."

"I want to play," Roarke told her.

"You've earned it." She caught herself before she grabbed him, kissed him, right in front of a corridor full of cops. Instead, she sent him a fierce grin. "Get me a tube of Pepsi, will you?"

In under ninety minutes, Eve had the pretty brick town house in the West Village covered. Cops in soft clothes sat at a bistro table outside a tiny restaurant, hunched in vehicles, strolled the sidewalks. Eve bought a soy dog from a glide-cart manned by Jenkinson.

"Some of them give tips," he said. "I'm keeping the tips."

"I don't want to hear about it."

"Maybe he rabbited, LT." He handed her the dog.

"No reason to. The son didn't make a call, hasn't asked to yet. If he thinks about it, makes the demand, we can stall him. As far as Pauley knows, the fruit of his fucking loins is busy killing an old woman."

Roarke took the second dog, strolled away with Eve. "I could easily get in the place."

"Yeah, and that's what we'll do if he doesn't show in another hour. We've got our warrant. But since the sensors show the place is empty, I'd rather wait."

She bit into the dog. "We wait until he comes back, until he's in that little gated area. Nowhere to run. Jesus, Louise's place is only a block away. I practically walked by this place a few days ago. I might've passed the bastard on the street."

Roarke took her hand, laced his fingers

with hers. "Part of our cover," he said easily.

"Sure. He's not home because he's out somewhere he can be seen, where he can buy something, get a time-stamped receipt. Just in case. It's always been about covering his own ass."

A difficult topic for a pretty summer evening, Roarke thought, but she needed to talk it through. "Why mold the boy into a killer?"

"Maybe he didn't have to mold that much. Hell if I know. That's for Mira or someone like her. I have to figure, maybe it ate at him some. Maybe it was his way to turn it around, not just so he'd be a hero to Darrin, but so he could believe what he was spewing. Everyone else's fault, everyone else is to blame. Punish them."

"Will the reasons matter to you?"

"No. I don't think they will."

"Dallas?"

She turned, saw Charles Monroe, groom-to-be, smiling as he hurried toward them. "Shit."

"What in the world are you two doing around here? I left your place less than an hour ago. I thought there were major plans for the ladies tonight."

"There are. They should be doing some . . . thing right now." What the hell, she thought, it was good cover. Just some friends running into each other on the street. "This isn't your block."

"No. I'm just out walking off some nerves. Tomorrow's . . . it."

"You don't look a bit nervous to me," Roarke commented.

He didn't, Eve agreed. He looked stupid with happy, just like Louise. And elegant despite the casual shirt and pants.

"I take it the rehearsal went off okay. Sorry about needing stand-ins."

"No problem, and it went very well. As far as I could tell." He laughed a little. "I want it to be perfect for her. I caught myself checking the weather forecasts every ten minutes on my way home, and once I got there. So I got out of the house. You should come back, come have a drink, save me from my weather obsession."

"Can't. I'm on an op, and subject sighted," she said. "Hold positions. Let him get inside the gate, then move in."

"What?"

"Just keep talking," she said to Charles. "Roarke, talk to Charles."

"Have you made your honeymoon plans?" Roarke asked pleasantly even as his eyes tracked over to the man who strolled down the sidewalk carrying a shopping bag.

"Ah, yes. We're going to Tuscany."

"Don't look around, Charles. Talk to Roarke."

"We . . . have a villa there for a couple of weeks. Then we—"

"It was great to see you." Eve shot him a huge smile, lifting her voice as Pauley reached out for his garden gate. "Wish we had more time, but we have to . . . Go!"

She sprinted, caught the gate Pauley left to swing shut behind him. And pressed her weapon to the back of his neck. "You don't want to move."

Ten armed officers surrounded the courtyard, weapons aimed. The bag Pauley held fell to the ground, shattering the contents.

"What's going on? What's the problem?"

"Hands behind your back. Oh, please hesitate. Please try to run or resist. Give me an excuse."

"I'm cooperating." He put his hands behind his back, and Eve cuffed him. "I don't want any trouble. I don't understand."

"Then I'll explain." She jerked him around to face her. "Vance Pauley, you're under arrest for conspiracy to commit murder, two counts, and conspiracy with intent to murder, one count. You have the right to remain silent."

"I don't—"

"Shut up. Didn't I just tell you you have the right to remain silent?" She completed the Revised Miranda, then kicked at the shards of glass on the ground. "Bought some prime brew. I guess you planned a little celebration for your son when he got home tonight. The thing is, he won't be coming home, for the rest of his life. And he flipped on you, Daddy."

He went pale, and his eyes dark and angry. "I don't know what you're talking about. Where is my son? I have a right to—"

"I gave you all the rights you're going to

get. Like father, like son. When push came to shove, he covered his own ass."

"That's bullshit. He'd never say anything against me."

She smiled. "Take this delusional asshole into Central. Book him on the counts charged and put him in a cage. We'll be talking soon, Vance. Real soon."

She turned to Roarke and a fascinated Charles. "Now you and the e-geeks can bypass security. By the numbers, people," she called out. "Records on, I want top to bottom, inside and out. Bag it, tag it, log it."

"Well." Charles smiled at her. "This was certainly an exciting walk around the neighborhood."

"Making your streets safer for newlyweds. I gotta go. I'll see you tomorrow."

"I'll be there. Oh, tell Louise, when you see her, tell her I can't wait."

"I'll do that."

She took him alone. She saw no reason to keep any of the team on the clock any longer. Carrying a large box, she went into Interview.

"Record on," she began.

"This is some sort of ridiculous mistake. I

haven't asked for a lawyer—yet—because I don't want to make it more complicated. Now, I demand to see my son."

"No. Shut up and listen, because this really isn't going to take that long. And I've got things to do. We've confiscated all your electronics, and we already have all the data you accumulated on Deena Mac-Masters, Karlene Robins, Charity Mimoto, Elysse—well, you know who they are. You kept excellent records of your research, your video documentation. Oh, just for the hell of it, we're throwing in the ID fraud charges and all that. We brought your workshop in, too. Plus, there's the illegals. It just keeps piling on, Vance."

"Look, you don't understand." He spread his hands, a man of perfect reason. "I have to see my boy. I have to make sure he's all right. You . . . something's wrong with him. I'm afraid he might have done something. He might have done something horrible. I've tried to take care of him, but he's been—"

"Do you think I'm going to buy that bull-shit?" She let her fury go, just go, and hauled him out of the chair. "You disgusting fucker. You made him, and now you'd let him fry. Just like you let her. To save your-self."

She all but threw him back into the chair. "You have no idea what I'd like to do to you, with my bare hands. So don't fuck with me. You made a monster out of him. You raped his mind, filled it with hate and loathing and lies. What makes people like you, fathers like you who'd do that to their children?"

She stepped away, stared at herself in the two-way mirror. Her heart beat too fast, and her hands wanted to tremble. It was getting away from her, she thought. She couldn't let it get away from her.

She lifted one hand, laid her palm on the glass. A mirror on one side, a window on the other. And she imagined Roarke's palm pressed to hers.

He knew her, she reminded herself. All there was. He was there, and he'd keep being there. She could handle this. She could handle anything.

Okay, she thought. *I'm okay.*

For another moment, she stared into her own eyes. "She didn't love him either, or not enough. He was . . . secondary to her. It was all about you." Steady again, she turned back. "She protected you and didn't spare him a backward glance. And when you got over your head with the Stallions, you offered her. She was secondary to you, after your own ass. She was someone to be used. That's all she was to you. A bargaining chip."

"That's not true." He said it slowly, his voice thickening, his eyes taking on a sheen. "I loved my son's mother."

"You can't even say his name. You don't know which name to use. He never really had one," she added. Neither had she. They hadn't named her so she'd remain nothing.

"He told us everything."

"He wouldn't do that."

"Oh yes, he would." Some of her fatigue came through, so she used it and angled it toward a kind of boredom. "In his twisted way, he was making you a hero." She walked back, leaned down. "He was bragging about you, Vance. How you taught him everything, told him everything. How you found your targets together. How you did the stalking, the research, shared that with him. How you planned it all out.

"And even if I didn't have all that—on the record . . ."

She began pulling items out of the box. "Discs—with data on the two people he murdered, the woman he tried to kill just today, on the one he planned to kill next week, and so on. On their families, their habits, their work, their friends.

"Very thorough."

She pulled out stacks of photos. "Visuals of same—including the ones he took of Deena and Karlene after he'd finished with them, so he could share the triumph with you. There's more. There's so much more. It's just a freaking banquet of evidence. I know an APA who's going to be shedding tears of joy."

"I can make a deal." He gestured with his hands, like a politician, she thought, emphasizing a talking point. "There's a lot you don't know. I'll give you information."

"Gee, that's some offer. But, no thanks. I've got more than I need, and jeez, it's been a long day already. Your prints are all over this stuff. All over it."

He rubbed a hand over his mouth. "I'm showing remorse. He pulled me into it. He's my son, and he needed my help. I raised him on my own, just him and me. And losing his mother the way we did, it . . . marked us. I was going to talk him into turning himself in, to get help."

"Would that be after he killed Judge Mimoto's mother today, or maybe just one or two more?"

"I didn't know about today. About Mimoto. I . . . thought he was at work. He consults for Biodent, he's a data analyst. I thought he was at work."

"Jesus, Vance." She paused, let out a belly laugh. "You're so completely screwed. You have today's hit marked on your freaking datebook like a dentist appointment."

"I couldn't stop him."

"Are you just going to keep throwing this shit at the wall until something sticks?"

"I never killed anybody. That has to mean something. I helped him, sure. Okay, I helped him set it all up, but that's all. And I'm remorseful. You can cut me a break. I never killed anybody."

"Yes, you did." The fatigue vanished, the boredom flipped into icy rage. "And if I could, I'd charge you with the murder of Illya Schooner, and with a kid of about four who died and became what you wanted him to be. The only break you'll get from me is the recommendation you be placed in a cage in another sector of Omega, so you never have contact with your son. Because he'll figure it out sooner or later, I gave him a start on that today. And once he does, he'll turn his talents on you. So the break you get, Vance? You live."

"I want a lawyer."

"Subject has requested representation. Interview end."

"There's money," he said as she began loading the box. "I have a lot of money hidden away. Secure. I can make it worth your while if you lose that evidence."

"Really? My while's worth a lot."

"Five million."

"So, if I tamper with this evidence so you get off, you'll give me five million dollars?"

"Cash."

"Thanks." She tapped her lapel. "I

guess you didn't notice my recorder. We'll add attempting to bribe a police office to the roll."

He screamed at her as she walked out, ugly invectives that were music to her ears. "Walk this down to Evidence." She passed the box to the uniform she had waiting. "And you can take that ball of puss. He wants a lawyer."

She kept walking. Roarke met her with a tube of Pepsi.

"God, that felt good. Now I feel good." She cracked the tube and drank deep. "Now bright sounds right."

"Peabody called to check. I told her I thought you were wrapping things up. I'm to tell you Trina's waiting for you."

"Shit. That was mean of you."

He walked with her. "You did well. You . . . decimated him."

"You were in Observation? I . . . I felt you."

"Where else would I be?"

This time she took his hand, laced her fingers with his. Palm to palm, she thought. He was there. He always would be.

"I know it sounds weird, but when I started to fill up with him, with my father, I felt you. I guess you could say I leaned on you. It helped me stay steady."

He brought her hand to his lips. "Let's you and I go find some of that bright."

EPILOGUE

The room smelled like a garden and sounded like a flock of birds—possibly chickadees—had just taken roost. Why, she wondered, did women so often sound like songbirds when they gathered together for one of their rites?

She sat, because she'd told herself it was her job to sit, in what Peabody had gleefully dubbed the Bridal Suite, while Trina slathered God-knew-what all over her face.

"Stop squirming." Trina, her hair a puzzling maze of braids and twists in screaming red, kept slathering.

"When, by all that's holy, are you going to stop?"

"When I'm finished. This product is going to help ease the bruising and cover it up. You could've at least tried not to get hit in the face right before the wedding."

"Oh yeah, I should've tried harder not to get caught in a human stampede since a black eye doesn't go with my dress."

"What I'm saying," Trina agreed. "It's not so bad. We got a lot of it treated last night when you finally got here."

"Would you get off my ass? Murderers, two vicious killers behind bars."

"I'll add it to your scorecard," Trina said and snapped her gum.

Peabody, her hair glossed and curled, her square-jawed face polished and painted, peered over Trina's shoulder. "You can hardly see it. Plus, it makes her skin all dewy."

"Wait till I add the base."

"More? I already have an inch troweled on. Why can't I—"

"Quit bitching. Why don't you get her some champagne," Trina suggested. "This can soak in while I start on Louise."

She gave Eve a hard grin. "She doesn't need as much work."

"Sure." Peabody strolled off in her floaty blue dress and bare feet.

Mavis, in a skintight mini nearly as red as Trina's hair zipped up on matching sandals with the teetering heels shaped like open hearts. "Looking flip, Dallas. Is this the most total day ever? Here hold Bellamina a minute. I want to get bubbly for the bride."

So saying, she dropped her six-month-old daughter in Eve's lap. "Hey, Mavis, don't—"

But it was too late as Eve had an armful of chubby baby in foaming, lacy pink. Blonde curls in pink ribbons danced as Bella bounced. She said, "Gah," and grinned.

"Okay. God. Okay. Why are you always smiling?" Eve demanded. "What do you know?"

Bella squealed, gave a kind of push and straightened her legs until she was standing, weaving and bobbing with a maniacal look in her eyes as an ice pick of panic rammed into Eve's stomach.

"What's she doing? For God's sake, somebody do something."

"She's just trying out her legs." Efficiently, Peabody snatched the giggling baby, balanced Bella on her hip, then passed Eve a flute of champagne.

Eve drank half of it down in one swallow.

APA Cher Reo breezed in, sleek and cool in pale lavender. "Everything looks amazing! The flowers, the candles, the—"

"Are you sure?" Louise demanded from her chair as Trina fussed and brushed. "I feel like I should pop down and just make sure everything's in place."

"Believe me. It's like a fairy tale. Oh God, yes," she said when Mavis scooted up with another glass of champagne. "I wanted to come up, let you know the status, Dallas. Darrin Pauley, against advice of counsel, waives a trial. Counsel's trying to pull a 'he's mentally incapable,' which won't fly. That's according to Mira. He understands the difference between right and wrong, is legally competent to make decisions. He just doesn't give a rat's ass. That's paraphrasing Mira. They don't have a prayer. He's going in, and staying in."

"That calls for another drink. Vance Pauley?"

"Wants a trial. Refused an offer of twenty-five for each conspiracy count, consecutively. That's added on to time for the fraud, and the bribery."

"What the hell did you make an offer for?"

"Dallas, seventy-five years plus puts him in for the rest of his life. He knows it, and he's gambling. He's going to lose. The good guys won. So." She lifted her glass. "Oh, Nadine's on her way. She just finished a live update on the arrests. We're— Trina, what kind of eyeshadow is that? It's gorgeous!"

Law and order forgotten under enhancements, Reo scrambled over to watch Trina transform the bride.

Women came in, went out in what seemed to Eve a blur of summer color. She struggled to sit stoically while she herself was transformed. Painted, buffed, fluffed, and polished. She could only feel relief when she could escape Trina's hands, shrug off the protective cape, the robe, and get dressed.

"You look really mag," Peabody said and brushed her fingers over the tissue-thin layers of Eve's dress. "It's like sunlight, the color. Summer sunlight."

"My huggie bear's a genius," Mavis proclaimed. "I'm playing handmaid so, I've got your glitters."

"Serious glitters." Peabody whistled at the long dangles of diamonds Eve fixed to her ears.

"Ice really sets off the dress. Pendant, bracelets," Mavis continued.

"I don't need all that stuff."

"Trust Leonardo. He worked out the look. See for yourself." Mavis circled her finger so Eve turned to look in the long mirror.

"Hmmm." The dress was more female than her usual, with all the sheer layers shimmering down, but she had to admit it wasn't fussy. And the diamonds, clear and clean, probably did add something. "Fine. Good."

"Total," Mavis corrected.

"You need to help Louise dress now," Peabody told her.

"Why? She's a big girl. She's probably been dressing herself for years."

"It's tradition."

Eve rolled her eyes. "Okay, okay." She walked over to where Louise stood unbelting her robe. And cocked her eyebrows at the frilly white corset and blue garter. "That'll make a statement."

"It will later. Right now its job is to make the dress fit perfectly." She winced. "There's that perfect again."

"Well, let's see." Eve started to remove the dress from its hanger. "Man, there's a lot of it. No wonder you can't do it yourself."

"Oh God. I'm putting on my wedding dress."

Eve looked over sharply. "Don't start leaking! It'll do something to your face, then Trina will start up again."

"I'm waterproofed." She turned her back so Eve could fasten the back of the dress.

"Your grandmother's earrings." Peabody handed Louise the delicate pearl drops. "Something old."

"New, the dress, blue, the garter." Louise put on the earrings. "And the necklace Leonardo picked from Dallas's treasure box for something borrowed." She glanced back at Eve before Peabody helped her fasten it. "Thanks."

"No problem. Nearly done here. One more button. There, Jesus, there must be two dozen buttons."

"No, don't turn around yet! Don't look yet!" Peabody ordered. "We have to attach the veil, then you can look."

"You do it. I'll mess up her hair, then Trina will kill me." And Eve had to admit, the soft, loose curls were pretty, and well, perfect, she decided when Peabody hooked the veil to the tiny, sparkling tiara nestled in them.

Peabody sniffled, blinked, but tears spilled out anyway.

"Cut it out," Eve ordered.

"I can't help it." She stepped back, where she and Mavis wrapped arms around each other's waist and sniffled in accord.

Louise took a deep breath, turned.

"Well, holy shit." Eve stared. "I think you went a couple clicks up from perfect."

Romantic, Eve thought, but almost otherworldly with acres of white foamy, filmy, floating skirts, the sparkle of beads on the strapless bodice. The dress was a winner, no question, but the look on Louise's face outshone even that.

"I look like a bride," Louise murmured.

"Here." Tears trickling, Trina offered Louise her bouquet of sweetheart roses in shades of the palest pink to the deepest red. Then gave Eve and Peabody their smaller rounds. "Come on, Mavis, we'd better get down there."

Mavis scooped up the baby. "Say bye, Bellarina. You're all seriously beautiful." She sighed and hurried out.

"Ready?" Eve asked Louise.

"Dallas." She held out a hand, took Eve's for a hard squeeze. "I'm so ready."

The sun shone, and the quietest of breezes whispered under the music of flutes and violins. Masses of flowers sweetened the air. Peabody walked first down the white runner forming an aisle between the seated guests toward the arbor of white roses where Charles stood with Roarke and McNab.

Eve followed her. Her eyes met Roarke's. And there, she thought, right there was the reason for this. The reason for the flowers and the pomp, the fuss and the formality.

There was love.

Only you, she remembered. She'd walked to him on a summer day once before, and he'd seen only her.

He smiled at her as he had when she'd walked down a white runner to an arbor of white roses toward him. As it had then, her heart gave one quick leap.

Sometimes, she thought as she took her place, turned, life could be pretty damn perfect.